Devil's Bride

STEPHANIE LAURENS

Devil's Bride

A Cynster Novel

AVON

An Imprint of HarperCollinsPublishers

The names Stephanie Laurens and Cynster are registered trademark of Savdek Management Proprietary Ltd.

DEVIL'S BRIDE. Copyright © 1998 by Savdek Management Proprietary Ltd. All rights reserved. Printed in the United States of America. No part of this book may be used or reproduced in any manner whatsoever without written permission except in the case of brief quotations embodied in critical articles and reviews. For information, address HarperCollins Publishers, 195 Broadway, New York, NY 10007.

HarperCollins books may be purchased for educational, business, or sales promotional use. For information, please write: Special Markets Department, HarperCollins Publishers, 195 Broadway, New York, NY 10007.

First Avon Books paperback printing: August 2014
First Avon Books mass market printing: March 1998

Library of Congress Cataloging-in-Publication Data is available upon request.

ISBN 978-0-06-233623-1

14 15 16 17 18   OV/RRD   10 9 8 7 6 5 4 3 2 1

Devil's Bride

The Cynster Family Tree

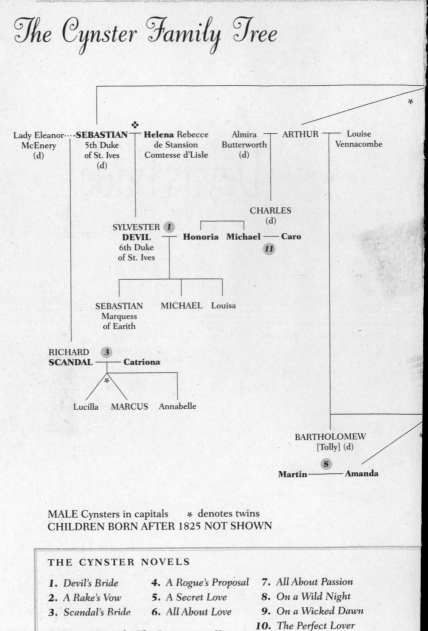

Lady Eleanor····**SEBASTIAN** ❖ **Helena** Rebecce   Almira ─┬─ ARTHUR ─┬─ Louise
McEnery   5th Duke   de Stansion   Butterworth   Vennacombe
(d)   of St. Ives   Comtesse d'Lisle   (d)
        (d)

                           CHARLES
                             (d)

SYLVESTER **1**
DEVIL ─ **Honoria**   **Michael** ─── **Caro**
6th Duke   **11**
of St. Ives

SEBASTIAN   MICHAEL   Louisa
Marquess
of Earith

RICHARD **3**
SCANDAL ─── **Catriona**
    *

Lucilla   MARCUS   Annabelle

                                    BARTHOLOMEW
                                    [Tolly] (d)

                                      8
                             Martin ─────── **Amanda**

MALE Cynsters in capitals   * denotes twins
CHILDREN BORN AFTER 1825 NOT SHOWN

THE CYNSTER NOVELS

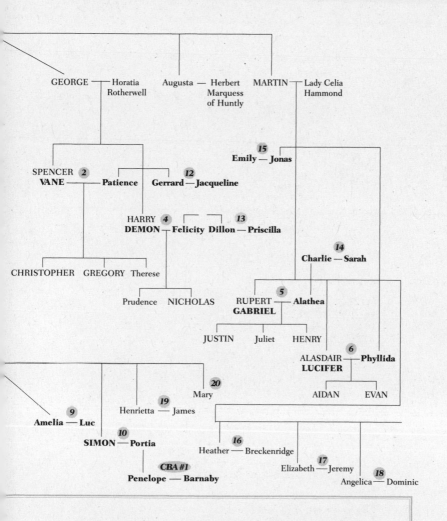

GEORGE — Horatia Rotherwell   Augusta — Herbert Marquess of Huntly   MARTIN — Lady Celia Hammond

15 Emily — Jonas

SPENCER **2** **VANE** — **Patience**   **12** **Gerrard** — **Jacqueline**

HARRY **4** **DEMON** — **Felicity**   Dillon — Priscilla **13**

14 Charlie — Sarah

CHRISTOPHER   GREGORY   Therese

Prudence   NICHOLAS   RUPERT **5** **GABRIEL** — **Alathea**

JUSTIN   Juliet   HENRY

ALASDAIR **6** **LUCIFER** — **Phyllida**

AIDAN   EVAN

Mary **20**

Henrietta **19** — James

9 **Amelia** — Luc

SIMON **10** — Portia

Heather **16** — Breckenridge

Elizabeth **17** — Jeremy

CBA #1 Penelope — Barnaby

Angelica **18** — Dominic

Chapter 1

Somersham, Cambridgeshire
August 1818

"The duchess is so very . . . very . . . well, really, most *charming*. So . . ." With an angelic smile, Mr. Postlethwaite, the vicar of Somersham, gestured airily. "*Continental*, if you take my meaning."

Standing by the vicarage gate while she waited for the gig to be brought around, Honoria Wetherby only wished she could. Wringing information from the local vicar was always one of her first actions on taking up a new position; unfortunately, while her need for information was more acute than usual, Mr. Postlethwaite's comments were unhelpfully vague. She nodded encouragingly—and pounced on the one point which might conceivably mean something. "Is the duchess foreign-born?"

"*Dowager* Duchess." Mr. Postlethwaite beamed. "She likes to be called that now. But foreign?" Head to one side, he considered the point. "I suppose some might call her so—she *was* French-born and -bred. But she's been amongst us so long, she seems a part of our landscape. Indeed"—his eyes brightened—"she's something of a *feature* on our limited horizon."

That much, Honoria had gleaned. It was one reason she needed to know more. "Does the Dowager join the congregration here? I didn't see any ducal arms about." Glancing at the neat stone church beyond the vicarage, she recalled numerous commemorative inscriptions honoring the deceased from various lordly houses, including some scions of the Claypoles, the family whose household she joined last Sunday. But no ducal plaques, helpfully inscribed with name and title, had she discovered anywhere.

"On occasion," Mr. Postlethwaite replied. "But there's a private church at the Place, quite *beautifully* appointed. Mr. Merryweather is chaplain there. The duchess is always reliable in her devotions." He shook his head sadly. "Not, I'm afraid, a general characteristic of that family."

Honoria resisted a strong urge to grind her teeth. *Which family?* She'd been chasing that information for the past three days. Given that her new employer, Lady Claypole, seemed convinced that her daughter Melissa, now Honoria's charge, was destined to be the next duchess, it seemed the course of wisdom to learn what she could of the duke and his family. The family name would help.

By choice, she had spent little time amongst the *haut ton* but, thanks to her brother Michael's long letters, she was reliably informed of the current status of the families who made up that gilded circle—the circle into which she'd been born. If she learned the name, or even the major title, she would know a great deal more.

However, despite spending an hour on Sunday explaining in excruciating detail just why Melissa was destined to be a duchess, Lady Claypole had not used the lucky duke's title. Assuming she would learn it easily enough, Honoria had not specifically questioned her ladyship. She'd only just met the woman; advertising her ignorance had seemed unnecessary. After taking stock of Melissa and her younger sister Annabel, she'd vetoed any idea of asking them; showing ignorance to such was inviting trouble. The same reason had kept her from inquiring of the Claypole Hall staff. Sure that she would learn all she wished while being welcomed to the local Ladies Auxiliary, she'd arranged for her afternoon off to coincide with that most useful of village gatherings.

She'd forgotten that, within the local area, the duke and Dowager Duchess would always be referred to in purely generic terms. Their neighbors all knew to whom they referred—she still did not. Unfortunately, the patent scorn with which the other ladies viewed Lady Claypole's ducal aspirations had made asking a simple question altogether too awkward. Undaunted, Honoria had endured a lengthy meeting over raising sufficient funds to replace the church's ancient roof, then scoured the church, reading every plaque she could find. All to no avail.

Drawing a deep breath, she prepared to admit to ignorance. "To which—"

"There you are, Ralph!" Mrs. Postlethwaite came bustling down the path. "I'm so sorry to interrupt, my dear." She smiled at Honoria, then looked at her spouse. "There's a boy come from old Mrs. Mickleham—she's asking for you urgently."

"Here you are, miss."

Honoria whirled—and saw the vicar's gardener leading the bad-tempered grey the Claypole Hall groom had harnessed to the gig. Shutting her lips, she nodded graciously to Mrs. Postlethwaite, then sailed through the gate the vicar held wide. Taking the reins with a tight smile, she allowed the gardener to assist her to the seat.

Mr. Postlethwaite beamed. "I'll look to see you on Sunday, Miss Wetherby."

Honoria nodded regally. "Nothing, Mr. Postlethwaite, could keep me away." *And*, she thought, as she set the grey in motion, *if I haven't found out by then who this blessed duke is, I won't let go of you until I have!*

Brooding darkly, she drove through the village; only as the last of the cottages fell behind did she become aware of the heaviness in the air. Glancing up, she saw thunderclouds sweeping in from the west.

Tension gripped her, locking her breath in her chest. Abruptly looking forward, Honoria focused on the intersection immediately ahead. The road to Chatteris led straight on, then curved north, into the path of the storm; the long lane to Claypole Hall gave off it three miles on.

A gust of wind plucked at her, whistling mockingly. Honoria started; the grey jibbed. Forcing the horse to a halt, Honoria berated herself for remaining out so long. A ducal name was hardly of earth-shattering importance. The approaching storm was.

Her gaze fell on the lane joining the road at the signpost. It wended away through stubbled fields, then entered a dense wood covering a low rise. She'd been told the lane was a shortcut, ultimately joining the Claypole Hall lane mere yards from the Hall gates. It seemed her only chance of reaching the Hall before the storm broke.

One glance at the roiling clouds growing like a celestial tidal wave to her right made up her mind. Stiffening her spine, Honoria clicked the reins and directed the grey left. The beast stepped out eagerly, carrying her past the golden fields, darkening as the clouds thickened.

A dull *crack!* cut through the heavy stillness. Honoria looked ahead, scanning the trees swiftly drawing nearer. Poachers? Would they be out in such weather when the game was in deep cover, sheltering from a storm? She was still puzzling over the odd sound when the wood rose before her. The grey trotted on; the trees engulfed them.

Determined to ignore the storm, and the unease it raised within her, Honoria turned to contemplation of her latest employers, and the niggle of doubt she felt over their worth as recipients of her talents. Beggars couldn't be choosers, which was what any *other* governess would say. Fortunately, she wasn't just any governess. She was wealthy enough to live idly; it was by her own eccentric will that she eschewed a life of quiet ease for one which allowed her to use her skills. Which meant she *could* choose her employers, and usually did so most reliably. This time, however, fate had intervened and sent her to the Claypoles. The Claypoles had failed to impress.

The wind rose in a bansheelike screech, then died to a sobbing moan. Branches shifted and swayed; boughs rubbed and groaned.

Honoria wriggled her shoulders. And refocused her thoughts on the Claypoles—on Melissa, their eldest daughter, the prospective duchess. Honoria grimaced. Melissa was slight and somewhat underdeveloped, fair, not to say faded. In terms of animation, she had taken the "to be seen and not heard" maxim to heart—she never had two words to say for herself. Two intelligent words, anyway. The only grace Honoria had yet discovered in her was her carriage, which was unconsciously elegant—on all the rest she'd have to work hard to bring Melissa up to scratch. To a duke's scratch at that.

Taking comfort from her irritation—it distracted her from the thought of what she could not see through the thick canopy overhead—Honoria set aside the vexing question of the duke's identity to reflect on the qualities Lady Claypole had ascribed to the phantom.

He was thoughtful, an excellent landowner, mature but not old, ready, so her ladyship assured her, to settle down and begin filling his nursery. This paragon had no faults to which any might take exception. The picture her ladyship had painted was of a sober, serious, retiring individual, almost a recluse. That last was Honoria's addition; she couldn't imagine any duke other than a reclusive one being willing, as Lady Claypole had declared this one was, to apply for Melissa's hand.

The grey tugged. Honoria kept the ribbons taut. They'd passed the entrance to two bridle paths, both winding away into trees so dense it was impossible to glimpse anything beyond a few yards. Ahead, the lane swung left, around a virtually blind curve. Tossing his head, the grey paced on.

Honoria checked for the curve, noting that their upward climb had ended. As the weight of his load lessened, the grey surged. Honoria's grip slipped—the reins slithered through her fingers. Cursing, she grabbed wildly and caught the ribbons firmly; leaning back, she wrestled with the beast.

The grey shied. Honoria shrieked and yanked hard, for once uncaring of the horse's mouth. Her heart racing, she forced the grey to a halt. Abruptly, the horse stood stockstill, quivering, coat aflicker. Honoria frowned. There'd been no thunderclaps yet. She glanced along the lane. And saw the body slumped beside the verge.

Time stood still—even the wind froze.

Honoria stared. *"Dear God."*

At her whisper, the leaves sighed; the metallic taint of fresh blood wafted along the lane. The grey sidled; Honoria steadied him, using the moment to swallow the knot of shock in her throat. She didn't need to look again to see the dark, glistening pool growing beside the body. The man had been shot recently—he might still be alive.

Honoria eased from the gig. The grey stood quietly, head drooping; edging to the verge, Honoria looped the reins about a branch and pulled the knot tight. Stripping off her gloves, she stuffed them in her pocket. Then she turned and, taking a deep breath, walked down the lane.

The man was still alive—she knew that the instant she knelt on the grass beside him; his breathing was rattly and harsh. He was lying on his side, slumped forward; grasping his right shoulder, she rolled him onto his back. His breathing eased—Honoria barely noticed, her gaze transfixed by the jagged hole marring the left side of his coat. With every ragged breath the man drew, blood welled from the wound.

She had to staunch the flow. Honoria looked down; her handkerchief was already in her hand. Another glance at the wound confirmed its inadequacy. Hurrying, she stripped off the topaz-silk scarf she wore over her dun-colored gown and wadded it into a pad. Lifting the sodden coat, she left the man's ruined shirt undisturbed and pressed her improvised dressing over the gaping hole. Only then did she glance at his face.

He was young—surely too young to die? His face was pale; his features were regular, handsome, still holding traces of youthful softness. Thick brown hair lay disheveled across a wide brow; brown brows arched over his closed eyes.

Sticky dampness rose beneath Honoria's fingers, her kerchief and scarf no match for the relentless flow. Her gaze fell on the youth's cravat. Unhooking the pin securing the linen folds, she unwound the cravat, folded it, then positioned the thick wad and carefully pressed down. She was bent over her patient when the thunder struck.

A deep resounding *boom*, it rent the air. The grey screamed, then shot down the lane, a sharp crack accompanying the thud of hooves. Heart pounding, Honoria watched in helpless dismay as the gig rushed past, the branch with the reins still wrapped about it bumping wildly in its wake.

Then lightning cracked. The flash was hidden by the canopy yet still lit the lane in garish white. Honoria shut her eyes tight, blocking her memories by sheer force of will.

A low moan reached her. Opening her eyes, she looked down, but her charge remained unconscious.

"Wonderful." She glanced around; the truth was impossible to avoid. She was alone in a wood, under trees, miles from shelter, without means of transport, in a countryside she'd first seen four days ago, with a storm lashing the leaves from the trees—and beside her lay a badly wounded man. How on earth could she help him?

Her mind was a comfortless blank. Into the void came the sound of hoofbeats. At first, she thought she was dreaming, but the sound grew steadily louder, nearer. Giddy with relief, Honoria rose. She stood in the lane, fingertips on the pad, listening as the hoofbeats drew rapidly nearer. At the last minute, she stood upright, turning and stepping boldly to the center of the lane.

The ground shook; thunder engulfed her. Looking up, she beheld Death.

A massive black stallion screamed and reared over her, iron-tipped hooves flailing within inches of her head. On the beast's back sat a man to match the horse, black-clad shoulders blocking out the twilight, dark mane wild, features harsh—satanic.

The stallion's hooves thudded to the ground, missing her by a bare foot. Furious, snorting, eyes showing white, the beast hauled at the reins. It tried to swing its huge head toward her; denied, it attempted to rear again.

Muscles bunched in the rider's arms, in the long thighs pressed to the stallion's flanks. For one eternal minute, man and beast did battle. Then all went still, the stallion acknowledging defeat in a long, shuddering, horsy sigh.

Her heart in her throat, Honoria lifted her gaze to the rider's face—and met his eyes. Even in the dimness, she was sure of their color. Pale, lucent green, they seemed ancient, all-seeing. Large, set deep under strongly arched black brows, they were the dominant feature in an impressively strong face. Their glance was penetrating, mesmerizing—unearthly. In that instant, Honoria was sure that the devil had come to claim one of his own. And her, too.

Then the air about her turned blue.

Chapter 2

"**W**hat in the devil's own name are you about, woman?"
Ending a string of decidedly inventive curses, that question, delivered with enough force to hold back the storm itself, jerked Honoria's wits into place. She focused on the commanding figure atop the restless stallion, then, with haughty dignity, stepped back, gesturing to the body on the verge. "I came upon him a few minutes ago—he's been shot, and I can't stop the bleeding."

The rider's eyes came to rest on the still figure. Satisfied, Honoria turned and headed back to the injured man, then realized the rider hadn't moved. She looked back, and saw the broad chest beneath what she now recognized as a dark hacking jacket expand—and expand—as the rider drew in an impossibly deep breath.

His gaze switched to her. "Press down on that pad—hard."

Without waiting to see if she obeyed, he swung down from his horse, the movement so eloquent of harnessed power, Honoria felt giddy again. She hurriedly returned to her patient. "That's precisely what I *was* doing," she muttered, dropping to her knees and placing both hands on the pad.

The rider, busy tying the stallion's reins about a tree, glanced her way. "Lean over him—use all your weight."

Honoria frowned but shuffled closer and did as he said. There was a note in the deep voice that suggested he expected to be obeyed. Given that she was counting on him to help her deal with the wounded man, now, she decided, was not the time to take umbrage. She heard him approach, footsteps firm on the packed earth. Then the footfalls slowed, became hesitant, then stopped altogether. She was about to glance up when he started forward again.

He came to the other side of the wounded man, avoiding the large pool of blood. Hunkering down, he gazed at the youth.

From beneath her lashes, Honoria gazed at him.

At closer range, the effect of his face diminished not one whit—if anything, the impact of strong, angular planes, decidedly patrician nose, and lips that were long, thin, and provocatively mobile was even more pronounced. His hair was indeed midnight black, thick and wavy enough to form large locks; his eyes, fixed on their common charge, were hooded. As for the rest of him, Honoria decided it was wiser not to notice—she needed all her wits for helping the wounded man.

"Let me see the wound."

Was that a quaver she heard running through that dark voice, so deep it half resonated through her? Honoria glanced swiftly at her rescuer. His expression was impassive, showing no hint of any emotion—no, she'd imagined the quaver.

She lifted the sodden wad; he bent closer, angling his shoulders to let light reach the wound. He grunted, then nodded, rocking back on his heels as she replaced the pad.

Looking up, Honoria saw him frown. Then his heavy lids

lifted and he met her gaze. Again she was struck by his curious eyes, transfixed by their omniscient quality.

Thunder rolled; the echoes were still reverberating when lightning lit up the world.

Honoria flinched, struggling to control her breathing. She refocused on her rescuer; his gaze hadn't left her. Raindrops pattered on the leaves and spattered the dust of the lane. He looked up. "We'll have to get him—and ourselves—under cover. The storm's nearly here."

He rose, smoothly straightening his long legs. Still kneeling, Honoria was forced to let her eyes travel upward, over top boots and long, powerfully muscled thighs, past lean hips and a narrow waist, all the way over the wide acreage of his chest to find his face. He was tall, large, lean, loose-limbed yet well muscled—a supremely powerful figure.

Finding her mouth suddenly dry, she felt her temper stir. "To where, precisely? We're miles from anywhere." Her rescuer looked down, his disturbing gaze fixing on her face. Honoria's confidence faltered. "Aren't we?"

He looked into the trees. "There's a woodsman's cottage nearby. A track leads off a little way along the lane."

So he was a local; Honoria was relieved. "How will we move him?"

"I'll carry him." He didn't add the "of course," but she heard it. Then he grimaced. "But we should pack the wound better before shifting him."

With that, he shrugged off his jacket, tossed it over a nearby branch, and proceeded to strip off his shirt. Abruptly, Honoria transferred her gaze to the wounded man. Seconds later, a fine linen shirt dangled before her face, suspended from long, tanned fingers.

"Fold the body of the shirt and use the arms to tie it about him."

Honoria frowned at the shirt. Lifting one hand, she took it, then looked up, directly into his face, studiously ignoring the tanned expanse of his bare chest and the crisply curling black hair that adorned it. "If you can take over here and keep your eyes on the wound, I'll donate my petticoat. We'll need more fabric to bind against the hole."

His black brows flew up, then he nodded and hunkered down, placing long strong fingers on the pad. Honoria withdrew her hand and stood.

Briskly, trying not to think about what she was doing, she crossed to the other side of the lane. Facing the trees, she lifted the front of her skirt and tugged at the drawstring securing her lawn petticoat.

"I don't suppose you've a penchant for underdrawers?"

Stifling a gasp, Honoria glanced over her shoulder, but her devilish rescuer was still facing in the opposite direction. When she didn't immediately answer, he went on: "It would give us even more bulk."

Honoria's petticoat slithered down her bare legs. "Unfortunately not," she replied repressively. Stepping free, she swiped up her offering and stalked back across the lane.

He shrugged. "Ah, well—I can't say I'm a fan of them myself."

The vision his words conjured up was ridiculous. Then Honoria's wits clicked into place. The look she cast him as she dropped to her knees should have blistered him; it was wasted—his gaze was trained on the wounded man's face. Inwardly humphing, Honoria ascribed the salacious comment to ingrained habit.

Folding the petticoat, she combined it with the shirt; he removed his hand, and she applied the thick pad over her earlier insignificant one.

"Leave the sleeves hanging. I'll lift him—then you can reach under and tie them tight."

Honoria wondered how even he would cope with the long, heavy weight of their unconscious charge. Amazingly well was the answer; he hefted the body and straightened in one fluid movement. She scrambled to her feet. He held the youth against his chest; with one sleeve in her hand she ducked and felt about for the other. Her searching fingertips brushed warm skin; muscles rippled in response. She pretended not to notice. Locating the wayward sleeve, she pulled it taut, tying the ends in a flat knot.

Her rescuer expelled a long breath through his teeth. For one instant, his strange eyes glittered. "Let's go. You'll have to lead Sulieman." With his head, he indicated the black monster cropping grass beside the lane.

Honoria stared at the stallion. "Sulieman was a treacherous Turk."

"Indeed."

She transferred her gaze back to the man. "You're serious, aren't you?"

"We can't leave him here. If he gets loose, panicked by the storm, he could damage something. Or someone."

Unconvinced, Honoria retrieved his jacket from the branch. She studied the stallion. "Are you sure he won't bite?" When no answer came, she turned to stare, openmouthed, at her rescuer. "You expect me to—?"

"Just take the reins—he'll behave himself."

His tone held enough irritated masculine impatience to have her crossing the lane, albeit with no good grace. She glared at the stallion; he stared levelly back. Refusing to be intimidated—by a horse—Honoria crammed the jacket under the saddle, then tugged the reins free. Holding them firmly, she started along the lane. And came to an abrupt halt when the stallion didn't budge.

"Sulieman—walk."

At the command, the huge horse started forward. Honoria scurried ahead, trying to keep beyond the range of the monster's teeth. Her rescuer, after one comprehensive glance, turned and strode on.

They were deep within the densest part of the wood, thickly leaved canopies interwoven overhead. As if flexing its muscles, the wind gusted, riffling the leaves and flinging a shower of raindrops upon them.

Honoria watched as her rescuer angled his awkward burden through a tight curve. As he straightened, the muscles in his back shifted, smoothly rippling under taut skin. A single raindrop fell to tremble, glistening, on one tanned shoulder, then slowly slid down his back. Honoria tracked it all the way; when it disappeared beneath his waistband, she swallowed.

Why the sight affected her so, she couldn't understand—men's bare torsos, viewed from childhood in the fields and forge, had never before made it difficult to breathe. Then again, she couldn't recall seeing a chest quite like her rescuer's before.

He glanced back. "How did you come to be in the lane alone?" He paused, shifted the youth in his arms, then strode on.

"I wasn't exactly alone," Honoria explained to his back. "I was returning from the village in the gig. I saw the storm coming and thought to take a shortcut."

"The gig?"

"When I saw the body I went to investigate. At the first thunderclap, the horse bolted."

"Ah."

Honoria narrowed her eyes. She hadn't seen him glance heavenward, but she knew he had. "It wasn't my knot that came undone. The branch I tied the reins to broke."

He glanced her way; while his face was expressionless, his lips were no longer perfectly straight. "I see."

The most noncommittal two words she had ever heard. Honoria scowled at his infuriating back, and trudged on in awful silence. Despite his burden, he was forging ahead; in her kid half boots, not designed for rough walking, she slipped and slid trying to keep up. Unfortunately, with the storm building by the second, she couldn't hold the pace he was setting against him.

The disgruntled thought brought her mentally up short. From the instant of encountering her rescuer, she'd been conscious of irritation, a ruffling of her sensibilities. He'd been abrupt, distinctly arrogant—quite impossible in some ill-defined way. Yet he was doing what needed to be done, quickly and efficiently. She ought to be grateful.

Negotiating a tangle of exposed tree roots, she decided it was his assumption of command that most irked—she had not before met anyone with his degree of authority, as if it was his unquestionable right to lead, to order, *and* to be obeyed. Naturally, being who she was, used to being obeyed herself, such an attitude did not sit well.

Finding her eyes once more glued to his back, entranced by the fluid flexing of his muscles, Honoria caught herself up. Irritation flared—she clung to its safety. He was impossible—in *every* way.

He glanced back and caught her black frown before she had a chance to wipe it from her face. His brows quirked; his eyes met hers, then he faced forward. "Nearly there."

Honoria released the breath that had stuck in her throat. And indulged in a furious scowl. Who the devil *was* he?

A gentleman certainly—horse, clothes, and manner attested to that. Beyond that, who could tell? She checked her impressions, then checked again, but could find no hint of underlying unease; she was perfectly certain she was safe with this man. Six years as a governess had honed her instincts well—she did not doubt them. Once they gained shelter, introductions would follow. As a well-bred lady, it wasn't her place to demand his name, it was his duty to make himself known to her.

Ahead, the dimness beneath the trees lightened; ten more steps brought them into a large clearing. Directly in front, backing onto the wood, stood a timber cottage, its thatch in good repair. Honoria noted the opening of two bridle paths, one to the right, one to the left. His stride lengthening, her rescuer headed for the cottage door.

"There's a stable of sorts to the side. Tie Sulieman in there." He flicked a glance her way. "To something unbreakable."

The glare she sent him bounced off his broad back. She quickened her pace, egged on by the rising whine of the wind. Leaves whirled like dervishes, clutching at her skirts; the black monster trotted at her heels. The stable was little more than a rude shack, built against the cottage wall.

Honoria scanned the exposed timbers for a hitching post. "I don't suppose it's what you're accustomed to," she informed her charge, "but you'll have to make do." She spied an iron ring bolted to the cottage wall. "Ah-hah!"

Looping the reins through, she hung on the ends to tighten the knot. She grabbed the jacket and was about to turn away when the huge black head swung toward her, one large eye wide, its expression strangely vulnerable. Briskly, she patted the black nose. "Stay calm."

With that sage advice, she picked up her skirts and fled for the cottage door. The storm chose that precise moment to rend the sky—thunder rolled, lightning crackled, the wind shrieked—so did Honoria.

She flew through the open door, whirled, and slammed it shut, then slumped back against it, eyes closed, hands clutching the soft jacket to her breast. Rain drummed on the roof and pelted the panels at her back. The wind shook the shutters and set the rafters creaking. Honoria's heart pounded; on the inside of her eyelids she saw the white light she knew brought death.

Catching her breath on a hiccup, she forced her eyes open.

And saw her rescuer, the youth in his arms, standing beside a pallet raised on a crude frame. The cottage was dark, lit only by dim remnants of light leaking through the slatted shutters.

"Light the candle, then come and set the covers."

The simple command prodded Honoria into action. She crossed to the table that dominated the single-roomed abode. A candle stood in a simple candlestick, tinder beside it. Laying the jacket aside, she struck a spark and coaxed the candle into flame. A soft glow spread through the room. Satisfied, she headed for the pallet. An odd assortment of furniture crowded the small cottage—an old wing chair sat beside the stone hearth, a huge carved chair with faded tapestry cushions facing it. Chairs, bed, and table took up much of the available space; a chest and two rough dressers hugged the walls. The bed stood out into the room, its head against one wall; Honoria reached for the neatly folded blankets left on its end. "Who lives here?"

"A woodsman. But it's August so he'll be in the woods by Earith. These are his winter quarters." He leaned forward, lowering his burden, as Honoria flipped the blanket out along the bed.

"Wait! He'll be more comfortable if we remove his coat."

Those unearthly eyes held hers, then he looked down at the body in his arms. "See if you can ease the sleeve off."

She'd been careful not to catch the coat when she'd secured their improvised bandage. Honoria gently tugged; the sleeve shifted inch by inch.

Her rescuer snorted. "Silly clunch probably took an hour to get into it."

Honoria looked up—this time she was sure. His voice had shaken on the "clunch." She stared at him, a dreadful premonition seeping through her. "Pull harder—he can't feel anything at the moment."

She did; between them, by yanking and tugging, they managed to free one arm. With a sigh of relief, he laid the body down, drawing the coat off as he eased his hands free. They stood and stared at the deathly pale face, framed by the faded blanket.

Lightning cracked; Honoria shifted and glanced at her rescuer. "Shouldn't we fetch a doctor?"

Thunder rolled, echoing and booming. Her rescuer turned his head; the heavy lids lifted, and his strange eyes met hers. In the clear green—timeless, ageless, filled with desolate bleakness—Honoria read his answer. "He's not going to recover, is he?"

The compelling gaze left her; his black mane shook in a definite negative.

"Are you sure?" She asked even though she suspected he was right.

His long lips twisted. "Death and I are well acquainted." The statement hung in the suddenly chill air. Honoria was grateful when he elaborated: "I was at Waterloo. A great victory we were later told. Hell on earth for those who lived through it. In one day I saw more men die than any sane man sees in a lifetime. I'm quite certain—" Thunder crashed, nearly drowning out his words. "He won't see out the night."

His words fell into sudden silence. Honoria believed him; the bleakness that hung about him left no room for doubt.

"You saw the wound—how the blood kept pulsing? The ball nicked the heart—either that, or one of the big vessels close by. That's why we can't stop the bleeding." He gestured to where blood was staining the thick pad. "Every time his heart beats, he dies a little more."

Glancing at the youth's innocent face, Honoria drew in a slow breath. Then she looked at her rescuer. She wasn't sure she believed the impassive face he wore. His very stoicism fed her suspicion; compassion stirred.

Then he frowned, black brows slashing down as he held up the youth's coat. Honoria watched as he examined the button opposite the bloody hole. "What is it?"

"The button deflected the ball. See?" He held the button to the light so she could see the dent in its rim, the scorching beside it. Eyes measuring the coat against the youth, he added: "If it hadn't been for the button, it would have been a clean shot through the heart."

Honoria grimaced. "A pity perhaps." When he glanced her way, green eyes strangely empty, she gestured helplessly. "In the circumstances, I mean—a slow death, rather than a fast one."

He said nothing but continued to frown at the button. Honoria pressed her lips together, trying to deny the impulse, and failed. "But?"

"But . . ." He hesitated, then went on: "A clean shot through the heart with a long-barreled pistol—small bore, so it wasn't a shotgun or even horse pistol—at reasonable range—closer would have left more of a burn—is no mean feat. Pulling off such a shot takes remarkable skill."

"And remarkable cold-bloodedness, I imagine."

"That, too."

Rain beat against the walls, the shutters. Honoria straightened. "If you light the fire, I'll heat some water and wash away the worst of the blood." The suggestion earned her a surprised look; she met it with implacable calm. "If he has to die, then at least he can die clean."

For an instant, she thought she'd shocked him—his gaze appeared truly arrested. Then he nodded, his permission so clearly implied she could not doubt that he considered the injured youth in his care.

She headed for the hearth; he followed, soft-footed for such a large man. Pausing before the fire, Honoria glanced over her shoulder—and nearly swallowed her heart when she found him directly beside her.

He was big—bigger than she'd realized. She was often referred to as a "Long Meg"; this man towered over her by a full head, cutting her off from the candlelight, his dramatic face in deep shadow, his black hair a dark corona about his head. He was the Prince of Darkness personified; for the first time in her life, she felt small, fragile, intensely vulnerable.

"There's a pump near the stable." He reached past her; candlelight glimmered on the curved contours of his arm as he lifted the kettle from its hook. "I'd better check Sulieman, too, but I'll get the fire going first."

Honoria quickly shifted to the side. Only when he had crouched before the hearth, laying logs from the woodbox in the grate, did she manage to breathe again. At close range, his voice reverberated through her, a decidedly unnerving sensation.

By the time he had a blaze established, she had her attention firmly fixed on the dressers, discovering clean cloths and a canister of tea. She heard him move past; reaching high, he lifted a bucket from a hook. The latch clicked; Honoria glanced around—he stood in the doorway, bare to the waist, silhouetted by a searing flash of light—an elemental figure in an elemental world. The wind funneled in, then was abruptly cut off; the door shut and he was gone.

She counted seven rolls of thunder before he returned. As the door closed behind him, the tension gripping her eased. Then she noticed he was dripping wet. "Here." She held out the largest of the cloths she'd found and reached for the kettle. She busied herself by the fire, setting the kettle to boil, quite sure she didn't need to watch him drying that remarkable chest. The kettle hissed; she reached for the bowl she'd set ready.

He was waiting by the bed; she considered ordering him to dry himself by the fire, then decided to save her breath. His gaze was fixed on the youth's face.

Setting the bowl on the chest by the bed, she squeezed out a cloth, then gently sponged the youth's face, removing the grit and dust of the lane. Cleanliness emphasized his innocence, and highlighted the obscenity of his death. Pressing her lips together, Honoria bent to her task. Until she came to the badly stained shirt.

"Let me."

She shifted back. Two well-judged rips, and the left side of the shirt was free.

"Give me a cloth."

She squeezed one out and handed it over. They worked side by side in the flickering light; she was amazed by how gentle such large hands could be, was moved by how reverently one so powerfully alive dealt with the dying.

Then they were done. Settling another blanket over their silent charge, she gathered the soiled cloths and loaded them into the bowl. He preceeded her to the fire; she set the bowl on the table and straightened her back.

"Devil?"

The call was so faint she only just heard it. Honoria whirled and flew back to the bed. The youth's lids fluttered. "Devil. Need . . . Devil."

"It's all right," she murmured, laying her hand on his brow. "There's no devil here—we won't let him get you."

The youth frowned; he shook his head against her hand. "No! Need to *see* . . ."

Hard hands closed about Honoria's shoulders; she gasped as she was lifted bodily aside. Freed of her touch, the youth opened glazed eyes and struggled to rise.

"Lie back, Tolly. I'm here."

Honoria stared as her rescuer took her place, pressing the youth back to the bed. His voice, his touch, calmed the dying man—he lay back, visibly relaxing, focusing on the older man's face. "Good," he breathed, his voice thin. "Found you." A weak smile flickered across his pale face. Then he sobered. "Have to tell you—"

His urgent words were cut off by a cough, which turned into a debilitating paroxym. Her rescuer braced the youth between his hands, as if willing strength into the wilting frame. As the coughing subsided, Honoria grabbed up a clean cloth and offered it. Laying the youth down, her rescuer wiped the blood from the boy's lips. "Tolly?"

No answer came—their charge was unconscious again.

"You're related." Honoria made it a statement; the revelation had come the instant the youth opened his eyes. The resemblance lay not only in the wide forehead but in the arch of the brows and the set of the eyes.

"Cousins." Animation leached from her rescuer's harsh face. "First cousins. He's one of the younger crew—barely twenty."

His tone made Honoria wonder how old *he* was—in his thirties certainly, but from his face it was impossible to judge. His demeanor conveyed the impression of wordly wisdom, wisdom earned, as if experience had tempered his steel.

As she watched, he put out one hand and gently brushed back a lock of hair from his cousin's pallid face.

The low moan of the wind turned into a dirge.

Chapter 3

She was stranded in a cottage with a dying man and a man known to his intimates as Devil. Ensconced in the wing chair by the fire, Honoria sipped tea from a mug and considered her position. It was now night; the storm showed no sign of abating. She could not leave the cottage, even had that been her most ardent desire.

Glancing at her rescuer, still seated on the pallet, she grimaced; she did not wish to leave. She'd yet to learn his name, but he'd commanded her respect, and her sympathy.

Half an hour had passed since the youth had spoken; Devil— she had no other name for him—had not left his dying cousin's side. His face remained impassive, showing no hint of emotion, yet emotion was there, behind the facade, shadowing the green of his eyes. Honoria knew of the shock and grief occasioned by sudden death, knew of the silent waiting and the vigils for the dead. Returning her gaze to the flames, she slowly sipped her tea.

Sometime later, she heard the bed creak; soft footfalls slowly neared. She sensed rather than saw him ease into the huge carved chair, smelled the dust that rose from the faded tapestry as he settled. The kettle softly hissed. Shifting forward, she poured boiling water into the mug she'd left ready; when the steam subsided, she picked up the mug and held it out.

He took it, long fingers brushing hers briefly, green eyes lifting to touch her face. "Thank you."

He sipped in silence, eyes on the flames; Honoria did the same.

Minutes ticked by, then he straightened his long legs, crossing his booted ankles. Honoria felt his gaze on her face.

"What brings you to Somersham, Miss . . . ?"

It was the opening she'd been waiting for. "Wetherby," she supplied.

Instead of responding with his name—Mr. Something, Lord Someone—he narrowed his eyes. "Your *full* name?"

Honoria held back a frown. "Honoria Prudence Wetherby," she recited, somewhat tartly.

One black brow rose; the disturbing green gaze did not waver. "Not Honoria Prudence *Anstruther*-Wetherby?"

Honoria stared. "How did you know?"

His lips quirked. "I'm acquainted with your grandfather."

A disbelieving look was her reply. "I suppose you're going to tell me I look like him?"

A short laugh, soft and deep, feathered across her senses. "Now you mention it, I believe there is a faint resemblance—about the chin, perhaps?"

Honoria glared.

"Now that," her tormentor remarked, "is very like old Magnus."

She frowned. "What is?"

He took a slow sip, his eyes holding hers. "Magnus Anstruther-Wetherby is an irascible old gentleman, atrociously high in the instep and as stubborn as bedamned."

"You know him well?"

"Only to nod to—my father knew him better."

Uncertain, Honoria watched him sip; her full name was no

state secret—she simply didn't care to use it, to claim relationship with that irascible, stubborn old gentleman in London.

"There was a second son, wasn't there?" Her rescuer studied her musingly. "He defied Magnus over . . . I remember—he
married against Magnus's wishes. One of the Montgomery girls.
You're their daughter?"

Stiffly, Honoria inclined her head.

"Which brings us back to my question, Miss Anstruther-
Wetherby. What the deuce are you doing here, gracing our quiet
backwater?"

Honoria hesitated; there was a restlessness in the long limbs,
a ripple of awareness—not of her, but of the body on the pallet
behind them—that suggested conversation was his need. She
lifted her chin. "I'm a finishing governess."

"A *finishing* governess?"

She nodded. "I prepare girls for their come-out—I only remain
with the families for the year before."

He eyed her with fascinated incredulity. "What in all the
heavens does old Magnus think of that?"

"I've no idea. I've never sought his opinion."

He laughed briefly—that same throaty, sensuous sound; Honoria suppressed an urge to wriggle her shoulders. Then he sobered. "What happened to your family?"

Inwardly, Honoria shrugged. It couldn't hurt to tell her tale,
and if it distracted him, well and good. "My parents died in an
accident when I was sixteen. My brother was nineteen. We lived
in Hampshire, but after the accident, I went to stay with my
mother's sister in Leicestershire."

He frowned. "I'm surprised Magnus didn't intervene."

"Michael informed him of the deaths, but he didn't come down
for the funeral." Honoria shrugged. "We hadn't expected him. After

the falling-out between him and Papa, there'd been no contact."
Her lips lifted fleetingly. "Papa swore he'd never ask for quarter."

"Stubbornness is clearly a family trait."

Honoria ignored the comment. "After a year in Leicestershire,
I decided to try my hand at governessing." She looked up, into
far-too-perceptive green eyes.

"Your aunt wasn't exactly welcoming?"

Honoria sighed. "No—she was *very* welcoming. She married
beneath her—not the mild *mesalliance* the Anstruther-Wetherbys
got so heated over but truly out of her class."

She paused, seeing again the rambling house filled with dogs
and children. "But she was happy and her household was welcoming *but . . .*" She grimaced and glanced at the dark face watching her. "Not for me."

"Fish out of water?"

"Precisely. Once I came out of mourning, I considered my options. Funds, of course, were never a problem. Michael wanted
me to buy a small house in some safe country village and live
quietly *but . . .*"

"Again, not for you?"

Honoria tilted her chin. "I couldn't conceive of a life so tame. I
think it unfair that women are forced to such mild existences and
only gentlemen get to lead exciting lives."

Both black brows rose. "Personally, I've always found it pays
to share the excitement."

Honoria opened her mouth to approve—then caught his eye.
She blinked and looked again, but the salacious glint had disappeared. "In my case, I decided to take control of my life and work
toward a more exciting existence."

"As a governess?" His steady green gaze remained ingenuously interested.

"No. That's only an intermediary stage. I decided eighteen was too young to go adventuring in Africa. I've decided to follow in Lady Stanhope's footsteps."

"*Good God!*"

Honoria ignored his tone. "I have it all planned—my burning ambition is to ride a camel in the shadow of the Great Sphinx. One would be ill-advised to undertake such an expedition too young; governessing in a manner that requires spending only a year with each family seemed the ideal way to fill in the years. As I need provide nothing beyond my clothes, my capital grows while I visit various counties, staying in select households. That last, of course, eases Michael's mind."

"Ah, yes—your brother. What's he doing while you fill in your years?"

Honoria eyed her inquisitor measuringly. "Michael is secretary to Lord Carlisle. Do you know him?"

"Carlisle? Yes. His secretary, no. I take it your brother has political ambitions?"

"Lord Carlisle was a friend of Papa's—he's agreed to stand as Michael's sponsor."

His brows rose fleetingly, then he drained his mug. "What made you decide on governessing as your temporary occupation?"

Honoria shrugged. "What else was there? I'd been well educated, prepared for presentation. Papa was adamant that I be presented to the *ton*, puffed off with all the trimmings—paraded beneath my grandfather's nose. He hoped I'd make a wonderful match, just to show Grandfather no one else shared his antiquated notions."

"But your parents were killed before you were brought out?"

Honoria nodded. "Lady Harwell, an old friend of Mama's, had a daughter two years younger than I. After putting off black gloves, I broached my idea to her—I thought with my background, my preparation, I could teach other girls how to go on. Lady Harwell agreed to a trial. After I finished coaching Miranda, she landed an earl. After that, of course, I never wanted for positions."

"The matchmaking mama's delight." An undercurrent of cynicism had crept into the deep voice. "And who are you coaching around Somersham?"

The question returned Honoria to reality with a thump. "Melissa Claypole."

Her rescuer frowned. "Is she the dark one or the fair one?"

"The fair one." Propping her chin in her hand, Honoria gazed into the flames. "An insipid miss with no conversation—God knows how I'm supposed to render her attractive. I was booked to go to Lady Oxley but her six-year old caught chicken pox, and then old Lady Oxley died. I'd declined all my other offers by then, but the Claypoles' letter arrived late, and I hadn't yet replied. So I accepted without doing my usual checks."

"Checks?"

"I don't work for just anyone." Stifling a yawn, Honoria settled more comfortably. "I make sure the family is good *ton*, well connected enough to get the right invitations and sufficiently beforehand not to make a fuss over the milliner's bills."

"Not to mention those from the modistes."

"Precisely. Well"—she gestured briefly—"no girl is going to snare a duke if she dresses like a dowd."

"Indubitably. Am I to understand the Claypoles fail to meet your stringent requirements?"

Honoria frowned. "I've only been with them since Sunday, but I've a nasty suspicion . . ." She let her words trail away, then shrugged. "Luckily, it appears Melissa is all but spoken for—by a duke, no less."

A pause followed, then her rescuer prompted: "A duke?"

"So it seems. If you live about here you must know of him— sober, reserved, rather reclusive, I think. Already tangled in Lady Claypole's web, if her ladyship speaks true." Recollecting her burning question, Honoria twisted around. "Do you know him?"

Clear green eyes blinked back at her; slowly, her rescuer shook his head. "I can't say I've had the pleasure."

"Humph!" Honoria sank back in her chair. "I'm beginning to think he's a hermit. Are you sure—"

But he was no longer listening to her. Then she heard what had caught his attention—the rattly breathing of the wounded youth. The next instant, he was striding back to the bed. He sat on the edge, taking one of the youth's hands in his. From the chair, Honoria listened as the youth's breathing grew more ragged, more rasping.

Fifteen painful minutes later, the dry rattle ceased.

An unearthly silence filled the cottage; even the storm was still. Honoria closed her eyes and silently uttered a prayer. Then the wind rose, mournfully keening, nature's chant for the dead.

Opening her eyes, Honoria watched as Devil laid his cousin's hands across his chest. Then he sat on the pallet's edge, eyes fixed on the pale features that would not move again. He was seeing his cousin alive and well, laughing, talking. Honoria knew how the mind dealt with death. Her heart twisted, but there was nothing she could do. Sinking back in the chair, she left him to his memories.

She must have dozed off. When next she opened her eyes, he was crouched before the hearth. The candle had guttered; the only light in the room was that thrown by the flames. Half-asleep, she watched as he laid logs on the blaze, banking it for the night.

During their earlier conversation, she'd kept her eyes on his face or the flames; now, with the firelight sculpting his arms and shoulders, she looked her fill. Something about all that tanned male skin had her battling a fierce urge to press her fingers to it, to spread her hands across the warm expanse, to curve her palms about hard muscle.

Arms crossed, hands safely clutching her elbows, she shivered.

In one fluid motion he rose and turned. And frowned. "Here." Reaching past her, he lifted his soft jacket from the table and held it out.

Honoria stared at it, valiantly denying the almost overwhelming urge to focus, not on the jacket, but on the chest a yard behind it. She swallowed, shook her head, then dragged her gaze straight up to his face. "No—you keep it. It was just that I woke up—I'm not really cold." That last was true enough; the fire was throwing steady heat into the room.

One black brow very slowly rose; the pale green eyes did not leave her face. Then the second brow joined the first, and he shrugged. "As you wish." He resumed his seat in the old carved chair, glancing about the cottage, his gaze lingering on the blanket-shrouded figure on the bed. Then, settling back, he looked at her. "I suggest we get what sleep we can. The storm should have passed by morning."

Honoria nodded, immensely relieved when he spread his jacket over his disturbing chest. He laid his head against the chairback, and closed his eyes. His lashes formed black crescents above his high cheekbones; light flickered over the austere planes of his face. A strong face, hard yet not insensitive. The sensuous line of his lips belied his rugged jaw; the fluid arch of his brows offset his wide forehead. Wild locks of midnight black framed the whole—Honoria smiled and closed her eyes. He should have been a pirate.

With sleep clouding her mind, her body soothed by the fire's warmth, it wasn't hard to drift back into her dreams.

Sylvester Sebastian Cynster, sixth Duke of St. Ives, known as That Devil Cynster to a select handful of retainers, as Devil Cynster to the *ton* at large and simply as Devil to his closest friends, watched his wife-to-be from beneath his long lashes. What, he wondered, would his mother, the Dowager Duchess, make of Honoria Prudence Anstruther-Wetherby?

The thought almost made him smile, but the dark pall that hung over his mind wouldn't let his lips curve. For Tolly's death there was only one answer; justice would be served, but vengeance would wield the sword. Nothing else would appease him or the other males of his clan. Despite their reckless propensities, Cynsters died in their beds.

But avenging Tolly's death would merely be laying the past to rest. Today he had rounded the next bend in his own road; his companion for the next stretch shifted restlessly in the old wing chair opposite.

Devil watched her settle, and wondered what was disturbing her dreams. Him, he hoped. She was certainly disturbing him—and he was wide-awake.

He hadn't realized when he'd left the Place that morning that he was searching for a wife; fate had known better. It had placed Honoria Prudence in his path in a manner that ensured he couldn't pass her by. The restless dissatisfaction that had gripped him of late seemed all of a piece, part of fate's scheme. Jaded by the importunities of his latest conquest, he'd come to the Place, sending word to Vane to meet him for a few days' shooting. Vane had been due to join him that evening; with a whole day to kill, he'd thrown a saddle on Sulieman and ridden out to his fields.

The wide lands that were his never failed to soothe him, to refocus his mind on who he was, what he was. Then the storm had risen; he'd cut through the wood, heading for the back entrance to the Place. That had put him on track to find Tolly—and Honoria Prudence. Fate had all but waved a red flag; no one had ever suggested he was slow to see the light. Seizing opportunity was how he'd made his name—he'd already decided to seize Honoria Prudence.

She would do very well as his wife.

For a start, she was tall, with a well-rounded figure, neither svelte nor fleshy but very definitely feminine. Hair of chestnut brown glowed richly, tendrils escaping from the knot on the top of her head. Her face, heart-shaped, was particularly arresting, fine-boned and classical, with a small straight nose, delicately arched brown brows, and a wide forehead. Her lips were full, a soft blush pink; her eyes, her finest feature, large, wide-set and long-lashed, were a misty grey. He'd told true about her chin—it was the only feature that reminded him of her grandsire, not in shape but in the determination it managed to convey.

Physically, she was a particularly engaging proposition—she'd certainly engaged his notoriously fickle interest.

Equally important, she was uncommonly level-headed, not given to flaps or starts. That had been clear from the first, when she'd stood straight and tall, uncowering beneath the weight of the epithets he'd so freely heaped on her head. Then she'd favored him with a look his mother could not have bettered and directed him to the matter at hand.

He'd been impressed by her courage. Instead of indulging in a fit of hysterics—surely prescribed practice for a gentlewoman

finding a man bleeding to death in her path?—she'd been resourceful and practical. Her struggle to subdue her fear of the
storm hadn't escaped him. He'd done what he could to distract
her; her instantaneous response to his commands—he'd almost
seen her hackles rising—had made distracting her easy enough.
Taking his shirt off hadn't hurt, either.

His lips twitched; ruthlessly he straightened them. That, of
course, was yet another good reason he should follow fate's advice.

For the past seventeen years, despite all the distractions the
ton's ladies had lined up to provide, his baser instincts had remained subject to his will, entirely and absolutely. Honoria Prudence, however, seemed to have established a direct link to that
part of his mind which, as was the case with any male Cynster,
was constantly on the lookout for likely prospects. It was the
hunter in him; the activity did not usually distract him from
whatever else he had in hand. Only when he was ready to attend
to such matters, did he permit that side of his nature to show.

Today, he had stumbled—more than once—over his lustful
appetites.

His question over underdrawers was one example, and while
taking off his shirt had certainly distracted her, that fact, in turn,
had also distracted him. He could feel her gaze—another sensitivity he hadn't been prey to for a very long time. At thirty-two,
he'd thought himself immune, hardened, too experienced to fall
victim to his own desires.

Hopefully, once he'd had Honoria Prudence a few times—
perhaps a few dozen times—the affliction would pass. The fact
that she was Magnus Anstruther-Wetherby's granddaughter,
rebellious granddaughter at that, would be the icing on his
wedding cake. Devil savored the thought.

He hadn't, of course, told her his name. If he had, she wouldn't have fallen asleep, restlessly or otherwise. He'd realized almost immediately that she didn't know who he was. There was no reason she should recognize *him*. She would, however, recognize his name.

Her peculiar profession would make keeping up with *ton* gossip imperative; he had not a doubt that, had he favored her with his name, she would have made the connection and reacted accordingly. Which would have been trying for them both.

Convincing her that she had no reason to fret would have taken a great deal of effort, which he did not, at the moment, have to spare. He still had Tolly's murder to contend with—he needed her calm and composed. He found her directness, her unfussy, almost wifely matter-of-factness, refreshing and strangely supportive.

The fire glowed, gilding her face. Devil studied the delicate curve of her cheek, noted the vulnerable softness of her lips. He would confess his identity in the morning—he wondered what she would say. The possibilities were, he judged, wide-ranging. He was mulling over the most likely when she whimpered and stiffened in her chair.

Devil opened his eyes fully. And simultaneously became aware of the renewed ferocity of the storm. Thunder rolled, rumbling ever nearer. The wind rose on a sudden shriek; a sharp crack echoed through the wood.

Honoria gasped and came to her feet. Eyes closed, hands reaching, she stepped forward.

Devil surged from his chair. Grabbing her about the waist, he lifted her away from the fire.

With a wrenching sob, she turned and flung herself against him. Her arms slipped about him; she clung tightly, pressing her cheek to his chest. Reflexively, Devil closed his arms about her and felt the sobs that racked her. Off-balance, he took a step back; the old chair caught him behind his knee.

He sat down; Honoria did not slacken her hold. She followed him down, drawing up her legs; she ended curled in his lap. Sobbing silently.

Tilting his head, Devil peered at her face. Her eyes were closed but not tightly. Tears coursed down her face. She was, in fact, still asleep.

Trapped in her nightmare, she shuddered. She gulped down a sob, only to have another rise in its place.

Watching her, Devil felt a sharp ache twist through his chest. The tears welled from beneath her lids, gathered, then rolled slowly, steadily, down her cheeks.

His gut clenched. Hard. Gently, he tipped up her face. She didn't wake; the tears continued to fall.

He couldn't stand it. Devil bent his head and set his lips to hers.

Engulfed in sorrow so black, so dense, not even lightning could pierce it, Honoria became aware of lips warm and firm pressed against her own. The unexpected sensation distracted her, breaking the hold of her dream. Blackness receded; she pulled back and caught her breath.

Strong fingers curved about her jaw; the distracting lips returned. Warmth seeped into her bones, her skin, driving out death's chill. The lips held to hers, reassuringly alive, a link from one dream to the next. She made the transition from nightmare to a sense of peace, of rightness, reassured by the strength surrounding her and the steady beat of a heart not her own.

She was no longer alone in misery. Someone was here, keeping her warm, holding the memories at bay. The ice in her veins melted. Her lips softened; tentatively, she returned the kiss.

Devil caught his baser instincts an instant before they bolted.

She was still asleep—the last thing he intended was to scare her awake. The battle to resist his demons, clamoring for him to deepen the caress into something far from innocent, was furious, as ferocious as the storm. He won—but the effort left him shaking.

She drew back. Lifting his head, he heard her sigh softly. Then, lips curving in a distinctly feminine smile, she shifted, settling herself in his lap.

Devil caught his breath; he bit his lip.

Pressing her cheek once more to his chest, she slid into peaceful slumber.

At least he'd stopped her tears. Jaw clenched, Devil reminded himself that that—and only that—had been his aim. Thanks to fate, he'd have time and more to claim recompense for the pain she was causing him, to claim a suitable reward for his remarkable rectitude. His halo, for once, ought to be glowing.

It took half an hour of thinking of something else before he could risk relaxing. By then she was deeply asleep. Shifting carefully, he settled more comfortably, then noticed the fire was dying. Reaching down, he snagged his jacket, then draped it carefully over his wife-to-be.

Lips curving, he rested his head against the chairback and closed his eyes.

He woke with his cheek pillowed on her curls.

Devil blinked. Sunlight slanted through the shutters. Honoria was still asleep, snuggled against him, legs curled across his thighs. Then he heard the clop of hooves approaching. Vane, no doubt, come to seek him out.

Straightening, Devil winced as cramped muscles protested. His wife-to-be did not stir. Gathering her in his arms, he stood;

Honoria mumbled, resettling her head against his shoulder. Devil gently deposited her in the wing chair, tucking his jacket about her. A frown fleetingly puckered her brows as her cheek touched the cold chintz, then her features eased and she slid deeper into sleep.

Devil stretched. Then, running his fingers across his chest, he headed for the door. Yawning, he opened it.

His breath hissed in through his teeth. "Hell and the devil!" Taking stock of the arrivals, he cursed beneath his breath. He'd been right about Vane—his cousin, mounted on a black hunter, had just pulled up. Another horseman halted alongside. Devil's features blanked as he nodded to his only older cousin, Charles—Tolly's half brother.

That, however, was not the worst. From the other bridle path, a party of four trotted forward—Lord Claypole, Lady Claypole, and two grooms.

"Your *Grace*! How surprising to come upon you here." A sharp-featured woman with crimped hair, Lady Claypole barely glanced at Vane and Charles before returning her gaze to Devil, her protruberant blue eyes widening.

"I was stranded by the storm." Bracing one forearm against the doorframe, Devil blocked the doorway.

"Indeed? Beastly night." Lord Claypole, a short, rotund gentleman, wrestled his bay to a halt. "Might I inquire, Your Grace, if you've seen anything of our governess? Took the gig out to Somersham yesterday—gig came home without her—haven't seen hide nor hair of her since."

Devil looked blank. "The storm was quite wild."

"Quite, quite." His lordship nodded briskly. "Daresay the horse got loose and bolted home. Testy brute. Sure to find Miss Wetherby safe and sound at the vicarage, what?" His lordship looked at his wife, still absorbed with the view. "Don't you think so, m'dear?"

Her ladyship shrugged. "Oh, I'm sure she'll be all right. So terribly inconsiderate of her to put us to all this fuss." Directing a weary smile at Devil, Lady Claypole gestured to the grooms. "We felt we should mount a search, but I daresay you're right, my lord, and she'll be sitting snug at the vicarage. Miss Wetherby," her ladyship informed Devil archly, "comes with the *highest* recommendations."

Devil's brows rose. "Does she indeed?"

"I had it from Mrs. Acheson-Smythe. Of the *highest* calibre—*quite* exclusive. Naturally, when she learned of my Melissa, she set aside all other offers and—" Lady Claypole broke off, protruberant eyes starting. Her mouth slowly opened as she stared past Devil's bare shoulder.

Heaving an inward sigh, Devil lowered his arm, halfturning to watch Honoria's entrance. She came up beside him, blinking sleepily, one hand pressed to her back; with the other, she brushed errant curls from her face. Her eyes were heavy-lidded, her topknot loose, releasing wispy tendrils of gold-shot brown to wreathe auralike about her head. She looked deliciously tumbled, her cheeks lightly flushed, as if they had indeed been entertaining each other in the manner the Claypoles were imagining.

Honoria looked past him—momentarily, she froze. Then she straightened, cool grace dropping like a cloak about her. Not a glimmer of consternation showed in her face. Devil's lips quirked—in approval, in appreciation.

"*Well*, miss!"

Lady Claypole's strident tones overflowed with indignant outrage. Devil fixed her with a clear, very direct glance that any sane person would have read as a warning.

Her ladyship was not so acute. "A *fine* broiling, indeed! Well, Miss Wetherby—if *this* is what you get up to when you *say* you're visiting the vicar, you need not think to cross the Claypole Hall threshold again!"

"Ahem!" More observant than his lady, Lord Claypole plucked at her sleeve. "My dear—"

"To *think* that I've been so misled! Mrs. Acheson-Smythe will hear about—"

"*No*! Really, Margery—" One eye on Devil's face, Lord Claypole fought to restrain his wife from committing social suicide. "No need for any of that."

"No *need*?" Lady Claypole stared at him as if he'd taken leave of his senses. Shaking off his hand, she drew herself up and haughtily declaimed: "If you will send word of your direction, we'll send your boxes on."

"How kind." Devil's purring murmur held sufficient steel to succeed where Lord Claypole had failed. "You may send Miss Anstruther-Wetherby's boxes to the Place."

A long silence greeted his edict.

Lady Claypole leaned forward. "*Anstruther*-Wetherby?"

"The Place?" The soft echo came from Charles Cynster; his horse shifted and stamped.

Abruptly, Lady Claypole switched her gaze to Honoria. "Is this true, miss? Or is it merely a piece of flummery you've succeeded in coaxing His Grace to swallow?"

His *Grace*? For one discrete instant, Honoria's brain reeled. She glanced sideways at the devil beside her—his eyes, cool green, fleetingly met hers. In that moment, she would have given all she possessed to rid herself of everyone else and take to him as he deserved. Instead, she lifted her chin and calmly regarded Lady Claypole. "As His Grace," she invested the title with subtle emphasis, "has seen fit to inform you, I am, indeed, one of the Anstruther-Wetherbys. I choose to make little of the connection, to avoid unwarranted, ill-bred interest."

The comment failed to rout her ladyship. "I really don't know *how* I'm going to explain this to my daughters."

"I suggest, madam,"—his gaze on Lady Claypole's face, Devil caught Honoria's hand, squeezing her fingers warningly as he raised them to his lips—"that you inform your daughters that they've had the honor of being instructed, albeit for so short a time, by my duchess."

"Your *duchess*!" The exclamation burst from three throats—of the gentry, only Vane Cynster remained silent.

Honoria's brain reeled again; the grip on her fingers tightened. Her expression serene, her lips gently curved, she glanced affectionately at her supposed fiancé''s face; only he could see the fell promise in her eyes.

"*Really*, Your Grace! You *can't* have considered." Lady Claypole had paled. "This matter hardly warrants such a sacrifice— I'm sure Miss Wetherby will be only too happy to reach some agreement . . ."

Her voice trailed away, finally silenced by the expression on Devil's face. For one, long minute, he held her paralyzed, then switched his chill gaze to Lord Claypole. "I had expected, my lord, that I could count on you and your lady to welcome my duchess." The deep flat tones held a definite menace.

Lord Claypole swallowed. "Yes indeed! No doubt of it—none whatever. Er . . ." Gathering his reins, he reached for his wife's. "Felicitations and all that—daresay we should get on. If you'll excuse us, Your Grace? Come, m'dear." With a yank, his lordship turned both his and his wife's horses; with remarkable speed, his party quit the clearing.

Relieved, Honoria studied the remaining horsemen. One glance was enough to identify the one nearest as a relative of . . . the duke called Devil. Her mind tripped on the thought, but she couldn't catch the connection. The horseman in question turned his head; hands negligently crossed on the pommel, he was strikingly handsome. His coloring—brown hair, brown brows—was less dramatic than Devil's, but he seemed of similar height and nearly as large as the man beside her. They shared one, definitive characteristic—the simple act of turning his head had been invested with the same fluid elegance that characterized all Devil's movements, a masculine grace that titillated the senses.

The horseman's gaze traveled rapidly over her—one comprehensive glance—then, lips curving in a subtle smile, he looked at Devil. "I take it you don't need rescuing?"

Voice and manner confirmed their relationship beyond question.

"Not rescuing—there's been an accident. Come inside."

The horseman's gaze sharpened; Honoria could have sworn some unspoken communication passed between him and Devil. Without another word, the horseman swung down from his saddle.

Revealing his companion, still atop his horse. An older man with pale thinning hair, he was heavily built, his face round, his features more fleshy than the aquiline planes of the other two men. He, too, met Devil's eye, then he hauled in a breath and dismounted. "Who are they?" Honoria whispered, as the first man, having secured his horse, started toward them.

"Two other cousins. The one approaching is Vane. At least, that's what we call him. The other is Charles. Tolly's brother."

"Brother?" Honoria juggled the image of the heavyset man against that of the dead youth.

"Half brother," Devil amended. Grasping her elbow, he stepped out of the cottage, drawing her with him.

It had been some time since anyone had physically compelled Honoria to do anything—it was certainly the first time any man had dared. His sheer presumption left her speechless; his sheer power rendered noncompliance impossible. Her heart, having finally slowed after the jolt he'd given it by kissing her fingers, started racing again.

Five paces from the door, he halted and, releasing her, faced her. "Wait over there—you can sit on that log. This might take a while."

For one pregnant instant, Honoria hovered on the brink of open rebellion. There was something implacable behind the crystal green, something that issued commands in the absolute certainty of being obeyed. She ached to challenge it, to challenge him, to take exception to his peremptory dictates. But she knew what he faced in the cottage.

Lips compressed, she inclined her head. "Very well."

She turned, skirts swirling; Devil watched as she started toward the log, set on stumps to one side of the clearing. Then she paused; without looking back, she inclined her head again. "Your Grace."

His gaze fixed on her swaying hips, Devil watched as she continued on her way. His interest in her had just dramatically increased; no woman before had so much as thought of throwing his commands—he knew perfectly well they were autocratic—back in his teeth. She'd not only thought of it—she'd nearly done it. If it hadn't been for Tolly's body in the cottage, she would have.

She reached the log. Satisfied, Devil turned; Vane was waiting at the cottage door.

"What?"

Devil's face hardened. "Tolly's dead. Shot."

Vane stilled, his eyes fixed on Devil's. "Who by?"

"That," Devil said softly, glancing at Charles as he neared, "I don't yet know. Come inside."

They stopped in a semicircle at the foot of the rude pallet, looking down on Tolly's body. Vane had been Devil's lieutenant at Waterloo; Charles had served as an adjutant. They'd seen death many times; familiarity didn't soften the blow. In a voice devoid of emotion, Devil recounted all he knew. He related Tolly's last words; Charles, his expression blank, hung on every syllable. Then came a long silence; in the bright light spilling through the open door, Tolly's corpse looked even more obscenely wrong than it had the night before.

"My *God. Tolly!*" Charles's words were broken. His features crumpled. Covering his face with one hand, he sank to the edge of the pallet.

Devil clenched his jaw, his fists. Death no longer possessed the power to shock him. Grief remained, but that he would handle privately. He was the head of his family—his first duty was to lead. They'd expect it of him—he expected it of himself. And he had Honoria Prudence to protect.

The thought anchored him, helping him pull free of the vortex of grief that dragged at his mind. He hauled in a deep breath, then quietly stepped back, retreating to the clear space before the hearth.

A few minutes later, Vane joined him; he glanced through the open door. "She found him?"

Devil nodded. "Thankfully, she's not the hysterical sort." They spoke quietly, their tones subdued. Glancing at the bed, Devil frowned. "What's Charles doing here?"

"He was at the Place when I arrived. Says he chased Tolly up here over some business matter. He called at Tolly's rooms—Old Mick told him Tolly had left for here."

Devil grimaced. "I suppose it's as well that he's here."

Vane was studying his bare chest. "Where's your shirt?"

"It's the bandage." After a moment, Devil sighed and straightened. "I'll take Miss Anstruther-Wetherby to the Place and send a cart."

"And I'll stay and watch over the body." A fleeting smile touched Vane's lips. "You always get the best roles."

Devil's answering smile was equally brief. "This one comes with a ball and chain."

Vane's eyes locked on his. "You're serious?"

"Never more so." Devil glanced at the pallet. "Keep an eye on Charles."

Vane nodded.

The sunshine outside nearly blinded him. Devil blinked and squinted at the log. It was empty. He cursed and looked again—a terrible thought occurred. What if she'd tried to take Sulieman?

His reaction was instantaneous—the rush of blood, the sudden pounding of his heart. His muscles had already tensed to send him racing to the stable when a flicker of movement caught his eye.

She hadn't gone to the stable. Eyes adjusting to the glare, Devil watched her pace back and forth, a few steps to the side of the log. Her dun-colored gown had blended with the boles of the trees, momentarily camouflaging her. His panic subsiding, he focused his gaze.

Honoria felt it—she looked up and saw him, bare-chested still, the very image of a buccaneer, watching her, unmoving, irritation in every line. Their gazes locked—a second later, she broke the contact. Nose in the air, she stepped gracefully to her right—and sat primly on the log.

He waited, sharp green gaze steady, then, apparently satisfied that she'd remain where she'd been put, he headed for the stable.

Honoria ground her teeth, and told herself that he didn't matter. He was an expert in manipulation—and in intimidation—but why should that bother her? She would go to this Place of his, wait for her boxes, and then be on her way. She could spend the time meeting the Dowager Duchess.

At least she'd solved one part of the mystery plaguing her—she'd met her elusive duke. The image she'd carried for the past three days—the image Lady Claypole had painted—of a mild, unassuming, reclusive peer, rose in her mind. The image didn't fit the reality—the duke called Devil was not mild or unassuming. He was a first-class tyrant. And as for Lady Claypole's claim that he was caught in her coils, her ladyship was dreaming.

But at least she'd met her duke, even if she had yet to learn his name. She was, however, having increasing difficulty believing that the notion of introducing himself had not, at some point in the past fifteen hours, passed through his mind. Which was a thought to ponder.

Honoria wriggled, ruing the loss of her petticoat. The log was rough and wrinkly; it was making painful indentations in her flesh. She could see the stable entrance; from the shifting shadows, she surmised Devil was saddling his demon horse. Presumably he would ride to the Place and send conveyances for her and his cousin's body.

With the end of her unexpected adventure in sight, she allowed herself a moment's reflection. Somewhat to her surprise, it was filled with thoughts of Devil. He was overbearing, arrogant,

domineering—the list went on. And on. But he was also strikingly handsome, could be charming when he wished and, she suspected, possessed a suitably devilish sense of humor. She'd seen
enough of the duke to accord him her respect and enough of the
man to feel an empathetic tug. Nevertheless, she had no desire to
spend overmuch time in the company of a tyrant called Devil.
Gentlemen such as he were all very well—as long as they weren't
related to you and kept a respectful distance.

She'd reached that firm conclusion when he reappeared, leading Sulieman. The stallion was skittish, the man somber. Honoria
stood as he neared.

Stopping in front of her, he halted Sulieman beside him; with
the log immediately behind her, Honoria couldn't step back.
Before she could execute a sideways sidle, Devil looped the reins
about one fist—and reached for her.

By the time she realized his intention, she was perched pre-
cariously sidesaddle on Sulieman's back. She gasped, and locked
her hands about the pommel. "What on *earth* . . . ?"

Unlooping the reins, Devil threw her an impatient frown. "I'm
taking you home."

Honoria blinked—he had a way with words she wasn't sure
she appreciated. "You're taking me to *your* home—the Place?"

"Somersham Place." The reins free, Devil reached for the
pommel. With Honoria riding before him, he wasn't intending to
use the stirrups.

Honoria's eyes widened. "*Wait!*"

The look Devil cast her could only be achieved by an impatient man. "What?"

"You've forgotten your jacket—it's in the cottage." Honoria
fought to contain her panic, occasioned by the thought of his

chest—bare—pressed against her back. Even within a foot of her back. Within a foot of any of her.

"Vane'll bring it."

"*No!* Well—whoever heard of a duke riding about the country-side bare-chested? You might catch cold—I mean . . ." Aghast, Honoria realized she was looking into pale green eyes that saw far more than she'd thought.

Devil held her gaze steadily. "Get used to it," he advised. Then he vaulted into the saddle behind her.

Chapter 4

The only benefit Honoria could discover in her position on Sulieman's back was that her tormentor, behind her, could not see her face. Unfortunately, he could see the blush staining not only her cheeks but her neck. He could also feel the rigidity that had gripped her—hardly surprising—the instant he'd landed in the saddle behind her, he'd wrapped a muscled arm about her and pulled her against him.

She'd shut her eyes the moment he'd touched her; panic had cut off her shriek. For the first time in her life she thought she might actually faint. The steely strength surrounding her was overwhelming; by the time she subdued her flaring reactions and could function rationally again, they were turning from the bridle path into the lane.

Glancing about, she looked down—and clutched at the arm about her waist. It tightened.

"Sit still—you won't fall."

Honoria's eyes widened. She could *feel* every word he said. She could also feel a pervasive heat emanating from his chest, his arms, his thighs; wherever they touched, her skin burned. "Ah . . ." They were retracing the journey she'd taken in the gig; the curve into the straight lay just ahead. "Is Somersham Place your principal residence?"

"It's home. My mother remains there most of the year."

There was no duke of Somersham. As they rounded the curve, Honoria decided she had had enough. Her hips, her bottom, were wedged firmly between his rock-hard thighs. They were exceedingly close, yet she didn't even know his name. "What *is* your title?"

"Titles." The stallion tried to veer to the side of the lane but was ruthlessly held on course. "Duke of St. Ives, Marquess of Earith, Earl of Strathfield, Viscount Wellsborough, Viscount Moreland, . . ."

The recital continued; Honoria leaned back against his arm so she could see his face. By the time names ceased to fall from his lips, they'd passed the place of yesterday's tragedy and rounded the next bend. He looked down; she narrowed her eyes at him. "Are you quite finished?"

"Actually, no. That's the litany they drummed into me when I was in shortcoats. There are more recent additions, but I've never learned where they fit."

He glanced down again—Honoria stared blankly back at him. She'd finally caught the elusive connection.

Cynsters hold St. Ives. That was a line of the rhyme her mother had taught her, listing the oldest families in the *ton*. And if Cynsters still held St. Ives, that meant . . . Abruptly, she focused on the chiseled features of the man holding her so easily before him. "You're *Devil Cynster?*"

His eyes met hers; when she continued to stare in dumbfounded accusation, one black brow arrogantly rose. "You want proof?"

Proof? What more proof could she need? One glance into those ageless, omniscient eyes, at that face displaying steely strength perfectly melded with rampant sensuality, was enough to settle all doubts. Abruptly, Honoria faced forward; her mind had reeled before—now it positively whirled.

Cynsters—the *ton* wouldn't be the same without them. They were a breed apart—wild, hedonistic, unpredictable. In company with her own forebears, they'd crossed the Channel with the Conqueror; while her ancestors sought power through politics and finance, the Cynsters pursued the same aim through more direct means. They were and always had been warriors supreme— strong, courageous, intelligent—men born to lead. Through the centuries, they'd thrown themselves into any likely-looking fray with a reckless passion that made any sane opponent think twice. Consequently, every king since William had seen the wisdom of placating the powerful lords of St. Ives. Luckily, by some strange quirk of nature, Cynsters were as passionate about land as they were over battle.

Added to that, whether by fate or sheer luck, their heroism under arms was matched by an uncanny ability to survive. In the aftermath of Waterloo, when so many noble families were counting the cost, a saying had gone the rounds, born of grudging awe. The Cynsters, so it went, were invincible; seven had taken the field and all seven returned, hale and whole, with barely a scratch.

They were also invincibly arrogant, a characteristic fueled by the fact that they were, by and large, as talented as they thought themselves, a situation which engendered in less-favored mortals a certain reluctant respect.

Not that Cynsters demanded respect—they simply took it as their due.

If even half the tales told were true, the current generation were as wild, hedonistic, and unpredictable as any Cynsters ever were. And the current head of the clan was the wildest, most hedonistic, and unpredictable of them all. The present duke of St.

Ives—he who had tossed her up to his saddle and declared he was taking her home. The same man who'd told her to get used to his bare chest. The piratical autocrat who had, without a blink, decreed she was to be his duchess.

It suddenly occurred to Honoria that she might be assuming too much. Matters might not be proceeding quite as she'd thought. Not that it mattered—she knew where life was taking her. Africa. She cleared her throat. "When next you meet them, the Claypole girls might prove trying—they are, I'm sorry to say, their mother's daughters."

She felt him shrug. "I'll leave you to deal with them."

"I won't be here." She made the statement firmly.

"We'll be here often enough—we'll spend some of the year in London and on my other estates, but the Place will always be home. But you needn't worry over me—I'm not fool enough to face the disappointed local aspirants without availing myself of your skirts."

"I beg your pardon?" Turning, Honoria stared at him.

He met her gaze briefly; his lips quirked. "To hide behind."

The temptation was too great—Honoria lifted an arrogant brow. "I thought Cynsters were invincible."

His smile flashed. "The trick is not to expose oneself unnecessarily to the enemy's fire."

Struck by the force of that fleeting smile, Honoria blinked—and abruptly faced forward. There was, after all, no reason she should face *him* unnecessarily either. Then she realized she'd been distracted. "I hate to destroy your defense, but I'll be gone in a few days."

"I hesitate to contradict you," came in a purring murmur just above her left ear, "but we're getting married. You are, therefore, not going anywhere."

Honoria gritted her teeth against the shivery tingles that coursed down her spine. Turning her head, she looked directly into his mesmerizing eyes. "You only said that to spike Lady Claypole's guns." When he didn't respond, just met her gaze levelly, she looked forward, shrugging haughtily. "You're no gentleman to tease me so."

The silence that followed was precisely gauged to stretch her nerves taut. She knew that when he spoke, his voice deep, low, velvet dark. "I never tease—at least not verbally. And I'm not a gentleman, I'm a nobleman, a distinction I suspect you understand very well."

Honoria knew what she was meant to understand—her insides were quaking in a thoroughly distracting way—but she was not about to surrender. "I am not marrying you."

"If you think that, my dear Miss Anstruther-Wetherby, I fear you've overlooked a number of pertinent points."

"Such as?"

"Such as the past night, which we spent under the same roof, in the same room, unchaperoned."

"Except by a dead man, your cousin, who everyone must know you were fond of. With his body laid out upon the bed, no one will imagine anything untoward occurred." Convinced she'd played a winning card, Honoria wasn't surprised by the silence which followed.

They emerged from the trees into the brightness of a late-summer morning. It was early; the crisp chill of the night had yet to fade. The track followed a water-filled ditch. Ahead, a line of gnarled trees lay across their path.

"I had intended to ask you not to mention how we found Tolly. Except, of course, to the family and the magistrate."

Honoria frowned. "What do you mean?"

"I'd rather it was thought that we found him this morning, already dead."

Honoria pursed her lips, and saw her defense evaporate. But she could hardly deny the request, particularly as it really mattered not at all. "Very well. But why?"

"The sensationalism will be bad enough when it becomes known he was killed by a highwayman. I'd rather spare my aunt, and you, as much of the consequent questioning as possible. If it's known he lived afterward and we found him before he died, you'll be subjected to an inquisition every time you appear in public."

She could hardly deny it—the *ton* thrived on speculation. "Why can't we say he was already dead when we found him yesterday?"

"Because if we do, it's rather difficult to explain why I didn't simply leave you with the body and ride home, relieving you of my dangerous presence."

"Given you appear impervious to the elements, why didn't you leave after he died?"

"It was too late by then."

Because the damage to her reputation had already been done? Honoria swallowed an impatient humph. Between the trees, she could see a stone wall, presumably enclosing the park. Beyond, she glimpsed a large house, the roof and the highest windows visible above tall hedges. "Anyway," she stated, "on one point Lady Claypole was entirely correct—there's no need for any great fuss."

"Oh?"

"It's a simple matter—as Lady Claypole will not give me a recommendation, perhaps your mother could do so?"

"I think that's unlikely."

"Why?" Honoria twisted around. "She'll know who I am just as you did."

Pale green eyes met hers. "That's why."

She wished narrowing her eyes at him had some effect—she tried it anyway. "In the circumstances, I would have thought your mother would do all she can to help me."

"I'm sure she will—which is precisely why she won't lift a finger to help you to another position as governess."

Stifling a snort, Honoria turned forward. "She can't be that stuffy."

"I can't recall her ever being described as such."

"I rather think somewhere to the north might be wise—the Lake District perhaps?"

He sighed—Honoria felt it all the way to her toes. "My dear Miss Anstruther-Wetherby, let me clarify a few details. Firstly, the tale of us spending the night alone in my woodsman's cottage will out—nothing is more certain. Regardless of all injunctions delivered by her put-upon spouse, Lady Claypole will not be able to resist telling her dearest friends the latest scandal involving the duke of St. Ives. All in absolute confidence, of course, which will ensure the story circulates to every corner of the *ton*. After that, your reputation will be worth rather less than a farthing. Regardless of what they say to your face, not a single soul will believe in your innocence. Your chances of gaining a position in a household of sufficient standing to set your brother's mind at rest are currently nil."

Honoria scowled at the trees, drawing ever nearer. "I take leave to inform you, Your Grace, that I'm hardly a green girl. I'm a mature woman of reasonable experience—no easy mark."

"Unfortunately, my dear, you have your cause and effect confused. If you had, indeed, been a fresh-faced chit just out of the schoolroom, few would imagine I'd done anything other than sleep last night. As it is . . ." He paused, slowing Sulieman as they neared the trees. "It's well-known I prefer more challenging game."

Disgusted, Honoria humphed. "It's ridiculous—there wasn't even a bed."

The chest behind her quaked, then was still. "Trust me— there's no requirement for a bed."

Honoria pressed her lips shut and glared at the trees. The path wended through the stand; beyond stood the stone wall, two feet thick and eight feet high. An archway gave onto an avenue lined with poplars. Through the shifting leaves, she sighted the house, still some way to the left. It was huge—a long central block with perpendicular wings at each end, like an E without the middle stroke. Directly ahead lay a sprawling stable complex.

The proximity of the stables prompted her to speech. "I suggest, Your Grace, that we agree to disagree over the likely outcome of last night. I acknowledge your concern but see no reason to tie myself up in matrimony to avoid a few months' whispers. Given your reputation, you can hardly argue." That, she felt, was a nicely telling touch.

"My dear Miss Anstruther-Wetherby." His gentle, perfectly lethal purr sounded in her left ear; tingles streaked down her spine. "Let me make one point perfectly clear. I don't intend to argue. You, an Anstruther-Wetherby, have been compromised, however innocently, by me, a Cynster. There is, therefore, no question over the outcome; hence, there can be no argument."

Honoria gritted her teeth so tightly her jaw ached. The struggle to suppress the shudder that purring murmur of his evoked distracted her all the way to the stable arch. They rode beneath it, Sulieman's hooves clattering on the cobbles. Two grooms came running but pulled up short of where Devil reined in his black steed.

"Where's Melton?"

"Not yet about, Y'r Grace."

Honoria heard her rescuer—or was that captor?—curse beneath his breath. Entirely without warning, he dismounted—by bringing his leg over the pommel, taking her to the ground with him. She didn't have time to shriek.

Catching her breath, she realized her feet had yet to reach earth—he was holding her still, firmly caught against him; another shudder threatened. She drew breath to protest—on the instant, he gently set her down.

Lips compressed, Honoria haughtily brushed down her skirts. Straightening, she turned toward him—he caught her hand, grabbed the reins, and headed for the stable block, towing her and his black demon behind him.

Honoria swallowed her protest; she'd rather go with him than cool her heels in the stable yard, a prey to his grooms' curiosity. Gloom, filled with the familiar smells of hay and horses, engulfed her. "Why can't your grooms brush him down?"

"They're too frightened of him—only old Melton can handle him."

Honoria looked at Sulieman—the horse looked steadily back.

His master stopped before a large stall. Released, Honoria leaned against the stall door. Arms crossed, she pondered her predicament while watching her captor—she was increasingly certain that was a more accurate description of him—rub down his fearsome steed.

Muscles bunched and relaxed; the sight was positively mesmerizing. He'd told her to get used to it; she doubted she ever could. He bent, then fluidly straightened and shifted to the horse's other side; his chest came into view. Honoria drew in a slow breath—then he caught her eye.

For one instant, their gazes held—then Honoria looked away, first at the tack hanging along the stable wall, then up at the rafters, inwardly berating herself for her reaction, simultaneously wishing she had a fan to hand.

It was never wise to tangle with autocrats, but, given she had no choice, she needed to remember that it was positively fatal to acknowledge he had any power over her.

Determined to hold her own, she ordered her mind to business. If he believed honor demanded he marry her, she'd need to try a different tack. She frowned. "I do not see that it's fair that, purely because I was stranded by a storm and took shelter in the same cottage as you, I should have to redirect my life. I am not a passive spectator waiting for the next occurrence to happen—I have plans!"

Devil glanced up. "Riding in the shadow of the Great Sphinx?" He could just imagine her on a camel—along with a hovering horde of Berber chieftains who looked remarkably like him and thought like him, too.

"Precisely. And I plan to explore the Ivory Coast as well—another exciting place so I've heard."

Barbary pirates and slave traders. Devil tossed aside the currying brush and dusted his hands on his breeches. "You'll just have to make do with becoming a Cynster—no one's ever suggested it's a mundane existence."

"I am not going to marry you."

Her flashing eyes and the set of her chin declared her Anstruther-Wetherby mind was made up; Devil knew he was going to seriously enjoy every minute it took to make her change it. He walked toward her.

Predictably, she backed not an inch, although he saw her muscles lock against the impulse. Without breaking stride, he closed his hands about her waist and lifted her, setting her down with her back against the stall wall. With commendable restraint, he removed his hands, locking one on the top of the half-closed door, bracing the other, palm flat, on the wall by her shoulder.

Caged, she glared at him; he tried not to notice how her breasts rose as she drew in a deep breath. He spoke before she could. "What have you got against the proposition?"

Honoria kept her eyes locked on his—standing as he was, her entire field of vision was filled with bare male. Once her heart had ceased to thud quite so loudly, she raised her brows haughtily. "I have no desire whatever to marry purely because of some antiquated social stricture."

"That's the sum of your objections?"

"Well, there's Africa, of course."

"Forget Africa. Is there any reason other than my motives in offering for you that in your opinion constitutes an impediment to our marriage?"

His arrogance, his high-handedness, his unrelenting authority—his chest. Honoria was tempted to start at the top of her list and work her way down. But not one of her caveats posed any serious impediment to their marriage. She searched his eyes for some clue as to her best answer, fascinated anew by their remarkable clarity. They were like crystal clear pools of pale green water, emotions, thoughts, flashing like quicksilver fish in their depths. "No."

"Good."

She glimpsed some emotion—was it relief?—flash through his eyes before his heavy lids hid them from view. Straightening, he caught her hand and headed for the stable door. Stifling a curse, she grabbed up her skirts and lengthened her stride. He made for the main archway; beyond lay his house, peaceful in the morning sunshine.

"You may set your mind at rest, Miss Anstruther-Wetherby." He glanced down, the planes of his face granite-hard. "I'm not marrying you because of any social stricture. That, if you consider it, is a nonsensical idea. Cynsters, as you well know, do not give a damn about social strictures. Society, as far as we're concerned, can think what it pleases—*it* does not rule *us*."

"But . . . if that's the case—and given your reputation I can readily believe it is—why insist on marrying me?"

"Because I want to."

The words were delivered as the most patently obvious answer to a simple question. Honoria held on to her temper. "Because you *want* to?"

He nodded.

"That's it? Just because you want to?"

The look he sent her was calculated to quell. "For a Cynster, that's a perfectly adequate reason. In fact, for a Cynster, there *is* no better reason."

He looked ahead again; Honoria glared at his profile. "*This* is ridiculous. You only set eyes on me yesterday, and now you want to marry me?"

Again he nodded.

"*Why?*"

The glance he shot her was too brief for her to read. "It so happens I need a wife, and you're the perfect candidate." With that, he altered their direction and lengthened his stride even more.

"I am *not* a racehorse."

His lips thinned, but he slowed—just enough so she didn't have to run. They'd gained the graveled walk that circled the house. It took her a moment to replay his words, another to see their weakness. "That's still ridiculous. You must have half the female population of the *ton* waiting to catch your handkerchief every time you blow your nose."

He didn't even glance her way. "At least half."

"So why *me*?"

Devil considered telling her—in graphic detail. Instead, he gritted his teeth and growled: "Because you're unique."

"*Unique?*"

Unique in that she was arguing. He halted, raised his eyes to the heavens in an appeal for sufficient strength to deal with an Anstruther-Wetherby, then looked down and trapped her gaze. "Let me put it this way—*you* are an attractive Anstruther-Wetherby female with whom I've spent an entire night in private—and I've yet to bed you." He smiled. "I assume you would prefer we married before I do?"

The stunned shock in her eyes was balm to his soul. The grey orbs, locked on his, widened—then widened even more. He knew what she was seeing—the sheer lust that blazed through him had to be lighting his eyes.

He fully expected her to dissolve into incoherent, ineffectual, disjointed gibberings—instead, she suddenly snapped free of his visual hold, blinked, drew a quick breath—and narrowed her eyes at him.

"I am *not* marrying you just so I can go to bed with you. I mean—" She caught herself up and breathlessly amended, "So that you can go to bed with me."

Devil watched the telltale color rise in her cheeks. Grimly, he nodded. "Fine." Tightening his grip on her hand, he turned and stalked on.

All the way from the cottage, she'd shifted and wriggled

against him; by the time they'd reached the stable, he'd been agonizingly aroused. How he'd managed not to throw her down in the straw and ease his pain, he had no idea. But he now had a roaring headache, and if he didn't keep moving—keep her moving—temptation might yet get the upper hand. *"You,"* he stated, as they rounded the corner of the house, "can marry me for a host of sensible, socially acceptable reasons. *I'll* marry you to get you into my bed."

He felt her dagger glance. "That is—*Good God!"*

Honoria stopped; stock-still, she stared. Somersham Place lay spread before her, basking in the morning sunshine. Immense, built of honey-colored stone at least a century before, it sprawled elegantly before her, a mature and gracious residence overlooking a wide lawn. She was dimly aware of the lake at the bottom of the lawn, of the oaks flanking the curving drive, of the stone wall over which a white rose cascaded, dew sparkling on the perfumed blooms. The clack of ducks drifted up from the lake; the air was fresh with the tang of clipped grass. But it was the house that held her. Durable, inviting, there was grandeur in every line, yet the sharp edges were muted, softened by the years. Sunbeams glinted on row upon row of lead-paned windows; huge double oak doors were framed by a portico of classic design. Like a lovely woman mellowed by experience, his home beckoned, enticed.

He was proposing to make her mistress of all this.

The thought flitted through her mind; even though she knew he was watching, she allowed herself a moment to imagine, to dwell on what might be. For this had she been born, reared, trained. What should have been her destiny lay before her. But becoming his duchess would mean risking . . .

No! She'd promised herself—never again.

Mentally shutting her eyes to the house, the temptation, she drew a steadying breath, and saw the crest blazoned in stone on the portico's facade, a shield sporting a stag rampant on a ground of fleur-de-lis. Beneath the shield ran a wide stone ribbon bearing a carved inscription. The words were Latin—it took her a moment to translate. "To have . . . and to hold?"

Hard fingers closed about hers. "The Cynster family motto."

Honoria raised her eyes heavenward. An irresistible force, he drew her toward the steps. "Where are you taking me?" A vision of silk cushions and gauze curtains—a pirate's private lair—flashed into her mind.

"To my mother. Incidentally, she prefers to be addressed as the Dowager."

Honoria frowned. "But you're not married."

"Yet. It's her subtle way of reminding me of my duty."

Subtle. Honoria wondered what the Dowager—his mother, after all—would do if she wished to make a point forcefully. Whatever, it was time and past to make a stand. It would be unwise to cross his threshold—beyond which, she had not the slightest doubt, he ruled like a king—without coming to some agreement as to their future relationship, or lack thereof.

They reached the porch; he halted before the doors and released her. Facing him, Honoria straightened. "Your Grace, we must—"

The doors swung inward, held majestically wide by a butler, one of the more imposing of the species. Cheated of her moment, Honoria only just managed not to glare.

The butler's eyes had gone to his master; his smile was genuinely fond. "Good morning, Your Grace."

His master nodded. "Webster."

Honoria stood her ground. She was not going to cross his

threshold until he acknowledged her right to ignore—as he did whenever it suited him—society's dictates.

He shifted to stand beside her, gesturing for her to precede him. Simultaneously, Honoria felt his hand at the back of her waist. Without her petticoat, only a single layer of fabric separated her skin from his hard palm. He didn't exert any great pressure; instead, seductively questing, his hand traveled slowly, very slowly, down. When it reached the curve of her bottom, Honoria sucked in a quick breath—and stepped quickly over the threshold.

He followed. "This is Miss Anstruther-Wetherby, Webster." He looked her way; Honoria glimpsed triumph in his eyes. "She'll be staying—her boxes should arrive this morning."

Webster bowed low. "I'll have your things taken to your room, miss."

Stiffly, Honoria inclined her head—her heart was still fluttering in her throat; her skin felt hot and cold in the strangest places. She couldn't fault the butler's demeanor; he seemed unsurprised by his master's lack of attire. Was she the only one who found his bare chest at all remarkable? Stifling an urge to sniff disbelievingly, she elevated her nose another inch and looked about the hall.

The impression created by the exterior extended within doors. A sense of graciousness pervaded the high-ceilinged hall, lit by sunlight pouring through the fanlight and the windows flanking the front doors. The walls were papered—blue fleur-de-lis on an ivory ground; the paneling, all light oak, glowed softly. Together with the blue-and-white tiles, the decor imparted an airy, uncluttered atmosphere. Stairs of polished oak, their baluster ornately carved, led upward in a long, straight sweep, then divided into two, both arms leading to the gallery above.

Webster had been informing his master of the presence of his cousins. Devil nodded curtly. "Where's the Dowager?"

"In the morning room, Your Grace."

"I'll take Miss Anstruther-Wetherby to her. Wait for me."

Webster bowed.

The devil glanced down at her. With a languid grace that set her nerves on end, he gestured for her to accompany him. She was still quivering inside—she told herself it was due to indignation. Head high, she swept down the hall.

His instruction to his butler to wait had recalled what their sparring had driven from her mind. As they neared the morning-room door, it occurred to Honoria that she might have been arguing for no real reason. Devil reached for the doorknob, his fingers closing about hers—she tugged. He looked up, incipient impatience in his eyes.

She smiled understandingly. "I'm sorry—I'd forgotten. You must be quite distracted by your cousin's death." She spoke softly, soothingly. "We can discuss all this later, but there's really no reason for us to wed. I daresay, once the trauma has passed, you'll see things as I do."

He held her gaze, his eyes as blank as his expression. Then his features hardened. "Don't count on it." With that, he set the door wide and handed her through. He followed, closing the door behind him.

A petite woman, black hair streaked with grey, was seated in a chair before the hearth, a hoop filled with embroidery on her lap. She looked up, then smiled—the most gloriously welcoming smile Honoria had ever seen—and held out her hand. "There you are, Sylvester. I'd wondered where you'd got to. And who is this?"

His mother's French background rang clearly in her accent;

it also showed in her coloring, in the hair that had once been as black as her son's combined with an alabaster complexion, in the quick, graceful movements of her hands, her animated features and the candid, appraising glance that swept Honoria.

Inwardly ruing her hideously creased skirts, Honoria kept her head high as she was towed across the room. The Dowager hadn't so much as blinked at her son's bare chest.

"*Maman.*" To her surprise, her devilish captor bent and kissed his mother's cheek. She accepted the tribute as her due; as he straightened, she fixed him with a questioning glance every bit as imperious as he was arrogant. He met it blandly. "You told me to bring you your successor the instant I found her. Allow me to present Miss Honoria Prudence Anstruther-Wetherby." Briefly, he glanced at Honoria. "The Dowager Duchess of St. Ives." Turning back to his mother, he added: "Miss Anstruther-Wetherby was residing with the Claypoles—her boxes will arrive shortly. I'll leave you to get acquainted."

With the briefest of nods, he proceeded to do just that, closing the door firmly behind him. Stunned, Honoria glanced at the Dowager, and was pleased to see she wasn't the only one left staring.

Then the Dowager looked up and smiled—warmly, welcomingly, much as she had smiled at her son. Honoria felt the glow touch her heart. The Dowager's expression was understanding, encouraging. "Come, my dear. Sit down." The Dowager waved to the *chaise* beside her chair. "If you have been dealing with Sylvester, you will need the rest. He is often very trying."

Resisting the temptation to agree emphatically, Honoria sank onto the chintz.

"You must excuse my son. He is somewhat . . ." The Dowager paused, clearly searching for the right word. She grimaced. "*De-tressé.*"

"I believe he has a number of matters on his mind."

The Dowager's fine brows rose. "His mind?" Then she smiled, eyes twinkling as they rested once more on Honoria's face. "But now, my dear, as my so-*detressé* son has decreed, we will get acquainted. And as you are to be my daughter-in-law, I will call you Honoria." Again, her brows rose. "Is that not right?"

Her name became "'Onoria"—the Dowager couldn't manage the "H." Honoria returned her smile, and sidestepped the leading question. "If you wish it, ma'am."

The Dowager's smile grew radiant. "My dear, I wish it with all my heart."

Chapter 5

A fter an hour of subtle interrogation, Honoria escaped the Dowager, pleased that, while she'd parted with her life history, she'd successfully avoided all mention of Tolly's death. Shown to an elegant suite, she washed and changed; her self-confidence renewed, she descended—into mayhem.

The magistrate had arrived; while Devil dealt with him, Vane had broken the news to the Dowager. When Honoria entered the drawing room, the Dowager was in full histrionic spate. While grief was certainly present, it had been overtaken by indignant fury.

Instantly, the Dowager appealed to her for details. "You need not apologize for not telling me before. I know just how it was— that oh-so-male son of mine sought to keep the matter from me, Cynster that he is."

Waved to a chair, Honoria dutifully complied. She'd barely finished her tale when the scrunch of wheels on gravel heralded Devil's reappearance.

"What's the verdict?" Vane asked.

Devil met his gaze levelly. "Death through shooting by some person unknown. Possibly a highwayman."

"A highwayman?" Honoria stared at him.

Devil shrugged. "Either that or a poacher." He turned to the Dowager. "I've sent for Arthur and Louise."

Lord Arthur Cynster and his wife Louise proved to be Tolly's parents.

There followed a detailed discussion of who to notify, the appropriate arrangements, and how to accommodate the expected crowd, which encompassed a goodly proportion of the *ton*. While Devil undertook the first two aspects, organizing rooms and sustenance fell to the Dowager.

Despite her firm intention to remain aloof from Devil's family, Honoria simply could not stand by and allow such a weight to descend on the Dowager's fragile shoulders. Especially not when she was more than well qualified to lighten the load. As, however reluctantly, an Anstruther-Wetherby who had been present when Tolly had died, she would be expected to attend the funeral; she would need to remain at the Place at least until after that. That being so, there was no reason not to offer her aid. Besides which, to sit idly in her room while about her the household ran frantic, would be entirely beyond her.

Within minutes, she was immersed in lists—initial lists, then derived lists and eventually lists for cross-checking. The afternoon and evening passed in intense activity; Webster and the housekeeper, a matronly woman known as Mrs. Hull, coordinated the execution of the Dowager's directives. An army of maids and footmen labored to open up rooms. Helpers from the nearby farms tramped in to assist in the kitchens and stables. Yet all the bustle was subdued, somber; not a laugh was heard nor a smile seen.

Night fell, restless, disturbed; Honoria awoke to a dull day. A funereal pall had settled over the Place—it deepened with the arrival of the first carriage.

The Dowager met it, taking her grieving sister-in-law under her wing. Honoria slipped away, intending to seek refuge in the summerhouse by the side of the front lawn. She was halfway across the lawn when she caught sight of Devil, heading her way through the trees. He had gone with the chaplain, Mr. Merryweather, and a party of men to mark out the grave. Devil had seen her; Honoria halted.

He came striding out of the shade, long legs encased in buckskin breeches and shiny top boots. His fine white shirt with billowing sleeves, opened at the throat, was topped by a leather waistcoat. Despite his less-than-conventional attire, with his dramatic coloring, he still looked impressive—and every inch a pirate.

His gaze traveled swiftly over her, taking in her gown of soft lavender-grey, a color suitable for half-mourning. His expression was set, impassive, yet she sensed his approval.

"Your aunt and uncle have arrived." She made the statement while he was still some yards away.

One black brow quirked; Devil didn't pause. "Good morning, Honoria Prudence." Smoothly collecting her hand, he placed it on his arm and deftly turned her back toward the house. "I trust you slept well?"

"Perfectly, thank you." With no choice offering, Honoria strolled briskly beside him. She suppressed an urge to glare. "I haven't made you free of my name."

Devil looked toward the drive. "An oversight on your part, but I'm not one to stand on ceremony. I take it *Maman* has my aunt in hand?"

Her eyes on his, Honoria nodded.

"In that case," Devil said, looking ahead, "I'll need your help." Another crepe-draped carriage came into view, rolling slowly toward the steps. "That will be Tolly's younger brother and sisters."

He glanced at Honoria; she exhaled and inclined her head. Lengthening their strides, they reached the drive as the carriage rocked to a halt.

The door burst open; a boy jumped down. Eyes wide, he looked dazedly toward the house. Then he heard their footsteps and swung their way. Slender, quivering with tension, he faced them, his face leached of all color, his lips pinched. Recognition flared in his tortured eyes. Honoria saw him tense to fly to Devil, but he conquered the impulse and straightened, swallowing manfully.

Devil strode to the boy, dropping a hand on his shoulder and squeezing reassuringly. "Good lad."

He looked into the carriage, then beckoned to the occupants. "Come."

He lifted first one silently sobbing girl, then another, down. Both possessed a wealth of chestnut ringlets and delicate complexions, presently blotchy. Four huge blue eyes swam in pools of tears; their slender figures shook with their sobs. They were, Honoria judged, about sixteen—and twins. Without any show of consciousness or fear, they clung to Devil, arms locking about his waist.

One arm about each, Devil turned them to face her. "This is Honoria Prudence—Miss Anstruther-Wetherby to you. She'll look after you both." He met Honoria's gaze. "She knows how it feels to lose someone you love."

Both girls and the boy were too distressed to render the prescribed greeting. Honoria didn't wait for it but smoothly took her cue. Devil deftly detached himself from the girls' clinging arms; gliding forward, she took his place. Slipping a comforting arm around each girl, she turned them toward the house. "Come—I'll show you to your room. Your parents are already inside."

They allowed her to shepherd them up the steps. Honoria was aware of their curious glances.

On the porch, both girls paused, gulping back their tears. Honoria cast a swift glance behind and saw Devil, his back to them, one arm draped across the boy's slight shoulders, head bent as he spoke to the lad. Turning back, she gathered her now shivering charges and urged them on.

Both balked.

"Will we have to . . . I mean—" One glanced up at her.

"Will we have to look at him?" the other forced out. "Is his face badly damaged?"

Honoria's heart lurched; sympathy—long-buried empathy—welled. "You won't have to see him if you don't want to." She spoke softly, reassuringly. "But he looks wonderfully peaceful—just like I imagine he always did. Handsome and quietly happy."

Both girls stared at her, hope in their eyes.

"I was there when he died," Honoria felt compelled to add.

"You were?" There was surprise and a touch of youthful skepticism in their tones.

"Your cousin was there as well."

"Oh." They glanced back at Devil, then both nodded.

"And now we'd better get you settled." Honoria glanced back; a maid had hopped down from the carriage; footmen had materialized and were unstrapping boxes from the boot and the roof. "You'll want to wash your faces and change before the rest of the family arrives."

With sniffs and watery smiles for Webster, encountered in the hall, they allowed her to usher them upstairs.

The chamber allotted to the girls was near the end of one

wing; promising to fetch them later, Honoria left them in their maid's care and returned downstairs.

Just in time to greet the next arrivals.

The rest of the day flew. Carriages rolled up in a steady stream, disgorging matrons and stiff-necked gentlemen and a goodly sprinkling of bucks. Devil and Vane were everywhere, greeting guests, fielding questions. Charles was there, too, his expression wooden, his manner stilted.

Stationed by the stairs, Honoria helped the Dowager greet and dispose of family and those friends close enough to claim room within the great house. Anchored to her hostess's side, the keeper of the lists, she found herself introduced by the Dowager, with a gently vague air.

"And this is Miss Anstruther-Wetherby, who is keeping me company."

The Cynster cousin to whom this was addressed, presently exchanging nods with Honoria, immediately looked intrigued. Speculation gleamed in the matronly woman's eyes. "Indeed?" She smiled, graciously coy. "I'm very pleased to make your acquaintance, my dear."

Honoria replied with a polite, noncommittal murmur. She'd failed to foresee her present predicament when she'd offered her aid; now she could hardly desert her post. Fixing a smile on her lips, she resolved to ignore her hostess's blatant manipulation. The Dowager, she'd already realized, was even more stubborn than her son.

The family viewing of the body was held late that afternoon; remembering her promise, Honoria went to fetch Tolly's sisters from the distant wing.

They were waiting, pale but composed, intensely vulnerable in black muslin. Honoria ran an experienced eye over them, then nodded. "You'll do." They came forward hesitantly, clearly dreading what was to come. Honoria smiled encouragingly. "Your cousin omitted to mention your names."

"I'm Amelia, Miss Anstruther-Wetherby." The closest bobbed a curtsy.

Her sister did the same, equally gracefully. "I'm Amanda."

Honoria raised her brows. "I presume calling 'Amy' will bring you both?"

The simple sally drew two faint smiles. "Usually," Amelia admitted.

Amanda had already sobered. "Is it true—what Devil said? About you knowing about losing one you love?"

Honoria met her ingenuous gaze levelly. "Yes—I lost both my parents in a carriage accident when I was sixteen."

"Both?" Amelia looked shocked. "That must have been terrible—even worse than losing a brother."

Honoria stilled, then, somewhat stiffly, inclined her head. "Losing any family member is hard—but when they leave us, we still have to go on. We owe it to them—to their memory—as much as to ourselves."

The philosophical comment left both girls puzzling. Honoria seized the moment to get them headed downstairs, to the private chapel off the gallery.

Halting in the doorway, the twins nervously surveyed the black-clad ranks of their aunts and uncles and older male cousins, all silent, most with heads bowed.

Both girls reacted as Honoria had hoped: their spines stiffened— they drew deep breaths, straightened their shoulders, then paced slowly down the quiet room. Hand in hand, they approached the coffin, set on trestles before the altar.

From the shadows by the door, Honoria watched what was, in

essence, a scene from her past. The somber peace of the chapel held her; she was about to slip into the back pew when Devil caught her eye. Commandingly formal in black coat and black trousers, white shirt and black cravat, he looked precisely what he was—a devilishly handsome rake—and the head of his family. From his position beyond the coffin, he raised one brow, his expression a subtle melding of invitation and challenge.

Tolly was no relative of hers, but she'd been present when he died. Honoria hesitated, then followed Tolly's sisters down the aisle.

Clinging to each other, the twins moved on, slipping into the pew behind their weeping mother. Honoria paused, looking down on an innocence not even death could erase. As she had said, Tolly's face was peaceful, serene; no hint of the wound in his chest showed. Only the grey pallor of his skin bore witness that he would not again awake.

She'd seen death before, but not like this. Those before had been taken by God; they had only needed to be mourned. Tolly had been taken by man—a vastly different response was required. She frowned.

"What is it?" Devil's voice came from beside her, pitched very low.

Honoria looked up. Frowning, she searched his eyes. He *knew*—how could he not? Why, then . . . ? A chill touched her soul—she shivered and looked away.

"Come." Devil took her arm; Honoria let him hand her to a pew. He sat beside her; she felt his gaze on her face but did not look his way.

Then Tolly's mother rose. Supported by her husband, she placed a white rose in the coffin; the viewing was at an end. No one spoke as they slowly filed out, following the Dowager and Tolly's parents to the drawing room.

In the front hall, Devil drew Honoria aside, into the shadows of the stairs. As the last stragglers passed, he said, his voice low: "I'm sorry—I shouldn't have insisted. I didn't realize it would remind you of your parents."

Honoria looked up, directly into his eyes. They were not, she realized, particularly useful for *hiding* emotions—the clear depths were too transparent. Right now, they looked contrite.

"It wasn't that. I was simply struck—" She paused, again searching his eyes. "By how *wrong* his death was." Impulsively, she asked: "Are you satisfied with the magistrate's verdict?"

His face hardened into a warrior's mask. His lids lowered, screening those too-revealing eyes, his lashes a distracting veil. "Perfectly." Languidly, he gestured toward the drawing room. "I suggest we join the others."

His abrupt dismissal was not quite a slap in the face, but it certainly gave Honoria pause. Cloaked in her customary poise, she allowed him to lead her into the drawing room, then inwardly cursed when so many eyes swung their way. Their entrance together, separate from the earlier crowd, supported the image Devil and the Dowager were intent on projecting—the image of her as Devil's bride. Such subtle nuances were life and breath to the *ton*, Honoria knew it—she was usually adept at using such signals to her own advantage, but, in the present case, she was clearly fencing with a master.

Make that two masters, simultaneously—the Dowager was no newcomer to the game.

The drawing room was full, crowded with family, connections and close acquaintances. Despite the subdued tones, the noise was substantial. The Dowager was seated on the *chaise* beside Tolly's mother. Devil steered Honoria to where Amelia and Amanda were nervously conversing with a very old lady.

"If you need help with names or connections, ask the twins. It'll make them feel useful."

Honoria inclined her head and coolly returned: "Much as I'd like to distract them, there's really no need. It is, after all, unlikely I'll meet any of your family again." Regally aloof, she raised her head—and met the dark, frowning glance Devil sent her with implacable calm.

Amanda and Amelia turned as they came up, an identical look of pleading in their eyes.

"Ah—Sylvester." The old lady put out a crabbed hand and gripped Devil's sleeve. "A shame it has to be such a sad occasion on which I see you again."

"Indeed, Cousin Clara." Fluidly, Devil drew Honoria into their circle, trapping her hand on his sleeve the instant before she removed it. "I believe," he drawled, "that you've already met . . ." An untrustworthy gleam lit his eyes; inwardly aghast, her gaze locked with his, Honoria held her breath—and saw his lips curve as he looked down at Cousin Clara. "Miss Anstruther-Wetherby?"

Honoria almost sighed with relief. Her serene smile somewhat strained, she trained it on Clara.

"Oh, yes! Dear me, yes." The old lady visibly brightened. "Such a *great* pleasure to meet you, dear. I've been looking forward to—" Catching herself up, Clara glanced impishly at Devil, then smiled sweetly at Honoria. "Well—you know." Reaching out, she patted Honoria's hand. "Suffice to say we're all *perfectly delighted*, my dear."

Honoria knew one person who was less than perfectly delighted, but, with Amanda and Amelia looking on, she was forced to allow Clara's transparent supposition to pass with nothing more than a gracious smile. Looking up, she fleetingly met Devil's gaze—she could have sworn she detected a satisfied gleam in his eyes.

He immediately broke the contact. Releasing her, he covered Clara's hand with his, stooping so she did not have to look up so far. "Have you spoken to Arthur?"

"Not yet." Clara glanced about. "I couldn't find him in this crush."

"He's by the window. Come—I'll take you to him."

Clara beamed. "So kind—but you always were a good boy." With brief nods to the twins, and a gracious one for Honoria, the old lady allowed Devil to lead her away.

Honoria watched them go, Devil so large and powerful, so arrogantly commanding, making not the smallest fuss over the creases Clara's sparrowlike claws were leaving in his sleeve. A good boy? She inwardly humphed.

"Thank goodness you came." Amanda swallowed. "She wanted to talk about Tolly. And I—we—didn't know how to . . ."

"Stop her?" Honoria smiled reassuringly. "Don't worry—it's only the very old who'll ask such questions. Now—" She glanced around—"tell me who the younger ones are—Devil told me their names, but I've forgotten."

That was untrue, but the exercise served to distract the twins. Aside from themselves, Simon, and their two younger sisters, Henrietta and Mary, ten and three, they had three younger cousins.

"Heather's fourteen. Elizabeth—we call her Eliza—is thirteen, and Angelica's ten, the same as Henrietta."

"They're Uncle Martin's and Aunt Celia's daughters. Gabriel and Lucifer are their older brothers."

Gabriel and Lucifer? Honoria opened her mouth to request clarification—simultaneously, the Dowager caught her eye.

The Dowager's expression was an outright appeal for help. Her sister-in-law's hands still gripped hers tightly. With her eyes, the Dowager signaled to Webster, standing unobtrusively before the door. The tension in his stately figure conveyed very clearly that something was amiss.

Honoria looked back at the Dowager—she understood what was being asked of her, and that a positive response would be interpreted as confirmation of another understanding—a matrimonial understanding between Devil and herself. But the appeal in the Dowager's eyes was very real, and of all the ladies present, she was unquestionably in the best state to deal with whatever disaster had befallen.

Torn, Honoria hesitated, then inwardly grimaced and nodded. She stepped toward the door, then remembered the twins. She glanced over her shoulder. "Come with me."

She swept regally across the room. Webster opened the door and stood back; Honoria sailed through. After waiting for her two escorts to pass, Webster followed, closing the door behind him.

In the hall, Honoria found Mrs. Hull waiting. "What's happened?"

Mrs. Hull's gaze flicked to Webster's face, then returned to Honoria's. The significance of that glance was not lost on Honoria; Webster had confirmed that she'd been deputed by the Dowager.

"It's the cakes, miss. What with all we've had to do, we sent out for them to the village. Mrs. Hobbs is excellent with cakes. We've often used her in such circumstances."

"But this time she hasn't lived up to expectations?"

Mrs. Hull's face tightened. "It's not that, miss. I sent two grooms with the gig, like I always do. Hobbs had the cakes ready—the boys loaded them in their trays. They were most of the way back"—Mrs. Hull paused to draw in a portentous breath—"when that *demon* horse of the master's came racing up, rearing and screaming, and spooked the old mare in the gig. The cakes went flying"—Mrs. Hull's eyes narrowed to flinty shards—"and that *devil* horse ate most of them!"

Pressing her fingers to her lips, Honoria looked down. Then she glanced at Webster. His face was expressionless.

"His Grace did not have time to ride the horse today, miss, so the head stableman turned him out for a run. The track from the village runs through the stable paddock."

"I see." Honoria's jaw ached. Despite all—the solemnity of the occasion and the impending crisis—the vision of Sulieman chomping on delicate petit fours was simply too much.

"So, you see, miss, I don't know what we're to do, with all these visitors and not even enough biscuits to go around." Mrs. Hull's expression remained severe.

"Indeed." Honoria straightened, considering possibilities. "Scones," she decided.

"Scones, miss?" Mrs. Hull looked surprised, then her expression turned calculating.

Honoria glanced at the clock on the wall. "It's just four—they won't be expecting tea for at least half an hour. If we arrange some distraction . . ." She looked at Webster. "What time were you intending to serve dinner?"

"Seven, miss."

Honoria nodded. "Put dinner back to eight—notify the valets and ladies' maids. Mrs. Hull, you've an hour to produce scones in quantity. Take whatever helpers you need. We'll have plain scones with jam—do you have any blackberry jam? That would be a nice touch."

"Indeed, miss." Mrs. Hull was transformed. "We have our own blackberry jam—there's no other like it."

"Very good—we'll have cream for those that wish it, and we'll have cheese scones and spiced scones as well."

"I'll get onto it immediately, miss." With a quick bob, Mrs. Hull sped back to her kitchen.

"You spoke of a distraction, miss—to gain half an hour for Mrs. Hull?"

Honoria met Webster's eye. "Not an easy task, given the cause of this gathering."

"Indeed not, miss."

"Can we help?"

Both Honoria and Webster turned to view the twins.

Amanda colored. "With the distraction, I mean."

Slowly, Honoria's brows rose. "I wonder . . . ?" She looked along the hall. "Come with me."

With Webster following, they entered the music room, next to the drawing room. Honoria waved at the instruments ranged along one wall. "What do you play?"

Amelia blinked. "I play the pianoforte."

"And I play the harp," Amanda supplied.

Excellent examples of both instruments stood before them; Webster hurried to maneuver the required pieces into place. Honoria turned to the girls. "You play together?" They nodded. "Good. What pieces can you play? Think of slow, mournful pieces—requiems or sections thereof."

To her relief, the twins were true to their class, well taught and with decent repertoires. Five minutes later, she'd also discovered they possessed considerable skill.

"Excellent." Honoria exchanged a relieved glance with Webster. "Don't let anyone distract you—we need you to play for at least forty minutes. Start at the beginning of your list and start repeating once you've finished. You can stop when the tea trolley arrives."

The girls nodded, and commenced a liturgical excerpt.

"Shall I open the doors, miss?" Webster whispered.

"Yes—the ones to the terrace as well." Both the music room and the drawing room gave onto the long terrace. Webster set the two doors flanking the fireplace wide, joining the two rooms. Heads turned as the haunting chords flowed over the conversations.

Gradually, tempted by the music, both ladies and gentlemen strolled in. The twins, used to performing before their elders, did not falter. There were chairs aplenty; gentlemen obligingly set them out, the ladies subsiding in groups, the gentlemen standing beside them.

From her position by the open terrace door, Honoria watched her distraction take hold. Suddenly, she felt a familiar presence behind her.

"*This* was inspired."

Glancing back, she met Devil's green eyes; they scanned her face.

"What was wrong?"

Honoria wondered if there was anyone in the entire assembly who had missed her assumption of the Dowager's authority. She'd been prepared to swear Devil had been deep in conversation at the far side of the room at the time. "Your devil-horse ate the tea cakes. Mrs. Hull is not impressed. I believe she has visions of turning your steed into cat's meat."

He was close, his shoulder propped against the doorframe behind her; she felt his chest quake with suppressed laughter. "Hully wouldn't do that."

"Just mention your horse and watch her reach for her cleaver."

He was silent, looking out over the room. "Don't tell me you don't play?"

Honoria caught herself just in time—and reframed her answer. "I play the harpsichord, but I'm not Tolly's sister. Incidentally," she continued, in the same mild tone, "I give you fair warning that regardless of whatever imbroglio you and your mother concoct, I will *not* be marrying you."

She felt his gaze on her face; when he spoke, the words feathered her spine. "Would you care to wager on that?"

Honoria lifted her chin. "With a reprobate like you?" She waved dismissively. "You're a gamester."

"One who rarely loses."

The deep words reverberated through her; Honoria abandoned speech and opted for a haughty shrug.

Devil didn't move. His gaze swept her face, but he said nothing more.

To Honoria's relief, her strategem worked. The tea, when it arrived, was perfect, the scones fresh from the oven, the jam sweet. The twins retired to subdued but sincere applause; one glance at their faces showed just how much their contribution had meant to them.

"We'll get them to play again tomorrow," Devil murmured in her ear.

"Tomorrow?" Honoria fought to quell an unhelpful shiver.

"At the wake." Devil met her eyes. "They'll feel better to be doing something useful again."

He left her musing—and returned with a cup of tea for her. She took it, only then realizing how much in need of refreshment she was. Other than understanding her too well, Devil behaved himself, smoothly introducing her to family friends. Honoria didn't need to exercise her imagination over how the company viewed her—their deference was marked. The events of the afternoon, orchestrated by Devil and the Dowager, aided and abetted by Devil's demon horse, had conveyed a clear message—that she was to be Devil's bride.

The evening passed swiftly; dinner, attended by everyone, was a somber meal. No one was inclined to entertainment; most retired early. A brooding, melancholy silence descended over the house, as if it mourned, too.

In her chamber, cocooned in down, Honoria thumped her pillow and ordered herself to fall asleep. Five minutes of restless rustling later, she turned onto her back, and glared at the canopy.

It was all Devil's fault, his and his mother's. She'd *tried* to avoid acting as his duchess-to-be, unfortunately unsuccessfully. Worse, as Devil had stated, on a superficial level, she was perfect for the position, a fact apparently obvious to any who considered the matter. She was starting to feel like she was fighting fate.

Honoria shuffled onto her side. She, Honoria Prudence *Anstruther*-Wetherby, was not going to be pressured into anything. It was patently obvious both Devil and the Dowager would do everything possible to tempt her, to convince her to accept his proposal—the proposal he hadn't made. That last was not a fact she was likely to forget—he'd simply taken it for granted that she would marry him.

She'd known from the first he was impossible, even when she'd thought him a mere country squire; as a duke, he was doubly— triply—so. Aside from anything else—his chest, for example— he was a first-class tyrant. Sane women did not marry tyrants.

She clung to that eminently sound declaration, drawing strength from its unarguable logic. Keeping Devil's image in mind helped enormously—one glance at his face, at the rest of him, was all it took to reinforce her conclusion.

Unfortunately, that image, while helpful on the one hand, brought the source of her deeper unease into stronger focus. No matter how she tried, she couldn't escape the conclusion that for all his vaunted strength of character, for all his apparent family feeling, even despite his Cousin Clara's belief, Devil was turning his back on his dead cousin. Sweeping his death under the proverbial rug, presumably so it wouldn't interfere with his hedonistic pursuit of pleasure.

She didn't want to believe it, but she'd heard him herself. He'd stated that Tolly had been killed by a highwayman or a poacher. Everyone believed him, the magistrate included. He was the head of the family, one step removed from a despot; to them and the *ton*, what Devil Cynster, duke of St. Ives, stated, was.

The only one inclined to question him was herself. Tolly hadn't been shot by a highwayman, nor a poacher.

Why would a highwayman kill an unarmed young man? Highwaymen ordered their victims to stand and deliver; Tolly had carried a heavy purse—she'd felt it in his pocket. Had Tolly been armed and, with the impetuosity of youth, attempted to defend himself? She'd seen no gun; it seemed unlikely he could have flung it far from him while falling from the saddle. A highwayman did not seem at all likely.

As for a poacher, her devilish host had narrowed the field there. Not a shotgun, he had said, but a pistol. Poachers did not use pistols.

Tolly had been murdered.

She wasn't sure when she had reached that conclusion; it was now as inescapable as the dawn.

Honoria sat up and thumped her pillow, then fell back and

stared into the night. Why was she so incensed by it—why did she feel so involved? She felt as if a responsibility had been laid upon her—upon her soul—to see justice done.

But that wasn't the cause of her sleeplessness.

She'd heard Tolly's voice in the cottage, heard the relief he'd felt when he'd realized he'd reached Devil. He'd thought he'd reached safety—someone who would protect him. In the cottage, she would have sworn Devil cared—cared deeply. But his behavior in ignoring the evidence of Tolly's murder said otherwise.

If he truly cared, wouldn't he be searching for the murderer, doing all he could to catch him? Or was his "caring" merely an attitude, only skin-deep? Beneath that facade of strength, was he truly weak and shallow?

She couldn't believe it. She didn't want to believe it.

Honoria closed her eyes. And tried to sleep.

Chapter 6

It was an illusion—all an illusion—a typically arrogant sleight of hand. The scales fell from Honoria's eyes late the next morning, right in the middle of Tolly's funeral.

The crowd attending was considerable. A short service had been held in the church in the grounds, a stone building ringed by ancient trees shading monuments to Cynsters long gone.

Then the pallbearers—Devil and his cousins—had carried the coffin to the grave, set in a small clearing beyond the first circle of trees. Contrary to her intention to merge with the crowd, Honoria had been partnered first by Vane, who had given her his arm, thus including her in the family procession to the church, then later claimed by Amanda and Amelia, who had steered her to the grave, admitting they were acting on Devil's orders. A funeral was no place to make a stand. Resigned, Honoria had capitulated, accepting a position behind the twins at the graveside.

It was then the truth struck her.

The males of the family lined the other side of the grave. Directly opposite stood Tolly's brothers, Charles, with Simon beside him. Devil stood next to Simon; as Honoria watched, he placed a hand on Simon's shoulder. The boy looked up; Honoria witnessed their shared glance, that silent communication at which Devil excelled.

Vane stood next to Devil; behind and around them stood a solid phalanx of male Cynsters. There was no doubt of their connection—their faces, seen all together, held the same unyielding planes, their features the same autocratic cast. They numbered six, not counting Simon and Charles, both set apart, one by age, the other by character. Between the six, hair color varied, from Devil's black to light chestnut; eye color, too, differed. Nothing else did.

There was enormous strength in the group facing her powerful, masculine, it emanated from them. Devil was their leader yet they were a group of individuals, each contributing to the whole. Elsewhere about the grave, grief was amorphous. The grief of Tolly's male cousins held purpose, melding into a cohesive force, directed, focused.

Focused on Tolly's grave.

Honoria narrowed her eyes. People were still shifting, finding places in the crowd; both Amelia and Amanda were tense. Honoria leaned forward and whispered: "Tell me the names of your older male cousins."

The twins glanced at her, then across the grave. Amelia spoke first. "Vane's next to Devil, but you know him."

"That can't be his real name."

"His real name's *Spencer*," Amanda whispered. "But don't *ever* call him that."

"The one behind Devil is Richard—he's called Scandal. He's Devil's brother."

"And the one behind Vane is his younger brother, Harry. They call him Demon."

"Demon Harry?"

"That's right." Amanda nodded. "The one next to Vane is Gabriel."

"His real name's Rupert—he's Uncle Martin's eldest son."

"And I suppose the one behind Gabriel is Lucifer?" Honoria asked. "His brother?"

"That's right—he's really Alasdair."

Straightening, Honoria spent one minute wondering how they'd come by their pseudonyms—one question she was not about to ask the twins. She looked across the grave at those six male faces, and saw them clearly. No force on earth would stop them bringing Tolly's murderer to justice.

Being Cynsters, they could be counted on to avenge Tolly's death. Also being Cynsters, they would ensure their women-folk, their elders and juniors—all those they considered in their care—were not disturbed or touched by such violence. Death and vengeance was their province, the home fires for the rest.

Which was all very well, *but* . . .

The last prayer was said; earth struck the coffin. Tolly's mother sagged in her sisters-in-law's arms; her husband hurried to her side. Amelia and Amanda tugged at Honoria's hands. Reluctantly, she turned from the grave—from the tableau on its opposite side.

Charles and the older Cynsters had left, but Simon, Devil, and the five others remained, their gazes still locked on the coffin. Just before she turned, Honoria saw Simon look up, into Devil's face, a question in his wide eyes. She saw Devil's response, the tightening of his hand on Simon's shoulder, the quiet promise he bent his head to give.

She had no doubt of the substance of that promise.

In company with the twins, Honoria crossed the lawns, musing on her situation. She would send for her brother Michael tomorrow, but he would take some days to reach her. Those days could be useful.

She needed to see justice done; she had a duty to avenge innocence—that was doubtless why Tolly's face haunted her. Impossible to send adult Cynster males to avenge innocence; their vengeance would be fueled by their warriors' reasons— the defending of their family, their clan. *She* would be the defender of innocence—she had a role to play, too.

She'd been looking for excitement, for adventure and intrigue— fate had landed her here. Far be it from her to argue.

The wake was a crush. Many of the bucks and bloods who had come up from London stayed for the final scene. In half an hour, Honoria had been introduced to more dangerous blades than she'd thought to meet in a lifetime. Luckily, her inclusion within the family group had sent a clear message; she was not troubled by any of the visitors.

The twins again took to their instruments; the crowd filled the music room and the drawing room and overflowed onto the terrace.

While chatting with Cynster relatives and *ton*nish family acquaintances, Honoria kept a careful eye on Devil and his five accomplices. A pattern was soon apparent. Devil stood in the drawing room, his back to the open terrace doors; the others roamed the crowd, every now and then either stopping by Devil's side quietly to impart some information or catching his eye.

She could do nothing to intercept that silent communication; as for the other, however, . . . Honoria focused on Lady Sheffield, her present interrogator.

"Of course," her ladyship intoned, "this distressing business will delay matters somewhat."

Deliberately vague, Honoria raised her brows. "Indeed?"

Lady Sheffield eyed her consideringly. "Three months of mourning—that makes it December."

"Winter," Honoria helpfully observed. She smiled at Lady Sheffield, and gave her something for her pains. "Pray excuse me, ma'am—I must speak with Webster."

With a smile, she glided to the door, quite certain how her words would be interpreted. In the hall, she wove through the knots of guests. Plates piled with tiny sandwiches sat waiting on a sideboard; picking one up, she proceeded through the music room and onto the terrace.

Reaching the spot immediately behind Devil's back, she took up her position, her back to the drawing room. The sandwiches on her plate instantly attracted suitable cover.

"Lady Harrington," an older lady introduced herself. "Know your grandfather well, miss. Haven't seen him for a while. Daresay he's keeping well?"

"I daresay," Honoria replied, keeping her voice low.

"Hurst knows nothing, nor does Gilford."

Without turning around and risking one of Devil's cousins noticing her, Honoria couldn't tell which one was reporting. But she knew Devil's voice. "Vane's checked with Blackwell. Try Gelling."

"Nice sandwiches, these." Lady Harrington took another. "There's Lady Smallworts—she knows your grandfather, too. Here—Dulcie!"

Lady Harrington waved at another bedizened lady; behind Honoria, another report was coming in. "Nothing from Dashwood and yes, I leaned heavily. He's not holding anything back. Not his style, this sort of caper."

There was silence, then Devil asked: "Anyone else here from that part of town?"

"I'll try Giles Edgeworth."

Some older gentleman approached Devil, and he was forced to converse; Honoria grasped the opportunity to give her attention to Lady Smallworts.

"Dear me, yes!" Lady Smallworts was examining her face through lorgnettes. "There's a definite likeness there, don't you think, Arethusa? About the chin."

Making a mental note to examine her chin when next she glanced in her mirror, Honoria plastered a smile on her lips and set herself to getting the two old dames chatting. Then she tuned her ears to the activity behind her.

"No luck with Farnsworth, nor Girton either."

Devil sighed. "There has to be something, somewhere."

"Must be—we'll just have to keep looking until we find it." After a pause, whichever cousin it was said: "I'll try a touch on Caffrey."

"Careful—I don't want this all over town by morning."

"Trust me."

Honoria could almost see the Cynster smile that went with the words.

Again Devil's attention was claimed by others; Honoria put her tuppence worth into the discussion over whether sprigged muslin would still be all the rage next Season.

It was some time before another of his cousins came to Devil's side. Guests were starting to depart when Vane reported; Honoria recognized his voice. "Forget Hillsworth or, I suspect, any of that ilk. If the problem's in that line, we'll need to get Harry to dig deeper."

"Speak of the Demon . . ."

"No go with any of my lot."

"Here come the others," Vane said.

"Not a whisper—not so much as a twitch."

"No luck."

"Not so much as a hint of a suspicion."

"Which means," Devil said, "that we'll have to go hunting."

"But in which direction?"

"In all directions." Devil paused. "Demon, you take the tracks and all connected enterprises. Vane, the guards and the taverns. Gabriel, the dens and finance in general. Scandal—you can do what you do best—chat up the ladies. Which leaves the catteries to Lucifer."

"And you?" Vane asked.

"I'll take the local angle."

"Right—I'm for London tonight."

"So am I."

"And me—I'll give you a lift if you like. I've got a prime 'un between the shafts."

Their deep voices faded, blending with the murmurs of the crowd. Lady Smallworts and Lady Harrington had moved onto the mysteries of the latest poke bonnets. It was time for Honoria to retreat—she'd heard all she needed. "If you'll excuse me, ladies?"

"Actually, my dear." Lady Harrington grasped Honoria's wrist. "I had meant to ask whether it's true."

"True?"

On the word, Honoria heard from behind her: "Dear me, coz—what trouble you do get into when you don't have me covering your back."

It was Vane's drawl; Honoria knew the instant Devil turned and saw her—she felt his gaze on her neck, her shoulders. She stiffened. She longed to swing about, but her ladyship clung tight.

"Why, yes." Lady Harrington smiled. "About you and—" She

broke off, gaze lifting to a point beyond Honoria's left shoulder, eyes widening with delight. "Ah—good afternoon, St. Ives."

"Lady Harrington."

It wasn't his voice, and the subtle menace beneath it, that sent shock waves coursing through Honoria—it was the large hand that curved possessively about her waist.

Devil captured the hand Lady Harrington freed. Honoria watched her fingers, trapped in his, rise inexorably toward his long lips. She steeled herself to feel his lips on her fingers.

He reversed her hand and pressed his lips to her wrist.

If she'd been a weaker woman, she'd have fainted.

Smoothly, Devil turned to Lady Harrington. "You were saying, ma'am?"

Lady Harrington beamed. "Nothing of any importance— think you've given me all the answer I need." She all but winked at Honoria, then jabbed Lady Smallworts in the arm. "Come along, Dulcie—I saw Harriet on the lawn. If we hurry, we might catch her before she leaves. Your Grace." Her ladyship nodded to Honoria. "We'll see you in town, my dear. Give my regards to your grandfather."

"Yes, of course," Honoria half gasped. Her lungs had seized, courtesy of the long fingers spread over her ribs. If he kissed her wrist again, she *would* faint.

"Wave to their ladyships," her tormentor instructed.

"With what," she hissed back. "The plate?"

"I really don't think you need the plate anymore—Thomas will take it."

A footman appeared and relieved her of the plate. There were few people left on the terrace. Honoria waited, but the grip on her waist did not ease. Instead, Devil wrapped his other arm about her waist, too, her hand still held in his. She could feel him, his chest, his thighs, steely-hard behind her, his arms an unbreakable cage about her.

"Did you learn much, out here on the terrace?" The words, soft, deep and low, tickled her ear.

"Reams about sprigged muslin. And did you know that the latest poke bonnets have a ruched rim?"

"Indeed? What next?"

"Precisely what Lady Smallworts wanted to know."

"And what do you want to know, Honoria Prudence?"

He had a distinctly lethal way of saying her name—he rolled the "r"s, just slightly, so the perfectly prim English words transformed into something more sensuous. Honoria fought down a shiver. "I want to know what you're about."

She felt him sigh. "What am I to do with you, you meddlesome woman?" He rocked her, slightly, to and fro.

The sensation of losing touch with the earth made Honoria gasp. He hadn't even shifted his grip. "You can put me *down* for a start!"

She was saved by the Dowager. "Sylvester! What on earth are you doing? Put Honoria down *at once*!"

He obeyed—reluctantly; the second Honoria's feet touched earth, the Dowager took her arm. "Come, my dear—there's someone I want you to meet."

Without a backward glance, Honoria escaped with the Dowager.

She took care to play least-in-sight for the rest of the day. While most guests left directly after the wake, many of the family lingered. Honoria had no intention of finding herself unexpectedly alone with Devil in his present mood. The summerhouse, a white-timber hexagon wreathed by a yellow rambler, became her refuge.

Her embroidery in her lap, she watched the carriages roll down the drive—watched Devil play the host and wave them on their way. Afternoon was fading to evening when Charles Cynster descended the front steps and started across the lawn, heading straight for the summerhouse.

Inclining his head gravely, he entered. "Good evening, my dear. I wanted to speak with you before I left—Sylvester told me where to find you."

So much for her refuge. Honoria studied Tolly's older brother critically. He was certainly older than Devil, which made him the oldest of the Cynster cousins. He cut an impressive figure, six feet tall and solidly built, but lacked the lean Cynster lines. His face was rounder, with heavy jowls. His eyes, resting on her, were plain brown; given his recent loss, Honoria was surprised by how intent his expression was.

The summerhouse boasted a long wickerwork settee with chintz cushions, and nothing else. With a wave, she invited Charles to sit; somewhat to her relief, he declined the settee to settle on a windowsill. Facing her. Honoria raised a polite brow. Presumably, Devil had sent Charles to persuade her to leave Tolly's death to the Cynsters.

"I wanted to thank you for aiding Tolly. Sylvester mentioned you'd helped." Charles's lips twisted in a fleeting smile. "To use his phrase, 'above and beyond what might reasonably be expected of a lady of your station.' "

Graciously, Honoria inclined her head. "Despite your cousin's beliefs, I did nothing more than any lady of practical sensibilities."

"Be that as it may . . ." Charles's words trailed away; Honoria glanced up and met his gaze. "My dear Miss Anstruther-Wetherby, I hope you will excuse me if I speak plainly?"

"I would prefer you did so." Setting aside her embroidery, Honoria folded her hands and gave him her full attention.

"It appears to me that, rather than being rewarded for your help, you have been placed in an invidious position." Charles glanced at her. "Forgive me—this is a delicate subject. But I understand that, by virtue of rendering assistance to Tolly and thus being stranded by the storm, you were forced to spend the night in company with Sylvester, and thus now find yourself compromised and, not to put too fine a point on it, forced to accept his offer."

Honoria opened her lips—Charles raised his hand. "No, if you please—allow me to finish. I realize that many ladies would be *aux anges* over becoming the duchess of St. Ives, whatever the circumstances. I can see, however, that you are not of that giddy ilk. You're an Anstruther-Wetherby, daughter of an old and ancient line—quite as proud as we Cynsters. You are a woman of sound sense, independence, and—as you acknowledged—of a practical bent.

"You have, I believe, chosen to live life quietly—it hardly seems fair that in return for your good offices, you should be forced to become Sylvester's wife, a role that will not only be demanding but also very likely less than rewarding." He paused, then added: "For a lady of sensitivity." He hesitated, weighing his words, then continued: "Sylvester bears a very specific reputation, as do most of the Cynsters. It seems unlikely that a leopard so devoted to hunting will readily change his spots."

He looked at Honoria; she raised her brows haughtily. "There is little in your assessment with which I would argue, Mr. Cynster."

Charles's brief smile did not light his eyes. "Indeed, my dear, I believe we are two who would understand each other well, which is why I hope you will understand my motives in proposing an alternative solution to your undeserved predicament."

"An alternative?" Honoria was conscious of increasing unease. She had not expected Charles to undermine Devil; she was truly surprised that he had.

"A more acceptable alternative to a lady of your sensibility."

Honoria looked her question.

"Marrying Sylvester would not be in your best interests—anyone with understanding can see that. You stand, however, in need of an offer, in restitution if nothing else. As Tolly was my brother, in order to retrieve your standing, I would be happy to offer you my hand. My estate, of course, is nothing compared to Sylvester's; it is, however, not inconsiderable."

Honoria was stunned; only years of training kept the fact from her face. She did not have to think to frame her reply—the words came spontaneously to her lips. "I thank you for your offer, sir, but I am not of a mind to marry—not for this nor, indeed, any other foreseeable reason."

Charles's face blanked. After a moment, he asked, "You don't intend to accept Sylvester's offer?"

Lips compressed, Honoria shook her head. "I have no intention of marrying at all." With that firm declaration, she reached for her embroidery.

"You will be pressured to accept Sylvester's offer—both by the Cynsters and your own family."

Honoria's eyes flashed; she raised her brows haughtily. "My dear sir, I am not at all amenable to unwarranted interference in my life."

Silence ensued, then Charles slowly stood. "I apologize, Miss Anstruther-Wetherby, should I have given offense." He paused, then added: "However, I urge you to remember that, should a time come when you feel it necessary to marry to escape the situation arising from Tolly's death, you have an alternative to marrying Sylvester."

Engrossed in jabbing her needle into her canvas, Honoria did not look up.

"Your humble servant, Miss Anstruther-Wetherby."

Barely glancing at Charles's bow, Honoria stiffly inclined her head. Charles turned on his heel and descended the steps; Honoria watched, narrow-eyed, as he returned to the house. When he disappeared, she frowned and wriggled her shoulders.

If she ever had to marry a Cynster, she'd rather try taming the tyrant.

The tyrant came knocking on her door late that evening.

Devil's uncles, aunts, and younger cousins had stayed for dinner, then all except Tolly's family had departed, letting the staff catch their collective breath. A cloak of calm had settled over the Place, a restful silence only found in those houses that had seen birth and death many times.

Leaving the Dowager and Tolly's parents swapping bittersweet memories, Honoria had retired to her chamber. She had intended to compose her letter to Michael. Instead, the peace outside drew her to the window; she sank onto the window seat, her mind sliding into the night.

The knock that interrupted her undirected reverie was so peremptory she had no doubt who was there. She hesitated, then, stiffening her spine, rose and crossed to the door.

Devil was standing in the corridor, looking back toward the stairs. As she set the door wide, he turned and met her gaze. "Come for a walk."

He held out his hand; Honoria held his gaze steadily—and slowly raised one brow. His lips twitched, then he fluidly sketched a bow. "My dear Honoria Prudence, will you do me the honor of strolling with me in the moonlight?"

She preferred his order to his request; the effortless charm lurking beneath his words, uttered in that soft, deep voice, was enough to turn any lady's head. But it needed no more than the blink of an eye to decide why he was here. "I'll get my shawl."

The swath of fine Norwich silk lay on a chair; draping it about her shoulders, Honoria pinned the ends, then headed for the door. She intended making it plain that she was not about to pull back from her interest in Tolly's murder.

Devil took her hand and drew her over the threshold and shut the door, then settled her hand on his sleeve. "There's another stairway that gives onto the side lawn."

In silence, they left the house to stroll beneath the huge trees dotting the lawn, passing from shadow to moonlight and back again.

The silence was soothing; the pervasive tang of leaves, green grass, and rich earth, scents Devil always associated with his home, was tonight spiced with a subtle fragrance, an elusive scent he had no difficulty placing.

It was her—the fragrance of her hair, of her skin, of her perfume—lily of the valley with a hint of rose—an expensive, alluring mix. Beneath all wafted the heady scent of woman, warm and sensual, promising all manner of earthly delights. The evocative scent teased his hunter's senses and heightened the tension gripping him.

Tonight, he was prey to two driving desires—at the moment, he could pursue neither goal. There was nothing he could do to avenge Tolly's death—and he could not take Honoria Prudence to his bed. Not yet. There was, however, one point he could address—he could do something about her chin.

He had no intention of letting her involve herself with Tolly's murder, but his action on the terrace had been ill-advised. Intimidation would not work with this particular lady. Luckily, an alternative strategy lay to hand, one much more to his liking. Using it would kill two birds with one stone. Cloaked in shadow, Devil smiled—and turned their steps toward the summerhouse.

She lost patience before they reached it. "What steps are you taking to apprehend your cousin's killer?"

"The matter will be dealt with—rest assured of that."

He felt her glare. "That's not what I asked."

"That is, however, all the answer you need."

She stiffened, then sweetly inquired: "Has anyone informed you, Your Grace, that you are without doubt the most arrogant man in Christendom?"

"Not in those precise words."

The comment robbed her of speech long enough for him to lead her up the summerhouse steps. He halted in the pavillion's center, releasing her. Shafts of moonlight streaked the floor, patterned with the shadows of the leaves. Through the dimness, he saw her breasts swell.

"*Be* that as it may—"

Honoria's words ended on a half squeak; one instant, her tormentor was standing, loose-limbed and relaxed, before her—the next, long fingers had firmed about her chin. And he was suddenly much closer. "What are you *doing*?" Her eyes had flown wide; she was breathless. She didn't try to free her chin; his grip felt unbreakable.

His lids lifted; his eyes, even paler in the weak light, met hers. "Distracting you."

His deep murmur was certainly distracting; Honoria felt it in her bones. Other than on her chin, he wasn't touching her, yet she felt herself sliding into his hold. He drew her upward and she stretched, her head tilting further; her heart tripped, then started to race. His eyes held hers, mesmerizing in the moonlight, ageless, seductive, all-knowing. His head slowly lowered—her lips softened, parted.

She could not have pulled back had the heavens fallen.

The first touch of his lips sent an aching shudder through her; his arms immediately closed about her, drawing her against him. Hardness surrounded her; muscles with less give than steel caged her. His head angled; the pressure of his lips increased.

They were hard, like the rest of him—commanding, demanding; a heartbeat later they were warm, enticing, seductively persuasive. Honoria stilled, quivering, on some invisible threshold—then he tugged and she plunged forward, into the unknown.

It was not the first time she'd been kissed, yet it was. Never before had there been magic in the air, never before had she been taken by the hand and introduced to a world of sensation. Pleasure rose, warm and enthralling, then whirled through her, a kaleidoscope of delight, leaving her giddy. Pleasurably giddy.

What little breath she managed to catch, he took, weaving his web until she was caught beyond recall. The tip of his tongue traced her lips, a beguilingly artful caress. She knew she'd be wise to ignore it; he was leading her into realms beyond her knowledge, where he would be her guide. A most unwise situation—a dangerous situation.

His lips firmed; heat welled, melting all resistance. On a sigh, she parted her lips farther, yielding to his arrogant demand.

He took what he wanted—the intimate caress sent sensation

streaking through her, a bolt of lightning striking to her core. Shocked, Honoria drew back on a gasp.

He let her retreat—just so far. Stunned, her wits reeling, she searched his face. One black brow slowly arched; his arms tightened.

"No." Honoria braced against his hold—or tried to; her muscles had the consistency of jelly.

"There's no need to panic—I'm only going to kiss you."

Only? Honoria blinked wildly. "That's bad enough. I mean—" She hauled in a breath and tried to focus her wayward wits. "You're dangerous."

He actually chuckled; the sound shredded her hard-won control—she shivered.

"I'm not dangerous to you." His hands stroked soothingly, seductively, down her back. "I'm going to marry you. That puts the shoe on the other foot."

Had her wits been completely addled? Honoria frowned. "What shoe—and which foot?"

His teeth gleamed. "According to all precepts, Cynster wives are the only beings on earth of whom Cynster men need be wary."

"Really?" He was pulling her leg. Honoria tried to whip up her indignation, an impossible task given he had bent his head and was gently nibbling her lips.

"Just kiss me." He whispered the words against her lips as he drew her hard against him. The contact set her nerves quivering again; his lips, lightly teasing, left her mind in no state to quibble.

Devil kissed her again, waiting with the patience of one who knew, until she yielded completely. Her melting surrender was all the more sweet, knowing as he did that she would prefer it was otherwise. Too wise, too experienced, he did not push her too far, keeping a tight rein on his passions. She lay softly supple in his arms, her lips his to enjoy, the sweet cavern of her mouth his to taste, to plunder, to claim; for tonight, that would have to be enough.

He would much rather have claimed her—taken her to his bed and filled her, celebrated life in that most fundamental of ways—a natural response to death's presence. But she was innocent—her skittering reactions, her quiescence, spoke to him clearly. She would be his and his alone—but not yet.

The reality of his need impinged fully on his mind; Devil mentally cursed. Her softness, pressed from breast to thigh against him, was a potent invocation, feeding his demons, calling them, inciting them. He drew back; chest swelling, he studied her face, wondering . . . even while he shackled his desires. Her eyes glinted beneath her lashes.

Her mind still adrift, Honoria let her gaze roam his face. There was no softness in his features, no hint of gentleness, only strength and passion and an ironclad will. "I am not going to marry you." The words went directly from her brain to her lips—an instinctive reaction.

He merely raised a brow, irritatingly supercilious.

"I'm going to send for my brother tomorrow to come and escort me home."

His eyes, silver in the night, narrowed fractionally. "Home—as in Hampshire?"

Honoria nodded. She felt unreal, out of touch with the world.

"Write a note for your brother—I'll frank it tomorrow."

She smiled. "And I'll put it in the post myself."

He smiled back—she had a premonition he was laughing at her though his chest, so close, was not quaking. "By all means. We'll see what he thinks of your decision."

Honoria's smile turned smug; she felt quite lightheaded. He, Cynster that he was, thought Michael would support his cause. Michael, of course, would agree with her—he would see, as instantly as she had, that for her, marrying Devil Cynster was not a good idea.

"And now, if we've settled your immediate future to your satisfaction . . ." His lips brushed hers; instinctively, Honoria tracked them.

A twig cracked.

Devil raised his head, every muscle tensing. He and Honoria looked out into the night; the sight that met their incredulous eyes had him straightening. "What the . . . ?"

"*Sssh!*" Honoria pressed her hand to his lips.

He frowned and caught her hand, but remained silent as the small procession drew nearer, then passed the summerhouse. Through moonlight and shadow, Amelia, Amanda and Simon led the little band. Henrietta, Eliza, Angelica and Heather with Mary in tow followed. Each child carried a white rose. Devil's frown deepened as the dense shadow of the trees swallowed them; of their destination there could be little doubt. "Wait here."

Honoria stared at him. "You must be joking." She picked up her skirts and hurried down the steps.

He was on her heels as they slipped from shadow to shadow, trailing the small band. The children halted before Tolly's freshly filled grave. Honoria stopped in the deep shadows beneath an oak; Devil stopped behind her. Then his hands gripped her waist; he lifted her to put her aside.

She twisted in his hold and flung herself against him. "*No!*" Her furious whisper made him blink. Her hands gripping his shoulders, she whispered: "You mustn't!"

He frowned at her, then lowered his head so he could whisper in her ear: "Why the hell not? They're not frightened of me."

"It's not that!" Honoria frowned back. "You're an adult—not one of them."

"So?"

"So this is their moment—their time to say good-bye. Don't spoil it for them."

He searched her face, then his lips thinned. Lifting his head, he looked at the contingent lined up at the foot of the grave but made no further move to join them.

Honoria wriggled and he let her go; she turned to watch. The chill beneath the trees penetrated her thin gown—she shivered. The next instant, Devil's arms came around her, drawing her back against him. Honoria stiffened, then gave up and relaxed, too grateful for his warmth to quibble.

A conference had taken place at the graveside; now Amelia stepped forward and threw her rose on the mound. "Sleep well, Tolly."

Amanda stepped up. "Rest in peace," she intoned, and flung her rose to join her twin's.

Next came Simon. "Good-bye, Tolly." Another rose landed on the grave.

One by one, the children added their roses to the small pile, each bidding Tolly farewell. When they were done, they looked at each other, then re-formed their procession and hurried back to the house.

Honoria held Devil back until the children passed by. He sent her an unreadable, distinctly Cynster look when she finally let him loose, then took her hand; together, they trailed the children back to the lawn.

There was dew on the grass; it was heavy going, particularly for little Mary. Devil grunted and lengthened his stride—Honoria flung herself at him again. "No!" She glared furiously and pressed him back under the trees.

Devil glared back. "They'll get wet feet—I can carry two of them."

He gripped her waist: Honoria clung to his shoulders. "They'll guess you know where they've been—they'll guess you watched. It'll spoil it for them. A little water won't hurt them—not if they're true Cynsters."

A gleam marked Devil's reluctant smile. He waited, grudgingly, until the children disappeared through the side door, then, her hand locked in his, strode for the house. The children were still negotiating the stairs when they reached the foot. Devil went straight on, treading close by the wall. When they reached the upper landing, the children were only partway up the next flight—Devil yanked Honoria into an alcove.

She gasped as she landed against his chest. One arm locked about her; hard fingers lifted her face. His lips were on hers before she drew breath; she tried to hold firm, but beneath the pleasure he lavished upon her, her resistance wilted, then melted away.

To be replaced by something so insidious, so soul-stealingly compulsive, so innately enthralling, she couldn't pull back. He was hungry—she sensed it in the leashed passion that hardened his lips, that, when she opened to him, set him plundering more rapaciously than before. The tension investing his every muscle spoke of rigid control; the turbulence behind it frightened and fascinated. His tongue tangled with hers, intimately enticing, then settled to a slow, repetitive, probing rhythm. Her mouth was his; his possession set her senses whirling—no man had touched her like this. A warm flush rushed through her, a sweet fever unlike anything she'd known. Beyond that and the shocking intimacy of his caress, she knew only one thing. He was ravenously hungry—for her. The sudden, almost overwhelming impulse to give herself to him, to assuage that rampant need, shook her to the core—and still she could not pull back.

How long they stood locked together in the dark she had no idea; when he lifted his head, she'd lost touch with the world.

He hesitated, then brushed her lips with his. "Do I frighten you?"

"Yes." In a way he did. Wide-eyed, her pulse tripping, Honoria searched his shadowed eyes. "But it's not you I'm frightened of." He was making her feel, making her yearn. "I—" Frowning, she stopped, for once lost for words.

In the dark, Devil smiled crookedly. "Don't worry." He took her mouth in one last, searching kiss before putting her from him. "Go. Now." It was a warning—he wasn't sure she understood.

She blinked up at him through the dimness, then nodded. "Good night." She slipped out of the alcove. "Sleep well."

Devil nearly laughed. He wouldn't have a good night—he wouldn't sleep well. He could feel another headache coming on.

Chapter 7

Next morning, Honoria attended Sunday service in the church in the grounds, then strolled back with Louise Cynster. Tolly's mother thanked her for helping her son; Honoria politely disclaimed. With little encouragement, Louise spoke of Tolly and his relationship with Devil. Hero worship seemed the most apt description.

The object of Tolly's reverence had not seen fit to attend church. When the ladies reached the breakfast table, it was apparent he'd been there before them. Honoria made quick work of tea and toast, then headed upstairs.

Devil, she felt sure, would have gone riding. It was a perfect day—he would be out surveying his fields astride his cake-eating demon. Which should leave nearer precincts clear.

It was the work of three minutes to don her stylish topaz riding habit. Her clothes were the one item she'd always insisted lived up to her Anstruther-Wetherby background. She flicked the feather on her matching toque so that it draped rakishly over one temple, then headed for the door.

There was no one in the stable yard. Unperturbed, she entered the main stable. The stall walls were high; she couldn't see over them. The tack room was at the end—she stepped purposefully down the aisle.

A large hand reached out and hauled her into a stall.

"What . . . ?" Warm steel encircled her. Honoria focused—and realized her danger. "Don't you *dare* kiss me—I'll scream if you do!"

"And who do you imagine will rescue you?"

Honoria blinked—and tried to think of the right answer.

"Anyway, you won't be able to scream while I'm kissing you."

She parted her lips and hauled in a deep breath.

By the time she realized that was not a wise move, it was too late—he'd taken full advantage. A vague notion of struggling wafted into her mind—then out, as heat, warmth and insidious pleasure burgeoned within her. His lips moved on hers, arrogantly confident; his tongue slid between in a deliciously languid caress, an unhurried caress that went on and on, until she was heated through. Honoria felt the fever rise—she tried to tell herself this was wrong—scandalously wrong—while every sense she possessed purred in appreciation.

She couldn't think or hear when he kissed her. She made that discovery when Devil finally raised his head; up until the instant his lips left hers, her mind had been thought-free, blissful in its vacancy. The sounds of the stable rushed in on her, compounding her breathlessness. Her bones had liquefied, yet she was still upright—then she realized it was due to him that she was so. He was holding her against himself; her toes only just touched the floor.

"Great heavens!" Blinking wildly, she lowered her heels to earth. Had she labeled him dangerous? He was lethal.

"Good morning, Honoria Prudence." His deep purr sent a shiver down her spine. "And where are you headed?"

"Ah . . ." Gazing, wide-eyed, into his too-knowing green eyes, Honoria marshaled her wits. "I was looking for a horse. Presumably you have more than one?"

"I believe there's a hoity, wilful mare that should suit. But where were you thinking of riding?"

"Oh—just out about the lanes." He was holding her too securely for her to pull away; she tried to ease back—his hold gave not an inch.

"You don't know this country—you'll get lost. You'll be safer riding with me."

Dispensing with all subtlety, Honoria reached behind her and tried to pry his arms loose. He chuckled and let her tug—all to no avail. Then he bent his head and feathered delicate kisses about her left ear.

Breathless, quite ridiculously flustered, Honoria glared. "Whoever called you Devil had the right of it!"

"Hully?"

Honoria blinked, directly into his eyes. "Mrs. *Hull* gave you your nickname?"

He grinned—devilishly. "She used to be my nursemaid. I was three when she christened me 'That Devil Cynster.' "

"You must have been a tyrant even then."

"I was."

A furious clearing of a throat spared Honoria the necessity of replying. Devil looked around, then released her, turning so he hid her from view. "What is it, Martin?"

"Sorry t'interrupt, Y'r Grace, but one of the flanges on the North Number One's split—Mister Kirby was a-wondering if you'd swing past that way. He was hoping you'd check the lay before he reset the blade."

The message made no sense to Honoria; she peered around

Devil's shoulder. A workman, his cap in his hands, stood waiting in the aisle. She glanced up—and discovered his master's green gaze on her.

"Tell Kirby I'll be there within the half-hour."

"Yes, Y'r Grace." Martin hurried out.

Honoria straightened. "What was that about?"

"One of the windmills is out of action."

"Mills?" Honoria recalled numerous windmills dotting the fields. "There seem to be a lot about."

Devil's lips twitched. He reached for her hand. "This is fen country, Honoria Prudence—the mills drive pumps which drain the land."

"Oh." Honoria found herself being towed down the aisle. "Where are you taking me?"

He raised both brows at her. "To find a horse. Wasn't that what you wanted?"

Ten minutes later, atop a frisky chestnut mare, Honoria clattered out of the stable yard—in Devil's wake. The notion of a surreptitious detour occurred only to be dismissed; he'd overtake her in an instant.

They left the park by a different route from that which led through the woods; beyond the park walls, the clack of windmills became noticeable, steadily increasing as they headed north. The mill in question was a large one; Devil dismounted in its shadow to confer with his foreman.

For Honoria, their discussion held little interest. As they cantered back to the Place, she took the devil by the horns. "Have you any idea who the 'highwayman' might be?" It seemed a clear enough question.

His response was a dissertation on the mechanics of fen drainage. By the time they reached the stable yard, Honoria had heard enough to verify the adage about Cynsters being as passionate about their land as they were in their other pursuits. She'd also gained a very firm idea of what her host thought of her interest in his cousin's murder.

The next morning, she watched from her window until she *saw* her nemesis ride out. Then she headed for the stables. The grooms saw nothing odd in her request that the mare be saddled again. When she passed under the arch leading out of the park, Honoria whooped with delight. Smiling inanely, she headed for the wood.

She ended going the long way around via the village. It was an hour and more before she finally reached the straight where Tolly had been shot. The mare seemed to sense the fatal spot; Honoria drew rein and slid from the saddle, tethering the horse some yards down the lane.

Brisk and full of purpose, she crossed the lane—the rumble of hoofbeats reached her. Halting, she listened; the unknown horseman was heading her way. "Damn!" She whisked about and hurried back to the mare.

She couldn't remount. In disbelief, Honoria looked right and left. The hoofbeats drew steadily nearer. In that moment, she would have traded her entire wardrobe for a suitable log; none was to be found.

The unknown presence was likely some local no more threatening than Mr. Postlethwaite. Honoria stepped to the mare's head and assumed a haughty, nonchalant expression. If she wished to stand beside her horse in the lane, who had the right to gainsay her?

The oncoming horse rounded the curve and burst into view. The rider wasn't Mr. Postlethwaite.

The black demon halted beside her; Devil looked down at her. "What are you doing here?"

Honoria opened her eyes wide—even wider than they already were. "I stopped to stretch my legs."

He didn't blink. "And admire the view?"

They were hemmed in on all sides by the wood. Honoria narrowed her eyes at him. "What are *you* doing here?"

Devil met her look, his expression implacable, then swung down from the saddle. Jaw set, he knotted the reins about a tree; without a word, he turned and strode to the spot where Tolly had fallen.

Honoria marched determinedly in his wake. "You don't believe it was a highwayman any more than I do—and it certainly wasn't a poacher."

Devil snorted. "I'm not daft." He shot her a piercing glance, then looked away, flexing his shoulders as if throwing off some restraint.

Honoria watched him study the ground. "Well? Who do you think did it?"

"I don't know, but we'll find out."

"We'll?" Honoria was perfectly certain he didn't mean *her* and him. "You're all searching, aren't you—you and your cousins?"

The look he cast her brimmed with masculine long suffering; his short sigh underscored it. "As you've so accurately deduced, it wasn't a highwayman; nor was it a poacher—Tolly was murdered. Behind such a murder there must be a reason—we're looking for the reason. The reason will lead us to the man."

"From what I heard, you haven't any clue as to what the reason might be." His glance, razor-sharp, touched her face; Honoria tried not to look conscious.

"Tolly lived a full life. While I'm going over the ground here,

the others are quartering London—the balls, the hells—anywhere a Cynster might have been."

Recalling the assignments he'd delegated to his cousins, Honoria frowned. "Was Tolly particularly partial to cats?"

Devil stared at her, his expression utterly blank.

"The catteries?"

He blinked, slowly, then his gaze, devoid of expression, met
hers. "The salons. Of the *demimonde*."

Honoria managed to keep the shock from her eyes. "He was
only twenty."

"So?" The word dripped arrogance. "Cynsters start young."

He was the archetype—presumably he knew. Honoria decided
to leave that subject—Devil had stepped into the undergrowth.
"What are you looking for? A gun?"

"Tolly didn't carry a gun."

"So?" Her version dripped impatience.

His lips thinned. "I'm looking for anything that shouldn't be
here." He stopped and looked around. "The wind could have
blown things either side of the lane."

It was a daunting task. While Devil tramped back the undergrowth close by where Tolly had fallen, Honoria peered and
poked at the verges farther along the lane. A strong stick in one
hand, she followed in his wake, prodded likely-looking clumps
of grass and lifted leaf mold. Devil glanced around and grunted,
then continued more swiftly, scanning the area as he went, leaving the finer details to her.

When they'd covered an area going back a yard from the lane,
Honoria straightened and pushed back the feather trying to poke
her in the eye. "Why do you think Tolly was in the lane?"

Devil answered without looking up. "I assume he was coming
to the Place."

"Your aunt thought it likely he was coming to seek your advice."

He looked up at that. "You asked Aunt Louise?"

His tone had Honoria straightening to attention. "We were just chatting—she doesn't suspect anything." His censorious expression didn't alter; gesturing airily, she shrugged. "You said it was a highwayman, so it was a highwayman. Everyone believes it—even your mother."

"Thank God for that." With a last, saber-edged glance, Devil returned to his search. "The last thing I need is females interfering."

"Indeed?" Wielding her stick, she scattered a pile of leaves. "I suppose it never occurred to you that we females might contribute something?"

"If you saw the contribution my mother thought of making you wouldn't ask. She penned a note to the magistrate that would have made his hair stand on end—if he could have deciphered it."

Honoria flicked over a clod. "If we weren't left feeling so frustratingly helpless—set to one side and told to knit mittens—perhaps we wouldn't react quite so wildly." Swinging about, she waved her stick at him. "Just think how frustrated *you* would feel if you knew you, personally, could never achieve *anything*."

He looked at her—steadily—for what seemed a long time. Then his features hardened; he gestured at the ground. "Just keep searching."

Though they searched both sides of the lane, they found precisely nothing. Remounting, they cantered through the fields, then through the gate into the park, both absorbed with thoughts of Tolly's death.

As they rode between the ranks of golden poplars, Honoria

glanced at Devil. "Your aunt intends to give you the silver hip flask you gave Tolly for his birthday as a keepsake—he had it on him when he was shot." When he merely nodded, his gaze fixed ahead, she added somewhat tartly: "It seems the 'highwayman' forgot it."

That got her a glance—a warning one.

"Your aunt also mentioned," she plowed on, "that if he was in trouble, Tolly would turn to you first, as head of the family, rather than to his father or Charles. Do you think that the reason he was killed could be the same as his reason for seeking you?"

Devil's gaze sharpened; in that instant, Honoria knew triumph. She'd beaten him to that conclusion, and he thought she was right. He said nothing, however, until they reached the stable yard. Lifting her down, he held her before him. "Don't say anything to *Maman* or Aunt Louise—there's no need to start hares."

Honoria met his gaze with one of bland hauteur.

"And if you should hear or discover anything, tell me."

She opened her eyes innocently wide. "And you'll tell me whatever you discover?"

His expression turned grim. "Don't press your luck, Honoria Prudence."

Chapter 8

Two mornings later, Devil descended the main stairs, tugging on his driving gloves. As he started down the last flight, Webster appeared, heading for the front door.

"Your curricle should be waiting, Your Grace."

"Thank you." Reaching the front door, Devil looked back.

Hand on the latch, Webster paused. "Is anything amiss, Your Grace?"

Devil turned as Webster opened the door—revealing his curricle drawn up before the steps, along with a figure in pale lilac. Devil smiled. "No, Webster—everything's as I expected."

Strolling out, Devil paused in the shadows of the porch to relish the picture Honoria presented. His bride-to-be had a certain style, an innate elegance. Her hair was piled high in a fashionable knot, fine errant curls wreathing her face. A frilled parasol protected her complexion; her hands and feet were encased in tan leather. Her lilac carriage dress had been cut with skill, neatly fitting her slender waist, emphasizing the ripe swell of her hips and the generous curves of her breasts. It took conscious effort to wipe the wolfish smile from his face.

Adopting a bland, impassive expression, he strolled down the steps.

Twirling her parasol, Honoria watched him approach. "I gather you intend driving to St. Ives, Your Grace. I wonder if I might accompany you? I have a keen interest in old chapels—I believe the bridge-chapel at St. Ives is a particularly fine example of its kind."

"Good morning, Honoria Prudence." Halting before her, Devil claimed her right hand; smoothly raising it, he pressed his lips to her inner wrist, left bare by her glove.

Honoria nearly dropped her parasol. She shot him a glare and tried to calm her racing heart. "Good morning, Your Grace."

Without another word—without the argument she had primed herself to win—he led her to the curricle's side and lifted her to the seat. Effortlessly. She had to calm her wayward heart all over again. Shifting along, she clung to the rail as the seat tipped as he climbed up. Once it resettled, she rearranged her skirts, then fussed with her parasol.

Devil took the reins, dismissed his groom, then they were bowling down the drive. Honoria drew a deep breath; the cool air beneath the oaks revived her wits—and brought the last minutes into sharper focus. Abruptly narrowing her eyes, she turned them on Devil. "You *knew*!"

He glanced her way, his expression mildly indulgent. "I'm generally considered a fast learner."

An unnerving suspicion leapt to mind. "Where are you taking me?"

This time his expression was innocence incarnate. "To St. Ives—to see the bridge-chapel."

Honoria looked into his eyes—they were crystal-clear. Twisting about, she looked behind—and saw a horse on a leading rein following the curricle. She turned back. "You're going to St. Ives to return the horse Tolly was riding the afternoon he was shot."

Devil's gaze turned sharp, his expression irritated. "I don't suppose I can persuade you to leave the matter in my hands?"

Honoria frowned. "Is it Tolly's horse—or could it be the murderer's?"

Devil's jaw firmed. "It must be the horse Tolly was riding—it was found fully saddled in a field near the wood the day after the storm. It's from the stables Tolly usually used. And the murderer presumably left the scene on horseback." A straight stretch lay before them; he slowed his matched bays and looked at Honoria. "Honoria Prudence, you might have come upon Tolly a few minutes before I did, but there's no reason you should take an active role in tracking down his killer."

Honoria put her nose in the air. "I take leave to disagree, Your Grace."

Devil scowled. "For God's sake, stop 'Your Gracing' me—call me Devil. We are, after all, going to be man and wife."

"That," Honoria declared, her chin rising another notch, "is unlikely."

Devil eyed the tip of her chin, and debated the wisdom of arguing. Instead, he said, his tone edged but even: "Honoria, I'm the head of this family—my shoulders are broader than yours and my back is a good deal stronger. Finding Tolly's murderer is *my* responsibility—rest assured I'll fulfill it."

She looked at him. "You do realize you've just contradicted yourself? One minute, you declare I'm to be your bride—the next you forbid me to act as either your wife or your bride should."

"As far as I'm concerned my wife, prospective or actual, which is to say *you*, should refrain from all dangerous activities." Forced to look to his horses, Devil heard his own growl; his frown deepened. "Murder is violent; tracking a murderer is dangerous. *You* should not be involved."

"Entrenched opinion states that a wife should give her husband aid and succor in all his enterprises."

"Forget the aid—I'll settle for the succor."

"I'm afraid you cannot separate the two—they come as a package. Besides," Honoria added, her eyes widening, "if I'm to stay away from all danger, however could we wed?"

He glanced at her, his expression arrested; he searched her face, then narrowed his eyes. "You know you stand in no danger from me. You wouldn't be here if you did."

That, Honoria inwardly admitted, was true; he was far too potent a force to challenge without cast-iron assurances. But her position was unassailable—given he viewed her as his bride, he would uphold her honor, even against himself. She could have no more formidable protector. Secure in that knowledge, she smiled serenely. "Have your cousins learned anything yet?"

He muttered something and looked ahead—she didn't try too hard to catch his words. His jaw was set—granite would have been softer. He took the next turn at speed, then whipped up his horses. Unperturbed, she sat back, idly scanning the flat fields past which they flew.

Devil barely checked his team for Somersham.

Honoria glimpsed Mr. Postlethwaite by the vicarage. She waved; he blinked, then smiled and waved back. Had it really been only a week since she'd taken the lane through the wood?

Tolly's family had left the previous day, having spent the days since the funeral coming to terms with their grief. She had taken the twins in hand, encouraging them to turn their thoughts to the futures that lay before them. She had also broken one of her golden rules and taken the younger girls, Henrietta and little Mary, under her wing; there'd been no one else suited to the task. Supporting Tolly's sisters had only strengthened her resolution to ensure that his killer was brought to justice.

The roofs of St. Ives lay ahead before Devil finally spoke. "Vane sent a messenger yesterday—no one has unearthed the smallest clue or heard the slightest whisper. Nothing to suggest what sent Tolly this way or why he might have been killed."

Honoria studied his profile. "You were expecting more, weren't you?"

"I put off returning the horse, hoping to have a description of the man we're seeking. He must have got to the wood somehow. If he followed Tolly or came earlier from London, he may have hired a horse in St. Ives."

"Perhaps he drove?"

Devil shook his head. "If he had, he would have had to drive out of the wood *away* from Somersham. Otherwise, he would have encountered you. There was a group of my laborers in the fields below the wood—any carriage going that way would have passed them. None did."

"What about a horseman?"

"No, but the wood's riddled with bridle paths. There are any number a horseman could have taken."

"Is it possible to ride up from London?"

"Possible but not likely." Devil checked his pair; the first houses of St. Ives were before them. "A horse ridden that far at any reasonable speed could not have participated in any subsequent flight."

They'd reached the main street; Devil slowed the bays to a walk.

"So," Honoria concluded, "we're looking for a man, identity

and description unknown, who hired a horse on the day of the shooting."

She felt Devil's gaze on her face—and heard the short, irritated, aggravated sigh he gave before saying: *"We're* looking for precisely that."

Five minutes later, sitting in the curricle, listening as he questioned the stablemaster, Honoria was still struggling with her triumph. She knew better than to let it show—the last thing she wanted was to bruise his masculine sensibilities and have him rescind his decision. Yet victory was so sweet it was hard to keep the smile from her lips—every time she was sure he couldn't see it, she gave in to the urge and smiled.

The curricle rocked as Devil climbed up. "You heard?"

"No horseman except Tolly. Are there other stables in town?"

There were two, but the answers there were the same as at the first. No man had hired a horse on that day—no one had noticed any horseman riding through. "What now?" Honoria asked as Devil headed his team back up the main street.

"I'll send men to check at Huntingdon, Godmanchester, and Ely. Chatteris as well, though that's even less likely."

"What about Cambridge?"

"That," Devil stated, "is the main chance. It's closer to town, and the coaches are more frequent on that route."

Honoria nodded. "So when are we going there?"

Devil flicked her a glance. *"We* aren't—any more than we're going to the other towns."

Honoria narrowed her eyes at him—only to see his lips twitch.

"I'm too well known to ask questions without inviting comment. St. Ives is different—it's the family town and has few other major families living close. And *you* can't ask either. But my grooms can chat up the ostlers over a pint or two and learn all we need without anyone being the wiser."

"Hmm." Honoria eyed him suspiciously.

"I'll send Melton to Cambridge."

"Your head stableman?"

"So to speak."

Honoria had yet to sight the man. "He doesn't seem to be much about."

"Melton is *never* around when I need him. It's a point of honor with him."

Honoria stared. "Why do you put up with him?"

Devil shrugged. "He's old."

"That's it? Because he's old?"

"No."

Intrigued, Honoria watched the hard face soften, not a great deal, but enough to show.

"Melton put me on my first pony—you could say he taught me to ride. He's been at the Place all his life, and no one knows more about horses—not even Demon. I couldn't turn him out to grass, not after a lifetime in the position. Luckily, his son-in-law, Hersey, is a sensible man—he's my understableman and actually does all the work. Other than on special occasions—and with handling Sulieman—Melton's position is purely titular."

"But he never turns up when you bring Sulieman in."

"Or when I take him out. As I said, it's a point of honor with him." Devil glanced at Honoria, his lips twisting wryly. "To make sure I don't forget all he's taught me. According to him, just because I'm a duke doesn't excuse me from currying my horse."

Honoria choked, then gave up and laughed unrestrainedly.

Devil cast her a disgusted glance—and drove on.

She was wiping her eyes, still racked by the occasional giggle, when he checked his team. They were a mile or so short of Somersham; Honoria sobered when Devil turned the horses off the road, eased them along a narrow lane, then swung onto a wide grassy patch and reined in.

"Behold—north Cambridgeshire."

She could hardly miss it—the county lay spread before her, a tapestry of greens and golds, edged with the darker hues of woods and hedgerows.

"This is the closest we come to a lookout in these parts."

Honoria studied the landscape—while her wariness escalated in leaps and bounds. They were on a grassy plateau, a stand of trees screening them from the road. Essentially private.

"Over there," Devil pointed to the right, "you can see the roofs of Chatteris. The first dark green line beyond is the Forty-Foot Drain, the second is the Old Nene."

Honoria nodded; she recalled the names from his earlier lecture on the fens.

"And now . . ." Devil secured the reins. "It's time for lunch."

"Lunch?" Honoria swung around, but he'd already leapt down from the curricle. An instant later, she heard him rummaging in the boot. He reappeared, a rug in one hand, a picnic basket in the other.

"Here." He tossed the rug at her. Reflexively, she caught it— then caught her breath as his free arm snaked about her waist and he swung her to the ground. He smiled down at her, pure wolf in his eyes. "Why don't you chose a suitable place to spread the rug?"

Honoria glared—she couldn't speak; her heart was blocking her throat, her breathing had seized. She barely had enough strength to whisk herself free of his encircling arm. Marching across the grass as determindedly as her suddenly shaky limbs allowed, all too aware he prowled close behind, she spread the rug over the first reasonable patch, then, remembering her parasol, returned to the safety of the curricle to retrieve it.

The move gave her time to calm her senses, to take a firm grip on her wayward wits—to remind herself of how safe she really was. As long as she didn't allow him to kiss her again, all would be well.

She could hardly be held responsible for the previous kisses he'd stolen—like the buccaneer he reminded her of, he'd surprised her, captured her and taken what he wished. This time, however, while she might unwittingly have walked into his trap, she did know it was a trap. He hadn't sprung it yet—as a virtuous lady it was clearly her duty to ensure his planning came to nought.

His kisses, and the desire behind them, were far from innocent; she could not, in all conscience, indulge in such scandalous dalliance.

Which made her role very clear—circumspection, caution, and unassailable virtue. She headed back to the rug, repeating that litany. The sight of the repast he'd unpacked—the two wineglasses, the champagne, cool in a white linen shroud, the delicacies designed to tempt a lady's palate—all bore testimony to his intent. She narrowed her eyes at him. "You planned this."

Lounging on the rug, Devil raised his brows. "Of course—what else?"

He caught her hand and gently tugged; she had no choice but to sink, gracefully, onto the other half of the rug. She was careful to keep the basket between them. "You didn't even know I was going to join you."

His answer was a single raised brow and a look so outrageously patronizing she was literally lost for words.

He grinned. "Here." He reached into the basket. "Have a chicken leg."

Honoria drew in a deep breath. She looked at the portion he held out, the bone wrapped neatly in a napkin—then reached out, took it, and sank her teeth into it.

To her relief, he made no effort to converse. She shot a glance his way. He lay stretched on the rug, propped on one elbow as he worked steadily through the basket. Honoria took a long draft of champagne—and focused on distracting them both.

"Why," she asked, "did Tolly come by way of St. Ives rather than Cambridge? If he wanted to see you, why didn't he come by the faster route?"

Devil shrugged. "All of us travel via St. Ives."

"For obvious reasons?"

He grinned. "We do, of course, feel a certain link with the town." He caught Honoria's eye. "One of my ancestors built the bridge-chapel, after all."

The chapel she had entirely forgotten to demand a glimpse of. Honoria humphed. "As a penance, no doubt."

"Presumably." Devil sipped his champagne.

Honoria returned to her cogitations. "When did Charles arrive at the Place?"

"I don't know—Vane said he was there when he arrived, late that evening, just before the worst of the storm."

Honoria frowned. "If Charles followed Tolly from town, why didn't he come upon us in the lane?"

"Charles wouldn't come that way."

"I thought all Cynsters travel via St. Ives?"

"All except Charles." Sitting up, Devil started to repack the basket. He glanced at Honoria, then reached for her glass. He drained it in one gulp. "Charles, in case you hadn't noticed, is not really one of the pack."

Pack—a good word to describe them, the Cynster pack of wolves. "He does seem . . ." leaning on one arm, Honoria gestured, "in something of a different mold."

Devil shrugged. "He takes after his mother in looks *and* in disposition. Barely a Cynster trait to be discerned."

"Hmm." Honoria settled more comfortably, a warm glow spreading through her. "When did his mother die?"

"Twenty or so years ago."

"So your uncle remarried almost immediately?"

The basket repacked, Devil stretched out, crossed his arms behind his head, closed his eyes—and watched Honoria through his lashes. "Uncle Arthur's first marriage was little short of a disaster. Almira Butterworth did what no other has in the history of the family—she trapped a Cynster into marriage, much good did it do her. After twelve years of marital discord, she died of consumption—Arthur married Louise a bare year later."

"So how would Charles, not being a dyed-in-the-wool Cynster, have come to the Place? Did he drive?"

"He doesn't drive—don't ask me why. He always comes via Cambridge, hires a horse, then comes riding up the main drive. He once said something about a master always coming to the front door, rather than the back."

Charles, Honoria decided, sounded as insufferable as she'd thought him. "So it's unlikely he saw anything?"

"He said he didn't see anyone about."

Honoria tried to think, but could find no focus for further questions. It was pleasant in the sunshine. Her parasol lay furled in the grass beside her; she should open it, but could not summon the strength. A deliciously warm, relaxed sense of peace pervaded her—she was loath to break the spell.

Glancing at Devil, she noted his closed eyes, black lashes feathering his high cheekbones. Briefly, she let her gaze skim his long frame, conscious, as always, of the deep tug she'd never previously experienced, never felt for any other man. A *frisson* of pure excitement, it heightened every sense, sensitized every nerve, and set her pulse racing. Simultaneously, at some fundamental level, it drew her like a magnet, a potent attraction all too hard to deny. Every instinct she possessed screamed he was dangerous— specifically dangerous to her. Perversely, those selfsame instincts insisted that with him, she was safe. Was it any wonder she felt giddy?

Yet the last was as true as the first. Not even Michael eased her mind to the same degree nor conveyed the same certainty of inviolable protection. The devil might be a tyrant, an autocrat supreme, yet he was also to be relied on, predictable in many ways, rigid in his honor.

Her eyes once more on his face, Honoria drew in a slow breath. He was dangerous indeed, but the basket sat, large and cumbersome between them. Lips gently curving, she looked away, into the soft haze of the early afternoon to the green fields of his domain.

No field came close to the pale, clear green of his eyes.

She'd reached that conclusion when the horizon abruptly fell, leaving her flat on her back, gazing up at the cloudless sky. An instant later, half the sky vanished, replaced by a black mane, hard, angular features and a pair of eyes that saw far too much. And a pair of long, mobile lips, their contours reflecting the same laughing triumph she could see in his green eyes.

The basket was no longer between them. Nothing was.

Honoria's breath caught—her gaze locked on his. Her heart thudded wildly; an uncharacteristic panic streaked through her. Could he read minds? It seemed that he could—the green gaze grew more intense, the line of his lips deepened. Then his lids lowered; slowly, deliberately, he bent his head.

Anticipation rose, an insidious temptation, stealing through her, unlocking her defenses. Honoria felt the fever rise, felt the longing grow. Each time he kissed her, it waxed stronger, more willful, harder to deny. She felt herself sinking under its influence, her lips softening. "No." The word was a whisper—all she could manage. Her heartbeat filled her; her pulse all but deafened her.

He heard her and stopped, eyes glinting from under heavy lids. "Why not?" His brows quirked—his smile grew as he searched her eyes, her face. "You like it when I kiss you, Honoria Prudence."

Her name, uttered in his deep, velvety dark voice, the "r"s gently rolled, was a sensual caress. Honoria struggled to hold back a shiver—she lost the fight when he raised one finger and traced her lower lip.

"You like my kisses—and I like kissing you. Why deny ourselves such innocent pleasure?"

Innocent? Honoria's eyes widened—she might be safe with him, but his notion of safety and hers were not the same. "Ah . . . that's not the point."

The curve of his lips deepened. "Which point is that?"

She hadn't the faintest idea. Honoria blinked blankly up at him—and saw his pirate's smile flash. His head swooped—his lips covered hers.

This time, she ought to struggle. The thought flashed into her mind—and was lost in the same instant, as anticipation exploded and wiped her mental slate clean. Further thought was beyond her; his kiss connected with some other being—a sensual, sen-

sate being—hidden deep inside her. It was that being who reveled in the long-drawn caress, in the hard pressure of his lips
on hers, that being who opened her lips, brazenly inviting him
beyond, to taste, to sample, to plunder to his heart's content.

Other than through his lips, and the long fingers that framed
her face, he did not touch her, yet she was surrounded by his
strength, by his will, bent like a reed to his passion. Her body—
skin, quivering flesh, even her bones—was achingly aware of
him—of his strength, of the tense, sharply defined muscles mere
inches away, of the hardness to match her melting softness.

Their lips melded, their tongues twined, sliding sensuously
together. The kiss was as heady as the fine wine they'd drunk, as
warm as the sunshine about them. He shifted, leaning over her as
he deepened the kiss; Honoria tasted his desire. The compulsion
to feed his hunger rose, flaring like a fever, an impetus steadily
growing with each deep beat of her heart, a driving need to twine
her arms about him, about his shoulders, his neck—to run her
fingers through his thick hair. Her fingers literally itched. One
hand had fallen on his upper arm, the other on his shoulder;
clinging to caution, she flexed her fingers, sinking them deep in a
desperate bid to deny the urge to touch, to feel, to explore.

Instead, the steely feel of him, harder than she'd imagined,
something akin to warm resilient rock, seduced her; caught by
her discovery, she flexed her fingers again, enthralled when his
muscles shifted beneath her hands.

Immediately, his lips hardened; in a heartbeat, their kiss
changed from merely hungry to ravenous. He was closer, his
weight tantalizingly near yet not upon her; Honoria's senses
leapt. Their lips parted; she hauled in a gasping breath. Before
she could open her eyes, he took her mouth again, commanding,
demanding, ravaging her senses.

His hand closed over her breast.

The shock of his touch, of the sliding caress of long, strong fingers, was muted by the cambric of her carriage dress. There was nothing to mute the shock of her reaction—like lightning it speared through her, incandescent fire arcing through her veins. Beneath his hand, her breast swelled; her nipple had tightened to a firm bud even before his fingers found it. Honoria tried to gasp, but he was still kissing her; in desperation, she took her breath from him—and discovered that she could.

His fingers stroked, gently kneaded, and her abandoned senses sang. While the warmth of his caresses spread through her, heating her, heightening the melting sensation deep inside, Honoria mastered the art of breathing through their kiss—suddenly, she was no longer so giddy.

Suddenly she could think enough to know what she felt. Enough to appreciate the quivering excitement that held her, the thrill of anticipation that invested every nerve, every square inch of her skin. Enough to recognize the desire that thrummed heavily in her veins—the compulsion to actively return his kiss, to draw his hard body to hers, to invite, incite—do whatever she could—to quench and fill the molten void within her.

The knowledge rocked her, shocked her—and gave her the strength to draw back.

Devil sensed her withdrawal. Beneath his hand, her breast was hot and swollen, the furled bud of her nipple a hard button against his palm. Yet her retreat was obvious—in their kiss, in the sudden sinking of her senses. He knew women too well, too thoroughly, to miss the battle she waged—the battle to block her own inclination, to suppress the desire that had welled within her in answer to his need.

Inwardly, he cursed; she was causing him no end of pain. He

was sorely tempted to open her bodice and slide his hand in—to show her what that would do to her, what more there was yet to come. But her innocence was a cross he'd steeled himself to bear—the knowledge that he would be the one to school her in love's ways, the only man she would ever know intimately, was a powerful inducement.

She was no prude—she was attracted to him at a level so deep it excited him just to know it. She was ripe for seduction, by him; she would be his—his wife—there was no way he'd let her escape him. Raising his head, he watched as her lids fluttered, then rose, revealing misty grey eyes still silvered with passion. He trapped her gaze. "I should warn you that I've made myself four promises."

His voice, deepened by passion, gravelly with frustration, rumbled between them. Honoria blinked dazedly; Devil suppressed a feral grin. "I'm going to enjoy watching your face the first time I pleasure you." Dipping his head, he brushed her lips with his. "And the second and third time as well."

He drew back—Honoria's eyes were wide, startled. "Pleasure . . . ?"

"When I make that molten heat inside you explode."

"Explode?"

"In a cataclysmic starburst." Devil tightened the fingers that still lay about her breast, then let them slide in a languid caress, his thumb circling her ruched nipple. A quivering shiver raced through her. Deliberately, he caught her eye. "Trust me—I know all about it."

She searched his eyes, her own widening; suddenly, she drew a breath.

"And," Devil said, bending to taste her lips again, cutting off whatever she'd thought to say, "my fourth promise will be the culminating event."

He drew back and watched her debate her next move; eventually, she cleared her throat and asked: "What else have you promised yourself?"

Devil's face hardened. "That I'll be watching your face as I fill you, as you take me inside you, as you give yourself to me."

Honoria stilled—it took all her strength to suppress her reaction, a flaring impulse to passion and possession, a lancing desire so thrillingly vital, so compelling it literally stole her breath. The unexpected insight—into herself, into what might be—was shocking. Most shocking of all was the fact it didn't scare her. But she knew where her future lay—it couldn't be with him. Her eyes locked on his, she shook her head. "It won't happen. I'm not marrying you."

She pushed against him; he hesitated, then drew back, letting her sit up. The instant she did, his fingers closed about her chin; he turned her to face him. "Why not?"

Honoria looked into his narrowed eyes, then haughtily lifted her chin from his hold. "I have my reasons."

"Which are?"

She shot him a resigned glance. "Because you are who you are for a start."

His frown turned black. "What's that supposed to mean?"

Honoria struggled to her feet—instantly, his hand was there to help. He followed her up. She bent and picked up the rug. "You're a tyrant, an unmitigated autocrat, utterly used to your own way. But that's beside the point." The folded rug in her arms, she faced him. "I have no ambition to wed—not you, not any man."

She met his gaze and held it; he continued to frown. "Why not?" The demand, this time, was less aggressive.

Honoria swiped up her parasol and started toward the curricle. "My reason is my own and not one I need share with you."

He was a duke—dukes required heirs. Reaching the curricle, she glanced back—basket in hand, he was trailing in her wake, his expression frowningly intent. When he stopped in front of her, she looked him in the eye. "Please understand, I *won't* change my mind."

He held her gaze for an instant, then he reached for the rug, tossed it into the boot, and swung the basket after it. Letting down the flap, he followed her to the side of the carriage. Honoria turned and waited; she caught her breath as his hands slid about her waist.

They firmed, but he didn't lift her. Suddenly breathless, Honoria looked up—into crystal green eyes that belonged to a conqueror.

He held her, held her gaze, for a full minute, before saying: "We have a standoff, it seems, Honoria Prudence."

Honoria attempted a look of hauteur. "Indeed?"

His lips lengthened, compressed to a line. "Indeed—for I have *no intention* of changing my mind, either."

For one finite instant, Honoria met his gaze, then she raised her brows and looked away.

Jaw clenched, Devil lifted her to the carriage seat, then followed her up. A minute later, they were back on the road; he let his horses have their heads, the whipping wind soothing his overheated brain. Possessiveness had never gripped him so hard, never sunk its talons so deep. Fate had given her to him, to have and to hold. He would have her—take her to wife—there was no alternative.

She had a reason, she said—one she wouldn't tell him. So he'd find out and eradicate it. It was that or go mad.

Chapter 9

"Yes?" Devil looked up from a ledger as Webster entered the library.

"Chatham just rode in, Your Grace—the gentleman you were expecting is waiting as directed."

"Good." Shutting the ledger, Devil stood. "Where is Miss Anstruther-Wetherby?"

"I believe she's in the rose garden, Your Grace."

"Excellent." Devil headed for the door. "I'm going riding, Webster. I'll be back in an hour with our guest."

"Very good, Your Grace."

Two grooms ran up as Devil strode into the stable yard. "Saddle up the bay and get Melton to saddle Sulieman."

"Ah—we've not sighted Melton since early, Y'r Grace."

Devil raised his eyes to the skies. "Never mind—I'll get Sulieman. You fig out the bay."

When he led Sulieman into the yard, the bay was waiting. Mounting, Devil accepted the bay's reins and rode out. Six days had passed since Honoria had dispatched her summons to her brother.

Cresting a low rise, he saw a carriage halted in the road ahead, one of his grooms chatting to the coachman. Beside the carriage, a gentleman paced impatiently. Devil's eyes narrowed, then he sent Sulieman down the road.

The gentleman glanced up at the sound of hooves. He straightened, head rising, chin tilting to an angle Devil recognized instantly. Drawing rein, he raised a brow. "Michael Anstruther-Wetherby, I presume?"

The answering nod was curt. "St. Ives."

Michael Anstruther-Wetherby was in his mid-twenties, of athletic build, with the same steady assurance, the same directness, that characterized his sister. Used to sizing men up in an instant, Devil rapidly readjusted his image of his prospective brother-in-law. Honoria's smugness had painted her brother as weaker than she, perhaps lacking the true Anstruther-Wetherby character. Yet the man eyeing him straitly, challenge and skepticism very clear in his blue eyes, had a decidedly purposeful chin. Devil smiled. "I believe we have matters to discuss. I suggest we take a ride beyond the reach of interruptions."

The blue eyes, arrested, held his, then Michael nodded. "An excellent idea." He reached for the bay's reins, then he was in the saddle. "If you can *guarantee* no interruptions, you'll have achieved a first."

Devil grinned, and set course for a nearby hillock. He halted on the crest; Michael drew up alongside. Devil glanced his way. "I've no idea what Honoria wrote, so I'll start at the beginning."

Michael nodded. "That might be wise."

Gazing over his fields, Devil outlined the events leading to Honoria's presence at the Place. "So," he concluded, "I've suggested that getting married is appropriate."

"To you?"

Devil's brows flew. "Whom else did you have in mind?"

"Just checking." Michael's grin surfaced briefly, then he sobered. "But if that's the case, why have I been summoned to escort her to Hampshire?"

"Because," Devil replied, "your sister imagines she's so long in the tooth that a reputation is neither here nor there. She plans to be the next Hester Stanhope."

"Oh, lord!" Michael cast his eyes heavenward. "She's not *still* set on Africa, is she?"

"It's her dearest wish, so I've been informed, to ride in the shadow of the Sphinx, pursued, no doubt, by a horde of Berber chieftains, then to fall victim to Barbary Coast slave traders. I understand she believes she's starved of excitement and the only way she'll get any is to brave the wilds of Africa."

Michael looked disgusted. "I'd hoped she'd grown out of that by now. Or that some gentleman would appear and give her mind a new direction."

"As to the first, I suspect she'll grow more determined with age—she is, after all, an Anstruther-Wetherby, a family renowned for its stubbornness. But as to giving her mind a new direction, I already have that in hand."

Michael looked up. "Has she agreed to marry you?"

"Not yet." Devil's expression hardened. "But she will."

There was an instant's silence, then Michael asked: "Free of any coercion?"

Devil's eyes met his; one brow lifted superciliously. "Naturally."

Michael studied Devil's eyes, then his features relaxed. He looked out over the fields; Devil waited patiently. Eventually, Michael looked his way. "I'll admit I would be glad to see Honoria safely wed, especially to a man of your standing. I won't oppose the match—I'll support it however I can. But I won't agree to pressure her into any decision."

Devil inclined his head. "Aside from anything else your sister is hardly a biddable female."

"As you say." Michael's gaze turned shrewd. "So what do you want of me?"

Devil grinned. "My brand of persuasion doesn't work well at a distance. I need Honoria to remain within reach." With a gesture, he indicated that they should ride on, and touched his heels to Sulieman's flanks.

Michael cantered alongside. "If Honoria's set on returning home, I'll need some reason to gainsay her."

Devil shot him a glance. "Is she her own mistress?"

"Until she's twenty-five, she's in my care."

"In that case," Devil said, "I have a plan."

By the time they cantered into the stable yard, Michael was entirely comfortable with his brother-in-law to be. It appeared that his sister, usually an irresistible force, had finally met a sufficiently immovable object. He matched his stride to Devil's as they headed for the house.

"Tell me," Devil said, his gaze roving the house, checking for impending interruptions. "Has she always been frightened of storms?"

He glanced at Michael in time to see him wince.

"They still make her twitch?"

Devil frowned. "Rather more than that."

Michael sighed. "Hardly surprising, I suppose—I still get edgy myself."

"Why?"

Michael met his eyes. "She told you our parents were killed in a carriage accident?"

Devil searched his memory. "That they were killed in an accident."

"There was rather more to it than that." Michael drew a deep breath. "Neither Honoria nor I are frightened of storms—at least, we weren't. On that day, our parents took the other two for a drive."

"*Other* two?" Devil slowed his pace.

Michael looked up. "Meg and Jemmy. Our brother and sister." Devil halted, his expression blank. Michael stopped and faced him. "She didn't tell you about them?"

Devil shook his head; abruptly, he focused on Michael. "Tell me exactly what happened."

Michael looked away, across the lawns toward the house. "The pater wanted to take Mama for a drive—it started as a lovely day. Mama had been ill—she was going through one of her better patches—Papa wanted her to get some air. The little ones went with them. Honoria and I stayed home—we couldn't fit and we both had studies to attend to. Then the storm blew up—raced in out of nowhere. Honoria and I loved watching the clouds roll in. We ran up to the schoolroom to watch."

He paused, his gaze distant, fixed in the past. "The schoolroom was in the attics, overlooking the drive. We stood at the window and looked out. We never dreamed . . ." He swallowed. "We were laughing and joking, listening for the thunder, trying to spot the flashes. Then there was a massive crash overhead. In the same instant, we saw the curricle come racing up the drive. The children were frantic, clinging to Mama. The horses had panicked—Papa had his hands full managing them." He paused. "I can see them so clearly, even now. Then the lightning struck."

When he said nothing more, Devil prompted: "The carriage?"

Michael shook his head. "The bolt hit a huge elm beside the drive. It fell." Again he paused, then, drawing a deep breath, went on: "We watched it fall. The others didn't see it at first—

then they did." He shuddered. "I closed my eyes, but I don't think Honoria did. She saw it all."

Devil gave him a moment, then asked: "They were killed?"

"Instantly." Michael drew a shaky breath. "I can still hear the horses screaming. We had to put them down."

Very gently, Devil said: "Go back—what happened to Honoria?"

Michael blinked. "Honoria? When I opened my eyes, she was standing, absolutely still, before the window. Then she stretched out her hands and stepped forward. I grabbed her and pulled her away. She clung to me then." He shivered. "That's the one thing I remember most vividly—how she cried. She made no sound— the tears just rolled down her cheeks, as if her sorrow was so deep she couldn't even sob." After a pause, he added: "I don't think I'll ever forget how *helpless* her crying made me feel."

Devil didn't think he'd ever forget either.

Shoulders lifting on a deep breath, Michael glanced fully at Devil. "That's the sum of it—we sorted things out and got on with our lives. Of course, the loss was worse for Honoria." He fell in beside Devil as they continued toward the house. "As Mama had been so ill, Honoria had become more mother than sister to the younger two. Losing them was like losing her own children, I think."

Devil was silent as they crossed the last of the lawn; he glanced up as they neared the portico, briefly studying the inscription on its facade. Then he glanced at Michael. "You need a drink."

He needed one, too. Then he needed to think.

Honoria was descending the main staircase, a frown puckering her brows, when the front door opened and her brother walked in.

"Michael!" Face clearing, she hurried down. "I've been ex-pecting you for hours." Hugging him, she returned his affectionate buss. "I saw a carriage arrive and thought it must be you, but no one came in. I was wondering—" She broke off as a large shadow darkened the doorway.

Michael looked over his shoulder. "St. Ives was good enough to meet me. He's explained the situation."

"He *has?* I mean—" Her gaze trapped in crystal green, Honoria fought the urge to gnash her teeth. "How very helpful." She noted Devil's expression of guileless innocence—it sat very ill on his piratical features.

"You're looking well." Michael scanned her amethyst morning gown. "Not browbeaten at all."

Even with her gaze firmly fixed on her brother's teasing face, Honoria was aware of Devil's raised brow—and of the color that seeped into her cheeks. Tilting her chin, she linked her arm in Michael's. "Come and meet the Dowager." She steered him toward the drawing room. "Then we'll go for a walk in the grounds." So she could set the record straight.

To her chagrin, Devil strolled after them.

The Dowager looked up as they entered. With a brilliant smile, she laid aside her embroidery and held out her hand. "Mr. Anstruther-Wetherby—it is good to meet you at last. I trust your journey was without mishap?"

"Entirely, ma'am." Michael bowed over her hand. "It's indeed a pleasure to make your acquaintance."

"*Bon!*" The Dowager beamed at him. "And now we can be comfortable and talk, can we not?" Indicating the *chaise* beside her, she glanced at Devil. "Ring for tea, Sylvester. Now, Mr. Anstruther-Wetherby, you are with Carlisle, is that right? And how is the good Marguerite?"

Subsiding into an armchair, Honoria watched as her brother, who she could have sworn was impervious to all forms of flattery, fell under the Dowager's fire. Even more disturbing, time and again, she saw Michael exchange a glance with Devil; by the time Webster brought in the tea, it was clear that, somehow, Devil had succeeded in securing her brother's approval. Honoria bit into a cucumber sandwich and tried not to glower.

She dragged her brother from mother and son's seductive influence as soon as she possibly could.

"Let's go down by the lake." Tightening her hold on Michael's arm, she steered him along the terrace. "There's a seat, near the shore—it's peaceful and private there."

"It's a truly magnificent house," was Michael's only comment as they strolled down the lawn. They reached the seat, and she settled herself upon it; Michael hesitated, looking down at her, then sat beside her. "You could be very comfortable here, you know."

Honoria met his gaze levelly. "Just what has that devil told you?"

Michael grinned. "Not all that much—just the bare facts."

Honoria drew a relieved breath. "In that case, it should be clear that there's no need for any talk of marriage between myself and St. Ives."

Michael's brows rose. "Actually, that's not the impression I received."

"Oh?" Honoria made the syllable a challenge.

Michael tugged at his earlobe. "Perhaps we'd better retread events."

She was very ready to do so. While she recited her well-rehearsed version of events, Michael listened intently. "And then he left me with the Dowager," she concluded.

Michael met her eye. "That's what he told me."

Honoria had a premonition she'd just taken a wrong step.

Michael straightened, one hand clasping hers. "Honoria, you're an unmarried lady of twenty-four, of impeccable lineage and unblemished reputation. In this instance, I must agree with St. Ives—there's really no course open to you other than to accept his offer. He's behaved precisely as he should—no one could hold either of you to blame, yet the circumstances remain and require the prescribed response."

"No." Honoria made the word a statement. "You can't seriously imagine me happily married to Devil Cynster."

Michael raised his brows. "Actually, I find that easier to imagine than any other outcome."

"*Michael*! He's a tyrant! An unmitigatingly arrogant *despot*."

Michael shrugged. "You can't have everything, as Mama was wont to tell you."

Honoria narrowed her eyes; she let a pregnant moment pass before stating, categorically: "Michael, I do not wish to marry Devil Cynster."

Letting go of her hand, Michael leaned back against the seat. "So what do you see as an alternative?"

Honoria knew relief—at least they were *discussing* alternatives. "I'd thought to return to Hampshire—it's too late to get another post this year."

"You'll never get another post, not once this gets out. And it will. St. Ives is right about that—if you marry him, the only whispers will be jealous ones; without his ring on your finger, they'll be malicious. Destructively so."

Honoria shrugged. "That's hardly a disaster. As you know, I care little for society."

"True." Michael hesitated, then added: "You might, however, have a care for our name, and our parents' memory."

Slowly, Honoria turned to face him, her eyes very narrow. "*That* was uncalled for."

His expression stern, Michael shook his head. "No—it had to be said. You cannot simply walk away from who you are and the fact that you have family connections together with the responsibility that entails."

Honoria felt chilled inside, like a general informed he'd just lost his last ally. "So," she said, haughtily tilting her chin, "you would have me marry for the sake of the family—for the sake of a name I've never claimed?"

"I would see you wed first and foremost for your *own* sake. There's no future for you in Hampshire, or anywhere else for that matter. Look about you." He gestured to the sprawling bulk of the Place, displayed like a jewel in the grounds before them. "Here you could be what you were supposed to be. You could be what Papa and Mama always *intended* you to be."

Honoria pressed her lips tightly together. "I cannot live my life according to the precepts of ghosts."

"No—but you should consider the reasons behind their precepts. They may be dead, but the reasons remain."

When she said no more but sat mulishly looking down at her clasped hands, Michael continued, his tone more gentle: "I daresay this may sound pompous, but I've seen more of our world than you—that's why I'm so sure the course I urge you to is right."

Honoria shot him an irate glance. "I am *not* a child—"

"No." Michael grinned. "If you were, this situation wouldn't exist. *But—!*" he insisted, as she opened her mouth to retort, "just hold on to your temper and listen to what I have to say before you set your mind in stone."

Honoria met his eyes. "I only have to listen?"

Michael nodded. "To the proposition St. Ives put to me—and the reasons why I think you should agree to it."

Honoria's jaw fell. "You discussed *me* with *him*?"

Michael closed his eyes for an instant, then fixed her with a distinctly male look. "Honoria, it was necessary he and I talked. We've both lived in society much longer than you—you've never done more than stick a toe in society's sea. That's a point St. Ives, thank heavens, is aware of—it's that that's behind his proposition."

Honoria glared. "*Proposition*? I thought it was a proposal."

Michael closed his eyes tight. "His proposal's on the table and will remain there until you make your decision!" He opened his eyes. "His proposition concerns how we should go on until you do."

"Oh." Faced with his exasperation, Honoria shifted, then looked across the lake. "So what is this proposition?"

Michael drew a deep breath. "Because of his cousin's death, a wedding could not be held inside three months—the Dowager will be in full mourning for six weeks, then half-mourning for another six. As you have no suitable family with whom to reside, what would normally occur is that you would remain with the Dowager and she would introduce you to the *ton* as her son's fiancée."

"But I haven't agreed to marry him."

"No—so in this case, you'll simply remain under the Dowager's wing. She intends going to London in a few weeks—you'll go with her and she'll introduce you to the *ton*. That will give you a chance to see society from a perspective you've never had—if, after that, you still wish to refuse St. Ives's offer, he and I will accept your decision and *try* to come up with some acceptable alternative."

His emphasis made it clear he did not expect to find one. Honoria frowned. "What explanation will be given for my presence with the Dowager?"

"None—Cynsters don't need to tender explanations any more than Anstruther-Wetherbys."

Honoria looked skeptical. "Surely people will wonder?"

"People will *know*, of that you may be sure. However, given the Dowager's involvement, they'll imagine an announcement is in the offing and comport themselves appropriately." Michael grimaced. "I should warn you, the Dowager is something of a force to be reckoned with."

Honoria raised a questioning brow.

Michael waved at the house. "You saw her just now. She's a consummate manipulator."

Honoria's lips twitched. "I had wondered whether you'd noticed."

"I noticed, but there's precious little point trying to resist. You called St. Ives a tyrant—I don't doubt he is, but that's probably just as well. Within the *ton*, his mother's considered a holy terror—of inestimable help if her sympathies lie with you, an enemy to be feared if they don't. No one's going to invite her ire by circulating possibly groundless rumors concerning her son and the lady who might be his duchess. There's no safer place for you than under the Dowager's wing."

Honoria could see it; slowly, she nodded, then looked frowningly at Michael. "I still think it would be much simpler for me to retire to Hampshire until all this blows over. Even if I don't get another post, as you pointed out, I *am* twenty-four. It's time I started on my travel plans."

Michael sighed, and looked away. "You can't stay in Hampshire alone—we'll have to get Aunt Hattie down."

"*Aunt Hattie?*" Honoria wrinkled her nose. "She'll drive me distracted inside of a week."

Michael pursed his lips. "Can't think of anyone else, and you can't live alone, especially once your sojourn in the woods with Devil Cynster becomes public. You'll find yourself dealing with all manner of unwanted visitors."

Honoria shot him a darkling glance, then frowned, very hard, at the lake. Michael preserved a stoic silence.

Minutes ticked past; eyes narrowed, Honoria reviewed her options. She had, indeed, regretted sending for Michael so precipitously; it was clearly going to take time to track Tolly's murderer down. Devil, initially a large hurdle to her plans, had been overcome; he now behaved as a reluctant but resigned coconspirator. The idea of them, together, unmasking Tolly's killer was attractive—quite aside from the compulsion she felt to see justice done, the situation looked set to provide the excitement she'd craved all her life. Leaving now would see all that lost.

There was also the small matter of her burgeoning desire to experience—just once—the pleasure Devil had alluded to. His words, his caresses, like Tolly's face, now haunted her. He'd made it clear physical possession and pleasure were independent events—although the thought was guaranteed to bring a blush to her cheek, she was aware of an increasing compulsion to learn what he could teach her. Of pleasure. Possession, in this case, was out of the question, beyond all possibility. Cynsters never let go anything that became theirs—she was far too wise to become his on any level.

Given she'd determined never to wed, her virtue would never be in question. It seemed wise to gain some experience of the pleasure possible between a man and a woman *before* she set off on her travels. And there was no denying the pleasure she'd thus far experienced at Devil Cynster's hands had held an excitement all its own.

With all that on offer, currently on her plate, but for Devil's matrimonial fixation, her present situation suited her admirably. She didn't *want* to go to Hampshire but with him so set on marriage, it hadn't seemed possible to stay.

Now, however, with his devilish proposition, the devil himself had cleared her path. She could remain in his household, in his mother's care, safe from him and any other gentleman, for three full months—surely, by that time, they would have laid Tolly's murderer by the heels? And she would have learned all she'd need to know of pleasure.

Which left only one quibble—was she strong enough, clever enough, to avoid any traps Devil might set for her?

Honoria straightened, and summoned a resigned grimace. "Very well." She turned and met Michael's eye. "I'll agree to remain under the Dowager's wing for three months." Michael grinned—Honoria narrowed her eyes. "After that, I'll go to Hampshire."

With a long-suffering groan, Michael rose and drew her to her feet. Arm in arm, they strolled back to the house.

Later that evening, Honoria was seated in an armchair in the drawing room, her lap full of embroidery silks, when a shadow fell across her. The Dowager was on the *chaise*, similarly occupied in sorting brilliant hanks. Michael, pleading tiredness, had retired early; Devil had retreated to the library. The tea trolley had come and gone; the evening had slipped silently into night.

Stymied in her attempt to discriminate between azure and turquoise, Honoria looked up—all the way up to Devil's face. He stood directly before her, his expression inscrutable. For a long moment, he simply held her gaze, his own shadowed, impossible to read. Then he held out his hand. "Come for a walk, Honoria Prudence."

From the corner of her eye, Honoria noted that the Dowager had been struck deaf.

Devil's lips softened fleetingly; his gaze remained intense, focused on her face. "I promise not to bite."

Honoria considered the pros and cons—she needed to talk to him, to make sure, while Michael was still here, that their bargain—his proposition—was precisely as she thought. She searched his face. "Not to the summerhouse." She might wish to learn more of pleasure, but she wanted the lessons under her control.

This time, his pirate's smile materialized fully if briefly. "Only on the terrace—I wouldn't want to distract you."

Honoria quelled an incipient shiver, elicited by the deep purring tones of his voice, and shot him a disbelieving glance.

He raised his brows resignedly. "Word of a Cynster."

And in that she could trust. Gathering her silks, Honoria set them aside, then placed her hand in his. He drew her to her feet, then settled her hand on his arm. The Dowager ignored them, apparently absorbed in lilac silks to the exclusion of all else. They strolled to where long windows stood open to the terrace, the night a curtain of black velvet beyond.

"I wished to speak to you," Honoria began the instant they gained the flags.

"And I to you." Looking down at her, Devil paused.

Regally, Honoria inclined her head, inviting his comment.

"Michael has informed me you've agreed to remain with my mother for the next three months."

Reaching the balustrade, Honoria lifted her hand from his sleeve and swung to face him. "Until the period of mourning is over."

"After which time, you'll become my duchess."

She tilted her chin. "After which time, I'll return to Hampshire."

He'd halted directly before her, no more than a foot away. With the light behind him, it was all she could do to discern his expression—arrogantly impassive; his eyes, hooded and shadowed, fixed on hers, she couldn't read at all. Honoria kept her head high, her gaze unwavering, determined to impress on him how inflexible she was.

The moment stretched—and stretched; she started to feel light-headed. Then one of his brows rose.

"We appear to have a problem, Honoria Prudence."

"Only in your mind, Your Grace."

The planes of his face shifted; his expression held a warning. "Perhaps," he said, exasperation clear beneath the polite form, "*before* we decide what will occur at the end of the three months, we should agree on the three months themselves?"

Haughtily, Honoria raised her brows. "I've agreed to remain with your mother."

"And seriously consider my proposal."

The message in his tone was unmistakable—a bargain, or no deal. Drawing in a quick breath, she nodded. "And seriously consider the prospect of becoming your wife. I should, however, inform you that I am unlikely to change my stance on that matter."

"In other words, you're bone stubborn—and I have three months to change your mind."

She did not at all like the way he said that. "I am not a vacillating female—I have no intention of changing my mind."

His teeth flashed in his pirate's smile. "You've yet to experience my powers of persuasion."

Honoria shrugged; nose in the air, she shifted her gaze beyond his shoulder. "You may persuade away—I *won't* be marrying, you or anyone."

Again, silence was his ally, slowly stretching her nerves taut. She nearly jumped when hard fingertips slid beneath her chin, turning her face back to him.

Even in the dark she could sense the piercing quality of his gaze, feel its potency. "Women have been known, on occasion, to change their minds." He spoke slowly, softly, his tones deep and purring. "How much of a woman are you, Honoria Prudence?"

Honoria felt her eyes widen. His fingertips slid across the sensitive skin beneath her chin; sharp slivers of sensation shivered through her. Her lungs had seized; it took considerable effort to lift her chin free of his touch. Haughtily, she stated: "I'm too wise to play with fire, Your Grace."

"Indeed?" His lips curved. "I thought you wanted excitement in your life?"

"On *my* terms."

"In that case, my dear, we'll have to negotiate."

"Indeed?" Honoria tried for airy nonchalance. "Why so?"

"Because you're shortly to become my duchess—that's why."

The glance she bent on him held every ounce of exasperation she could summon, then, with a swish of her skirts, she turned and stepped out of his shadow, following the balustrade. "I've warned you—don't later say I haven't. I am *not* going to marry you at the end of three months." She paused, then, head rising; eyes widening, she swung back and waved a finger at him. "And I am *not* a challenge—don't you *dare* view me as such."

His laughter was that of a pirate—a buccaneer, a swashbuckling rogue who should have been safely on a deck in the middle of some ocean—nowhere near her. The sound, deep, rolling, and far too sure, held a threat and a promise; it enveloped her, caught her up, and held her—then he was there, before her once more.

"You are challenge personified, Honoria Prudence."

"*You* are riding for a fall, Your Grace."

"I'll be riding you before Christmas."

The deliberate reference shocked Honoria, but she wasn't about to let it show. Keeping her chin high, she narrowed her eyes. "You aren't, by any chance, imagining you're going to seduce me into marriage?"

One arrogant black brow rose. "The thought had crossed my mind."

"Well it won't work." When his second brow joined the first, Honoria smiled, supremely confident. "I cut my eyeteeth long ago—I know perfectly well you won't press me while I'm residing under your roof, in your mother's care."

For a long moment, he held her gaze. Then he asked: "How much do you know of seduction?"

It was Honoria's turn to raise her brows. Taking another step along the terrace, she shrugged lightly. "You won't be the first to try it."

"Possibly not, but I'll be the first to succeed."

Honoria sighed. "You won't, you know." Glancing up, she saw him frown. She narrowed her eyes. "*Succeed*, I mean." The frown disappeared. He paced slowly beside her as she strolled the flags. "I know you won't force me—I'll simply call your bluff."

She felt his glance; oddly, it was less intense, less disturbing than before. When he spoke, she detected faint amusement in his tone. "No force, no bluff." He met her gaze as she glanced up. "There's a lot you have to learn about seduction, Honoria Prudence, and this time, you'll be dealing with a master."

Honoria shook her head despairingly. Well, she'd warned him. He was so arrogantly confident it would do him good to be taken down a peg or two—to learn that not all things on this earth would meekly bow to his rule.

The evening reached chill fingers through her gown; she shivered.

Devil's hand on her arm halted her. "We should go in."

Honoria half turned—and found herself facing him. As she watched, his expression hardened; abruptly, he leaned closer. With a stifled shriek, she backed—into the balustrade. He set his hands on the stone parapet, one on either side of her, caging her between his arms.

Breathless, her heart racing, she blinked into his eyes, now level with hers. "You promised not to bite."

His expression was graven. "I haven't—yet." His eyes searched hers. "As you've been so ingenuously frank, the least I can do is return the favor—so that we understand each other fully." He held her gaze steadily; Honoria felt the full weight of his will. "I will not permit you to turn your back on who you are, on the destiny that was always intended to be yours. I will not let you turn yourself into a governessing drudge, nor an eccentric to titillate the *ton*."

Honoria's expression blanked.

Devil held her gaze ruthlessly. "You were born and bred to take a position at the head of the *ton*—that position now lies at your feet. You have three months to reconcile yourself to the reality. Don't imagine you can run from it."

Pale, inwardly quivering, Honoria wrenched her gaze from his. Turning, she yanked at his sleeve.

Letting go of the balustrade, Devil straightened, leaving her escape route clear. Honoria hesitated, then, her expression as stony as his, she turned and looked him straight in the eye. "You have *no right* to decree what my life is to be."

"I have *every* right." Devil's expression softened not at all; his gaze was mercilous. "You will be what you were meant to be— *mine.*"

The emphasis he placed on that single word shook Honoria to her toes. Barely able to breathe, she walked quickly back to the drawing room, head high, skirts shushing furiously.

Chapter 10

Three days later, Devil stood at the library windows, his gaze, abstracted, fixed on the summerhouse. Behind him, open ledgers littered his desk; a pile of letters begged for attention. He had a lot of unfinished business on his plate.

No trace had been found of Tolly's killer, and the simple task of securing his bride was proving remarkably complicated. The latter was more bothersome than the former—he was sure they'd eventually track Tolly's murderer down. He was also unshakably convinced Honoria would be his bride—he was simply no longer so sanguine about what state he'd be in by the wedding.

She was driving him demented. What power had goaded him into declaring his hand so forcefully, there, on the terrace in the moonlight? It had been sheer madness to act the tyrant as he had—yet he could feel the same emotion, the urge to conquer, to seize, to hold, flaring even now, simply at the thought of her.

Luckily, her stubbornness, her defiance, her unquenchable pride had forbidden her to flee before his heavy-handed declaration. She'd let Michael depart alone. Now, with her nose in the air, wrapped in a cloak of chill civility, she held him at a distance.

After learning of her past, common sense suggested he at least reconsider. Common sense stood not a chance against the deep-seated conviction that she was his. Where she was concerned he felt like one of his conquering ancestors preparing to lay siege to a much-desired prize. Given what he now suspected, her surrender, when it came, would need to be proclaimed from the battlements.

He'd wondered how she'd reached a succulently ripe twenty-four still unwed. Even hidden away as a governess, not all men were blind. Some must have seen her and appreciated her worth. A determination on her part to remain a spinster, childless, could, in this case, explain the inexplicable. Her stubbornness was a tangible thing.

In this case, her stubbornness would need to surrender.

He wasn't going to let her go. Ever.

At least she couldn't later say that *he* hadn't warned *her*. His gaze, still on the summerhouse, sharpened; Devil straightened and reached for the handle of the French doors.

Honoria saw him coming; her hand froze in midair, then she looked down and resumed her stitching. Devil climbed the steps two at a time; she looked up and met his gaze squarely. Slowly, she raised her brows.

He held her gaze, then glanced at the seat beside her.

She hesitated, then carefully gathered up her strewn silks. "Did your man learn anything in Chatteris?"

Devil stared at her.

Honoria laid the silks in her basket. "I saw him ride in."

Swallowing his irritation, Devil sat beside her, angling his shoulders so he faced her. "Nothing—no horseman came by way of Chatteris." Perhaps he should grow screening hedges about the summerhouse? She'd adopted it as her lair; he could see a number of pertinent advantages.

Honoria frowned. "So that's all the towns 'round about—and no gentleman hired a horse anywhere."

"Except for Charles, who came by way of Cambridge."

"Is there any other place—a tavern, or some such—where horses might be hired?"

"My people checked all the hedge-taverns within reach. Short of borrowing a horse, something we can't rule out, it seems likely the murderer rode away on his own horse."

"I thought you said that was unlikely?"

"Unlikely but not impossible."

"The storm came up shortly after. Wouldn't he have had to take shelter?"

"The others checked all the inns and taverns on their way back to London. No likely gentleman took refuge anywhere. Whoever shot Tolly was either exceedingly lucky or he covered his tracks exceptionally well."

"Riding his own horse, he could have come from anywhere, not just London. He might have been a hired assassin."

Devil looked at her, silently, for a full minute. "Don't complicate things."

"Well, it's true. But I had *meant* to ask you . . ." She paused to snip a thread; in the silence that followed, Devil got her message. She'd meant to ask him *before* he'd acted the despot. Setting aside her shears, she continued: "Was it common knowledge that Tolly habitually took the lane through the wood?"

Devil grimaced. "Not *common* knowledge, but widespread enough to be easily learned."

Honoria set another stitch. "Have your cousins discovered anything in London?"

"No. But there must be something—some clue—somewhere. Young gentlemen don't get murdered on country lanes for no reason." He looked out across the lawns—and saw his mother approaching. With a sigh, he uncrossed his legs and stood.

"Is this where you are hiding, Sylvester?" The Dowager came up the steps in a froth of black lace. She held up her face for a kiss.

Devil dutifully obliged. "Hardly hiding, *Maman*."

"Indeed—you are a great deal too large for this place." The Dowager prodded him. "Sit—don't tower."

As she promptly took his place beside Honoria, Devil was reduced to perching on a windowsill. The Dowager glanced at Honoria's work—and pointed to one stitch. Honoria stared, then muttered unintelligibly, set down her needle, and reached for her shears.

Devil grabbed the opportunity. "I wanted to speak to you, *Maman*. I'll be leaving for London tomorrow."

"London?" The exclamation came from two throats; two heads jerked up, two pairs of eyes fixed on his face.

Devil shrugged. "Purely business."

Honoria looked at the Dowager; the Dowager looked at her.

When she turned back to her son, the Dowager was frowning. "I have been thinking, *chéri*, that I should also go up to London. Now that I have dear 'Onoria to keep me company, I think it would be quite *convenable*."

Devil blinked. "You're in mourning. Full mourning."

"So?" The Dowager opened her eyes wide. "I'll be in full mourning in London—so appropriate—it is always so grey there at this time of year."

"I had thought," Devil said, "that you would want to remain here, at least for another week or so."

The Dowager lifted her hands, palms upward. "For what? It is a little early for the balls, I grant you, but I am not suggesting we go to London for dissipation. No. It is appropriate, I think, that I introduce 'Onoria, even though the family is in black. She is not affected; I discussed it with your aunt 'Oratia—like me, she thinks the sooner the *ton* meets 'Onoria, the better."

Devil glanced, swiftly, at Honoria; the consternation in her eyes was a delight to behold. "An excellent idea, *Maman*." Silver glinted in Honoria's eyes; he hurriedly looked away. "But you'll have to be careful not to step on the tabbies' tails."

The Dowager waved dismissively. "Do not teach your mother to suck eggs. Your aunt and I will know just how to manage. Nothing too elaborate or such as will . . . how do you say it?—raise the wind?"

Devil hid his grin. "Raise a dust—the wind is money."

The Dowager frowned. "Such strange sayings you English have."

Devil forebore to remind her that she'd lived in England for most of her life—and that her grasp of the language always deteriorated when she was hatching some scheme. In this case, it was a scheme of which he approved.

"Everything will be *tout comme il faut*," the Dowager insisted. "You need not concern yourself—I know how conservative you are growing—we will do nothing to offend your sensibilities."

The comment left Devil speechless.

"Indeed, just this morning I was thinking that I should be in London, with your aunt Louise. I am the matriarch, no? And a matriarch's duty is to be with her family." The Dowager fixed her undeniably matriarchal gaze on her silent son. "Your father would have wished it so."

That, of course, signaled the end to all argument—not that Devil intended arguing. Manufacturing an aggravated sigh, he held up his hands. "If that's what you truly wish, *Maman*, I'll give orders immediately. We can leave tomorrow at midday and be in town before nightfall."

"Bon!" The Dowager looked at Honoria. "We had best start our packing."

"Indeed." Honoria put her needlework in her basket, then glanced briefly, triumphantly, at Devil.

He kept his expression impassive, standing back as she and his mother exited the summerhouse. Only when they were well ahead did he descend the steps, strolling languorously in their wake, his gaze on Honoria's shapely curves, smug satisfaction in his eyes.

St. Ives House in Grosvenor Square was a great deal smaller than Somersham Place. It was still large enough to lose a battalion in, a fact emphasized by the odd individual of military mien who presided over it.

Honoria nodded at Sligo as she crossed the hall, and wondered at Devil Cynster's idiosyncracies. On arriving at dusk two days before, she'd been taken aback to find the stoop-shouldered, thin, and wiry Sligo acting as majordomo. He had a careworn face, moon-shaped and mournful; his attire was severe but did not quite fit. His speech was abrupt, as if he was still on a parade ground.

Later, she'd questioned the Dowager; Sligo, it transpired, had been Devil's batman at Waterloo. He was fanatically devoted to his erstwhile captain; on disbanding, he'd simply continued to follow him. Devil had made him his general factotum. Sligo remained at St. Ives House, acting as its caretaker when the family was not in residence. When his master was in residence, Honoria surmised, he reverted to his previous role.

Which, she suspected, meant that Sligo would bear watching. A footman opened the breakfast-parlor door.

"There you are, my dear." The Dowager beamed gloriously from one end of the elegant table.

Honoria bobbed a curtsy, then inclined her head toward the head of the table. "Your Grace."

The devil nodded back, his gaze roving over her. "I trust you slept well?" With a wave, he summoned Webster to hold a chair for her—the one beside his.

"Tolerably well, thank you." Perforce ignoring the nine other empty chairs about the immaculately laid table, Honoria settled her skirts, then thanked Webster as he poured her tea. The previous day had gone in unpacking and settling in. A rain squall had cut short the afternoon; she'd got no closer to the park in the Square than the drawing-room windows.

"I have been telling Sylvester that we plan to visit the modistes this morning." The Dowager waved a knife at her. "He tells me that these days the *ton* selects modistes by age."

"Age?" Honoria frowned.

Busy with toast and marmalade, the Dowager nodded. "Apparently, it is quite *convenable* that I continue with my old Franchot, but for you it must be . . ." She glanced at her son. "*Qu'est-ce que?*"

"Celestine," Devil supplied.

Honoria turned her frown on him.

He met her look with one of ineffable boredom. "It's simple enough—if you want bombazine and turbans, you go to Franchot. If frills and furbelows are your fancy, then Madame Abelard's is more likely to suit. For innocent country misses," he paused, his gaze briefly touching Honoria's fine lace fichu, "then I've heard Mademoiselle Cocotte is hard to beat. For true elegance, however, there's only one name you need know—Celestine."

"Indeed?" Honoria sipped her tea, then, setting down her cup, reached for the toast. "Is she on Bruton Street?"

Devil's brows flew. "Where else?" He looked away as Sligo approached, carrying a silver salver piled with letters. Taking them, Devil flicked through the stack. "I daresay you'll find any number of modistes that might take your fancy if you stroll the length of Bruton Street."

From the corner of her eye, Honoria watched him examine his mail. He employed a small army of agents; one had followed on their heels from the Place and spent all yesterday closeted with his master. Running estates as extensive as those of the dukedom of St. Ives would keep any man busy; thus far, from all she'd seen, business had prevented Devil from pursuing his investigations.

Reaching the bottom of the pile, he shuffled the letters together, then glanced at his mother. "If you'll excuse me, *Maman.*" Briefly, his eyes touched Honoria's. "Honoria Prudence." With a graceful nod, he stood; absorbed with his letters, he left the room.

Honoria stared at his back until the door hid it from view, then took another sip of her tea.

The St. Ives town carriage had just rumbled around the corner, bearing the Dowager and Honoria to Bruton Street, when Vane Cynster strolled into Grosvenor Square. His stride long and ranging, he crossed the pavements; cane swinging, he climbed the steps to his cousin's imposing door. He was about to beat an imperious tattoo when the door swung inward. Sligo rushed out.

"Oh! Sorry, sir." Sligo flattened himself against the doorjamb. "Didn't see you there, sir."

Vane smiled. "That's quite all right, Sligo."

"Cap'n's orders. An urgent dispatch." Sligo tapped his breast—rustling parchment testified to his cause. "If you'll excuse me, sir?"

Released by Vane's bemused nod, Sligo hurried down the steps and ran to the corner. He flagged down a hackney and climbed aboard. Vane shook his head, then turned to the still-open door. Webster stood beside it.

"The master is in the library, sir. I believe he's expecting you. Do you wish to be announced?"

"No need." Surrendering his cane, hat and gloves, Vane headed for Devil's sanctum. He opened the door, instantly coming under his cousin's green gaze.

Devil sat in a leather chair behind a large desk, an open letter in one hand. "You're the first."

Vane grinned. "And you're impatient."

"You're not?"

Vane raised his brows. "Until a second ago, I didn't know you had no news." He crossed the room and dropped into a chair facing the desk.

"I take it you have no insights to offer either?"

Vane grimaced. "In a word—no."

Devil grimaced back; refolding his letter, he laid it aside. "I just hope the others have turned up something."

"What's Sligo up to?" When Devil looked up, Vane elaborated: "I bumped into him on the steps—he seemed in a tearing hurry."

Devil waved dismissively. "A small matter of forward strategy."

"Speaking of which, have you managed to convince your bride-to-be that investigating murder is not a suitable hobby for a gentlewoman?"

Devil smiled. "*Maman* can always be counted on to visit the modistes within forty-eight hours of arriving in town."

Vane raised his brows. "So you *haven't* succeeded in striking murder from Miss Anstruther-Wetherby's agenda?"

Devil's smile turned feral. "I'm directing my fire at a different target. Once that falls, her agenda will no longer apply."

Vane grinned. "Poor Honoria Prudence—does she know what she's up against?"

"She'll learn."

"Too late?"

"That's the general idea."

A brief rap on the door heralded the appearance of Richard "Scandal" Cynster; he was followed by Gabriel and Demon Harry, Vane's brother. The comfortably spacious room was suddenly very full of very large men.

"Why the delay?" Harry asked, lowering his long frame to the *chaise*. "I expected to be summoned yesterday."

"Devil had to make sure the coast was clear," Vane replied—and earned a hard look from Devil.

"Lucifer sends his regrets," Gabriel informed the room at large. "He's exhausted from his efforts to discover any news of Tolly's peccadilloes—which efforts have thus far been completely unrewarding."

"That," Harry returned, "I find exceedingly hard to believe."

"Unrewarding in terms of our investigation," Gabriel amended.

"As to that," Harry continued, "I know exactly how he feels."

Despite considerable effort in their delegated spheres, none had uncovered any evidence that Tolly had been in trouble. Devil put forward the idea that Tolly might not personally have been in trouble at all. "He may have unwittingly stumbled on something he wasn't supposed to know—he might unsuspectingly have become a threat to someone."

Gabriel was nodding. "*That* scenario sounds a lot more like Tolly."

Harry snorted. "Silly beggar would have got all fired up with innocent zeal and hared off to lay the evidence at your feet."

"Before demanding that you fix it." Richard's smile went slightly awry. "That plot rings truer than any other."

His eyes on Richard's, Devil said, "The very fact that he was coming to see me may have been what led to his death."

Vane nodded. "*That* would explain why he was killed at Somersham."

"We'll have to recanvass all Tolly's friends." Under Devil's direction, Gabriel, Harry, and Richard agreed to take on the task.

"And me?" Vane raised his brows. "What fascinating piece of detecting am I to undertake?"

"You get to wring out Old Mick."

"*Old Mick?!*" Vane groaned. "The man drinks like a fish."

"You've the hardest head of the lot of us, and someone's got to speak to him. As Tolly's man, he's our most likely lead."

Vane grumbled, but no one paid him any heed.

"We'll meet here again in two days." Devil stood; the others followed suit. Gabriel, Harry, and Richard headed for the door.

"It's occurred to me," Vane said, as he strolled after the others, "that the latest addition to the family might not be so amenable to bowing to your authority."

Devil arched a brow. "She'll learn."

"So you keep saying." At the door, Vane glanced back. "But you know what they say—beware of loose cannon."

The look Devil sent him embodied arrogance supreme; Vane chuckled and left, closing the door behind him.

Wringing information from a devil was not an easy task, especially when he evinced no interest in her company. Poised at the top of the stairs, Honoria debated her next move.

She'd taken Devil's advice and visited Celestine's salon. Her suspicious nature had reared its head when a note, directed in bold black script and carrying a red seal, had arrived for Celestine hard on their heels. While Honoria tried on subtly understated morning gowns, fashionable carriage dresses, and delectably exquisite evening gowns, the modiste, in constant attendance from the instant she'd read the note, had made comments enough on *monsieur le duc's* partialities to confirm her suspicions. But by then she'd seen too many of Celestine's creations to contemplate cutting off her nose to spite her face.

Instead, she'd bought an entire wardrobe, all for the express purpose of setting *monsieur le duc* back on his heels. Celestine's evening gowns, while unquestionably acceptable, were subtly scandalous—her height and age allowed her to wear them to advantage. Nightgowns, peignoirs, and chemises, all in silks and satins, were similarly stunning. Everything, naturally, was shockingly expensive—luckily, her pocket was more than deep enough to stand the nonsense.

She'd spent the ride back to Grosvenor Square imagining the look on Devil's face when he saw her in a particularly *provoking* nightgown—only as the carriage reached St. Ives House did the anomaly in her thinking strike her. When would Devil see her in her nightgown?

Never if she was wise. She'd bundled the thought from her mind.

For the past two mornings, she'd entered the breakfast-parlor wearing an encouraging smile and one of Celestine's more fetching creations; while the devil had noticed her, other than a certain glint in his green eyes, he'd shown no inclination to commit himself beyond an absentminded nod. On both mornings, in an unflatteringly short space of time, he'd excused himself and taken refuge in his study.

She could imagine that he might be busy; she was not prepared to accept that as an excuse to ignore her, particularly as he must by now have learned *something* about his cousin's death.

Drawing a determined breath, she started down the stairs. Direct action was called for—she would beard the lion in his den. Or was that the devil in his lair? Luckily, his lair was also the library. Hand on the doorknob, she paused; no sound came from within. Mentally girding her loins, she plastered a breezily unconscious smile on her face, opened the door, and walked briskly in.

Without looking up, she closed the door and turned, taking two steps before letting her gaze reach the desk. "Oh!" Lips parting, eyes widening, she halted. "I'm sorry. I didn't realize . . ." She let her words trail away.

Her devilish host sat behind the large desk, his correspondence spread before him. By the windows, Sligo was sorting ledgers. Both men had looked up; while Sligo's expression was arrested, Devil's was unreadable.

With a longing glance at the bookshelves, Honoria conjured an apologetic smile. "I didn't mean to intrude. Pray excuse me."

Gathering her skirts, she half turned—a languid gesture halted her. "If it's distraction you seek, then by all means, seek it here."

Devil's eyes met hers; while his accompanying wave indicated the volumes and tomes, Honoria was not at all certain they were the distraction to which he referred. Lifting her chin, she inclined her head graciously. "I won't disturb you."

She already had. Devil shifted in his chair, then rearranged his letters. From the corner of his eye, he watched Honoria scan the shelves, pausing artistically here and there to raise a hand to this book or that. He wondered who she thought she was fooling.

The past two days had been difficult. Resisting the invitation in her eyes had required considerable resolution, but he'd won too many campaigns not to know the value of having her approach him. At last she'd weakened—impatience mounting, he waited for her to get to the point.

Picking up his pen, he signed a letter, blotted it, and laid it aside. Glancing up, he surprised her watching him—she quickly looked away. A sunbeam lancing through the windows burnished the gleaming chestnut knot atop her head; wispy tendrils wreathed her nape and forehead. In her cream-colored morning gown, she looked good enough to eat; for a ravenous wolf, the temptation was great. Devil watched as she put a hand to a heavy tome, one on agricultural practices; she hesitated, then pulled it out and opened it. She was vacillating.

Realizing what she was reading, she abruptly shut the book and replaced it, then drifted back to the shelves nearer the door, selecting another book at random. With an inward sigh, Devil put down his pen and stood. He didn't have all day—his cousins were due later that afternoon. Rounding the desk, he crossed the carpet; sensing his approach, Honoria looked up.

Devil lifted the book from her hands, shut it, and returned it to the shelf—then met her startled gaze. "What's it to be—a drive in the park or a stroll in the square?"

Honoria blinked. She searched his eyes, then stiffened and raised her chin. "A drive." The park might be crowded but on the box seat of his curricle she could interrogate him without restriction.

Devil's eyes didn't leave hers. "Sligo—get the bays put to."

"Aye, Capt'n Y'r Grace." Sligo darted for the door.

Intending to follow, Honoria found herself trapped, held, by

Devil's green gaze. Forsaking her eyes, it slid down, lingering briefly but with a weight that sent heat rising to her cheeks.

He looked up. "Perhaps, my dear, you had better change—we wouldn't want you to catch cold."

Like she'd caught cold trying to fool him? Haughtily, Honoria raised her chin another inch. "Indeed, Your Grace. I shouldn't keep you above half an hour."

With a swish of her skirts, she escaped. Even forcibly dragging her heels, she was back in the hall in under ten minutes; to her relief, the devil forebore to comment, merely meeting her eye with a glance too arrogantly assured for her liking. His gaze swept her, neat and trim in green jaconet, then he gave her his arm; nose still high, she consented to be led down the steps.

Devil lifted her to the seat. They were bowling through the park gates, the carriages of the *ton* lining the curved avenue ahead, before she registered that a groom had swung up behind. Glancing back, she beheld Sligo.

Devil saw her surprise. "You'll no doubt be relieved that I've decided to observe the strictures wherever possible."

Honoria gestured behind. "Isn't *that* rather excessive?"

"I wouldn't let it dampen your enthusiasms, Honoria Prudence." He slanted her a glance. "Sligo's half-deaf."

A quick glance confirmed it; despite the fact Devil had not lowered his voice, Sligo's expression remained blank. Satisfied, Honoria drew a deep breath. "In that case—"

"That's the countess of Tonbridge to your right. She's a bosom-bow of *Maman's*."

Honoria smiled at the *grande dame* lounging in a brougham drawn up by the verge; a quizzing glass magnifying one protu-

berant eye, the countess inclined her head graciously. Honoria
nodded back. "What—"

"Lady Havelock ahead. Is that a turban she's wearing?"

"A toque," Honoria replied through her smile. "But—"

"Mrs. Bingham and Lady Carstairs in the landau."

It was difficult, Honoria discovered, to smile with clenched
teeth. Her breeding, however, dictated her behavior, even in
such trying circumstances; calmly serene, she smiled and
nodded with gracious impartiality—the truth was, she barely
focused on those claiming her attention. Not even the sight of
Skiffy Skeffington in his customary bilious green had the power
to divert her—her attention was firmly fixed on the reprobate
beside her.

She should have chosen the square. After the first three encounters, the interest directed their way registered; the glances
of the ladies whose nods she returned were not idle. They were
sharp, speculative—keenly acute. Her position beside Devil was
clearly making some statement; Honoria had a strong suspicion it
was not a statement she'd intended to make. Nodding to a beaming Lady Sefton, she asked: "How long is it since you last drove
a lady in the park?"

"I don't."

"Don't?" Honoria turned and stared. "Why not? You can
hardly claim you're misogynous."

Devil's lips twitched; briefly he met her eye. "If you think
about it, Honoria Prudence, you'll see that appearing beside me
in the park is tantamount to a declaration—a declaration no unmarried lady has previously been invited to make and one which
no married lady would care to flaunt."

Lady Chetwynd was waiting to be noticed; by the time she
was free again, Honoria was simmering. "And what about me?"

Devil glanced her way; this time, his expression was harder. "*You* are different. You're going to marry me."

An altercation in the park was unthinkable; Honoria seethed, but couldn't let it show, other than in her eyes. Those, only he could see, much good did her fury do her; with an infuriatingly arrogant lift to his brows, he turned back to his horses.

Denied the interrogation she'd planned *and* the tirade he deserved, Honoria struggled, not simply to contain her wrath but to redirect it. Losing her temper was unlikely to advance her cause.

She slanted a glance at Devil; his attention was on his horses, his profile clear-cut, hard-edged. Eyes narrowing, she looked ahead, to where a line of carriages had formed, waiting to turn. Devil drew in at the end; Honoria saw her chance and took it. "Have you and your cousins learned anything of the reason behind Tolly's murder?"

One black brow quirked upward. "I had heard . . ."

Breath bated, Honoria waited.

"That Aunt Horatia intends giving a ball in a week or so." Blank green eyes turned her way. "To declare the family once more on the town, so to speak. Until then, I suspect we should curb our excursions—the park and such mild entertainments are, I believe, permissible. Later . . ."

In utter disbelief, Honoria listened to a catalogue of projected diversions—the usual *divertissements* favored by the *ton*. She didn't bother trying to interrupt. He'd accepted her help in the lane; he'd told her that his people had turned up no clues in the towns about Somersham. She'd thought he'd capitulated—understood and accepted her right to involve herself in the solving of the crime, or, at the very least, accepted her right to know what had been discovered. As the litany of pleasures in store for her continued, Honoria readjusted her thinking.

Very straight, her expression blank, she held her tongue until, the turn accomplished, he ran out of entertainments. Then, and only then, did she glance sideways and meet his eye. "You are not being fair."

His features hardened. "That's the way our world is."

"Perhaps," Honoria declared, tilting her chin, "it's time our world changed."

He made no answer; flicking the reins, he sent the horses back along the avenue.

Honoria's head was so high she nearly missed seeing the gentleman standing by the verge; he raised his cane in greeting, then waved it.

Devil checked his team, drawing them to a stamping halt by the lawn's edge. "Good afternoon, Charles."

Charles Cynster inclined his head. "Sylvester." His gaze traveled to Honoria. "Miss Anstruther-Wetherby."

Resisting an instinctive retreat to haughtiness, Honoria returned his nod. "Sir. Might I inquire how your family is faring?" Charles wore the customary black armband, easily seen against his brown coat. Devil likewise wore the badge of mourning, virtually invisible against his black sleeve. Honoria leaned down and gave Charles her hand. "I've yet to meet your brother and sisters since coming to town."

"They are . . ." Charles hesitated. "Well, I think." He met Honoria's eyes. "Recovering from the shock. But how are you? I admit to surprise at seeing you here. I had thought your plans were otherwise?"

Honoria smiled—feelingly. "They are. *This*"—she gestured airily—"is merely a temporary arrangement. I've agreed to remain with the Dowager for three months. After that, I plan to begin my preparations for Africa. I'm considering a prolonged sojourn—there's so much to see." Her smile grew brittle. "*And* do."

"Indeed?" Charles frowned vaguely. "I believe there's a very good exhibition at the museum. If Sylvester's too busy to escort you, pray call on me. As I assured you before, I'll always hold myself ready to assist you in any way I can."

Regally, Honoria inclined her head.

After promising to convey their regards to his family, Charles stepped back. With a flick of his wrist, Devil set his horses trotting. "Honoria Prudence, you would try the patience of a saint."

Irritation ran beneath his smooth tones. "You," Honoria declared, "are no saint."

"A point you would do well to bear in mind."

Quelling a most peculiar shiver, Honoria stared straight ahead.

They ran the gauntlet—the long line of stationary carriages holding the *grandes dames* of the *ton*—once more, then Devil turned his horses for home. By the time they reached Grosvenor Square, Honoria had refocused on her day's objective. The objective she had yet to attain.

Devil drew up before his door. Throwing the reins to Sligo, he alighted and lifted Honoria down. By the time she caught her breath, she was on the porch; his front stoop, she decided, was no place for an argument.

The door opened; Devil followed her inside. The hall seemed crowded; as well as Webster, Lucifer was there.

"You're early."

Honoria glanced at Devil, surprised by the disapproval she detected in his tone. Lucifer's brows had quirked in surprise, but he smiled charmingly as he bowed over her hand. Straightening, he looked at Devil. "In recompense, if you will, for my previous absence."

Previous absence? Honoria looked at Devil.

His expression gave nothing away. "You'll have to excuse us, my dear. Business demands our attention."

Business her left foot. Honoria raced through her options, searching for some acceptable way to remain with them. There wasn't one. Swallowing a curse, she inclined her head regally, first to her nemesis, then to his cousin, then turned and glided up the stairs.

"I hesitate to state the obvious, but we're getting nowhere. I, for one, am finding failure a mite tedious." A general growl of agreement greeted Gabriel's pronouncement. All six cousins were present, long limbs disposed in various poses about Devil's library.

"Speaking personally," Vane drawled, "I'd prefer to have failure to report. As it is, Old Mick, longtime servitor to the second family, has departed these fair shores."

Harry frowned. "He's left England?"

"So Charles informs me." Vane flicked a speck of lint from his knee. "I went to Tolly's lodgings and found them relet. According to the landlord, who lives downstairs, Charles turned up the day after Tolly's funeral. No one had told Mick about Tolly—he was, needless to say, cut up."

Richard whistled soundlessly. "He'd been with the family forever—he was devoted to Tolly."

Vane inclined his head. "I assumed Charles would have ensured Mick was told in time to come up for the funeral—he must have been more distraught than we realized. As it transpired, there was something of a scene. According to the landlord, Mick stormed out. According to Charles, Mick was so cut up over Tolly's death that he decided to quit London and return to his family in Ireland."

Harry looked wary. "Do we know Mick's surname?"

"O'Shannessy," Richard supplied.

Devil frowned. "Do we know where his family live?"

Vane shook his head.

Harry sighed. "I'm due in Ireland within the week to look over some brood mares. I could see if I can ferret out *our* Mick O'Shannessy."

Devil nodded. "Do." His features hardened. "And when you find him, aside from our questions, make sure Charles took proper care of him. If not, make the usual arrangements and have the accounts sent to me."

Harry nodded.

"Incidentally," Vane said, "Charles's man, Holthorpe, has also left for greener fields—in his case, to America."

"America?" Lucifer exclaimed.

"Apparently Holthorpe had saved enough to visit his sister there. When Charles returned from Somersham, Holthorpe was gone. Charles's new man has rather less presence than Sligo and goes by the name of Smiggs."

Harry snorted. "Sounds like he'll suit Charles."

Lucifer sighed. "So where do we search next?"

Devil frowned. "We must be overlooking something."

Vane grinned wryly. "But not even the devil knows what it is."

Devil humphed. "Unfortunately not. But if Tolly stumbled on someone's illegal or scandalous secret, then, presumably, if we try hard enough, we can learn that same secret."

"And *whose* secret it is," Gabriel, somewhat grimly, added.

"It could be anything," Lucifer said. "Tolly could have heard it from a man on a corner or from some silly chit in a ballroom."

"Which is why we'll need to cast our net wide. Whatever it is must be out there somewhere—we'll have to trawl." Devil scanned their dissatisfied but still-determined faces. "I can't see that we have any choice other than to keep searching until we have some facts to work on."

Gabriel nodded. "You're right." He stood and met Devil's eye, a lilting smile curving his lips. "None of us are about to desert."

The others nodded; unhurriedly, they left, restrained impatience in their eyes. Devil saw them out. He turned back to the library, then hesitated. Frowning, he glanced over his shoulder. "Webster—"

"I believe Miss Anstruther-Wetherby is in the upstairs parlor, Your Grace."

Devil nodded and started up the stairs. Their lack of progress hung heavily on his mind; Honoria's wish to involve herself in the hunt was an added irritant—seducing her to his side was proving difficult enough without that complication. Gaining the top of the stairs, he smiled, grimly. There was more than one way of spiking a gun—presumably the same held true for loose cannon.

The parlor door opened noiselessly; Honoria was pacing before the hearth. She didn't hear him enter. She was muttering in distinctly forceful fashion; as Devil neared, he caught the words "fair" and "stubborn beast."

Honoria glanced up—and jumped back. Devil caught her by the elbows and yanked her to him, away from the fire.

Breathless, her heart in her mouth, Honoria pushed him away. He released her instantly; her inner shaking didn't stop. Furious, on any number of points, she put her hands on her hips and glared. "*Don't do* that!" She batted aside a distracting curl. "Hasn't anyone ever told you it's unacceptable to sneak up on people?"

"I wasn't sneaking." Devil's expression remained mild. "You didn't hear me—you were too busy rehearsing your lecture."

Honoria blinked; caution belatedly seeped into her mind.

"Now I'm here," Devil continued, "why don't you deliver it?" The invitation was the opposite of encouraging. "On the other hand," his brows quirked, "you might care to hear what my cousins had to report."

Honoria was bottling up so much spleen, she felt she might explode. There was, she understood, an "either or" buried in his words. If she poured out the tirade she'd spent the last hour preparing, she wouldn't hear what had been learned of Tolly's killer. Her head hurt. "Very well—tell me what you and your cousins have found out."

Devil gestured to the *chaise*; he waited until she sat, then settled his long frame in the opposite corner. "Unfortunately, thus far, despite considerable effort, we've turned up precisely nothing. No hint whatever of what it was that set Tolly on the road to Somersham."

"Nothing?" Honoria searched his face; there was no hint of evasion in his eyes. "Where did you look and what were you searching for?"

Devil told her; she drank in his description of the others' particular strengths and the gamut of their investigations. She was confident he wasn't lying; she did wonder if he was telling her the whole truth. She quizzed him, but his answers remained consistent. "So what now?"

In the distance, they heard the dinner gong boom. "Now," he said, rising gracefully and holding out his hand, "we keep searching." He'd explained they were looking for someone else's secret. "Until we have a scent to follow, we can do nothing more."

Honoria wasn't so certain of that. She allowed him to draw her to her feet. "Perhaps—"

One long finger slid beneath her chin; Devil tipped her face up to his. "I'll keep you informed of developments, Honoria Prudence."

His voice deepened on her name. Mesmerized, Honoria saw the color of his eyes change, a gleam silvering their depths. His gaze shifted, dropping to her lips; she felt them soften, part, felt her lids grow heavy.

"Ah . . . yes." Breathless, she lifted her chin from his finger and stepped sideways, bringing the door into view. "I'd better change."

One black brow rose, but beyond that and a quizzical glance, he made no comment, escorting her to the door and holding it while she made good her escape. It was only when, half an hour later, she sat before her mirror for her maid, Cassie, to do her hair, that understanding dawned.

He'd told her what they'd discovered—nothing. He'd promised to keep her apprised of developments—eyes narrowing, Honoria realized he meant *after* they'd been acted upon. Even more telling, he'd prevented her from offering to assist—so that he wouldn't have to refuse and make it plain that she was still not permitted any meaningful involvement.

When she entered the drawing room, she was poised and assured, able to meet Devil's eye with calm serenity. Throughout the meal, she remained distant, listening to the conversation with but half an ear, her mind busy formulating her investigative strategy.

Nothing useful had yet been discovered, which left the field wide open. As for His Grace's antiquated notions, she was sure that, when she discovered the vital secret, he wouldn't be able to deny her. How could he?—she wouldn't tell him until after, until it was too late for him to exclude her.

Chapter 11

Investigating Tolly's murder proved more difficult than she'd thought. While his cousins had entrée to Tolly's largely male world, Honoria did not. Likewise, they knew Tolly, his habits, his interests. On the other hand, she reasoned, she could view his last days impartially, the facts uncolored by preconceived notions. Besides, women were notoriously more observant than men.

Tolly's youngest aunt, Celia, had been elected by the conclave of Cynster wives to give the first "at home," a declaration to the *ton* that the family had emerged from deepest mourning. Even Louise was present, still in deadest black, her composure a shield against those proffering their condolences.

At St. Ives House, black crepe had wreathed the knocker ever since they had come up to town; on the Dowager's orders, it had been removed this morning. Their first week in the capital had been spent quietly, eschewing all social functions, but it was now three weeks since Tolly's death; his aunts had decreed their time in deep mourning past. They all still wore black and would for another three weeks, then they would go into half-mourning for another six weeks.

Honoria circulated amongst Celia's guests, noting those whose acuity might prove useful. Unfortunately, as it was the first time she'd ventured into society, there were many eager to claim her attention.

"Honoria." Turning, Honoria found Celia beside her, a plate of cakes in her hand, her eye on a *chaise* on the opposite side of the room. "I hate to ask, but I know you can handle it." With a smile, Celia handed her the plate. "Lady Osbaldestone—she's a veritable tartar. If I go, she'll shackle me to the *chaise*, and I'll never get free. But if one of the family doesn't appear to appease her curiosity, she'll batten on Louise. Here, let me take your cup."

Relieved of her empty teacup, Honoria was left with the cake plate. She opened her lips to point out she wasn't "family"—but Celia had disappeared into the crowd. Honoria hesitated, then, with a resigned sigh, straightened her shoulders and bore down on Lady Osbaldestone.

Her ladyship greeted her with a basilik stare. "And about time, too." A clawlike hand shot out and snaffled a petit four. "Well, miss?" She stared at Honoria. When she simply stared back, politely vacant, her ladyship snorted. "Sit down, do! You're giving me a crick. Daresay that devil St. Ives chose you for your height—I can just imagine why." This last was said with a definite leer—Honoria swallowed an urge to request clarification. Instead, she perched, precisely correct, on the edge of the *chaise*, the cake plate held where Lady Osbaldestone could reach it.

Her ladyship's black eyes studied her carefully while the petit four was consumed. "Not just in the usual way and an Anstruther-Wetherby to boot, heh? What's your grandfather say to this match, miss?"

"I have no idea," Honoria answered calmly. "But you're laboring under a misapprehension. I'm not marrying anyone."

Lady Osbaldestone blinked. "Not even St. Ives?"

"*Particularly* not St. Ives." Deciding she might as well eat, Honoria selected a small tea cake and nibbled delicately.

Her declaration had struck Lady Osbaldestone dumb. For a full minute, her black eyes, narrowed, rested on Honoria's profile, then her ladyship's face cracked in a wide smile; she cackled gleefully. "Oh, you'll do. Keep up that pose, miss, and you'll do for Devil Cynster nicely."

Haughtily, Honoria looked down her nose. "I have no interest in His Grace of St. Ives."

"Oh-*ho*!" Her ladyship poked her arm with a bony finger. "But has His Grace an interest in *you*?"

Her eyes trapped in her ladyship's black gaze, Honoria wished she could lie. Lady Osbaldestone's grin grew wider. "Take my advice, girl—make sure he never loses it. Never let him take you for granted. The best way to hold such men is to make them work for their pleasure."

Adopting a martyred expression, Honoria sighed. "I really am *not* going to marry him."

Lady Osbaldestone, suddenly terrifyingly sober, looked at Honoria through old black eyes. "Girl—you don't have a choice. *No*—!" She pointed a skeletal finger. "Don't poker up and stick that Anstruther-Wetherby chin in the air. There's no benefit in running from fate. Devil Cynster has all but declared he wants you—which means he'll have you—and if that chin is any guide, it'll be a good thing, too. And as he's too experienced to pursue where there's no reciprocating sentiment, you needn't think to deny it." Her ladyship snorted. "You'd have to be dead to be immune to his temptation—and you don't look too desiccated to me."

A blush stole into Honoria's cheeks; Lady Osbaldestone

nodded. "Your mother's dead—so's your grandmother—so I'll give you the right advice in their stead. Accept fate's decree— marry the devil and *make it work*. Handsome may be as handsome is, but underneath it all he's a good man. You're a strong woman—that's the way it should be. And despite any thoughts of yours, the devil, in this case, is right. The Cynsters need you; the Anstruther-Wetherbys, strange to tell, need you as a Cynster, too. Fate has landed you precisely where you're supposed to be."

Leaning forward, she held Honoria's gaze mercilously. "And besides, if you don't take him on, who do you imagine will? Some namby-pamby chit with more hair than wit? Do you hate him so much you'd condemn him to that—a marriage with no *passion*?"

Honoria couldn't breathe. A gust of laughter reached them; the rustle of silk heralded an approaching lady. "There you are, Josephine. Are you grilling poor Miss Anstruther-Wetherby?"

Lady Osbaldestone finally consented to release Honoria; she glanced up at the newcomer. "Good afternoon, Emily. I was merely giving Miss Anstruther-Wetherby the benefit of my experienced counsel." She waved Honoria to her feet. "Off you go— and remember what I said. And take those cakes away—they're fattening."

Shaken, her features stiff, Honoria bobbed a curtsy to Emily, Lady Cowper, then, head high, let the crowd swallow her. Unfortunately, many ladies were waiting to waylay her, to quiz her on her new relationship.

"Has St. Ives taken you to Richmond yet? The trees are quite lovely at present."

"And where are you planning to spend the festive season, my dear?"

Sidestepping such inquiries required tact and skill, difficult with her mind reeling from Lady Osbaldestone's lecture. Spying

Amanda and Amelia half-hidden by a palm, Honoria sought refuge with them. Their eyes lit up when they saw the cake plate; she handed it over without comment.

"Mama said we should come and see what 'at homes' are like," Amanda said around a miniature currant bun.

"We're to be brought out next year," Amelia added.

Honoria watched them eat. "How are you?"

Both girls looked up, openly, without any trace of pain. They both screwed up their faces in thought, then Amanda offered: "All right, I think."

"We keep expecting him to come for dinner—just like he always did." Amelia looked down and picked up a last crumb.

Amanda nodded. "Laughing and joking, just like that last night."

Honoria frowned. "Last night?"

"The night before he was shot."

Honoria blinked. "Tolly came to dinner the night before he died?"

Amelia nodded. "He was in great spirits—he usually was. He played spillikins with the young ones, then after dinner, we all played Speculation. It was great fun."

"That's . . ." Honoria blinked again. "Nice—I mean, that you have such good memories of him."

"Yes." Amanda nodded. "It is nice." She appeared to dwell on the fact, then looked at Honoria. "When are you going to marry Devil?"

The question hit Honoria right in the chest. She looked into the twins' eyes, four orbs of innocent blue, and cleared her throat. "We haven't decided."

"Oh," they chorused, and smiled benignly.

Honoria beat a hasty retreat and headed for an empty alcove.

Inwardly, she cursed, First Lady Osbaldestone, now Tolly's sisters. Who else was lining up to shake her resolution? The answer was unexpected.

"How are you coping with being absorbed into the clan?"

The soft question had Honoria turning, to meet Louise Cynster's still-weary eyes. Tolly's mother smiled. "It takes a little getting used to, I know."

Honoria drew a deep breath. "It's not that." She hesitated, then, encouraged by Louise's calm expression, forged on: "I haven't actually *agreed* to marry Devil—just to consider the idea." With a gesture that encompassed the room, she added: "I feel like a fraud."

To her relief, Louise didn't laugh or turn the comment lightly aside. Instead, after a moment scrutinizing her face, she put a hand on her arm. "You're not certain, are you?"

"No." Her voice was barely a whisper. After a minute, she added: "I *thought* I was." It was the truth—plain, unvarnished; the realization left her stunned. What had he—they—done to her? What had happened to Africa?

"It's normal to feel hesitant." Louise spoke reassuringly, with no hint of condescension. "Especially in such a case, where the decision is so much your own." She glanced at Honoria. "My own case was similar. Arthur was there, ready to lay his heart and all that came with it at my feet—everything hung on my whim." Her lips curved, her gaze becoming lost in reminiscence. "It's easy to make decisions when no one but yourself is involved, but when there are others to consider, it's natural to question your judgment. Particularly if the gentleman concerned is a Cynster." Her smile deepened; she glanced again at Honoria. "Doubly so if he's Devil Cynster."

"He's a tyrant," Honoria declared.

Louise laughed. "You'll get no argument from me on that score. All the Cynsters are dictatorially inclined, but Devil dictates to all the rest."

Honoria humphed. "He's inflexible—and far too used to getting his own way."

"You should ask Helena about that someday—she has stories that will curl your hair. You won't need the tongs for a week."

Honoria frowned. "I thought you were encouraging me."

Louise smiled. "I am—but that doesn't mean I can't see Devil's faults. But for all those—and you won't find a Cynster wife who's not had to cope with the same—there's a great deal to be said for a man who will unfailingly be there to shoulder the burdens, who, regardless of all else, is devoted to his family. Devil may be the leader of the pack—the president of the Bar Cynster—but give him a son or a daughter, and he'll happily sit in Cambridgeshire and play spillikins every night."

Unbidden, the image Louise's words conjured up took shape in Honoria's mind—a large, black-haired, harsh-featured male sprawled on a rug before a blazing fire with a child in petticoats clambering over him. Watching the scene, she felt a warm glow of pride, of satisfaction; she heard the child's shrill giggles over a deeper rumbling laugh—she could almost reach out and touch them. She waited—waited for the fear that had always dogged her to rise up and swallow the image whole, to banish it to the realm of unattainable dreams. She waited—and still the image glowed.

Firelight sheened on both black heads, unruly locks thick and wild. It gilded the child's upturned face—in her mind, Honoria stretched out her hand to the man's familiar shoulder, hard and stable as rock beneath her fingers. Unable to help herself, fascinated beyond recall, she reached, hesitantly, so hesitantly, for the child's face. It shrieked with laughter and ducked its head; her fingers touched hair like silky down, soft as a butterfly's wing. Emotion welled, unlike any she'd known. Dazed, she shook her head.

Then she blinked rapidly and hauled in a quick breath. She focused on Louise, idly scanning the crowd. What had she said? "The Bar Cynster?"

"Ah!" Louise sent her an arch look, then glanced about. No one was close enough to hear. "They think we don't know, but it's a standing joke among the gentlemen about town. Some wit coined the term when Richard and Harry followed Devil and Vane to London, supposedly to denote a . . . certain rite of passage. With Richard and Harry, of course, there was never any doubt that they would follow Devil and Vane into the *customary* Cynster pursuits." Her emphasis and the look in her eye left no doubt as to what those pursuits were. "Later, when Rupert and Alasdair went on the town, it was merely a matter of time before they, too, were called to the Bar Cynster."

"Like a barrister being called to Temple Bar?" Honoria kept her mind focused on the point.

"Precisely." Louise's smile faded. "Tolly would have been next."

It was Honoria's turn to lay a hand on Louise's arm and squeeze reassuringly. "I'd imagined the name derived from the heraldic term."

"The *bar sinister*?" Louise shook off her sorrow and pointedly met Honoria's gaze. "Between you, me, and the other Cynster ladies, I'm quite certain many gentlemen about town refer to our sons as 'noble bastards.' " Honoria's eyes widened; Louise grinned. "That, however, is not something anyone, gentleman or lady, would be willing to admit in our presence."

Honoria's lips twitched. "Naturally not." Then she frowned. "What about Charles?"

"Charles?" Louise waved dismissively. "Oh, he was never part of it."

Two ladies approached to take their leave; when the hand-clasps were over and they were private once more, Louise turned to Honoria. "If you need any support, we're always here—the others in a similar bed. Don't hesitate to call on us—it's an absolute rule that Cynster wives help each other. We are, after all, the only ones who truly understand what it's like being married to a Cynster."

Honoria glanced over the thinning crowd, noting the other family members, not just the Dowager, Horatia, and Celia, but other cousins and connections. "You really do stick together."

"We're a *family*, my dear." Louise squeezed Honoria's arm one last time. "And we hope very much that you'll join us."

"There!" Heaving a relieved sigh, Honoria propped the parchment inscribed with her brother's direction against the pigeon-holes of the escritoire. Describing her doings to Michael without letting her troubled state show had proved a Herculean task. Almost as difficult as facing the fact that she might be wrong—and that Devil, the Dowager, Michael, and everyone else might be right.

She was in the sitting room adjoining her bedchamber. The windows on either side of the fireplace overlooked the courtyard below. Propping her elbow on the desk, she put her chin in her hand and stared outside.

Eight years ago she'd suffered her loss; seven years ago she'd made up her mind never to risk losing again. Until three days past, she hadn't reviewed that decision—she'd never had reason to do so. No man, no circumstance, had been strong enough to force a reevaluation.

Three days ago, everything had changed. Lady Osbaldestone's sermon had shaken her, setting the consequences of refusing Devil firmly in her mind.

Louise and the twins had compounded her uncertainty, showing her how close to the family she'd already become.

But the most startling revelation had been the image evoked by Louise, the image she'd resurrected in every spare moment since—the image of Devil and their child.

Her fear of loss was still there, very real, very deep; to lose again would be devastating—she'd known *that* for eight years. But never before had she truly *wanted* a child. Never before had she felt this driving need—a desire, a want, that made her fear seem puny, something she could, if she wished, brush aside.

The strength of that need was unnerving—not something she could readily explain. Was it simple maternal desire gaining strength because Devil would be so protective, that, because he was so wealthy, their child would have every care? Was it because, as Cynsters, both she and their child would be surrounded by a loving, supportive clan? Or was it because she knew that being the mother of Devil's child would give her a position no other could ever have?

If she gave Devil a child, he would worship at her feet.

Drawing a deep breath, she stood and walked to the window, gazing unseeing at the weeping cherry, drooping artistically in the courtyard. Was wanting Devil, wanting him in thrall, the reason she wanted his child? Or had she simply grown older, become more of a woman than she had been at seventeen? Or both? She didn't know. Her inner turmoil was all-consuming, allconfusing; she felt like an adolescent finally waking up, but compared to growing up this was worse.

A knock on the door startled her. Straightening, she turned. "Come!"

The door swung inward; Devil stood on the threshold. One black brow rose; inherently graceful, he strolled into the room. "Would you care for a drive, Honoria Prudence?"

Honoria kept her eyes on his, refusing all other distractions. "In the park?"

His eyes opened wide. "Where else?"

Honoria glanced at her letter, in which she'd carefully skirted the truth. It was too early to make any admission—she wasn't yet sure where she stood. She looked at Devil. "Perhaps you could frank my letter while I change?"

He nodded. Honoria moved past him; without a backward glance, she retreated to her bedchamber.

Ten minutes later, clad in topaz twill, she returned to find him standing before one window, hands behind his back, her letter held between his long fingers. He turned as she approached. As always, whenever he saw her anew, his gaze swept her, possessively, from head to toe.

"Your letter." He presented the folded parchment with a flourish.

Honoria took it, noting the bold black script decorating one corner. It was, she would swear, the same script that had adorned the note Celestine had, so opportunely, received.

"Come. Webster will put it in the post."

As they traveled the long corridors, Honoria inwardly frowned. Celestine had not sent in her bill. It was over a week since the last gowns had arrived.

With her letter entrusted into Webster's care, they headed for the park, Sligo, as usual, up behind. Their progress down the fashionable avenue was uneventful beyond the usual smiles and nods; her appearance in Devil's curricle no longer created any great stir.

As they left the main knot of carriages, Honoria shifted—and glanced frowningly at Devil. "*What* are they going to say when I don't marry you?" The question had been bothering her for the past three days.

The look he shot her matched her own. "You *are* going to marry me."

"But what if I *don't*?" Honoria stubbornly fixed her gaze on his equally stubborn profile. "You ought to start considering that." The *ton* could be quite vicious; until Lady Osbaldestone's sermon, she'd viewed him as an adversary comfortably impervious to the slings and arrows of society. Her ladyship had changed her perspective; she was no longer comfortable at all. "I've warned you repeatedly that I'm unlikely to change my mind."

His sigh was full of teeth-gritted impatience. "Honoria Prudence, I don't give a damn what anyone says except you. And all I want to hear from you is 'Yes.' And as for our wedding, its occurrence is far more likely than you getting within *sight* of Cairo, let alone the Great Sphinx!"

His accents left no doubt that the subject was closed. Honoria stuck her nose in the air and stared haughtily down at a group of innocent passersby.

Grim silence reined until, the turn accomplished, they headed back toward the fashionable throng. Slanting a glance at Devil's set face, Honoria heard Lady Osbaldestone's words: *make it work.* Was it possible? Fixing her gaze in the distance, she airily inquired: "Was Tolly particularly good at hiding his feelings?"

Devil stared at her—she could feel his green gaze, sharp and penetrating; stubbornly, she kept her face averted. The next instant, they were drawing in to the verge. The carriage rocked to a halt; Sligo rushed to the horses' heads.

"Hold 'em—wait here." With that terse command, Devil tied off the reins, stood, stepped past her, and jumped to the ground. Fluidly, he turned and plucked her from the seat. Ignoring her gasp, he set her on her feet, hauled her hand through his arm, and strode off across the lawn.

Honoria hung on to her hat. "Where are we going?"

Devil shot her a black glance. "Somewhere we can talk freely."

"I thought you said Sligo was half-deaf?"

"He is—others aren't." Devil scowled discouragingly at a party of young people. The fashionable throng was rapidly thinning, left behind in their wake. "Anyway, Sligo knows all about Tolly and our search."

Honoria's eyes narrowed—then flew wide. The rhododendron walk loomed ahead. "I thought you said we were to observe the strictures?"

"Wherever possible," Devil growled, and whisked her into the deserted walk. Screened by the thick bushes, he halted and swung to face her. "Now!" Eyes narrowed, he captured her gaze. "Why the devil do you want to know if Tolly was a dab hand at hiding his feelings?"

Chin up, Honoria met his gaze—and tried not to notice how very big he was. He was tall enough and broad enough to screen her completely—even if someone strolled up on them, all they would see of her was a wisp of skirt. She tipped her chin higher. "Was he—or wasn't he?"

The eyes boring into hers were crystal-clear, his gaze sharp as a surgeon's knife. She saw his jaw clench; when he spoke, his voice was a deep feral growl. "Tolly couldn't dissemble to save himself. He never learned the knack."

"Hmm." Honoria shifted her gaze to the bushes.

"Why did you want to know?"

She shrugged. "I just . . ." She glanced up—her glib reply died on her lips, slain by the look in his eye. Her heart leapt to her throat; determinedly, she swallowed it. "I just thought it was of interest that he spent the evening before he was shot playing with his brother and sisters, apparently in excellent spirits." Elevating her nose, she let her gaze drift over the glossy green leaves.

Devil stared at her. "He did?"

Honoria nodded. Silence stretched; eyes on the bushes, she waited, barely breathing. She could feel his gaze, still intense, on her face; she knew when he looked away. Then, with a deep resigned sigh that seemed to come from his boots, he set her hand back on his sleeve, and turned her along the walk. "So—tell me—what have you learned?"

It wasn't the most gracious invitation to collusion, but Honoria decided it would do. "The twins mentioned their last dinner with Tolly when I saw them on Wednesday." Strolling beside him down the secluded walk, she related the twins' description. "I had the impression Tolly and the twins were close. If he was agitated, even if he was trying to hide it, I would have thought they'd have noticed."

Devil nodded. "They would have—they're as sharp as tacks." He grimaced. "Uncle Arthur told me Tolly went there for dinner. He gave me the impression Tolly was somewhat reserved. I'd forgotten how young men react to their fathers—it was probably no more than that."

He fell silent, pacing slowly down the serpentine path; Honoria held her tongue, content to let him ponder her findings. Although he walked by her side, she felt surrounded by his strength. What had Louise said? Unfailingly protective? That was, she had to admit, a comforting trait.

Eventually the rhododendrons ended; the walk debouched onto a wide sweep of lawn. "Your information," Devil said, as they stepped clear of the walk, "narrows the field rather drastically."

"Whatever Tolly learned, whatever sent him to find you, he must have stumbled on it *after* he left the family that evening." She looked up and saw Devil grimace. "What is it?"

He glanced at her, lips thin, his gaze considering. Then he answered. "Tolly's man went home to Ireland before we could talk to him. He'll know if Tolly was in the boughs when he came in that night." Honoria opened her mouth. "And *yes*—we're tracking him down. Demon's over there now."

Honoria glanced around, noting the many nursemaids and governesses, charges in tow, dotted across the lawn. "Where are we?"

Devil stopped. "In the nursery section. The rhododendrons keep the darlings out of sight and sound of their fond mamas." He half turned to retrace their steps—an earsplitting cry rent the peace.

"Deyyyyyyyy-vil!"

All heads turned their way, most displaying disapproving expressions. Devil turned back in time to catch Simon as he flung himself against his cousin.

"Hello! Didn't 'spect to see *you* here!"

"I didn't expect to see you either," Devil returned. "Make your bow to Honoria Prudence."

Simon promptly complied. Smiling in return, Honoria noted the boy's ruddy cheeks and bright eyes, and marveled at the resilience of youth. She looked up as two women, the twins, Henrietta, and little Mary came bustling up in Simon's wake. Devil made her known to Mrs. Hawlings, the younger girls' nurse, and Miss Pritchard, the twins' governess.

"We'd thought to take advantage of the weather while we may," Mrs. Hawlings explained. "The fogs and rains will be here soon enough."

"Indeed." Honoria saw Devil draw Simon aside. She could guess the subject under discussion. Left to deal with—or was that distract?—the governess and nurse, she exchanged polite nothings with a facility born of long practice. The expectant look in the twins' bright eyes as they glanced from her to Devil and back again did not escape her. She could only be thankful they did not voice the question clearly exercising their minds.

The sun found a chink in the clouds and beamed down; the twins and Henrietta fell to weaving daisy chains. Little Mary, her fingers too plump to manage the slim stems, sat beside her sisters on the grass, big blue eyes studying first the three women chatting nearby, then Devil, still talking to Simon. After a long, wide-eyed scrutiny, she picked up her doll and, on sturdy legs, stumped up to Honoria's side.

Honoria didn't know she was there until she felt a small hand slip into hers. Startled, she glanced down. Mary looked up and smiled—confidently, openly trusting—then tightened her pudgy-fingered grip and, looking back at her sisters, leaned against Honoria's legs.

It took all Honoria's years of practice to preserve her composure, to look back at Mrs. Hawlings and Miss Pritchard and continue to converse as if nothing had happened. As if there wasn't a hot, soft hand snuggled into hers, as if there wasn't a soft weight propped against her legs, a soft cheek pressed against her thigh.

Luckily, neither woman knew her well enough to know that her expression was not normally so blank.

Then Devil strolled up, one hand on Simon's shoulder. He saw Mary and glanced at Honoria. She kept her expression bland, determinedly uninformative under his sharp-eyed scrutiny; he looked down and held out a hand. Mary dropped Honoria's hand and went to him. Devil swung her up in his arms; Mary clung and snuggled her head down on his shoulder.

Honoria breathed deeply, her gaze locked on little Mary clinging close; the emotions rolling through her, sharp need, poignant desire swamping all fear, left her giddy.

Devil declared it was time for them to go. They made their farewells; as Mrs. Hawlings turned away, Mary in her arms, the little girl wriggled about to wave a pudgy hand. Honoria smiled softly and waved back.

"Come—Sligo's probably organizing a search by now."

Honoria turned; Devil took her hand and tucked it into his elbow, leaving his fingers, warm and strong, over hers. She found his touch both comforting and disturbing as, frowning slightly, she tried to settle her emotions. They walked briskly back to the main carriageway.

The curricle was in sight when Devil spoke. "As a governess, did you ever have younger children in your care?"

Honoria shook her head. "As a *finishing* governess, my role was specifically restricted to girls a year from their come-out. If the families I worked with had younger children, they always had another, ordinary governess to take charge of them."

Devil nodded, then looked ahead.

The drive back to Grosvenor Square gave Honoria time to marshal her thoughts. Their outing had been unexpectedly productive.

She'd verified Lady Osbaldestone's theory that she was strong enough to influence Devil, even over something he had a deep antipathy to—like her involvement in the search for Tolly's murderer. She'd had it confirmed that she did, very definitely, want to have his child. Of all men, he had to be the best-qualified mate for a woman with her particular fear—and she most assuredly wanted him, arrogant tyrant that he was, worshiping at her feet.

There remained one piece of Lady Osbaldestone's vision she had yet to verify, although he had, from the first, stated that he was marrying her to get her into his bed. Did that qualify as passion? Was that what lay between them?

Ever since their interlude on the terrace at the Place, she'd given him no chance to draw her close; his *"mine"* had effectively quashed her pursuit of his *"pleasure."* Over the last three days, however, her interest in the subject had returned. Even grown.

Webster opened the door; Honoria swept over the threshold. "If you have a moment, Your Grace, there's a matter I wish to discuss." Head high, she headed straight for the library door. A footman sprang to open it for her; she glided through—into the devil's lair.

Devil watched her go, his expression unreadable. Then he handed his driving gloves to Webster. "I suspect I won't want to be disturbed."

"Indeed, Your Grace."

Waving aside the hovering footman, Devil entered the library and shut the door.

Honoria stood before the desk, tapping her fingers on its edge. She heard the latch click; turning, she watched Devil slowly approach. "I want to discuss the *ton*'s likely reaction when it learns I'm not marrying you." That seemed a sufficiently goading topic.

Devil's brows rose. "Is that what this is about?"

"Yes." Honoria remembered to frown when he did not halt but continued his prowling advance. "It's pointless to close your eyes to the fact that such an outcome will cause a considerable stir." She turned to stroll, as slowly as he, around the edge of his desk. "You know perfectly well it will affect not just yourself but the family as well." Glancing over her shoulder, she saw him some steps behind her, following in her wake. She kept walking. "It's simply not sensible to allow the expectation to build."

"So what do you suggest?"

Rounding the desk, Honoria continued toward the fireplace. "You could hint that matters were not settled between us."

"On what grounds?"

"How should I know?" She flung a glance over her shoulder. "I'm sure you're imaginative enough to invent something."

From six feet behind, Devil's gaze remained steady.

"Why?"

"Why?"

"Why should I invent something?"

"Because . . ." Gesturing vaguely, Honoria walked into the corner of the room. She stopped and stared at the volumes level with her nose. "Because it's necessary." She drew a deep breath, mentally crossed her fingers, and swung around. "Because I don't want anyone held up to ridicule because of my decision."

As she'd hoped, Devil was no longer six feet away. His eyes held hers, mere inches distant. "*I'm* the only one risking the *ton*'s ridicule. And I'm not about to run shy."

Honoria narrowed her eyes at him, and tried not to notice she was trapped. "You are without doubt the most impossibly arrogant, conceited—" His eyes dropped from hers—Honoria caught her breath.

"Have you finished?"

The question was uttered in a conversational tone. His lids lifted and he met her gaze; Honoria managed a nod.

"Good." Again his gaze lowered; one hand rose to frame her face, then he bent his head.

Honoria's lids fell; in the instant his lips closed over hers, she gripped the bookshelves behind her tightly, fighting down her triumph. She'd got her wolf to pounce, and he hadn't even realized he'd been baited.

The thrill of success met the thrill of delight his kiss sent racing through her; she parted her lips, eager to learn of his passion, eager to experience again the pleasure she'd found in his arms. He shifted; she thought he groaned. For one instant, his weight pressed against her as his lips forced hers wider, his tongue tasting her voraciously. The sudden surge of desire surprised her; immediately, he shackled it, drawing back to a slow, steady plundering designed to reduce any resistance to dust.

That instant of raw, primitive emotion spurred Honoria on—she wanted to know it, taste it again; she needed to learn more. Her hands left the bookshelves and slid beneath his coat. His waistcoat effectively shielded his chest; the buttons, thankfully, were large. Her fingers busy, she angled her head against the pressure of his kiss. Their lips shifted, then locked; tentatively, then with greater confidence, she kissed him back.

It had been far too long since he'd kissed her.

Devil knew that was true; he was so famished, so caught up in drinking in the heady taste of her, that long minutes passed before he realized she was responding. Not passively allowing him to kiss her, not even merely offering her lips, her soft mouth. She was kissing him back. With untutored skill maybe, but also with the same determined forthrightness that characterized all she did.

The realization mentally halted him. She pressed closer, deepening the kiss of her own volition—shaking off his distraction, he took all she offered and greedily angled for more. Then he felt her hands on his chest. Palms gliding, fingers spread, she traced the heavy muscles, the fine linen of his shirt no real barrier to her touch.

She was setting him alight! Abruptly, Devil straightened, breaking off their kiss. It didn't work—Honoria's hands slid over his shoulders as she stretched upward against him; who initiated the next kiss was moot. With a groan, Devil took all she gave, his arms closing possessively about her. Did she know what she was doing?

Her eagerness, the alacrity with which she pressed herself against him, suggested she'd forgotten every maidenly precept she'd ever learned. It also suggested it was time to draw her deeper. Setting aside restraint, Devil kissed her deeply, hungrily, as ravenously as he wished, deliberately leaving her breathless. Raising his head, he drew her to the large armchair before the hearth; her hand in his, he freed the last two buttons on his waistcoat, then sat. Looking up at her, he raised one brow.

Her senses whirling, her hand clasped in his, Honoria read the question in his eyes. He'd asked it of her once before: *How much of a woman are you?* Her breasts, already heated, swelled as she drew breath. Deliberately, she stepped about his knees and sat, turning to him, sliding her hands over his chest, pushing his waistcoat wide.

Under her hands, his chest expanded; his lips found hers as he lifted her, settling her in his lap. A fleeting thought impinged on Honoria's mind—that she'd been here, like this, before. She dismissed it as nonsense—she could never have forgotten the sensation of being surrounded by him, his thighs hard beneath her, his arms a cage about her, his chest a fascinating wall of hard, shifting muscle bands over even harder bone. She pressed her hands against it, then slid them around, reaching as far as she could. His hands at her back urged her closer; her breasts brushed his chest. Then he changed the angle of their kiss and shifted her, laying her back against one arm.

Immediately, the tenor of their kiss changed; his tongue glided sensuously over hers, then alongside—she sensed his invitation. Responding, she was drawn deep into an intimate game, of thrust and parry, of artlessly evocative caresses, of steadily escalating desire. When his hand closed over her breast, she arched; his long fingers found her nipple, tantalizingly circling it before closing in a firm caress, which only left her aching for more.

Instead, his hand left her; her lips trapped beneath his, Honoria was considering pulling away to protest, when she felt her bodice give. An instant later, his hand slid beneath the twill, cupping her breast fully.

Heat seared her; as his fingers closed, then stroked, her breast grew heavy. Honoria tried to break their kiss to catch her breath; he refused to let her go, deepening the kiss instead as she felt his fingers tangle with the silk ribbons of her chemise. Giddy, her senses reeling, she felt the ribbons give, felt the silk shift and slide—then his hand, his fingers, stroked her bare skin, intimately, unhurriedly.

Sweet fever rose and spread through her; her senses sang. Every particle of awareness she possessed was fixed on where he caressed her. With each questing sweep of his fingers, he knew her more.

Devil broke their heady kiss so that he could move her back slightly and shift his attentions to her other breast. She dragged in a shuddering breath, but kept her eyes shut and didn't protest;

lips curving, he gave her what she wanted. Her skin was smooth as satin, rich to the touch; his fingertips tingled as he stroked her, his palm burned when he cupped the soft weight. Her height belied her curvaceousness; each breast filled his palm, a satisfyingly sensual sensation. His only complaint was that he couldn't see what his fingers traced; her carriage dress was too stiff, the style too well cut, to brush her bodice aside.

He returned to the first breast; his fingers tightened. Honoria's eyes glinted from beneath her lashes. He caught her gaze. "I want you, sweet Honoria." Gravelly with leashed desire, his voice was very deep. "I want to watch you, naked, writhing in my arms. I want to see you, naked, spread beneath me."

Honoria couldn't stop the shiver that raced through her. Eyes trapped in his, she struggled to draw breath, struggled to steady her giddy head. The planes of his face were hard-edged; desire glowed in his eyes. His fingers shifted; a shaft of pure delight streaked through her. She shivered again.

"There's much more that I can teach you. Marry me, and I'll show you all the pleasure I can give you—and all that you can give me."

If she'd needed any warning of how dangerous he was, how intent he was, it was there in that last phrase; Honoria heard his possessiveness ring. Any pleasure he gave her she would pay for—but would possessing her truly be such pleasure to him? And, given all she now knew, was being possessed, by him, any longer a destiny to be feared? Breathing shallowly, she raised her hand and sent it skating over his chest. Muscles shifted, then locked. Other than a hardening of his features, his face showed no reaction.

Honoria smiled knowingly; raising her hand, she boldly traced his jaw, traced the sensual line of his lips.

"No—I will go upstairs, I think."

They both froze, eyes locked on the other's. The Dowager's voice carried clearly from the hall as she issued instructions to Webster, then heels clicked as she swept past the library door.

Eyes wide, excruciatingly aware that his hand lay firm about her naked breast, Honoria swallowed. "I think I'd better go up." How long had they been here, scandalously dallying?

Devil's smile turned devilish. "In a minute."

It wasn't one, but ten. When she finally climbed the stairs, Honoria felt like she was floating. Reaching the gallery, she frowned. Devil's pleasure, she suspected, could be seriously addictive; of his possessiveness she had not a doubt. But passion?— that should be intense, uncontrollable, explosively powerful; Devil had been in control throughout. Her frown deepening, she shook her head and headed for the morning room.

Chapter 12

"**I** don't *believe* it!" Seated before her escritoire, Honoria stared at the single sheet of parchment in her hand. For the third time, she read the simple message, then, her jaw setting ominously, she rose and, letter in hand, headed for the library.

She didn't knock. She flung the door wide and marched in. Devil, seated in his accustomed place, raised his brows.

"I take it there's a problem."

"Indeed." Honoria's eyes glittered. *"This!"* With a flourish, she deposited her letter on the desk. "Explain *that*, if you would, Your Grace."

Devil picked up the letter and scanned it, lips firming as he realized its content. Dropping it on the blotter, he leaned back, studying Honoria still standing before the desk, arms crossed, eyes flashing—the very image of an intemperate virago. "I didn't actually think you'd ask."

"Didn't think I'd ask?" The look she bent on him overflowed with incredulous scorn. "When I spend a small fortune at a modiste's, I expect to receive a bill. Of *course* I asked!"

Devil glanced at the letter. "It appears you received an answer."

"Not an answer I wished to receive." Turning to pace, skirts swishing, Honoria paused long enough to inform him through clenched teeth: "It is, as you very well know, totally unacceptable for you to pay for my wardrobe."

"Why?"

Dumbfounded, she stopped and stared. *"Why?"* Then she narrowed her eyes at him. "You've been dealing with ladybirds too long, Your Grace. While it may be *de rigueur* to lavish Celestine's best on such women, it is not accepted practice for gentlemen to provide wardrobes for ladies of character."

"While I naturally hesitate to contradict you, Honoria Prudence, you're wrong on both counts." With unruffleable sangfroid, Devil picked up his pen, and his next letter. "It's perfectly acceptable for gentlemen to provide wardrobes for their wives. Ask any of *Maman's* acquaintances—I'm sure they'll verify that fact." Honoria opened her mouth—he continued before she could speak: "And as for the other, I haven't."

Honoria frowned. "Haven't what?"

Devil looked up and met her eye. "Haven't lavished Celestine's best on any of my ladybirds." Honoria's expression blanked; he lifted one brow. "That's what you meant, wasn't it?"

Honoria drew herself up. "That's irrelevant. What is relevant is the fact that I'm not your wife."

Devil looked down. "A minor inconsistency time will no doubt correct." With a series of bold strokes, he signed his letter.

Drawing a deep breath, Honoria clasped her hands before her and addressed the air above his head. "I am afraid, Your Grace, that I cannot acquiesce to the present situation. It is entirely inappropriate." Glancing down her nose, she watched as he reached for another letter. "Any *reasonable* being would instantly see, and acknowledge, that fact." With unimpaired calm, Devil picked up his pen and dipped it in the inkstand. Honoria set her teeth. "I must request that you inform me of the total of Celestine's bill and allow me to recompense you for the sum."

Devil signed his name, blotted it, set the pen back in its rack—and looked up. "No."

Honoria searched his eyes—his green gaze was jewel-clear, hard, and uncompromising. Her breasts swelled as she drew a portentous breath; she pressed her lips tightly together, then nodded. "Very well. I'll send everything back." She turned on her heel and headed for the door.

Devil swallowed an oath and came out of his chair. He was around the desk and striding in Honoria's wake long before she reached the middle of the room. She was reaching for the doorknob when he picked her up.

"What—!" Honoria batted at his hands, fastened about her waist. "Put me *down*, you arrogant oaf!"

Devil complied, but only long enough to swing her about so that she faced him. He kept his hands locked about her waist, holding her at a distance. For her own safety. The effect she had on him when in haughty mood was bad enough; haughty and angry together wound his spring far too tight. One unwary touch and he might unwind—which would certainly surprise her.

"Stop wriggling. Calm down." That advice was greeted with a furious glare. Devil sighed. "You know you can't send Celestine's things back—as I've already paid for them, she'll simply send them back here again. All you'll achieve is to inform Celestine, her staff, *and* my staff that you're throwing some incomprehensible tantrum."

"I am not throwing a tantrum," Honoria, declared. "I am behaving with exemplary reticence. If I gave vent to my feelings, I'd be *screaming!*"

Devil tightened his hold. "You are."

Honoria's glare turned baleful. "No I'm not. I can scream much louder than that."

Devil winced—and locked the muscles in his arms. He was definitely going to put that claim to the test. Later. He trapped her irate gaze in his. "Honoria, I am not going to divulge to you a figure you do not need to know, and you are not going to attempt to return Celestine's gowns."

Honoria's grey gaze turned steely. "You, my lord, are the most arrogant, overbearing, high-handed, tyrannical, dictatorial despot it has ever been my misfortune to meet."

Devil raised a brow. "You forgot autocratic."

She stared at him; he could feel the frustration mounting within her, swelling like a barely capped volcano.

"You are *impossible*!" The word came out in a hiss—like steam escaping. "I bought those gowns—I have a right and a duty to pay for them."

"Wrong—as your husband, that right and duty is mine."

"*Only* if I request your assistance! Which I haven't! And even if I did need help, I couldn't ask you *because*," Honoria drew a deep breath and carefully enunciated, "*we're . . . not . . . married!*"

"Yet."

Capping that terse syllable should have been impossible; Honoria resorted to a seething glare of operatic proportions and carried on regardless. "If you have some vague notion that I'm unable to pay such an amount, you're wrong. I'm perfectly willing to introduce you to Robert Child, of Child's Bank, who handles my estate. I'm sure he'll be happy to inform you that I'm no *pauper*!" She pushed again at Devil's arms; frowning, he let her go.

"I didn't pay because I thought you couldn't."

Honoria glanced at him; his eyes declared he was telling the truth. "Well," she said, somewhat mollified, "if that wasn't the reason, what was?"

Devil's jaw hardened. "I told you."

Honoria had to think back, then, her own features hardening, she shook her head. "No, no, *no*! *Even* if we were married, you have *no right* to pay bills that are *mine*, not unless I ask you to. In fact, I can't think why Celestine sent the bill to you at all." She tripped on the last words, and looked up, directly into his eyes. Abruptly, she narrowed hers. "It was you, wasn't it? Who sent that note to Celestine?"

Exasperated, Devil frowned at her. "It was just an introduction."

"As what? Your *wife*?" When he didn't answer, Honoria ground her teeth. "What on earth am I to *do* with you?"

Devil's features hardened. "Marry me." His voice was a frustrated growl. "The rest will follow naturally."

Honoria tilted her chin. "You are being deliberately obtuse. May I please have my account from Celestine?"

His frown deepening, darkening his eyes, Devil looked down at her. "No." The single syllable was backed by centuries of undisputed power.

Honoria held his gaze steadily—and felt her temper swell, felt indignation soar. Gazes locked, she could feel their wills, tangible entities, directly opposed, neither giving an inch. Slowly, she narrowed her eyes. "How," she inquired, her voice steely calm, "do you imagine I feel knowing that every stitch I have on was paid for by you?"

Instantly, she saw her mistake—saw it in his eyes, in the subtle shift that lightened the green, in the consideration that flashed through their depths.

He shifted closer. "I don't know." His voice had dropped to a gravelly purr; his gaze grew mesmerically intent. "Tell me."

Inwardly railing, Honoria saw any chance of getting Celestine's bill evaporate. "I do not believe we have anything further to discuss, Your Grace. If you'll excuse me?"

She heard her own words, cool and distant. His gaze hardened; his expression was as controlled as her own. He searched her eyes, then, rigidly formal, inclined his head, and stepped aside, clearing her path to the door.

Honoria's breath caught as she tried to draw it in. She bobbed a curtsy, then, regally erect, glided to the door, conscious of his gaze, shimmering heat on her back, until the door swung closed between them.

She shut the door with a definite click.

The weather, mimicking the atmosphere within St. Ives House, turned decidedly chilly. Three nights later, ensconced in one corner of the St. Ives town carriage, Honoria looked out on a dark and dreary landscape whipped by wind and incessant rain. They were on their way to Richmond, to the duchess of Richmond's ball; all the *haut ton* would be present, the Cynsters included. None of the family would dance, but appearance was mandatory.

It was not, however, the prospect of her first real ball that had knotted her nerves. The tension that held her was entirely attributable to the impressive figure, clothed in black, lounging directly opposite, his inner tension, a match for hers, radiating through the darkness. The Lord of Hell could not have had more complete command of her awareness.

Honoria's jaw tensed; her stubbornness swelled. Her gaze glued to the misery beyond the window, she conjured up an image of the Great Sphinx. Her destiny. She had started to waver, to wonder whether, perhaps . . . until his demonstration that a tyrant never changed his spots. It was, she acknowledged, deep disappointment that had left the odd emptiness inside her, as if a treat had been offered and then withdrawn.

Richmond House, ablaze with lights, shone through the darkness. Their carriage joined the long queue leading to the portico. Innumerable stop-start jerks later, the carriage door was opened; Devil uncoiled his long length and stepped down. He assisted the Dowager up the porch steps, then returned. Avoiding his eye, Honoria placed her fingers in his and allowed him to hand her down, then escort her in the Dowager's wake.

Negotiating the stairs proved an unexpected trial; the unyielding press of bodies forced them close. So close she could feel the heat of him reach for her, feel his strength envelop her. The flimsiness of her lavender-silk gown only heightened her susceptibility; as they reached the head of the stairs, she flicked open her fan.

The duchess of Richmond was delighted to receive them. "Horatia's near the conservatory." The duchess touched a scented cheek to the Dowager's, then held out a hand to Honoria. "Hmm—yes." Surveying her critically as she rose from her curtsy, the duchess broke into a beaming smile. "A pleasure to meet you, my dear." Releasing Honoria, she glanced archly at Devil. "And you, St. Ives? How are you finding life as an almost-affianced gentleman?"

"Trying." His expression bland, Devil shook her hand.

The duchess grinned. "I wonder why?" Slanting a laughing glance at Honoria, the duchess waved them on. "I'll rely on you, St. Ives, to ensure Miss Anstruther-Wetherby is suitably entertained."

With stultifying correctness, Devil offered his arm; in precisely the same vein, Honoria rested her fingertips upon it and allowed him to steer her in the Dowager's wake. She kept her head high, scanning the crowd for familiar faces.

Many were too familiar. She wished she could take her hand from Devil's sleeve, take just one step away, enough to put some distance between them. But the *ton* had grown so used to the idea she was his duchess-in-waiting, that she was his, that any hint of a rift would immediately focus every eye on them, which would be even worse.

Her serene mask firmly in place, she had to leave her nerves to suffer his nearness.

Devil led her to a position just beyond the *chaise* where the Dowager and Horatia Cynster sat, surrounded by a coterie of older ladies. Within minutes, they were surrounded themselves, by friends, acquaintances, and the inevitable Cynsters.

The group about them swelled and ebbed, then swelled and ebbed again. Then a suavely elegant gentleman materialized from the crowd to bow gracefully before her. "Chillingworth, my dear Miss Anstruther-Wetherby." Straightening, he smiled charmingly. "We've not been introduced, but I'm acquainted with your brother."

"Michael?" Honoria gave him her hand. She'd heard of the earl of Chillingworth; by reputation, he was Devil Cynster's match. "Have you seen him recently?"

"Ah—no." Chillingworth turned to greet Lady Waltham and Miss Mott. Lord Hill and Mr. Pringle joined the group, distracting the other two ladies; Chillingworth turned back to Honoria. "Michael and I share the same club."

And very little else, Honoria suspected. "Indeed? And have you seen the play at the Theatre Royal?" Lady Waltham had waxed lyrical about the production but couldn't remember its title.

The earl's brows rose. "Quite a *tour de force*." He glanced at Devil, absorbed with Lord Malmsbury. "If St. Ives is unable to escort you, perhaps I could get up a party, one you might consent to join?"

Classically handsome, well set, tall enough to look down into her eyes, Chillingworth was a damsel's dream—and a prudent mama's nightmare. Honoria opened her eyes wide. "But you've already seen the play, my lord."

"Watching the play would not be my aim, my dear."

Honoria smiled. "But it would be *my* aim, my lord, which might disappoint you."

An appreciative gleam lit Chillingworth's eyes. "I suspect, Miss Anstruther-Wetherby, that I wouldn't find you disappointing at all."

Honoria raised a brow; simultaneously, she felt a stir at her side.

Chillingworth looked up, and nodded. "St. Ives."

"Chillingworth." Devil's deep drawl held a subtle menace. "What cast of the dice landed you here?"

The earl smiled. "Pure chance—I stopped to pay my respects to Miss Anstruther-Wetherby." His smile deepened. "But speaking of gaming, I haven't seen you at the tables recently. Other matters keeping you busy?"

"As you say." Devil's tone was noncommittal. "But I'm surprised you haven't gone north for the hunting. Lord Ormeskirk and his lady have already left, I hear."

"Indeed—but one shouldn't cram one's fences, as I'm sure you appreciate."

Devil raised a brow. "Assuming one still has fences to overcome."

Honoria resisted an urge to raise her eyes to the heavens.

The following five minutes were a revelation; Devil and Chillingworth traded quips as sharp-edged as sabers, their rivalry self-evident. Then, as if they'd satisfied some prescribed routine, the conversation swung to horseflesh and thus into a more amicable vein. When that subject failed, Chillingworth turned the talk to politics, drawing her into the conversation. Honoria wondered why.

A squeaky screech was her first warning of impending difficulty. Everyone looked toward the dais at the end of the room. A whine followed by a handful of plucked notes confirmed the general supposition; a hum rose along with a bustling rush as partners were claimed for the first waltz.

Looking back at Chillingworth, Honoria saw him smile.

"Can I tempt you to the dance floor, Miss Anstruther-Wetherby?"

With that simple question, he put her on the spot. Fairly and squarely, with no room for maneuver. As she studied Chillingworth's quizzical hazel eyes, Honoria's mind raced, but she didn't need to think to know Devil's opinion. The arm under her fingers was rigid; while he appeared as languidly bored as ever, his every muscle had tensed.

She wanted to dance, had intended to dance—had looked forward to her first waltz in the capital. And she'd known that Devil, still wearing a black armband, would not take the floor. Until Celia's "at-home," she'd fully intended to waltz with others, thus making a clear statement that she would live her own life, make her own decisions, that she was her own mistress, not his. This waltz was to have been her declaration—and what better partner with which to underscore her point than Chillingworth?

He was waiting, outwardly charming but watching her like a hawk; the musicians were still tuning their strings. Devil was also watching her—he might be hedonistic, he might be unpredictable, but here, in the duchess of Richmond's ballroom, he was helpless to prevent her doing as she wished. So what did she wish?

Calmly, Honoria held out her hand. "Thank you, my lord." Satisfaction flared in Chillingworth's eyes; Honoria lifted a brow. "But I do not dance this evening."

To give him his due, the light in his eyes didn't fade although his triumphant expression certainly did. For an instant, he held Honoria's gaze, then glanced at the other ladies in their group. Looking back at Honoria, he raised a resigned brow. "How exceedingly cruel of you, my dear."

His words were too soft for anyone beyond Honoria or Devil to hear. Chillingworth raised his brows fleetingly at Devil, then, with a last nod to Honoria, he turned and, with faultless grace, solicited Miss Mott's hand.

Devil waited until the end of the dance to catch his mother's eye. She grimaced at him but when he persisted, reluctantly conceded. Setting his hand over Honoria's fingers, still resting on his sleeve, he turned her toward the *chaise*. Puzzled, she glanced up at him.

"*Maman* wishes to leave."

Collecting the Dowager, they took leave of their hostess. Taking Honoria's cloak from a footman, Devil draped it about her shoulders, fighting the urge to rest his hands, however briefly, on the smoothly rounded contours. His mother commandeered the Richmonds' butler, leaving him to lead Honoria down the steps and hand her into the carriage.

The door shut upon them, cloaking him in safe darkness; harness jingled, and they were on their way home. And he was still sane. Just.

Settled in his corner, Devil tried to relax. He'd been tense on the way to Richmond House, he'd been tense while there. He was still tense now—he didn't entirely know why.

But if Honoria had accepted Chillingworth, all hell would have broken loose. The possibility that she had refused the invitation purely to spare his feelings was almost as unacceptable as his relief that she had.

Protectiveness he understood, possessiveness he understood—both were an entrenched part of his makeup. But what the hell was this he was experiencing now—this compulsion she made him feel? He didn't know what it was but he knew he didn't like it. Vulnerability was a part of it, and no Cynster could accept that. Which begged one question—what was the alternative?

The carriage rumbled on. Devil sat in his corner, his shadowed gaze fixed on Honoria's face, and pondered the imponderable.

He'd reached no conclusion when the carriage rocked to a halt before his door. Footmen ran down the steps; his mother exited first, Honoria followed. Climbing the steps in her wake, Devil entered his hall on her heels.

"I am going straight up—I will see you tomorrow, my dears." With a regal wave, the Dowager headed up the stairs.

Cassie came running to relieve Honoria of her heavy cloak; Webster appeared at Devil's side. Devil shrugged off his evening cape.

"Master Alasdair is waiting in the library, Your Grace."

Webster delivered his message *sotto voce* but as he turned to look at his butler, Devil caught a glimpse of Honoria's face—and her arrested expression.

"Thank you, Webster." Resettling his sleeves, Devil turned to Honoria. "I bid you a good night, Honoria Prudence."

She hesitated, her eyes touching his briefly, then stiffly inclined her head. "And I bid *you* a good night, Your Grace."

With cool hauteur, she turned and climbed the stairs. Devil watched her ascend, hips swaying gently; when she passed from view, he hauled in a deep breath, slowly let it out—then headed for the library.

Wringing blood from a stone would doubtless be easier, but Honoria was not about to allow Devil to deny her the latest news. She wasn't going to marry him—she'd warned him repeatedly she would not—but she was still committed to unmasking Tolly's killer. She'd shared the information she had found; it was his turn to reciprocate.

She heard the latch of the morning-room door click; swinging to face it, she straightened. Devil entered and shut the door. His gaze swept her, then returned to her face; with his customary languid prowl, he approached.

"I've been told you wished to see me." His tone, and the elevation of one dark brow, suggested mild boredom.

Regally, Honoria inclined her head and kept her eyes on his. All the rest of him—his distant expression, his movements so smoothly controlled, all the elements of his physical presence—were calculated to underscore his authority. Others might find the combination intimidating; she simply found it distracting. "Indeed." He halted before her. Lifting her chin she fixed him with a gaze as incisive as his was bland. "I wish to know the latest news in the search for Tolly's murderer. What did Lucifer learn?"

Devil's brows rose higher. "Nothing of any importance."

Honoria's eyes narrowed. "He waited until one in the morning to see you to report 'nothing of any importance'?"

Devil nodded. Honoria searched his eyes; her own eyes widened. "You're lying!"

Inwardly, Devil cursed. What was it that gave him away? "There was nothing Lucifer discovered that might lead us to Tolly's murderer."

Honoria stared at him. "That's not true either."

Closing his eyes, Devil swore beneath his breath. "Honoria—"

"I can't *believe* it! I helped you—it was *I* who discovered Tolly was untroubled when he left his parents' house."

Opening his eyes, Devil saw her chin tilt, her gaze shift. Before she could begin her usual peregrinations, he locked both hands on the mantelpiece, one on either side of her. Caging her. Incensed, she glared at him.

"Believe me," he said, trapping her heated gaze, "I'm grateful for your help. The others are concentrating on discovering where Tolly went after he left Mount Street. What Lucifer came to report was something else entirely." He paused, choosing his words with care. "It may be nothing, but it's not anything you can help investigate."

Honoria considered the evidence of his eyes—they remained crystal-clear. Whenever he lied, they fogged. She nodded. "Very well. I shall continue with my own investigations, in my own way."

Devil's hands clenched on the mantelpiece. "Honoria, we're discussing tracking a murderer—a cold-blooded killer—not discovering who stole the Queen of Hearts's tarts."

"I had assimilated that fact, Your Grace." Honoria tilted her chin higher. "Indeed, *before* I leave for Africa, I intended seeing the villain taken in charge."

Devil's jaw set. "You are not going to Africa, and you'll stay well clear of this villain."

Her eyes flashed; she lifted her chin one last notch. "You're very good at giving orders, Your Grace, but you've forgotten one pertinent point. *I* am not subject to your authority. And never shall be."

Those last four words were Devil's undoing; lightning-fast, he straightened, hauled her into his arms, and set his lips to hers. In his present state, it was sheer madness to try to coerce her, to attempt to enforce his will in that way.

Sheer unmitigated *madness*.

It snatched Honoria up, buffeting her senses, ripping her from reality. Only her fury and an intuitive grasp of his aim allowed her to resist. His lips were hard, demanding, searching—for a response she longed to—ached to—give. She locked her lips against him.

His arms locked about her; unyielding steel, they tightened, impressing her soft flesh with the male hardness of his. Sensation streaked through her; her skin tingled. Still she held firm, holding to her anger, using it as a shield.

He tilted his head, his lips moved on hers, a powerful, elemental call to her senses. Inwardly reeling, Honoria clung to lucidity, sure of only one thing. He was kissing her into submission. And succeeding.

Fragment by fragment, she lost her grip on her fury; familiar heat flooded her. She felt herself soften, felt her lips lose their resolution, felt all resistance melt. Desperation gripped her. Surrender was too galling to contemplate.

Which left attack her only option. Her hands were trapped against his chest; sliding them up, she found the hard planes of his face. He stilled at her touch; before he could react, she framed his jaw—and kissed him.

His lips were parted—she slid her tongue between to tangle

challengingly with his. He tasted powerful—wonderfully, elementally male—a mind-whirling sensation gripped her. He hadn't moved—instinctively she deepened the caress, angling her lips against his.

Passion.

It burst upon her, upon her senses, in a hot flood tide. It rose from within him, from between them, pouring through her, cascade upon cascade of exquisite sensation, of deep, swirling emotion, of soul-stealing compulsion.

On one heartbeat, she was the leader, on the next, he resumed command, his lips hard, his body a steel cage surrounding her. A cage she no longer wished to escape. She surrendered, gladly yielding; ravenous, he stole her very breath. Breasts aching, heart thundering, Honoria stole it back.

Between them, desire smoldered, flared, then exploded, flames licking greedily, devouring all reticence. Honoria gave herself up to them, to the beckoning pleasure, to the thrill of desire, to the urge of molten need.

She pressed herself against him, flagrantly enticing, hips shifting in unconscious entreaty. Fingers sliding into his thick hair, she reveled in the raw hunger that rose, naked, elemental, between them.

Their lips parted briefly, for less than a heartbeat; who pressed the next kiss was moot. They were lost together, trapped in the vortex, neither in control, both beyond reason. Hunger welled, swelled; urgency mounted, inexorable, compelling.

An almighty crash shook them to their senses.

Devil lifted his head, arms tightening protectively as he looked toward the door. Gasping, literally reeling, Honoria clung to him; dazed, she followed his gaze.

From beyond the door came sounds of calamity—wails and

recriminations exchanged between two maids—then Webster's sonorous tones cut across the commotion, bringing the plaints to an end. The sound of tinkling glass and the scrape of a whisk on the polished boards followed.

Honoria could barely make out the sounds over the thundering in her ears. Her heart thudded heavily; she had yet to catch her breath. Eyes wide, she looked into Devil's face—and saw the same driving desire, the same inchoate longing gripping her, reflected in his silvered eyes. Flames lit the crystal cores; sparks flew.

His breathing was as ragged as hers. Every muscle in his body was taut, coiled. Like a spring about to break.

"Don't—move."

He bit the words out; his eyes blazed. Light-headed, barely able to drag in her next breath, Honoria didn't even think of disobeying. The planes of his face had never looked so hard, so graven. His eyes held hers steadily; she dared not blink as, rigid, he battled the force that threatened to consume them—the passion she had unleashed.

Degree by painful degree, the tension holding them decreased. His lids lowered, long lashes veiling the subsiding tempest. Gradually, his locked muscles eased; Honoria breathed again.

"The next time you do that, you'll end on your back."

There was no threat in his words; they were a statement of fact.

Hedonistic, unpredictable—she'd forgotten about the wild. A peculiar thrill shot through Honoria, immediately swamped beneath a tide of guilt. She had seen the effort her naive tactic had cost him; remnants of their passion still shimmered about them, licking at her nerves, shivering over her skin. His lids slowly rose; she met his gaze unflinchingly.

And put up a hand to touch his cheek. "I didn't know—"

Turbulence engulfed them as he brusquely drew back. *"Don't—"* His features hardened; his gaze transfixed her. "Go. *Now.*"

Honoria looked into his eyes—and obeyed. She stepped out of his arms; they fell from her but not readily. With one last, hesitant glance, she turned away; head high, shaken to her toes, she left him.

The three days that followed were the hardest Honoria had ever faced. Distracted, her nerves permanently on edge, her stomach a hard knot of reaction, she struggled to find some way out of the impasse that faced her. Hiding her state from the Dowager left her drained, yet being alone was not a desirable alternative; once free, her mind dwelled incessantly on what she had seen, what she had felt, what she had learned in the morning room.

Which only added to her distraction.

Her only consolation was that Devil seemed as distracted as she. By mutual consent, they met each other's eyes but briefly; each touch—when he took her hand or she placed it on his arm—rocked them both.

He'd told her from the first that he wanted her; she hadn't understood what he meant. Now she knew—instead of frightening her or shocking her, the physical depth of his need thrilled her. She gloried in it; at some fundamental level, her heart positively sang.

Which left her feeling exceedingly wary.

She was standing before her sitting-room window, mulling over her state, when a knock fell on the door.

Her heart skipped a beat. She straightened. "Come."

The door swung inward; Devil stood on the threshold. He raised a brow at her.

Honoria raised a brow back.

Lips thinning, he entered the room, shutting the door behind him. His expression was unreadable—not impassive so much as deliberately uninformative.

"I'm here to apologize."

Honoria met his gaze steadily, certain the word "apologize" rarely passed his lips. Her feelings took flight, only to plummet a second later. Her stomach hollow, her heart in her throat, she asked: "For what?

His quick frown was genuinely puzzled, then it evaporated; his gaze grew hard. "For appropriating Celestine's bill." His tone made it clear that if she wished for an apology for what had transpired in the morning room, she'd be waiting until hell froze.

Honoria's unruly heart sang. She fought to keep a silly—totally unnecessary—smile from her lips. "So you'll give me the bill?"

He studied her eyes, then his lips compressed. "No."

Honoria stared. "Why apologize if you won't give me the bill?"

For a long moment, he looked at her, frustration seeping into his expression. "I'm *not* apologizing for paying Celestine's account—I am apologizing for stepping on your independent toes—that was not my intention. But as you so rightly pointed out, the only reason such a bill would cross my desk was if you, as my wife, had referred it to me." His lips twisted. "I couldn't resist."

Honoria's jaw nearly dropped; rescuing it in time, she swallowed a gurgle of laughter. "You signed it . . . *pretending* to be my husband?" She had to struggle to keep a straight face.

The aggravation in Devil's eyes helped. "*Practicing* to be your husband."

Abruptly, Honoria sobered. "You needn't practice that particular activity on my account. *I'll* pay my bills, whether I marry you or not."

Her crisp "or not" hung between them; Devil straightened and inclined his head. "As you wish." His gaze wandered to the landscape above the fireplace.

Honoria narrowed her eyes at his profile. "We have yet to come to terms over this bill you *inadvertently* paid, Your Grace."

Both description and honorific pricked Devil on the raw. Bracing one arm along the mantelpiece, he trapped Honoria's gaze. "You can't seriously imagine I'll accept recompense—monetary recompense—from you. That, as you well know, is asking too much."

Honoria raised her brows. "I can't see why. If you'd paid a trifling sum for one of your friends, you'd allow them to repay you without fuss."

"The sum is not trifling, you are not 'one of my friends,' and in case it's escaped your notice, I'm not the sort of man to whom a woman can confess to being conscious of owing every stitch she has on, to him, and then expect to be allowed to pay him back."

Honoria's silk chemise suddenly grew hot; tightening her arms over her breasts, she tilted her chin. His conqueror's mask, all hard planes and ironclad determination, warned her she would win no concessions on that front. Searching his eyes, she felt her skin prickle. She scowled. "You . . . *devil*!"

His lips twitched.

Honoria took two paces into the room, then whirled and paced back. "The situation is beyond improper—it's outrageous!"

Pushing away from the mantelpiece, Devil raised an arrogant brow. "Ladies who dice with me do find situations tend to end that way."

"I," Honoria declared, swinging to face him and meeting his eyes, "am far too wise to play games with you. We need some agreement over this bill."

Devil eyed her set face, and inwardly cursed. Every time he glimpsed a quick escape from the dilemma his uncharacteristically fanciful self-indulgence had landed him in, she blocked it. And demanded he negotiate. Didn't she realize *she* was the besieged and *he* the besieger? Evidently not.

From the moment he'd declared his intention to wed her, she'd flung unexpected hurdles in his path. He'd overcome each one and chased her into her castle, to which he'd immediately laid siege. He'd succeeded in harrying her to the point where she was weakening, considering opening her gates and welcoming him in—when she'd stumbled on his moment of weakness and turned it into a blunt weapon. Which she was presently wielding with Anstruther-Wetherby stubbornness. His lips thinned. "Can't you overlook it? No one knows about it other than you and me."

"And Celestine."

"She's not going to alienate a valuable customer."

"Be that as it may—"

"Might I suggest," Devil tersely interpolated, "that, considering the situation between us, you could justifiably set the matter of this bill aside, to be decided after your three months have elapsed? Once you're my duchess, you can *justifiably* forget it."

"I haven't yet agreed to marry you."

"You will."

Honoria heard the absolute decree in his words. She eyed his stony face, then raised one brow. "I can hardly accept a proposal I haven't heard."

Conquerors didn't make polite requests; his instinct was to seize what he wanted—the more he wanted, the more forceful the seizure. Devil looked into her eyes, calmly watching, calmly waiting; he read the subtle challenge in her face, the underlying stubbornness in the tilt of her chin. How much did he want this prize?

He drew a deep breath, then stepped closer and reached for her hand; his eyes on hers, he brushed his lips across her fingertips. "My dear Honoria Prudence, will you do me the honor of being my wife, my duchess—" He paused, then deliberately added: "The mother of my children?"

Her gaze flickered; she looked away. Placing one fingertip under her chin, Devil turned her face back.

After a fractional hesitation, Honoria lifted her lids and met his eyes. "I haven't yet made up my mind." He might not be able to lie—she could. But he was too potent a force to surrender to without being absolutely certain. A few more days would give her time to check her decision.

He held her gaze; between them, passion lingered, shivering in the air.

"Don't take too long."

The words, uttered softly, could have been a warning or a plea. Retrieving her fingers from his clasp, Honoria lifted her chin free of his touch. "*If* I married you, I would want to be assured no incident similar to the present *contretemps* would occur again."

"I've told you I'm not daft." Devil's eyes glinted. "And I'm certainly no advocate of self-torture."

Ruthlessly, Honoria suppressed her smile.

The planes of Devil's face shifted; he caught her hand. "Come for a drive."

"*One* more point . . ." Honoria held firm. She met the aggravation in his eyes, and tried not to feel the warmth, the seductive strength in the fingers and palm clasping hers. "Tolly's murder."

Devil's jaw firmed. "I will not let you involve yourself in the search for his killer."

Honoria met his gaze directly; again, she sensed their wills locking, this time without heat. "I wouldn't need to actively search for clues if you told me what you and your cousins discover as soon as you discover it." She'd exhausted all avenues open to her; she needed his cooperation to go on.

He frowned, then looked away; she'd started to wonder what he was thinking before he looked back. "I'll agree on one condition."

Honoria raised her brows.

"That you promise that under no circumstances whatever will you personally go searching for Tolly's killer."

Honoria promptly nodded. Her ability to come up with any male felon was severely limited by the social code; her contribution to the investigation would have to be primarily deductive. "So what did Lucifer learn?"

Devil's lips thinned. "I can't tell you."

Honoria stiffened.

"No!" He squeezed her hand. "*Don't* rip up at me—I said 'can't,' not 'won't.' "

Honoria narrowed her eyes. "Why 'can't'?"

Devil searched her face, then looked down at their linked hands. "Because what Lucifer learned casts a far from flattering light on one of the family, probably Tolly. Unfortunately, Lucifer's information was rumor—we've yet to establish the facts." He studied her slim digits entwined with his, then tightened his grip and looked up. "However, if Tolly was involved, then it suggests a possible scenario whereby someone—someone capable of the act or of procuring the same—might have wanted him dead."

Honoria noted the fastidiousness that had crept into his expression. "It's something disreputable, isn't it?" She thought of Louise Cynster.

Slowly, Devil nodded. "Exceedingly disreputable."

Honoria drew in a long breath—then gasped as a tug set her on course for the door.

"You need some air," Devil decreed. He shot her a glance, then admitted through clenched teeth: "So do I."

Towed in his wake, Honoria grinned. Her gown was too thin, but she could don her pelisse at the front door. She had won a host of concessions; she could afford to be magnanimous. The day was fine; her heart was light. And her wolf had reached the end of his tether.

Chapter 13

"I make it 334." Honoria restacked the lists in her lap and started counting again.

His gaze on her profile, Devil raised his brows. They were in the morning room, Honoria at one end of the *chaise* while he sprawled elegantly at the other; she was adding up the acceptances for the grand ball his aunt Horatia was to host in Berkeley Square the next night, to declare the family out of mourning. Smiling, Devil retrieved a list from the floor. "That's a goodly number for this time of year. The weather's put back the shooting, so many have stayed in town. Like Chillingworth—it appears my aunt has seen fit to invite him."

"He is an earl." Honoria glanced up, frowned, then reached over and tugged at the list. "But I gather you've known him forever."

"It certainly seems like forever. We were at Eton together."

"Rivals from your earliest years?"

"I wouldn't class Chillingworth as a rival—more like a nuisance."

Honoria looked down, hiding her grin. Devil had taken to joining her in the morning room in the post-luncheon hour during which the Dowager habitually rested. He would stay for half an hour, long limbs disposed in the opposite corner of the *chaise*, his presence filling the room, dominating her senses. They would chat; if he had information from his cousins, he would tell her, simply and straightforwardly, without evasion.

From her own efforts, she'd learned nothing more. The Dowager had fulfilled her stated intention of introducing her to the *ton;* through a mind-numbing round of morning calls, "at-homes," and afternoon teas, she had met all the major hostesses and been accepted as one of their circle. But in all the gossip and scandalmongering abounding amongst the female half of the *ton*, not a single scrap had she heard regarding Tolly.

She looked up. "Have you heard anything?"

"As it happens, I have." Honoria opened her eyes wide; Devil's lips quirked wryly. "Don't get your hopes up, but Demon's back."

"Did he find Tolly's man?"

"Yes. Mick remembered that last night clearly—Tolly, to use Mick's words, was 'in a right spate' when he came in. Unfortunately, Tolly refused to tell him anything concerning the who, the why, or the what."

Honoria frowned. "Refused?"

"Mick—being Mick—asked."

"And?"

"Uncharacteristically got told, in no uncertain terms, to mind his own business."

"That was odd?"

Devil nodded. "Mick had been with Tolly since Tolly was in shortcoats. If he was troubled over something, the most likely occurrence is that Tolly would have talked it over, without reservation, with Mick."

"So." Honoria considered. "What sort of secret would Tolly refuse to discuss with Mick?"

"That, indeed, is the question." His gaze on her face, on the slight frown disturbing the sweeping arch of her brows, Devil added: "Along with the puzzle of the time."

"The time?"

"That night, Tolly got in less than an hour after he left Mount Street."

They'd assumed Tolly had been out half the night, at some function at which he'd learned the secret that led to his death. Honoria's frown deepened. "Is Mick sure?"

"Positive—he remembers particularly as he hadn't expected Tolly back so soon."

Honoria nodded. "How far is it from Mount Street to Tolly's lodgings?"

"His lodgings were in Wigmore Street—about twenty minutes from my uncle's house."

"Was there any particular house—of a friend, perhaps— where he might have stopped along the way?"

"Nothing directly in his path. And none close that we haven't checked. None of his friends saw him that night."

Honoria caught Devil's eye. "How does such a short time fit with Lucifer's discreditable rumor?"

"Not well." Devil hesitated, then added, "It doesn't rule it out, but it makes it unlikely. If Tolly had gone—" He broke off, then continued: "If what we *thought* had happened, then it most likely happened at some earlier date, which doesn't explain why Tolly only got agitated *after* he left Mount Street."

Studying his face, more revealing now that he didn't guard his expression in her presence, Honoria inwardly frowned. He remained disturbed by the discreditable rumor, even though it might now be unlinked to Tolly's death. "What is it?"

Devil looked up, then grimaced. "It's merely that, as the head of the family, I don't appreciate the idea of some skeleton not safely locked in a cupboard."

Honoria's lips softened; she looked away.

They sat silent for some minutes, Honoria puzzling over the questions Mick's recollections had raised, Devil outwardly relaxed, his gaze, gently pensive, resting on her face. Then Honoria looked at Devil. "Have you told the others?"

"They were on the doorstep with Demon. While I wrestle with our discreditable rumor, they're trying to shake information from any tree they can find. Richard and Demon have gone after the local jarveys; Gabriel, believe it or not, is hobnobbing with street sweepers. Vane and Lucifer are combing the likeliest taverns in the hope they might stumble upon some drunk who saw where Tolly went."

"That seems a very long bow to draw."

Devil sighed and leaned his head back against the *chaise*. "It is." After a moment of staring at the ceiling, he added: "I find it hard to credit but they seem as frustrated as I am." Slowly, he turned his head and looked at Honoria.

She met his gaze levelly. "Matters won't always fall into line just because you decree it."

His eyes on hers, Devil raised his brows. "So I apprehend." There was an undercurrent of subtle self-deprecation in his voice; it was followed almost immediately by a tangible ripple in the atmosphere about them. They stilled, then Devil smoothly reached out and lifted the topmost sheet from the piled lists. "I presume," he said, ostensibly scanning the list, "that every last one of the *grande dames* will be present?"

"Naturally." Equally smoothly, Honoria followed his lead, ruthlessly ignoring the breathlessness that had afflicted her. They spent the next five minutes trading inconsequential quips, while the restless hunger simmering between them subsided.

No matter how easy in each other's company they became, that flame still smoldered, ready to flare at the slightest touch, the least unwary comment. Honoria was sorely tempted to confess that she'd reached her decision, finally and firmly, incontrovertibly. She'd thought long and hard; she could see all the difficulties. She could also see the benefits, and the possibilities; she'd decided to accept the challenge.

And what better way than to start as she meant to go on? She'd determined to use Horatia's ball as the stage for her acceptance. Her speech was well rehearsed . . .

She blinked and returned to reality—and realized her voice had died in mid-sentence. Devil's gaze was on her face, too perceptive, too knowing. Heat rose in her cheeks.

He smiled—wolfishly—and fluidly rose. "I'd better see Hobden—he's come up from St. Ives with the tillage tallies." He met Honoria's eyes, then bowed elegantly. "I'll wish you a good afternoon, my dear."

"And I you, Your Grace." Honoria graciously inclined her head. As Devil strolled to the door, the black armband he still wore caught her eye. Honoria frowned. The six weeks the family had decreed as full mourning ended that night; presumably, tomorrow, he'd leave off his black armband.

Her frown deepened. He had better leave it off tomorrow night.

For Honoria, the next evening started auspiciously. Nerves wound tight, she descended the stairs, gowned for conquest. As usual, Webster materialized in the hall before she reached the last step; he crossed to the drawing-room door and placed a hand on the knob before glancing her way.

His jaw dropped—only momentarily, but the sight did wonders for Honoria's confidence. "Good evening, Webster. Is His Grace down?"

"Indeed, ma'am—I mean, miss." Webster drew in a quick breath and relocated his usual mask. "His Grace is waiting." With a deep bow, he set the door wide.

Smoothly, serenely, inwardly so tight she felt she might break, Honoria glided forward.

Standing before the fireplace, Devil swung around as she entered. As always, his gaze skimmed her, top to toe. Tonight, when he reached her silver sandals, peeking from beneath her hem, he stopped, then, excruciatingly slowly, traced his way back up her length, over the sweep of *eau de Nil* silk clinging sleekly to her long limbs. His eyes dwelled successively on each flatteringly draped curve, then rose higher, to caress her shoulders, concealed only where the simple, toga-style gown was anchored by a gold clasp on her left shoulder. The spangled silk shawl she carried over her elbows was flimsy; no real distraction. She wore no jewelry other than the gold comb in her hair, itself piled high, curl upon gleaming curl. Honoria felt the sudden intensity in his gaze.

Her breath caught.

With long, prowling stride, he crossed the room, his gaze steady on hers. As he neared, he held out one hand; without hesitation, she laid her fingers across his. Slowly, he turned her; dutifully, she twirled. She could feel the heat of his gaze as, at close quarters, it roamed her body, shielded only by gossamer silk. As she completed her revolution and faced him again, she saw his lips curve. His eyes met hers. "Celestine has my gratitude."

His voice reverberated through her; Honoria arched one brow.

"Celestine?" She let her gaze linger on his. "And what, pray tell, do I receive?"

"My attention." On the words, Devil drew her closer. His gaze lifted to her curls, then dropped to her eyes, then fell to her lips. "Unreserved."

Obedient to the pressure of his hand at her back, Honoria arched closer, lifting her lips to his. He met her halfway, yet she was sure she was floating as his lips settled, warm and firm, on hers.

It was the first kiss they'd shared since their confrontation in the morning room; beyond the fact their lips touched, this caress bore no relation to that previous embrace. This was all pleasure and warmth, delight spiced with enthralling fascination as lips melded and held, then firmed again.

Honoria's restless hands came to rest on Devil's lapels; his free hand curved possessively over one silk-clad hip. Beneath his palms, her skin burned, two layers of fine silk no real barrier to his touch. Willingly, she sank into his arms, yielding to the persuasion of his lips and her own flaring desire.

A form of magic held them fast; how many minutes they spent in that soul-stealing kiss neither could have said. The click of heels on the hall tiles brought it to an end.

Devil raised his head and looked at the door; Honoria waited, but he did not step away. His only concession as the door swung wide and his mother appeared in the doorway, was to remove his hand from her hip and, with the hand at her back, gently turn her to the door. Not by word nor, it was clear, even by deed, did he intend concealing the fact he'd been kissing her.

Honoria blinked. She was slow in following Devil's lead; when the Dowager's gaze reached them, she was still half-stretched on her toes, one hand lying on his chest. The Dowager, *grande dame* that she was, pretended not to notice. "If you are ready, my dears, I suggest we leave. There's no point waiting in *this* drawing room."

Inclining his head, Devil offered Honoria his arm; she placed her fingertips upon it. A great deal warmer than when she had entered, she left the room by his side.

The journey to Lord George Cynster's house in Berkeley Square took a bare five minutes. Another five saw Honoria, with Devil by her side, surrounded by Cynsters. The drawing room was full of them; tall, commandingly arrogant gentlemen and briskly imperious ladies, they threw the other members of the *haut ton* invited to dinner into the proverbial shade.

Her gown caused a stir—she hadn't been sure what to expect. What she received were wide smiles and nods of encouragement from the other Cynster ladies—and arrested looks from all the Cynster males. It was Lucifer who translated those looks into words. He shook his dark head at her. "You do realize, don't you, that if Devil hadn't snapped you up, you'd be facing a concerted siege?"

Honoria tried to look innocent.

Dinner had been moved forward to seven; the ball would start at nine. Across the sound of twenty conversations, Webster, borrowed for the occasion, announced that the meal was served.

Devil led his aunt into the dining room, leaving Honoria to be escorted thence by Vane. Remembering a like occasion, Tolly's funeral, Honoria glanced at Vane. "Do you always stand in for him?"

The look he sent her was startled, then his lips lifted. "It would," he murmured, with the cool hauteur that was his most notable characteristic, "be more accurate to say that we cover each other's backs. Devil's only a few months older than I am— we've known each other all our lives."

Honoria heard the devotion beneath the smooth tones and inwardly approved. Vane led her to the chair next to Devil's, taking the chair beside hers. Flanked by such partners, she looked forward to the dinner with unalloyed anticipation.

The conversation about her revolved about politics and the issues of the day; Honoria listened with an interest she hadn't previously known, registering Devil's views, reconciling them with what she knew of His Grace of St. Ives. While the second course was being served, she idly glanced around the table. And noticed the black strip about the arm of each of the Cynster cousins. Devil's left arm was by her side; she turned her head—the black band, barely noticeable against his black coat, was level with her chin.

Looking down at her plate, she swallowed a curse.

She bided her time until they were strolling the huge ballroom, ostensibly admiring the decorative wreaths. They were sufficiently private; the ball guests were only just arriving in the hall below. As they neared the ballroom's end, she slipped one finger beneath the black band and tugged. Devil looked down— and raised a brow.

"Why are you still wearing this?"

He met her gaze; she sensed his hesitation. Then he sighed and looked forward. "Because we haven't yet caught Tolly's murderer."

Given the dearth of clues, they might never catch Tolly's murderer; Honoria kept that thought to herself. "Is it really necessary?" She glanced at his stern profile. "Surely one little waltz won't addle your wits?"

His lips twisted as he glanced down, but he shook his head. "I just feel . . ." His words trailed away; frowning, he looked ahead. "I'm *sure* I've forgotten something—some key—some vital clue."

His tone made it clear he'd changed tack; Honoria followed

without quibble. She could understand that he felt guilty over his inability to bring Tolly's killer to justice; she didn't need to hear him admit it. "Do you remember anything about this clue?"

"No—it's the most damnable thing. I'm sure there's something I've seen, something I've already learned, but I simply can't fasten on it. It's like a phantom at the edge of my vision—I keep turning my head to look but can never bring it into view."

Frustration rang clearly in his tone; Honoria decided to change the subject. "Tell me, is Lady Osbaldestone a Cynster connection?"

Devil glanced to where her ladyship, gimlet gaze fixed on them, sat ensconced in one corner of a nearby *chaise*. "An exceedingly distant one." He shrugged. "But that description covers half the *ton*."

They strolled, chatting with those they came upon, their perambulation slowing as the *ton* rolled up, all eager to be seen at the only Cynster ball of the season. In a short half hour, the ballroom was awash with silks and satins; perfume hung heavy on the air. The sheen of curls was fractured by the sparkle and glint of jewels; hundreds of tongues contributed to the polite hum. Being on Devil's arm guaranteed Honoria space enough to breathe; none were game to crowd her. There were, however, a definite number who, sighting her, were impelled to pay their compliments. Some, indeed, looked set to worship at her feet, even in the teeth of the very real threat of receiving a swift and well-aimed kick from her escort.

Fixed by Honoria's side, compelled to witness her effect on other males, Devil set his jaw, and tried not to let it show. His mood was steadily turning black—not a good sign, given what he had yet to endure. He'd toyed with the idea of asking her not to dance, but she was not yet his wife. He'd transgressed once; she had, by some benign stroke of fate, consented to forgive him. He was not about to try for twice.

And she liked to dance. He knew that without asking; her attention to the music was proof enough. How he would force himself to let her waltz with some other gentleman, he did not know. He'd planned to get his cousins to stand in his place; instead, like him, they'd held to their resolution. Which left him wrestling with a rampant possessiveness he didn't at all wish to tame.

To his disgust, the musicians appeared early. Through the inevitable squeaks and plunks, Lord Ainsworth declaimed: "My dear Miss Anstruther-Wetherby, I would be most honored, indeed, overcome with gratification, should you consent to favor me with your hand and allow me to partner you in this measure." His lordship capped his period with a flourishing bow, then looked earnestly, with almost reverent devotion, at Honoria.

Devil tensed, ruthlessly denying the urge to plant his fist in Ainsworth's vacuous face. Tightening his hold on every wayward impulse, he steeled himself to hear Honoria's acceptance—and to let her go without causing a scene. Honoria held out her hand; Devil felt his control quake.

"Thank you, my lord." Her smile serene, Honoria barely touched fingers with Ainsworth. "But I won't be dancing tonight."

"My dear Miss Anstruther-Wetherby, your actions bear testimony to your exquisite sensibilities. Forgive me, dear lady, for being so gauche as to even *suggest* . . ."

Lord Ainsworth spouted on; Devil hardly heard him. When it finally dawned that the woman on his arm was in all likelihood not listening either, he cut his lordship's performance short. "Sorry, Ainsworth, but we must catch up with Lady Jersey."

As Sally Jersey had a well-developed dislike of the pompous Ainsworth, his lordship did not offer to accompany them. Crestfallen, he took his leave of them; the others in their circle smiled and dispersed, many taking to the floor as the strains of a waltz filled the room.

Devil placed his hand over Honoria's and ruthlessly drew her away. As they strolled the edge of the dance floor, their pace enough to discourage idle encounters, he searched for words, finally settling for: "There's no reason you can't dance."

His tone was dark; his delivery flat. He looked down; Honoria looked up. She studied his eyes; the smile that slowly curved her lips held understanding spiced with feminine satisfaction. "Yes, there is."

Her eyes challenged him to deny it; when he said nothing, her smile deepened and she looked ahead. "I think we should stop by Lady Osbaldestone, don't you?"

Devil didn't; the old tartar was guaranteed deliberately to bait him. On the other hand, he needed a major distraction. Dragging in a deep breath, he nodded, and set course for her ladyship's *chaise*.

"If there was ever any doubt, *that*—" with a nod, Vane indicated the group about the *chaise* on the opposite side of the ballroom, "settles it."

Standing beside Vane, one shoulder propped against the wall, Gabriel nodded. "Indubitably. Lady Osbaldestone hardly qualifies as a *desirable* interlocutor."

Vane's gaze was fixed on Devil's broad back. "I wonder what Honoria said to get him there?"

"Whatever," Gabriel said, pausing to drain his glass, "it looks like we've lost our leader."

"Have we?" Vane narrowed his eyes. "Or is he, as usual, leading the way?"

Gabriel shuddered. "What a hideous prospect." He wriggled

his broad shoulders. "That felt like someone walked over my grave."

Vane laughed. "No point in running from fate—as our esteemed leader is wont to say. Which raises the intriguing subject of *his* fate. When do you think?"

Considering the tableau opposite, Gabriel pursed his lips. "Before Christmas?"

Vane's snort was eloquent. "It damn well better be before Christmas."

"*What* had better be before Christmas?"

The question had them turning; instantly, restraint entered both their expressions. "Good evening, Charles." Gabriel nodded to his cousin, then looked away.

"We were," Vane said, his tone mild, "discussing impending nuptials."

"Indeed?" Charles looked politely intrigued. "Whose?"

Gabriel stared; Vane blinked. After an instant's pause, Vane replied: "Devil's, of course."

"Sylvester's?" Brow furrowing, Charles looked across the room, then his features relaxed. "Oh—you mean that old business about him marrying Miss Anstruther-Wetherby."

"*Old* business?"

"Good heavens, yes." His expression fastidious, Charles smoothed his sleeve. Looking up, he saw his cousins' blank faces—and sighed. "If you must know, I spoke to Miss Anstruther-Wetherby at some length on the matter. She's definitely not marrying Sylvester."

Vane looked at Gabriel; Gabriel looked at Vane. Then Vane turned back to Charles. "When did you speak to Honoria Prudence?"

Charles lifted a supercilious brow. "At Somersham, after the funeral. And I spoke with her shortly after she came up to town."

"Uh-huh." Vane exchanged another look with Gabriel.

Gabriel sighed. "Charles, has anyone ever pointed out to you that ladies are prone to change their minds?"

Charles's answering glance was contemptuous. "Miss Anstruther-Wetherby is an exceedingly well-educated lady of superior sensibilities."

"Who also happens to be *exceedingly* well-structured and as such is an *exceedingly* likely target for Devil's attentions, in this case, honorable." Gabriel gestured to the distant *chaise*. "And if you won't believe us, just open your eyes."

Following his gesture, Charles frowned. Honoria, her hand on Devil's arm, leaned close to say something; Devil bent his head the better to hear her. Their stance spoke eloquently of intimacy, of closeness; Charles's frown deepened.

Vane glanced at Charles. "Our money's on Devil—unfortunately, we haven't found any takers."

"Mmm." Gabriel straightened. "A wedding before Christmas," he slanted a questioning glance at Vane, "and an heir before St.Valentine's Day?"

"Now that," Vane said, "might find us some action."

"Yes, but which way should we jump?" Gabriel headed into the crowd.

Vane followed. "Fie on you—don't you have any faith in our leader?"

"I've plenty of faith in him, but you have to admit there's rather more to producing an heir than his sire's performance. Come and talk to Demon. He'll tell you . . ."

Their words faded. Left behind, Charles continued to frown, staring fixedly at the couple before Lady Osbaldestone's *chaise*.

Chapter 14

A s the evening wore on, the gaiety increased. Supper was served at one o'clock. Seated beside Devil at one of the larger tables, Honoria laughed and chatted. Smiling serenely, she studied Devil's cousins and their supper partners and knew what those ladies were feeling. The same expectation tightened her nerves, heightened her senses. Laughing at one of Gabriel's sallies, she met Devil's eye—and understood precisely why ladies of the *ton* deliberately played with fire.

The musicians summoned them back to the ballroom. The others all rose; Honoria fussed with her shawl, then untangled the ribbons of her fan. She'd intended informing Devil of her decision while sharing their first waltz; denied that opportunity, she was sure that, if she quietly suggested she had something to tell him, he would create another.

She looked up—Devil stood beside her, patient boredom in his face. She held out a hand; smoothly, he drew her to her feet. She glanced around; the supper room was empty. She turned to Devil—only to have him turn her still further, away from the ballroom. Startled, she looked up at him.

He smiled, all wolf. "Trust me."

He led her to a wall—and opened a door concealed within the paneling. The door gave onto a minor corridor, presently deserted. Devil handed her through, then followed. Blinking, Honoria looked around; the corridor ran parallel to the ballroom, leading toward its end. "Where . . . ?"

"Come with me." Taking her hand, Devil strode down the corridor.

As usual, she had to hurry to keep up; before she could think of a sufficiently pointed comment, they reached a set of stairs. Somewhat to her surprise, he took the downward flight. "Where are we going?" Why she was whispering she didn't know.

"You'll see in a minute," he whispered back.

The stairs debouched into another corridor, parallel to the one above; Devil halted before a door near its end. Opening it, he looked in, then stepped back and handed her over the threshold.

Pausing just inside, Honoria blinked. Behind her, the lock clicked, then Devil led her down three shallow stone steps and onto a flagged floor.

Eyes wide and widening, Honoria gazed about. Huge panes of glass formed half the roof, all of one wall and half of each sidewall. Moonlight, crystal white, poured in, illuminating neatly trimmed orange trees in clay pots, set in two semicircles about the room's center. Slipping her hand from Devil's, she entered the grove. In the moonlight, the glossy leaves gleamed; she touched them— their citrus scent clung to her fingers. In the grove's center stood a wrought-iron daybed piled with silk cushions. Beside it on the flags sat a wickerwork basket overflowing with embroideries and lace.

Glancing back, she saw Devil, a silvered shadow prowling in her wake. "It's an orangery."

She saw his lips twitch. "One of my aunt's fancies."

The tenor of his voice made her wonder what *his* fancy was.

An expectant thrill shot through her—a violin rent the peace. Startled, she looked up. "We're *under* the ballroom?"

Devil's teeth flashed as he reached for her. "My dance, I believe."

She was in his arms and whirling before she realized his intent. Not that she wished to argue, but a *soupçon* of warning might have helped, might have made the sudden impact of his nearness a little easier to absorb. As it was, with arms like iron about her and long thighs hard as oak parting hers, she immediately fell prey to a host of sensations, all distractingly pleasant. He waltzed as he did most things—masterfully, his skill so assured she need do nothing but glide and twirl. They precessed down the grove, then slowly revolved about its perimeter. As they passed the entrance to the enchanted circle, he looked down, into her eyes— and deliberately drew her closer.

Honoria's breath caught; her heart stuttered, then picked up its pace. The pale silk covering her breasts shifted against his coat; she felt her nipples tingle. Their hips met as they turned, silk shushing softly, sirenlike in the night. Hardness met softness, then slid tantalizingly away, only to return, harder, more defined, a heartbeat later. The ebb and sway of the dance teased her senses; they ached—for him. Eyes wide, her gaze trapped in the clear green of his, Honoria felt the silvery touch of the moonlight and tipped up her head. Her lips, parted, were oddly dry; they throbbed to her heartbeat.

Her invitation could not have been clearer. Caught in the moment, Devil did not even think of refusing. With practised ease, he lowered his head and tasted her, confident in his mastery, only to find his head swimming as she drew him in. With an inward curse, he hauled hard on his reins and wrested back control, settling to languidly sample the riches she offered, subtly stoking her flame.

They waltzed between the orange trees; the music stopped and still they revolved. Gradually, their steps slowed; they halted by the daybed.

Honoria quelled a shiver of anticipation. Their kiss unbroken, Devil released her hand; he slid both palms over her silk-clad curves until one rested on each hip, burning through her flimsy gown. Slowly, deliberately, his hands slid further, cupping her bottom, drawing her fully against him. Honoria felt his blatant need, his desire—an answering heat blossomed within her. Her breath was his; caught in their kiss, she lifted her arms and twined them about his neck. She pressed herself against him, soothing her aching breasts against the wall of his chest. The deep shudder that passed through him thrilled her.

She'd rehearsed an acceptance speech—this was even better; actions, after all, spoke far louder than words. With a sigh of pure delight, she sank deeper into his embrace, returning his kiss with unfeigned eagerness.

Tension gripped him. He lifted her; their kiss unbroken, he lowered her to the daybed. And followed her down; Honoria's breath fled. She knew his body was hard, but she'd never had it pressed against her, limb to limb, down her entire length. The shock was delicious; with a stifled gasp, she pushed aside his coat and eagerly spread her hands over his chest.

And felt the sudden hitch in his breathing, sensed his sudden surge of desire. From deep within, she answered it, flagrantly enticing his tongue to duel and dance with hers. She set her long legs tangling with his; her hands reached further. She would be no passive spectator; she wanted to feel, to experience, to explore.

Which was more encouragement than Devil could stand.

Abruptly, he pulled back, caught her hands and anchored them over her head. Immediately, he recaptured her lips, desire growing, escalating wildly, barely restrained. Ravenous, he deepened the kiss, searching for appeasement, fighting, simultaneously, to retain control.

Half-trapped beneath him, Honoria arched, responding to the intimacy, the steadily growing heat. Desire, a palpable entity, welled and swelled; she squirmed, silk sliding sensuously between them, then moaned and tugged against his hold. He broke their kiss only long enough to say: "No."

Twisting her head, she avoided his lips. "I only want to touch you."

"Forget it," he grated. He was dangerously overheated, driven by a desire he'd seriously underestimated; her wandering hands would be the last straw.

"Why?" Honoria tested his grip, then twisted, trying to gain greater purchase; one soft thigh pressed close, then slid downward, provocatively stroking that part of his anatomy he was desperately trying to ignore.

His breath hissed in; she pressed closer—Devil forgot why— forgot everything bar the need to assuage the driving force that filled him. Desire crystallized, hardening every muscle. Tightening every nerve. Obliterating the last remnants of caution. He caught her chin and captured her mouth in a searing kiss. He shifted, one leg trapping hers, using his weight to subdue her.

Not that she was struggling. Her lips clung to his, passionately enticing. She moaned again, this time in abandoned entreaty; her body arched, caressing his, inviting, inciting.

His hand dropped from her jaw to possessively cup one breast; he kneaded the firm mound, then rolled its tip to a tight bud.

Honoria gasped; her breast throbbed, then ached as his fingers played. She writhed, savoring his tensed muscles, shifting in response. His body was close—she ached to have him closer. Much closer. Heat flared wherever he touched her; she needed his hardness to quench the flame, to satisfy the fever that sang in her veins.

She wanted him, *needed* him—there was no longer any reason she couldn't have him. Desperately, she tugged at his grip—it firmed. His hand left her breast—before she could protest, she heard a muffled click. She stilled—the bodice of her gown peeled away. Her heart thudded, then raced. The drawstring of her chemise pulled tight, then released—the gossamer-fine fabric floated down, leaving her breasts bare.

Devil lifted his head; Honoria drew in a shuddering breath. She felt the cool touch of the moonlit air, felt the heat of his gaze. Her nipples crinkled tight. Lifting lids suddenly heavy, she looked up. His face was graven, harsh planes sharp-edged. Her breasts throbbed painfully; as if he could sense it, he bent his head.

And touched his lips to her heated skin. Honoria stiffened; her senses leapt. Devil dropped hot kisses around one aureole, then drew the soft flesh into his mouth. She tensed. He suckled—and she thought she would die. Sensation streaked through her; her toes curled. She gasped, her body tightening, lifting against him. Her fingers, still locked above her head, clenched tight.

He tortured her soft flesh until she cried out, then turned to her other breast. Only when that, too, was aching fiercely, when her body felt molten, pulsing with need, did he raise his head. From beneath her lashes, Honoria watched as he skimmed his hand down, possessively caressing the smooth curve of her hip, then tracing the long sweep of her thigh. Her lungs seized when his fingers slid beneath her hem; her heart stopped when, in one, smooth motion, he swept her skirts up to her waist.

Honoria trembled. Cool air caressed her fevered flesh; his gaze, hot as the sun, dispelled the chill, roaming comprehensively, surveying what he intended to possess. Then he turned his head and met her gaze. His hand tightened about her bare hip, then slid lower in a tantalizing caress, hard palm and long fingers stroking knowingly down, then up.

Her gaze trapped in his, Honoria shuddered. He leaned closer; she shut her eyes as his lips found hers. She gave herself up to him, up to their kiss, surrendered to the sweet wildfire that rose between them.

Devil's conqueror's soul relished the victory—he pressed on, eager for the final conquest. The long sweep of her ivory thighs was a potent attraction, her skin warm satin to his touch. Her softly rounded belly tensed beneath his hand; he slid his palm over her hip, his fingers curving about one firm buttock.

Knowingly, he traced, caressed; tangling his fingers in the soft curls at the apex of her thighs, he gently teased. Beneath him, Honoria shifted restlessly, her lips clinging to his. He drew back, fleetingly studying her face, passion-blank. At his whispered command, she parted her thighs—then gasped as he touched her, then cupped her. Only when that first flaring shock of awareness had died did he caress her, intimately stroking the delicate swollen folds, parting them to find the bud of her desire, already hard and throbbing. He circled it, and felt her passion rise—he found her slickness and gently probed, deliberately inciting the wave of desire building between them.

The higher the wave, the headier the ride, the more profound the final crash. Bringing years of experience to bear, he fed her passion until it became a raging tide.

Caught on the crest, Honoria knew nothing beyond her violent need, centered in the swollen, throbbing flesh he so knowingly stroked, so tantalizingly caressed. Then one long finger slid deeper, circled, then pressed deeper still. She caught her breath on a moan; her body lifted, helplessly seeking. He stroked—the heat within her ignited.

Again and again came that intimate invasion; eyes closed, senses raging, she wanted more. He knew her need; his lips returned to hers, his tongue claiming her mouth in the same, mesmerizingly languid rhythm with which he probed her heated body.

Her breasts swollen and heavy, Honoria arched against him, trying to ease their ache. Abruptly, he released her lips; a second later, his mouth fastened about one nipple.

A strangled shriek escaped her—lightning streaked through her; the conflagration within her roared. The hand locked about hers disappeared. Devil shifted; using one hand to ease the ache of one breast, he caressed the other with lips and tongue. Between her thighs, his fingers slid deep, and still deeper.

Her hands free, Honoria reached for him.

Immediately, events became more heated, more urgent. She wrestled his cravat from him, then set about undoing the buttons of his shirt. Frantic, she stopped halfway and, shifting, squirming and panting, struggled with his coat. Devil struggled to hold her still. With a muttered curse, he suddenly pulled back and shrugged, then flung his coat and waistcoat aside. Honoria welcomed him back with open arms, thrilled to her toes when she finally made contact with his naked chest. His muscles tensed, shifted—greedily, she explored. Crisp hair tangled about her fingers; beneath her palms, he burned.

Devil felt her yank his shirt free of his waistband, felt her small hands slide about him, reaching to caress the broad muscles of his back. He raised his head. She tightened her hold—the twin peaks of her breasts pressed against his bare chest; the heat between her thighs scalded him. That naked embrace left him shaking, gasping, struggling to regain any glimmer of control. Every instinct he possessed urged him on, urged him to take all she offered, to sink into her slick heat and take her, claim her beyond recall. The pressure of that instinct was overwhelming; his fingers were on the buttons of his trousers, his rake's instincts running a final cursory check—when he remembered her fear.

Her reason for not marrying.

He stilled. Then blinked. He heard his ragged breathing, felt his chest swell. Raging desire pounded at his senses; passion, unleashed, fought for release. But . . . In that crazed instant, lust and will collided. The shock was almost physical. The wrenching effort required to draw his hands from Honoria, to roll away and sit up, left him giddy.

With a whimper, Honoria pulled him back. Or tried to. She couldn't get a grip on his body—clenching her hands in his loose shirt, she tugged desperately. All she did was rock herself.

Devil didn't shift. Gently, he caught her hands and disengaged her fingers. "No."

"*No?*" The question came out as a muted wail; in utter disbelief, Honoria stared at him. "You're a rake—rakes don't say 'No'!"

He had the grace to grimace. "This isn't right."

Honoria drew a deep breath; her senses were whirling, clamoring with need. "You've been bedding women for God knows how long—you must by now know what to do!"

The look Devil cast her was exceedingly sharp. "What I meant was, this isn't how I intend bedding *you*."

Honoria opened her eyes wide. "Does it matter?"

"*Yes!*" His expression grim, he shook his head. "This wasn't supposed to happen yet!"

Her hands still trapped in his, Honoria stared at him. "Why did you bring me down here, then?"

"Believe it or not, I had merely envisaged an illicit waltz—not a full-scale seduction."

"Then what are we doing on this daybed?"

Devil clenched his jaw. "I got carried away—by you!"

"I see." She narrowed her eyes. "You're allowed to seduce me, but I'm not allowed the reciprocal privilege?"

The eyes that met hers were mere green shards. "Precisely. Seduction is an art best left to the experts."

"I'm obviously a quick learner—I've had an excellent teacher." Her hands immobilized in his, she tugged, trying to topple him back down; if she could just get him back on the bed alongside her . . .

"No!" Abruptly, Devil let go of her hands and stood; grimly, he looked down at her. She hadn't seduced him—something in him had accomplished that. Whatever it was, he didn't trust it—that force that whispered within him, urging him to capitulate, to toss aside his careful plans and fall in, lustily, with hers. "When you come to me as my wife, I want you to come of your own free will. Because you've *made* the decision to become my duchess. That's not a decision you've yet made."

Staggered, Honoria stared at him. "What do you imagine *this* is all about?" Her gesture encompassed her seminaked sprawl.

Devil narrowed his eyes. "Curiosity."

"*Curi . . . ?*" Honoria's mouth fell open, then shut; lips setting ominously, she came up on one elbow.

Devil spoke before she could. "Even if it wasn't—even if you'd made up your mind in cold blood—how the hell could I tell now, when you're so heated you're almost simmering?"

Honoria met his eyes—and wished she had an answer.

"You're all but drunk with passion—don't try to deny it."

She didn't—couldn't; just sitting up had nearly made her swoon. Her pulse thundered in her ears; she felt flushed one instant, then desperate for heat—his heat—the next. There was a curious, molten void pulsing within her; her breathing was so shallow it was difficult to think.

Devil's gaze, on her face, became more intent, then flicked down, swiftly scanning. The folds of her gown had slipped down, the hem floating on her thighs. Instantly, his eyes switched back to her face; she saw his jaw set, saw the iron shackles of his control lock.

He spoke through clenched teeth, frustration in his voice. "It's important to me to know that you've made a conscious decision— that you've decided to become my wife, the mother of my children, for your own reasons, not because I've seduced, coerced, or manipulated you into it."

"I've *made* my decision." Honoria struggled to her knees. "How can I convince you?"

"I need to hear you say it—state it—when you're fully *compos mentis.*" Devil held her gaze. "I want to hear you declare that you'll be my duchess, that you *want* to bear my children."

Through the haze of her passion, Honoria glimpsed an unexpected light. She narrowed her eyes. "Just why do you need this declaration?"

Devil looked down at her—and narrowed his eyes back. "Can you deny you've avoided marrying because of your decision not to risk losing children—like you lost your brother and sister?"

Stunned, she stared at him. "How did you know?"

Devil's jaw firmed. "Michael told me about your brother and sister. The rest's obvious. You must have had a reason for not marrying—you avoid young children."

His presumption in guessing her most private fear—correctly—was infuriating; Honoria knew she should react—do something to put him in his place. Instead, their talk of children had evoked a far stronger response, a surging, primitive urge to put him in his place, in quite a different way.

Their discussion had done nothing to quench the desire beating steady in her veins. They were both half-naked, both breathing rapidly; passion still throbbed between them. His every muscle was sharply defined, locked against that driving need. She had no such defense.

Realization swept her—and left her quivering. "I . . ." She searched his eyes, her own widening. She spread her arms helplessly. "You can't leave me like this."

Devil looked into her eyes—and mentally cursed—himself, her—and Celestine's damned gown, gathered in sheening folds about her waist, draping her thighs in silken splendor. As he watched, a telltale shiver racked her, an almost-imperceptible quiver rippling beneath her skin.

Reaching out, she locked her fingers in his shirt and pulled. Reluctantly, he shifted closer. He'd purposely aroused her, deliberately pushed her to a state bordering on the frantic.

"Please?" The soft plea lay on her bruised lips; it glowed in her eyes.

What could a gentleman do? With one last mental curse, Devil gathered her into his arms and set his lips to hers.

She opened to him instantly, sinking against him. He gave her what she wanted, steadily fanning her flames, holding himself rigidly aloof. His demons were once more under his control—he wasn't about to let the reins slip again.

Honoria sensed his decision; the muscles that surrounded her remained locked and unyielding. She would not be his wife tonight. But she had no will left to rail against fate—her entire being was focused on the fire that raged within her. Wave upon flaming wave it seared through her, leaving her empty and yearning, weak with need. How he was going to sate her hunger she did not know; adrift, she gave herself up to his kisses, surrendered to the inferno and put herself in his hands.

When he lifted his head she was reeling, and hotter than she'd been in her life. Her whole being was one heated, aching void. Gasping, she clung to his shoulders.

"Trust me."

He whispered the words against her throat, then trailed wicked kisses down one blue vein. Honoria let her head fall back, then shuddered. The next instant, he swung her into his arms. She waited to be laid on the daybed—instead, he carried her around it; his back to it, he set her on her feet before him, facing the long mirror on the wall.

Honoria blinked. The moonlight found her skin and set it shimmering; behind her, Devil appeared a dense shadow, his hands dark against her body. Honoria licked her lips. "What are you going to do?"

He bent his head and traced one earlobe with his tongue. "Satisfy you. Release you." His eyes met hers in the mirror. "Pleasure you."

The deep purring murmur sent a sharp thrill racing through her; his hands slid around to cup both breasts—his fingers tightened and she shuddered. "All you have to do is do exactly as I say." Again he met her gaze. "Keep your eyes open and watch my hands—and concentrate on what you feel, on the sensations . . ."

His words were low, hypnotic; Honoria couldn't drag her eyes from his hands, rhythmically kneading her breasts. She watched his long fingers reach for her nipples; they swirled, then squeezed—sharp shivers lanced through her. She sucked in a short breath and leaned back—and felt his bare chest behind her, crisp hair rasping against her bare shoulders.

His hands left her breasts—she refocused on the mirror. One dark hand splayed across her midriff, holding her against him; the other gripped her gown, gathered in folds about her hips. She realized his intention and stiffened—protest welled, but never made it past her lips. He drew both gown and chemise down, over her hips, baring her, then let them slither to the floor. The costly fabrics pooled about their feet—Honoria ignored them, shocked, entranced, mesmerized by the sight of dark hands freely roaming her body.

She heard a low moan, and knew it was hers. Her head fell back against his shoulder; her spine arched. Her senses, fully alive, registered every touch, every knowing caress; from under weighted lids, she watched every erotic move. Then he shifted, his arms coming around her, surrounding her, his left hand cupping her right breast, his right hand splaying over her stomach. From behind, his knee pressed hers apart; head bent, his lips grazed the soft skin beneath her ear. "Keep watching."

Honoria did—she watched as his hand slid lower, long fingers tangling in her curls, then sliding further, pressing inward. He touched her softness, found her molten heat and stroked. Breathless, aching, she felt the muscles in his arm shift as he reached further, felt the pressure of his hand between her thighs, felt the slow inexorable invasion as one long finger entered her.

Sensation upon sensation crashed through her; the hand at her breast fondled, fingers finding, then tightening about her budded nipple. Of their own volition, her hands found his, fastening over his broad wrists. The crisp hair of his forearms rasped the soft skin of her inner arms; beneath her fingers, hard muscle and steely sinew played.

Between her thighs, his hand shifted; as one finger slid deep, his thumb pressed, caressed.

Lightning, wildfire—pure streaks of elemental sensation lanced through her; her body tightened, arched; Honoria gasped. His caresses continued, increasingly forceful; within her, sensations swirled, then rose—a vortex of feeling.

"Keep watching."

Naked, on fire, she dragged her lids open—and saw his hand push deep between her thighs.

A starburst took her—exploded within her. Sensation crystallized, soared, then fractured, a million silver shards raining down, shooting through her, flying down overstretched nerves to melt, tingling, beneath her skin.

Release.

It swept her, washing away her tension, replacing it with a pleasure so deep she thought she'd died. She felt his lips at her temple, felt his hands soften in soothing, intimate caresses. Sweet oblivion claimed her.

When her wits reconnected with reality, Honoria discovered herself fully dressed, leaning against the daybed's back. Before her, Devil stood before the mirror, tying his cravat. She watched his fingers deftly crease and knot the wide folds, and smiled.

In the mirror, Devil's eyes met hers. Her smile widened; he raised a brow.

"I just realized," she said, leaning more heavily against the daybed, "why you don't have a valet. Being a rake necessarily means you can't rely on the services of a servant to turn you out in trim."

Settling the ends of his cravat, Devil cast her a jaundiced glance. "Precisely." He turned. "And if you've returned to the living enough to think that through, we'd better get back to the ballroom."

He stooped to snatch his coat from the floor; Honoria opened her lips to inform him that she had, indeed, made up her mind, then thought better of it. They'd been away from the ball for too long as it was—this was no longer the time and place. Tomorrow morning would do.

She felt like she was floating, in some strange way sundered from reality. She watched Devil shrug into his coat. As he settled the lapels, something caught her eye. Turning, she peered between the orange trees.

"What is it?" Devil followed her gaze.

"I thought I saw someone, but it must have been a shifting shadow."

Devil took her hand. "Come—the gossipmongers will have enough to talk about as it is."

They walked swiftly through the orange grove; a moment later, the latch clicked and all was still. The moon continued to lay its gentle beams in wide swaths across the flagged floor.

A shadow broke the pattern.

The outline of a man was thrown across the grove, distorted to menacing proportions. Then the figure slipped away, around the corner of the orangery, and the shadow was no more.

Moonlight bathed the scene in soft white light, illuminating the orange trees, the wickerwork basket, and the daybed with its rumpled cushions.

Chapter 15

"Thank you, Emmy." Standing, arms folded, before her sitting-room window, Honoria watched the tweeny tidy her luncheon tray. "Has His Grace returned to the house?"

"I don't believe so, miss." Emmy straightened, hefting her burden. "I could ask Webster, if you like?"

"No—thank you, Emmy." Honoria fabricated a smile. "It was merely an idle question."

Very idle. Turning back to the window, Honoria wondered how much more idleness she could take. They'd returned from Berkeley Square well after three o'clock; sleep, deep and dreamless, had claimed her. Devil's pleasure had obviously agreed with her; on waking, she'd determined to waste no time claiming more. Gowned in one of Celestine's most fetching creations, she'd headed downstairs.

Only to discover the breakfast room empty. Devoid of wolves. Webster informed her that His Grace had broken his fast early and departed for a long drive. After breakfasting in solitary splendor—the Dowager had, the night before, declared her intention of not rising until the afternoon—she'd retreated to her sitting room. To wait. Impatiently.

How dare he demand a declaration from her and then go for a drive? She set her teeth and heard the front door slam. The sound of raised voices reached her. Frowning, she went to the door, opened it, and recognized Webster's voice raised in exclamation.

Webster shaken from his habitual imperturbability? Honoria headed for the stairs. Surely nothing short of catastrophe—

Her breath caught; eyes widening, she picked up her skirts and ran.

Reaching the gallery, she leaned over the rail. The sight that met her eyes was the opposite of reassuring. In the hall below, footmen milled about a ragged figure, supporting, exclaiming. It was Sligo, pale, shaken, one arm in a makeshift sling, cuts and abrasions all over his face.

Her heart in her mouth, Honoria started down the stairs—and heard Devil's voice, deep, strong, a forcefully coherent rumble. Relief hit her so strongly she had to lean on the balustrade to let the giddiness pass. Drawing a steadying breath, she continued down.

Devil strode out of the library; Honoria clutched the banister again. His coat was ripped in countless places, in jagged little tears. His buckskin breeches, usually immaculate, were scraped and dusty, as were his boots. Disheveled black locks framed his frowning face; an angry scatch ran along his jaw. "Get the sawbones in for Sligo—that shoulder needs setting."

"But what about *you*, m'lord?" Webster, following on his heels, raised his hands, as if tempted to seize hold of his master.

Devil swung about—and saw Honoria on the stairs. His gaze locked on hers. "There's nothing wrong with me bar a few scratches." After a moment, he glanced to his left, frowning at Webster. "Stop fussing—Cynsters are invincible, remember?" With that, he set his boot on the first stair. "Just send up some hot water—that's all I need."

"I'll bring it up directly, Your Grace." With injured dignity, Webster headed for the kitchens.

Devil climbed the stairs; Honoria waited. There were slivers of wood, some painted, caught in the tears in his coat. Her chest felt so tight it hurt. "What happened?"

Drawing abreast of her, Devil met her gaze. "The axle on my phaeton snapped."

There were small bloodstains on his shirt; he was moving briskly but without his usual fluid grace. He kept climbing; Honoria turned and followed. "Where?"

"Hampstead Heath." Without waiting for her next question, he added: "I needed some air, so I went out there and let the horses have their heads. We were flying when the axle went."

Honoria felt the blood drain from her face. "Went?"

Devil shrugged. "Snapped—there was an almighty crack. We might have hit something, but I don't think we did."

Reaching the top of the stairs, he turned and strode down the corridor; picturing the scene, and not liking what she saw, Honoria hurried in his wake. "Your horses—the bays?"

"No." Devil threw her a glance. "I had a pair of young blacks put to—to try out their paces." His features contorted. "I shot one immediately, but I only carry one pistol. Luckily, Sherringham came along—I borrowed his pistol, then he drove us back here."

"But—" Honoria frowned. "What actually happened?"

A decidedly testy glance found her. "The axle snapped under the box seat—essentially, the phaeton came apart. By hell's own luck, both Sligo and I were thrown free. I bounce better than he does."

"The carriage?"

"Is kindling."

They'd reached the end of the long corridor; opening the heavy oak door at its end, Devil strode on. He stopped in the middle of the room, in the center of a richly hued carpet. Lifting one shoulder, he started to ease off his coat—and caught his breath on an indrawn hiss.

"Here." Behind him, Honoria reached over his shoulders and gently tugged, freeing first one shoulder, then the other, then easing the sleeves off. "Great heavens!" Dropping the ruined coat, she stared.

His shirt was badly torn, the fine linen shredded down the side of his back that had taken the brunt of his fall. The abrasions had bled, as had numerous little cuts. Thankfully, his breeches and boots had provided sterner protection; there were no rips below his waist.

Before she could react, Devil pulled the shirt free of his breeches and hauled it over his head. And froze. Then his head snapped around. "What the devil are you doing here?"

It took a moment to shift her gaze from his bleeding back to his face. The look in his eyes didn't, immediately, make sense, then she looked past him—to the massive, fully canopied four-poster bed that dominated the room. In one swift glance, she took in the sumptuous hangings, all in shades of green, the ornately carved headboard and barley-sugar posts, the silk sheets and thick feather-bed and the abundance of soft pillows piled high. Her expression mild, she looked back at him. "Your cuts are bleeding—they need salving."

Devil swore beneath his breath. "You shouldn't be in here." He wrestled with his shirt, trying to free his arms.

"Don't be ridiculous." Honoria caught his hands, now thoroughly tangled; deftly, she unlaced his cuffs. "The circumstances excuse the impropriety."

Devil stripped the shirt from his wrists and flung it aside. "I am not on my deathbed."

"You are, however, badly scraped." Honoria met his gaze calmly. "You can't see it."

Devil narrowed his eyes at her—then twisted, trying to look over his shoulder. "It doesn't feel that bad—I can take care of it myself."

"For goodness sake!" Honoria planted her hands on her hips and glared at him. "Stop acting like a six-year-old—I'm only going to bathe the cuts and apply some salve."

Devil's head whipped back. "That's just the point—I'm *not* a six-year-old—and I'm not dead, either."

"Naturally." Honoria nodded. "You're a Cynster—you're invincible, remember?"

Devil gritted his teeth. "Honoria, if you want to play ministering angel, you can damn well marry me first."

Honoria lost her temper—she'd been waiting to make the declaration he wanted and he turned up like this! Stepping forward, she planted her index finger in the center of his bare chest. "*If,*" she declared, emphasizing the word with a definite jab. "I *do* decide to marry you." She tried another jab; when he instinctively stepped back, she closed the distance. "I would want to be *assured.*" Another jab, another step. "That you will behave *reasonably.*" Her finger was starting to ache. "*In—all—situations!*" Three quick jabs, three quick steps; Devil's legs hit the end of his bed. Honoria pounced. "Like now!" Glaring defiantly up at him, she prodded him one last time. "*Sit!*"

The face she looked into was uncompromisingly set; his eyes, shadowed green, smoldered darkly. They stood, gazes locked, toe-to-toe, will against will—abruptly, Devil's gaze shifted to the door.

Honoria grabbed the moment. Placing both palms on the heavy muscles of his chest, she pushed. Hard.

With a muffled expletive, Devil toppled—and sat.

"Your water, Your Grace." Webster elbowed open the door, which had swung half-shut behind them.

Turning, Honoria held out her hands. "I'll need some salve, Webster."

"Indeed, miss." Without a blink, Webster relinquished the bowl into her care. "I'll fetch some immediately."

The instant he'd gone, Honoria turned—straight into a furious glower.

"This is *not* a good idea."

She raised a brow, then bent and placed the bowl on the floor. "Stop complaining—you'll survive."

Devil watched her gown draw tight over her bottom—abruptly, he shook his head. "Maybe—but will I be sane?"

Wringing out a cloth, Honoria cast him a measuring glance. Rising, she folded the cloth, then stepped up beside him, her legs almost touching his thigh. Placing one hand on his shoulder, she drew it forward, bringing a deep cut into view. Under her fingers, his skin was warm, resilient, very much alive. "Think of something else." Carefully, she started to bathe the cut.

Closing his eyes, Devil drew a deep breath. *Think of something else.* Just as well he was sitting, or she'd know for a fact just what his "else" was. His cuts and scrapes barely rated on his scale of afflictions; his major hurt was throbbing steadily, and was only going to get worse. She was so close, leaning over, reaching around his shoulder; her perfume surrounded him, wreathing his senses, leaving him giddy with need.

Small hands touched gently, hesitantly; she started when his muscles shifted, flickering beneath her fingers. Clenching his fists, Devil anchored them to his knees; when Webster returned, salve-pot in hand, he all but sighed with relief. "How's Sligo?"

It was an effort, but he managed to keep his butler talking until, with every last scratch bathed and salved, Honoria finally stepped back.

"There." Wiping her hands on the towel Webster held for her, she slanted him a questioning glance.

Devil returned it with a blank stare. He waited while Webster gathered ruined clothes, towels, salve, and basin, then swept magisterially out. Honoria turned to watch him go—silently, Devil rose and moved up behind her. He'd lost the battle with his demons five minutes before.

"Now!" Honoria turned—straight into Devil's arms. "What—?" Her words died as she looked into his eyes. A feeling of being about to be devoured washed over her. She felt his hand at the base of her throat. It rose, framing her jaw as his head lowered.

He waited for no permission, implied or otherwise, but took her mouth rapaciously. Honoria felt her bones melt; beneath that onslaught, resistance fled. He shifted and moved her; her legs hit the bed end. Lifting her against him, he knelt on the bed, then they were toppling together. She landed on her back—he landed on top of her.

Directly on top of her.

Any thought of struggling vanished; the hunger that roared through him, the sheer muscled weight of him, tense, rigid, and ready to claim her, lit her fires instantly. Honoria wrapped her arms about his neck and feverishly kissed him back.

He pressed his hands into the down covers and slid them beneath her hips, fingers firming, then tilting her against him. More definite, more fascinating than before, she felt the rigid column of his desire ride against her. Instinctively, she writhed beneath that throbbing weight—wanting, needing.

"God Almighty!"

Devil's weight left her—she was plucked rudely from the bed. Trapped in his arms in a froth of petticoats, blinking wildly, Honoria saw the door approaching; juggling her, Devil swung it wide.

And deposited her on her feet in the corridor.

"What . . . ?" Breasts swelling, Honoria whirled to face him, the rest of her question writ large in her eyes.

Devil pointed a finger at her nose. "Your declaration." He looked wild, dark hair disheveled, black brows slashing down, lips a thin, hard line. His chest rose and fell dramatically.

Honoria drew in a deep breath.

"Not now!" Devil scowled. "When you've thought it over properly."

With that, he slammed the door.

Honoria's jaw dropped; she stared at the oak panels. Abruptly snapping her mouth shut, she reached for the doorknob.

And heard the lock fall home.

In utter disbelief, she stared at the door, her mouth open once more. Then she gritted her teeth, screwed her eyes tight and, fists clenched, gave vent to a frustrated scream.

She opened her eyes—the door remained shut.

Jaw setting ominously, Honoria swung on her heel and stalked off.

Devil escaped from his house and sought refuge at Manton's. It was late afternoon, a time when many of his peers still in town could be counted on to look in, to spend an hour or two culping wafers in convivial company.

Scanning those occupying the shooting stalls, his gaze alighted on one dark head. He strolled forward, waiting until his mark discharged his pistol before drawling: "You haven't quite corrected for the kick, brother mine."

Richard turned his head—and raised one brow. "You offering to teach me, big brother?"

Devil's teeth gleamed. "I gave up teaching you years ago—I was thinking more along the lines of a little friendly competition."

Richard grinned back. "A tenner each wafer?"

"Why not just make it a monkey the lot?"

"Done."

In perfect amity, they set to culping wafer after wafer; acquaintances strolled up, making none-too-serious suggestions, to which the brothers replied in like vein. No one, seeing them together, could doubt their relationship. Devil was the taller by an inch or so; although Richard lacked his more developed musculature, much of the difference lay in the four years between them. Their faces, seen separately, were not obviously alike, Devil's features being leaner, harder, more austere, yet when seen side by side, the same patriarchal planes, the same arrogant nose and brow line, the same aggressive chin, were readily apparent.

Standing back to let Richard take his shot, Devil smiled to himself. Other than Vane, who was as familiar as his shadow, no one was closer to him than Richard. Their similarity went deep, much deeper than the physical. Of all the Bar Cynster, Richard was the one he could predict most easily—because Richard always reacted as he did.

The retort of Richard's pistol echoed in the stall; Devil looked up, noting the hole an inch to the left of the target's center. They were using a brace plus one of Manton's specials, wicked, long-barreled specimens. While well balanced, over the distance they were shooting, the longest permitted in the gallery, there was a definite difference between the guns; using the three in rotation meant they had to constantly readjust their aim.

The assistant waiting on them had reloaded the next pistol; Devil weighed it in his hand. Richard shifted positions; Devil swung into place and raised his arm. His shot holed the wafer between the center and Richard's shot.

"Tsk, tsk! Always impulsive, Sylvester—taking a fraction more time would yield a better result."

Richard, who'd been lounging against the stall wall, stiffened, then straightened, his previously relaxed expression leaching to impassivity. He nodded briefly to Charles, then turned to supervise the reloading.

In contrast, Devil's smile broadened wickedly. "As you know, Charles, wasting time's not my style."

Charles's pale lashes flickered; a frown showed fleetingly in his eyes.

Devil noted it; unfailingly urbane, he picked up a freshly loaded pistol. "Care to show us how?" Swinging the gun about, he laid the barrel across his sleeve and presented the butt to Charles.

Charles reached for it—his hand stopped in midair. Then his jaw firmed; wrapping his fingers about the polished butt, he hefted the pistol. Stepping past Devil, Charles took up his stance. He flexed his shoulders once, then lifted his arm. He sighted, taking, as he'd said, only a moment longer than Devil, before firing.

The wafer's center disappeared.

With a sincere "Bravo," Devil clapped Charles on the shoulder. "You're one of the few who can do that intentionally." Charles looked up; Devil grinned. "Care to join us?"

Charles did; despite his initial stiffness, even Richard studied his eldest cousin's style. Shooting was one of the few gentlemanly pursuits Charles shared with the members of the Bar Cynster; pistol shooting was an activity at which he excelled. Charles accepted Devil's easy compliments as his due, but after twenty minutes recalled another engagement and took his leave.

Watching Charles's retreating back, Richard shook his head. "If he wasn't such a prig, he might be bearable."

Devil studied the score sheets. "What's the tally?"

"I lost count when Charles appeared." Richard glanced at the sheets, then grimaced. "You probably won—you usually do."

"Let's declare it a draw." Devil laid the pistols aside. "For me, it served its purpose."

"Which was?" Brows rising, Richard followed Devil from the stall.

"Distraction." With a nod for Manton, who smiled and bowed in return, Devil led the way from the gallery.

Richard ambled in his wake, coming up with him on the pavement. Glancing into Devil's frowning face, Richard raised his brows higher. "Well, you're certainly that."

Devil blinked and focused. "What?"

"Distracted."

Devil grimaced. "It's just that . . . I've forgotten something—something about Tolly's murder."

Instantly, Richard sobered. "Something important?"

"I've an ominous feeling it might be crucial, but every time I try to catch hold of it, it slips back into the mist."

"Stop trying so hard." Richard clapped him on the shoulder. "Go talk to Honoria Prudence—distract yourself some more." He grinned. "Your vital clue will probably come to mind in the most unlikely situation."

Stifling the impulse to inform his brother that it was Honoria Prudence he needed distracting from, Devil nodded. They parted, Richard heading for his lodgings, Devil striding along the pavements toward Grosvenor Square.

In his present condition, the walk wouldn't hurt.

The wind had risen by the time Devil reached his front door in the small hours of the morning. After leaving Richard, he'd returned home only to dress for the evening. Like most of his recent evenings, the past night had been devoted to what, borrowing Honoria's description, he now mentally dubbed "Lucifer's discreditable rumor." It was not something he or his cousins could investigate directly—their views were too widely known. No one would talk openly in their presence for fear of repercussions. Which meant he'd had to find a pawn to do their investigating for them—he'd finally settled on one Viscount Bromley. His lordship was bored, dissipated, a hardened gamester, always on the lookout for distraction.

A renowned cardplayer himself, Devil had found no difficulty in dangling the right lure before his lordship's nose. As of tonight, the viscount was well on the way to losing his shirt. After which, his lordship was going to prove exceedingly helpful. And after that, he'd probably never play piquet again.

Grinning grimly, Devil paused, latchkey in hand; eyes narrowing, he scanned the night sky. It was dark, but not so dark he couldn't see the thunderheads rolling in, lowering blackly over the housetops.

He quickly let himself in. He hoped Webster had remembered his instructions.

The storm broke with an almighty crash.

It flung Honoria straight into hell. Only this time, it was a different hell, with a different scene of carnage.

From above, she looked down on the wreck of a carriage, all splintered wood and crushed leather seats. The horses, tangled and torn, were screaming. Beside the carriage lay the figure of a man, sprawled, long limbs flung in impossible angles. Black locks covered his eyes; his face was pale as death.

He lay unmoving, with the absolute stillness of one gone from this world.

The black misery that welled from Honoria's heart was stronger than ever before. It caught her, effortlessly whirled her, then dragged her down into a vortex of desolation, the vale of unending tears.

He was gone—and she couldn't breathe, couldn't find voice to protest, could find no strength to call him back. With a choking sob, hands outstretched, beseeching the gods, she stepped forward.

Her fingers met solid flesh. Warm flesh.

"Hush."

The nightmare shattered; despair howled, then slid away, slinking back into the darkness, relinquishing its hold. Honoria woke.

She was not in her bed but standing before the window, her feet cold on the boards. Outside, the wind shrieked; she flinched as rain stung the pane. Her cheeks were wet with tears she couldn't recall shedding; her fine lawn nightgown was no match for the room's chill. She shivered.

Warm arms surrounded her, steadied her. Wonderingly, she looked up—for one instant, she wasn't sure which was reality and which the dream—then the heat reaching through his fine shirt registered. With a sob, she flung herself against him.

"It's all right." Devil closed his arms about her; with one hand, he stroked her hair. She was quivering; her fists, tight balls, clutched his shirt. Slipping his hand beneath the heavy fall of her hair, he stroked her nape, leaning his cheek against the top of her head. "It's all right."

She shook her head furiously. "It's *not* all right." Her voice was choked, muffled in his chest. Devil felt her tears, hot against his skin. Gripping his shirt, she tried, ineffectually, to shake him. "You were *killed*! Dead."

Devil blinked. He'd assumed her nightmare concerned her parents' and siblings' deaths. "I'm not dead." He knew that for certain; she was wearing nothing bar a single layer of fine lawn, a fact his rakish senses had immediately noted. Luckily, he'd come prepared. Reaching out, he snagged the blanket he'd left on the window seat. "Come—sit by the fire." She was tense, cold and shivering; she wouldn't sleep until she was relaxed and warm.

"There's no fire—one of the footmen put it out. There's something wrong with the chimney." Honoria imparted the information without lifting her head. She had no idea what was going on; her heart was thumping wildly, sheer panic walked her nerves.

Devil turned her to the door. "In the sitting room."

He tried to set her from him; when she wouldn't let go, he heaved a sigh and draped the blanket about her back and shoulders, tucking it about her as best he could.

Honoria accepted his ministrations meekly—just as long as she didn't have to let go.

She felt him hesitate; he muttered something incomprehensible, then stooped and swung her into his arms. The movement broke her hold; she clutched two fresh handfuls of his shirt and pressed her cheek to his chest, relieved beyond measure when his arms tightened about her. The turbulence inside her was frightening.

As if she was a child, he carried her into the sitting room and sat in a large armchair facing the blazing fire. He settled her in his lap; she immediately curled close, pressing tightly into his hard body. Both chair and fire had changed since she'd retired, a fact she noted, but that was the most minor aspect of the confusion clouding her mind.

Her heart was still racing, high in her throat; her lips were dry. There was a metallic taste in her mouth; her skin felt coldly clammy. Her mind was awhirl, thoughts and fears, present and past, jostling for prominence, demanding responses. Reality and fearful fancy merged, then separated, then merged again, partners in a giddy dance.

She couldn't think, couldn't talk—she didn't even know what she felt.

Devil asked no questions but simply held her, stroking her hair, her back, his large palms moving slowly, hypnotically, yet without any sensual intent. His touch was pure comfort.

Honoria closed her eyes and leaned into his strength; a shuddering sigh escaped her, some of her tension drained. For countless minutes, she lay in his arms, listening to his heart, steady and sure, beating beneath her cheek. Like a rock, his strength anchored her; under its influence, the kaleidoscope of her emotions slowed, then settled—suddenly, everything was clear.

"Your phaeton." Twisting, she looked up at him. "It wasn't an accident—you were meant to die."

The flames lit his face; she could see his frown clearly. "Honoria, it was an accident. I told you—the axle broke."

"Why did it break? Do axles usually break—especially in carriages from the sort of carriagemaker you patronize?"

His lips firmed. "We might have hit something."

"You said you hadn't."

She felt his sigh. "Honoria, it was an accident—the rest is all nightmare. The fact is, I'm alive."

"But you're not *supposed* to be!" She struggled to sit up but his arms firmed, holding her still. "I don't have nightmares about deaths that didn't happen. You were *meant* to be killed. The only reason you're alive is . . ." Lost for words, she gestured.

"I'm a Cynster," he supplied. "I'm invincible, remember?"

He wasn't—he was a flesh-and-blood man, no one knew that better than she. Honoria set her lips mutinously. "If someone tampered with the axle, wouldn't it show?"

Devil looked into her eyes, unnaturally bright, and wondered if sleepwalkers got fevers. "The whole carriage, axle and all, was reduced to splinters." What could he, what should he, say to ease her mind? "Why would anyone want to kill me?"

He realized, instantly, that that wasn't a wise choice. Fighting his hold, Honoria squirmed and sat straighter. "Of course!" Eyes wide, she stared at him. "Tolly—Tolly was coming to *warn* you. Whoever's trying to kill you had to kill him before he did."

Briefly, Devil closed his eyes—in pain. Opening them, he lifted her and resettled her, clamping his arms about her. Then he met her gaze. "You are weaving this from whole cloth—and from the remnants of your nightmare. If you like, we can discuss this in the morning, when you can examine the facts in the cold light of day."

Even in her present state, he could sense the rebellion within her. Her chin firmed, then tilted. Turning her head, she settled back against his chest. "As you wish."

Too wise to take exception to her tone, he waited, patiently, for some of her haughty tension to leave her, then tightened his arms again.

Staring into the leaping flames, Honoria reexamined her new-found certainty and could not fault it. She knew what she knew, even if he refused to see it. He was a Cynster male—he believed he was invincible. She'd no intention of arguing the point, any more than she intended to change her perspective. Her "facts" might not appear all that substantial in daylight, but she wasn't about to deny them.

Her life, her purpose, was now crystal-clear. She knew, absolutely, with complete and utter conviction, precisely what she had to do. He'd challenged her to face her deepest fear; fate was now challenging her to face a deeper truth—the truth of what she felt for him.

She would give him what he asked, all he asked, and more; she would let nothing—*no one*—take him from her. She might be his, but he was hers. Nothing under heaven could change that.

Last time death had threatened those she loved, she'd been helpless, unable to save them. This time, she would not stand by; she would not let any mere mortal steal her destiny from her.

Conviction, total certainty, infused her. Her earlier confusion had passed; she felt calm, in control. Focused. Aware. She frowned. "Why are you here?"

He hesitated, then answered: "You always sleepwalk during storms."

"Always?" Then she remembered the night Tolly died. "In the cottage?"

She felt Devil nod. Safe in his arms, she considered, then shook her head. "That can't be right. It's been eight years since the accident. I haven't woken anywhere other than in my bed and I've slept in so many different houses, through so many different storms." It had only been when violent death had hovered close—at the cottage, and now, in the aftermath of his accident. Honoria mentally nodded, her conclusion confirmed. If death's presence was what evoked her nightmare, then death had stalked him that morning.

Behind her, Devil shrugged. "You walked tonight—that's all that matters. I'll stay until you sleep."

Her gaze on the flames, Honoria raised her brows. And considered that in some detail. Increasingly salacious detail. Then she grimaced. His muscles were locked, not tensed with passion but holding it at bay.

Turning her head, she looked up, into his face, all hard angles and austere planes. Raising a hand, she traced one lean cheek; at her touch, he froze. "I don't suppose you'd consider taking me to bed?"

His jaw locked; flames danced in his eyes. "No."

"Why not?"

Devil met her gaze; when he spoke, his tone was flat. "You're upset—distraught. And you haven't made your decision yet."

Honoria sat up and twisted to face him. "I'm not upset now. And I *have* made up my mind."

Devil winced. Teeth gritted, he lifted her and set her bottom back on his thigh. "I'm not taking you to bed—to wife—purely because you're afraid of lightning!"

Honoria narrowed her eyes at him—his expression was not encouraging. "This is ridiculous." She felt soft, warm and empty inside.

"Forget it." Devil ground the words out. "*Just—sit—still.*"

Honoria stared at him, then uttered a strangled, disgusted sound and slumped back against his chest.

"Go to sleep."

She bit her tongue. In the orangery, she'd surprised him; after the accident, her tending him had simply been too much. He wouldn't again make the mistake of letting her touch him— without that, she stood no chance of getting his body to change his mind.

The warmth surrounding her had unlocked her muscles. Safe, certain—determined to prevail—she slid into untroubled slumber.

She woke the next morning neatly tucked in her bed. Blinking her eyes wide, she was almost at the point of dismissing her memories of the night as dreams when her gaze alighted on the odd blanket draped across the bed's corner. She narrowed her eyes at the inoffensive plaid; her recollections became much clearer.

With a disgusted humph, she sat up and threw back the covers. It was clearly time she had a long talk with his Obstinate Grace of St. Ives.

Gowned appropriately, she swept into the breakfast parlor primed to declare herself won—only to discover he'd left the house early, ostensibly on business. He was not expected to return until shortly before dinner, after which he would escort her to the Theater Royal.

She amended her plans—he invited some country neighbors passing through town to join them in their box. The Draycotts were charming, and utterly unshakable. At Devil's invitation, Lord Draycott accompanied them back to Grosvenor Square, the better to discuss repairs to the Five-Mile fence.

There was no storm that night.

The next morning, Honoria rose early, determined to catch her worm. He didn't even appear, taking breakfast in his library, in the protective presence of his steward.

By evening, she'd reached the end of *her* tether. Why he was avoiding her she had no idea, but his actions left her no choice. There was one approach guaranteed to gain his complete and undivided attention—as far as she was concerned, there was no reason she couldn't employ it.

Chapter 16

*D*onnnnnnng.

Devil spared not a glance for the long-case clock as he passed it on the stairs. Crossing the gallery, he lifted his candle in insouciant salute to his father's portrait, then strode on, into the long corridor that led to his rooms.

His sire, he was sure, would applaud his night's work.

In his pocket lay three notes inscribed with Viscount Bromley's square script. Bromley was already deep in debt, although by how much he was probably unaware. Of course, the last hand had seen the luck change. Devil smiled. He'd have Bromley tied tight in less than a week.

Despite his success, as he drew nearer his door, he tensed; the frustration he continually held at bay exerted its power. An ache settled in his gut; muscle after muscle turned heavy, as if he was fighting himself. Grimacing, he reached for the doorknob. As long as he limited his time with Honoria to public, social venues, he could cope.

He'd told her the truth—he was more than capable of manipulating, coercing, or seducing her into marriage. Indeed, his very nature compelled him to do so, which was why he felt like a wild beast caged. He was a born conqueror—taking what he wanted came naturally. Subtleties, sensitivities, were usually of little consequence.

His expression hardening, he entered his room. Shutting the door, he crossed to the tallboy; setting the candlestick by the mirror on its top, he untied his armband, unbuttoned his waistcoat, then eased the diamond pin from his cravat. Reaching out to lay the pin in its box, his gaze slid past his reflection—white glimmered in the shadows behind him.

His head snapped around. Then, his tread utterly silent, he crossed to the chair by the fire.

Even before he touched the silk, he knew to whom it belonged. The fire, a mere glow of coals, was still warm enough to send her scent rising, wafting upward to ensorcel him. He only just stopped himself from lifting the soft silk to his face, from inhaling the beguiling fragrance. Stifling a curse, he dropped the peignoir as if it was as hot as the fire's coals. Slowly, he turned to the bed.

He couldn't believe his eyes. Even from this distance, he could see her hair, a rippling chesnut wave breaking across his pillows. She lay on her side, facing the center of the bed. The sight drew him like a lodestone. He was beside the bed, looking down on her, before he knew he'd moved.

No woman had ever slept in his bed—at least not during his tenure. His father had been of the stated opinion that a duke's bed was reserved for his duchess; he had agreed—no other woman had lain between his silken sheets. To return late at night to discover those sheets warmed by the one woman he wanted to find asleep there, breathing gently, soft, sleek limbs sunk deep into the down, left him reeling.

He couldn't think.

The realization left him shaking, battling a too-powerful urge to put aside all explanations and react—act—do what he wished with all his conqueror's soul to do.

But he needed to think—to be sure, *certain*, that he wasn't being led by the nose—no, not his nose, but another protuberant part of his anatomy—into committing a deed he would later regret. He'd taken his stance, one he knew was right. Demanding her knowing commitment, heart, mind, and soul, might not be a customary requirement, yet for him, with her, it simply had to be.

His gaze roamed her face, softly flushed, then slid lower, filling in what the sheet concealed. Swallowing a savage curse, he swung away. He fell to pacing, his footfalls cushioned by the carpet. Why the hell was she here?

He cast a glittering glance her way—it fell on her lips, slightly parted. He heard again the urgent, intensely feminine moans she'd uttered in the orangery while writhing beneath his hands. With a muted oath, he paced to the other side of the bed. From there, the view was less torturing.

Three minutes later, he still couldn't marshal a single unlustful thought. Muttering one last, disgusted expletive, he swung back to the bed. Sitting on it was too dangerous, given her hands and her propensity to get them on him. Standing beside the carved post at one end, he reached across and, through the covers, grasped her ankle. He shook it.

She muttered and tried to wriggle free. Devil closed his hand, locked his fingers about her slim bones and shook her again.

She opened her eyes—blinking sleepily. "You're back."

"As you see." Releasing her, Devil straightened. Folding his arms, he leaned against the bedpost. "Would you care to explain why, of all the beds in this house, you chose mine to fall asleep in?"

Honoria raised a brow. "I would have thought that was obvious—I was waiting for you."

Devil hesitated; his faculties remained fogged by seething lust. "To what purpose?"

"I have a few questions."

His jaw firmed. "One o'clock in the morning, in my bed, is neither a suitable nor wise choice of time and venue to ask questions."

"On the contrary"—Honoria started to sit up—"it's the perfect place."

Devil watched the covers fall, revealing her shoulders, clearly visible through translucent silk, revealing the ripe swell of her breasts—"Stop!" His jaw clenched hard. "Honoria, just—*sit—still.*"

Tartly, she hauled the covers up as she sat, then folded her arms beneath her breasts. She frowned at him. "Why have you been avoiding me?"

Devil returned the frown. "I would have thought *that* was obvious. You've a decision to make—I cannot conceive that private meetings between us, at present, would help. They certainly wouldn't help me." He'd intended giving her time—a week at least. The three days so far had been hell.

Honoria held his gaze. "About that decision—you've told me it's important to you—you haven't told me why."

For a long moment, he didn't move, didn't speak, then his folded arms lifted as he drew a deep breath. "I'm a Cynster—I've been raised to acquire, defend, and protect. My family is the core of my existence—without a family, without children, I'd have nothing to protect or defend, no reason to acquire. Given your past, I want to hear your decision declared. You're an Anstruther-

Wetherby—given all I know of you, if you make a declaration, you'll stick by it. Whatever the challenge, you won't back down."

Honoria held his gaze steadily. "Given what you know of me, are you sure I'm the right wife for you?"

The answer came back, deep and sure. "You're mine."

Between them, the atmosphere rippled; ignoring the breathlessness only he could evoke, Honoria raised her brows. "Would you agree that, at present, I'm free of your seductive influence? Free of coercion or manipulation?"

He was watching her closely; he hesitated, then nodded.

"In that case—" She flung back the covers and scrambled across the bed. Devil straightened—before he could move away, Honoria grabbed the front of his shirt, and hauled herself up on her knees. "I have a declaration to make!"

Locking her eyes on his, locking both hands in his shirt, she drew a deep breath. "I *want* to marry you. I want to be your wife, your duchess, to face the world at your side. I *want* to bear your children." She invested the last with all the conviction in her soul.

He'd stilled. She tugged and he moved closer, until his legs hit the bed. He stood directly before her as she knelt, knees wide, on the bed's edge.

"Most importantly of all." She paused to draw another breath; her eyes on his, she spread her hands across his chest. "I want *you*. Now." In case he hadn't yet got her message, she added: "Tonight."

Devil felt desire soar, triumphant, compelling. Excruciatingly aware of her hands sliding as his chest swelled, he forced himself to ask: "Are you sure?" Exasperation flared in her eyes; he shook his head. "I mean about tonight." Of the rest, he had not a doubt.

Her exasperation didn't die. "*Yes!*" she said—and kissed him.

He managed not to wrap his arms about her and crush her, managed to cling grimly to his reins as she wound her arms about his neck, pressed herself to him in utter abandon and flagrantly incited his possession. He locked his hands about her waist, steadying her—then responded to her invitation. She opened to him instantly, her mouth softening, a sweet cavern to fill, to explore, to claim.

She took him in and held him, took his breath, then gave it back. Devil set his hands skimming, fingers firming, thumbs pressing inward at the tops of her thighs. Her nightgown was a mere cobweb of gossamer silk; he let his hands fall, tracing her sleek thighs before closing one hand above each knee. Slowly, he slid his fingers upward, feeling the silk slide over satiny skin, his thumbs drawing lazy circles along her inner thighs. Higher and higher, inch by inch, he raised his hands—the long muscles of her thighs tensed, then locked, then quivered.

He stopped with his thumbs just below her soft curls. Drawing back from their kiss, he watched her—and waited for her lids to rise. When they did, he trapped her gaze with his—and drew two more circles. She shivered.

"Once I take you, there'll be no turning back."

Determination flared, steely blue in her eyes. "Hallelujah."

Their lips met again; Devil loosened his reins. Desire, hot and urgent, rose between them; passion rode in its wake.

Honoria sensed the change in him, felt his muscles harden, felt his hands, still gripping her thighs, tighten. An expectant quiver ran through her tensed muscles. He released them. One hand slid around to spread across her bottom; her skin turned feverish at his touch. He caressed her in slow, sensuous circles—her senses followed, distracted by the silk shifting between hand and naked skin.

Then his hand firmed, cupping her bottom—in the same instant, she felt his other hand slide between her parted thighs.

His head angled over hers; his kiss became more demanding. He stroked her through the gossamer silk, stroked and caressed and teased until the silk clung, a second skin, muting his touch, tantalizing her senses. Honoria tensed, fingertips sinking into the muscles of his back. She felt his hand shift; one long finger slid into her, probing gently, then more deliberately.

Suddenly, she couldn't breathe. She pulled back with a gasp—he let her go, his hands leaving her. Grasping her waist, he toppled her back on the bed.

"Wait."

Devil crossed to the door to his dressing room, opened it, confirmed Sligo had not waited up, then locked it. Striding back across the room, he shrugged out of his coat and threw it on the chair. Flicking the intricate folds of his cravat undone, he tugged the yard-long strip from his neck, then stripped off his waistcoat and sent it to join his coat, before unlacing his cuffs and pulling off his shirt. The flame from the candle on the tallboy gilded the muscles of his back, then he turned and picked up the candlestick.

Sprawled, breathless, across his bed, Honoria watched as he set flame to the two five-armed candelabra upon the mantelpiece. Concentrating on each graceful movement, on the play of the flames over his sculpted frame, she held back her thoughts, too scandalous for words. Anticipation had soared; excitement shivered over her skin. Her lungs had seized; a delicious panic had tightened every nerve.

Leaving the single candle on the mantelpiece, Devil carried one candelabra to the side of the bed, tugging the bedside table forward so that the candles' light fell across the covers. Blinking, aware that in the light she'd appear next to naked, Honoria watched as he placed the second candelabra similiarly on the bed's opposite side. She frowned. "Isn't it usually night? I mean dark?"

Devil met her gaze. "You've forgotten something."

Honoria couldn't think what and wasn't sure she cared; her gaze roamed his chest as he walked toward the bed, bathed in golden light. He stopped by her feet, then turned and sat. While he pulled off his boots, she distracted herself with his back. His cuts and scrapes had healed; she reached out a hand and traced one. His skin flickered at her touch; he muttered something beneath his breath. Honoria grinned and spread her fingers—he stood, casting one black glance back at her before stripping off his trousers. He sat to pull them free of his feet; Honoria stared at the long, broad muscles framing his spine, tailing into twin hollows below his waist. He reached, and muscles shifted; the view was almost as good as his chest.

Free of his last restriction, Devil half turned and fell back on the bed. He knew what would happen—Honoria didn't. With a valiantly smothered shriek, she rolled into him, into his arms, unable to gain any purchase on the slippery sheets. He lifted her over him, her legs tangling with his, her hair fanning over his naked chest.

He expected her to be shocked, expected her to hesitate—this had to be the first time she'd touched a naked male. The shock was certainly there—he saw it in her stunned expression; hesitation followed—it lasted a split second.

In the next, their lips met—there was no longer any distinction between him kissing her and her kissing him. He felt her hands on his chest, greedily exploring; he ravaged her mouth—and felt her fingers sink deep. He spread his hands over the firm mounds of her derriere and held her against him, easing the throbbing ache of his erection against her soft belly. She writhed, heated and eager, thin silk no barrier to his senses.

Some women were catlike, elusively seductive—she was far too bold to be a cat. She was demanding, aggressive, intent on, not just fraying his reins, but shredding them. Deliberately invoking his desire, his demons—all the possessiveness in his soul. Which, given she was a virgin, qualified as abject madness.

Breathing raggedly, he pulled back from their kiss. "For God's sake, slow down!"

Engrossed in caressing one flat nipple, Honoria didn't look up. "I'm twenty-four—I've wasted enough time."

She wriggled; Devil gritted his teeth. "You're twenty-four— you should know better. You should at least have some measure of self-preservation." Intent on impaling herself on her fate, she seemed to have no concept of how much he could hurt her, of how much his strength overshadowed hers, of how much harder than her he was.

She was intent on learning—her hands reached lower, exploring the ridges of his lower chest. Devil felt desire rise, full-blown, ravenous—too strong for her to handle. Releasing her buttocks, he grasped her upper arms.

Just as she grasped him.

The shock that lanced through him nearly shattered his control. He froze. So did Honoria.

She looked into his face—his eyes were shut, his expression graven. Carefully, she curled her fingers again, utterly fascinated by her discovery. How could something so hard, so rigid, so ridged, so blatantly, elementally male, be so silky smooth, so soft? Again, she touched the smoothly rounded head—it was akin to stroking hot steel through the finest peach silk.

Devil groaned; he reached down and closed his hand over hers—not to pull it away but to curl her fingers more tightly. Eagerly, she followed his unspoken instructions, obviously much more to her taste than slowing down.

He let her caress him until he thought his jaw would break—he had to pull her hand away. She fought him, squirming all over him, soft, hot, silk-encased flesh writhing over his by-now-painful erection.

With an oath, he caught her hands, one in each of his, and rolled, trapping her beneath him. He anchored her hands to the bed and kissed her, deeply and yet more deeply, letting his weight sink fully onto her—until she had no breath left to fight him, no strength to defy him.

They both stilled; in that instant, she was open to him, heated, her thighs spread, soft and welcoming, her hips a cradle in which he already lay. All he needed to do was reach down and rip the thin silk from between them, then sink his throbbing staff into her softness and claim her.

Simple.

Gritting his teeth, Devil let go of her hands and lifted away. He moved back. Knees spread, he sat back on his ankles in the middle of the bed. Locking his eyes on hers, he beckoned with both hands. "Come here."

Her eyes widened; they searched his, then fell—jaw locked, he suffered her scrutiny, saw the age-old question form in her eyes.

Giddy, not only from breathlessness, Honoria slowly blinked, then raised her eyes to his face. He looked like some god, seated in the candlelight, his maleness so flagrantly displayed. The soft light gilded the muscles of his arms, his chest—and the rest of him. She drew in a deep breath; her heartbeat thundered in her ears. Slowly, she rose on one elbow, then freed her legs from the folds of her nightgown and came up on her knees, facing him.

He took her hands in his and drew her closer, then closed his hands about her waist and lifted her. As he set her down astride his thighs, Honoria frowned into his eyes. "If you tell me we have to wait, I'll scream."

The planes of his face looked harder than granite. "You'll scream anyway."

She frowned harder—and saw his lips twitch.

"With pleasure."

The idea was new to her—she was still puzzling as Devil drew her closer. High on her knees as she was, her hips grazed his lower chest.

"Kiss me."

He didn't need to ask twice; willingly, she twined her arms about his neck and set her lips to his.

One hand at her back holding her upright, Devil deepened the kiss, skimming his other hand upward, over her taut abdomen, before closing it about her breast. The already heated flesh swelled and firmed; he kneaded and heard her moan. He drew back from the kiss; she let her head fall back, the exposed curve of her throat an offering he didn't refuse. He trailed hot kisses down the pulsing vein; she inched closer, pressing her breast to his palm.

Bending her back, he lowered his head. She stilled, her breathing harried. One long lick dampened the silk covering one nipple. She gasped as his lips touched the ruched peak—he suckled lightly and felt her melt.

He couldn't even remember the last time he'd bedded a virgin—even then, whoever she was, she hadn't been a gently reared, twenty-four-year-old capable of unexpected enthusiasms. He harbored no illusions over how difficult the next half hour would be; for the first time in his lengthy career, he prayed he'd be strong enough to manage—her, and the passion she unleashed in him. Head bent, he tortured one tightly budded nipple, then turned his attention to its mate.

Sinking her fingers into his upper arms, Honoria gasped and swayed. With her bones transmuted to warm honey, her weak grip, his hand at her back and the tantalizing tug of his lips were all that was keeping her upright. Hot and wet, his lips, his mouth, moved over her breasts, teasing first one aching peak, then the other until both were swollen tight. She ached to touch him, to send her hands searching, but didn't dare let go. His lips left her; a second later, his teeth grazed one crinkled nipple.

Sharp sensation lanced through her; she gave a muted cry. His lips returned, soothing her flesh, then he suckled hard—and within her heat rose. Wave upon wave, it answered his call, a primal urge building, swelling, surging ever stronger. With a long-drawn moan, she swayed forward, into his kiss.

It caught her, anchored her, as his hands roved her body, heated palms burning. Every curve she possessed, he traced; every square inch of her skin tingled, then ached for more. Her back, her sides, the curve of her stomach, the long muscles of her thighs, her arms, her bottom—none escaped his attention; her skin was flushed, dewed, when he lifted the edge of her gown.

The shiver that racked her came from deep within, a final farewell to the virgin she was but would be no more. His hands rose and he released her lips. From under weighted lids, Honoria saw the silk in his hands, already above her waist. Dragging in a huge breath that, for all her effort, was insufficient to steady her giddy head, she lifted her arms. The gown whispered from her. It screened the candles as it floated out beyond the bed; she traced its fall, feeling the air, then his hands, on her skin.

His arms closed about her.

Heat, warm skin, hard muscle surrounded her; his crisp mat of midnight black hair rasped her sensitized nipples. Hard lips found hers, demanding, commanding, ravishing her senses—no surrender requested, no quarter considered—he would take her, body and soul, and more.

For one instant, the onslaught swept her before it, then she shuddered in his arms, set her feet against desire's tide—and met his demands with her own. Passion stirred, stretched, unfolded between them; splaying her fingers, she sank the tips into his chest, and felt his muscles lock. She kissed him with a fervor to match his own, reveling in the urgency building between them, glorying in the heady rush, the growing vortex of their need.

Excitement whirled as their lips melded, each breath the other's, tongues entwined. She sank into his heat, drank it in, and felt it flood her. His hands roamed, as urgently demanding as his lips, hard palms sculpting, fingers flexing, possessing. Still on her knees, her thighs locked on either side of his, her hips pressed to his abdomen, she felt his hands curve and cup her bottom. One remained, holding her high, the other slid lower, long fingers questing. They found her heat and slid further, pressing between her thighs, probing the hot, slick folds, caressing, then pressing deep.

And deeper, igniting her fire.

The wild rush of flames seared her; she ached and burned. His only response was to deepen their kiss, holding her captive as the flames roared on. His fingers stroked slowly, deliberately—the flames grew in intensity, to a sheet, then a wall, finally erupting into an inferno, fueled by urgent need.

The inferno pulsed to her heartbeat; the same beat rang in her veins, in her ears, a tattoo of desire driving her on.

Abruptly, Devil drew back from their kiss. His fingers left her; he cupped her bottom with both hands. "Slide down."

Honoria couldn't believe the strength of the compulsion that gripped her—she needed him inside her more than she needed to breathe. Even so . . . She shook her head. "You're never going to fit."

His hands firmed about her hips. "Just slide."

She did, sinking lower, his hands guiding her. She felt the first touch of his staff, hot and hard, and stopped. He slipped his fingers between her thighs and opened her; she felt the first intimate intrusion of his body into hers. Catching her breath on a strangled gasp, she sank lower, and felt the rounded head slip inside.

He felt large, much larger than she'd expected. She sucked in a breath; under the weight of his hands, she sank still lower. Hard as forged iron, hot as unquenched steel, he pressed into her. She shook her head again. "This is not going to work."

"It will." She felt his words within her; he was, if anything, even tenser than she, rock-hard muscles flickering. "You'll stretch to take me—women's bodies are built that way."

He was the expert. Through the maelstrom of emotions besetting her—uncertainty, desire, and giddy need, laced with distant remnants of modesty, all subsumed beneath the most desperate longing she'd ever known—Honoria clung to that fact. The inferno inside her swelled; she sank down.

And stopped.

Immediately, Devil lifted her, not quite losing her clinging heat. "Sink down again." She did, until her maidenhead again impeded their progress. Under his hands, she repeated the maneuver again and again.

She was hot, slick and very tight; once she was moving freely, he brushed his lips against her temple. "Kiss me."

She lifted her head immediately, swollen lips parted, eager for more. He took her mouth voraciously, struggling to harness the wild passion that drove him, battling to remain in control long enough to avoid unnecessarily hurting her. He was going to hurt her enough as it was.

On the heels of the thought came the deed. One, powerful upward thrust, timed to meet her downward slide, enforced by the pressure of his hands on her hips, and it was done. He breached her in that single movement, forging deep into her body, filling her, stretching her.

She screamed, the sound smothered by their kiss. Her body tensed; so did his.

Focusing completely on her, waiting for her softening, the first sign of acceptance that he knew would come, Devil grimly denied the primal urge to lose himself in her heat, to plunder the scalding softness that clasped him, to assuage his driving need.

Their lips had parted; they were both breathing raggedly. From under his lashes, he watched as she moistened her lips with her tongue.

"Was that the scream you were talking about?"

"No." He touched his lips to the corner of hers. "There'll be no more pain—from now on, you'll only scream with pleasure."

No more pain. Her senses awash, overloaded with sensation, Honoria could only hope. The memory of the sharp agony that had speared her was so intense she could still feel it. Yet with every breath, with every heartbeat, the heat of him, the glow suffusing her, eased the ache. She tried to shift; his hands firmed, holding her still.

"Wait."

She had to obey. Until that moment, she hadn't appreciated how completely in his control she was. The hard, throbbing reality that had invaded her, intimately filling her, impinged fully on her mind. Vulnerability swept her, rippling through her, all the way to . . .

Her senses focused on the place where they joined. She heard Devil groan. Blinking, she looked up; his eyes were shut, his features like stone. Under her hands, the muscles of his shoulders were taut, locked in some phantom battle. Inside her, the steady throb of him radiated heat and a sense of barely reined urgency. Her pain had gone. On the thought, the last of her tension ebbed; the last vestiges of resistance fell away. Tentatively, her gaze on his face, she eased from his hold, and rose slowly on her knees.

"*Yes.*" The single word was heavy with encouragement.

He stopped her at the precise point beyond which their contact would break. She sensed his eagerness, the same compelling urgency that welled within her; she needed no direction to sink slowly down, enthralled by the feel of his steely hardness sliding, slick and hot, deep into her.

She did it again, and again, head falling back as she slid sensuously down, opening her senses completely, savoring every drawn-out second. Their guidance no longer required, his hands roved, reclaiming her breasts, the full curves of her bottom, the sensitive backs of her thighs. All awkwardness, all reticence, had vanished; lifting her head, Honoria draped her arms about his neck and sought his lips with hers. The glide of their bodies, uniting in a rhythm as old as the moon, felt exquisitely right. She gave him her mouth; as he claimed it, she tightened her arms, pressing herself to him, drawn to the promise contained within his powerful body, flagrantly demanding more.

He drew back from the kiss; under his lashes, she saw his eyes gleam.

"Are you all right?"

His hands traced mesmerizing circles over her bottom. At the peak of her rise, Honoria held his gaze—and slowly, concentrating on the rigid hardness invading her, sank down.

She felt his rippling shudder and saw his jaw firm. His eyes flashed. Greatly daring, she licked the vein pulsing at the base of his throat. "Actually, I find this quite . . ." She was so far past breathless her words shook.

"Surprising?" His voice was a rumble almost too low to be heard.

Catching a desperate breath, Honoria closed her eyes. *"Enthralling."*

His laugh was so deep she felt it in her marrow. "Trust me." His lips traced the curve of her ear. "There's a great deal more pleasure to come."

"Ah, yes," Honoria murmured, trying desperately to cling to sanity. "I believe you claim to be a past master at this exercise." Dragging in a tight breath, she rose upon him. "Does that make me your mistress?"

"No." Devil held his breath as she sank, excruciatingly slowly, down. "That makes you my pupil." It would make her his slave, but he'd no intention of telling her that, nor that, if she applied herself diligently, the connection might just work both ways.

On her next downward slide, she pressed lower; he nudged deeper. Her breath hitched; instinctively, she tightened about him. Devil set his teeth against a groan.

Eyes wide, she looked up at him, her breathing shallow and fast. "It feels . . . very strange . . . to have you . . . inside me." Breasts rising and falling, brushing his chest, she moistened her lips. "I really didn't think . . . you'd fit."

Devil locked his jaw—along with every other muscle he possessed. After a moment of fraught silence, he managed to say: "I'll fit—eventually."

"Event . . . ?"

Her eyes grew round—he didn't wait for more. He caught her lips in a ravishing kiss and, anchoring her hips against him, tumbled her back onto the pillows.

He'd chosen their earlier position to breach her, placing a limit on how deep he could go, helpful given the force of his instincts. But the time for limits had passed; his swift rearrangement landed her on her back among the pillows, his hips between her thighs, his staff still within her.

She tensed as his weight trapped her; instantly, he lifted his chest and shoulders from her, straightening his arms, his hands sinking into the down on either side. Their kiss broken, her eyes flew open.

He trapped her gaze in his. Slowly, deliberately, he withdrew from her, then, fluidly flexing his spine, he entered her.

Inexorably, inch by inch, he claimed her; heated and slick, her body welcomed him, stretching to take him in. He watched her eyes widen, the blue-grey transmuting to silver, then fracturing as he surged deeper. He sheathed himself in her softness, sinking into her to the hilt, nudging her womb. He came to rest embedded within her; she held him in a scorching silken vice.

Gazes locked, they both held still.

Honoria couldn't breathe, he filled her so completely; she could feel the steady beat of him at the base of her throat. Staring up at his face, she saw the hard planes shift, sharp-edged with reined passion. A conqueror looked down on her, green eyes dark, ringed with silver—the conqueror she'd given herself to. A sense of possession swamped her; her heart swelled, then soared.

He was waiting—for what? Some sign of surrender? On the thought, certainty bloomed within her; a glorious confidence filled her. She smiled—slowly, fully. Her hands had come to rest on his forearms; lifting them, she reached up and drew his face to hers. She heard him groan in the instant their lips met. He came down on his elbows, his hands flicking her hair aside, then framing her face.

He deepened their kiss and her senses went spinning; his body moved on her, within her, and pleasure bloomed.

Like waves piling on the shore, they surged together. Sensations swelled like the incoming tide, rolling ever higher. She caught the rhythm and matched him, letting her body welcome him, holding him tight for a heartbeat before reluctantly releasing him. Again and again they formed that intimate embrace; each time, each devastatingly thorough thrust pushed her higher, further, onward toward some beckoning shore she could only barely perceive. Her mind and senses merged, then soared, locked in dizzying flight. Heat and light spread through her, running down each vein, irradiating each nerve. Then heat changed to fire and light to incandescent glory.

Fed by their striving bodies, by each panting breath, by each soft moan, each guttural groan, the sunburst swelled, larger, brighter, more intense.

It exploded between them—Honoria lost herself in the primal energy, all fire and light and glorious, heart-stopping sensation. Blind, she couldn't see; deaf, she couldn't hear. All she could do was feel—feel him under her hands and know he was with her, feel the warmth that filled her and know she was his, feel the emotion that held them, forged strong in the sunburst's fire— and know nothing on earth could ever change it.

The sunburst died and they drifted back to earth, to the earthly pleasures of silk sheets and soft pillows, to sleepy murmurs and sated kisses, and the comfort of each other's arms.

Devil stirred as the last candle guttered. Even before he lifted his head, he'd assimilated the fact that there was a woman, sleeping the sleep of the sated, more or less beneath him. Before he levered his shoulders away from her and looked down, he'd recalled who that woman was.

The knowledge swelled the emotion that gripped him; his gaze roved her face, gently flushed, swollen lips slightly parted. Her bare breasts rose and fell; she was deeply asleep. Triumph roared through him; smug self-satisfaction swaggered in its wake. With a grin she would probably have taken exception to, had she been in any condition to see it, he lifted from her, careful not to wake her. He'd tried to withdraw from her earlier, before he'd succumbed, but she'd clung to him fiercely and muttered an injunction he'd had insufficient strength to disobey. Despite his weight, she'd wanted to prolong their intimacy, not an aim he could argue against with any conviction.

Their intimacy had been spectacular. Superb. Sufficiently remarkable to startle even him.

He settled on his stomach, feeling her soft weight against his side. The sensation had its inevitable effect; determinedly, he ignored it. He had time and more to explore the possibilities—the rest of his life, in fact. Anticipation had replaced frustration; from the first, he'd sensed in her an underlying awareness, a sensual propensity rare in women of her kind. Now he knew it was real, he would take care to nuture it; under his tutelage, it would blossom. Then he would have time and more to reap the rewards of his control, his care, his expertise, to slake his senses in her, with her—to make her his slave.

Turning his head on the pillow, he studied her face. Lifting his hand, he brushed a stray lock from her cheek; she snuffled, then wriggled onto her side, snuggling against him, one hand searching, coming to rest on his back.

Devil stilled; the emotion that stirred within him was not one he recognized—it stole his breath and left him curiously weak. Oddly shaken. Frowning, he tried to bring it into focus, but by then it had subsided. Not left him, but sunk deep again, into the depths where such emotions dwelled.

Shaking off the sensation, he hesitated, then, very gently, slid one arm across Honoria's waist. She sighed in her sleep, and sank more heavily against him. Lips curving gently, Devil closed his eyes.

When next he awoke, he was alone in his bed. Blinking fully awake, he stared at the empty space beside him in abject disbelief. Then he closed his eyes, dropped his head back into the pillows, and groaned.

Damn the woman—didn't she know . . . ? Obviously not—it was a point of wifely etiquette on which he'd have to educate her. She wasn't supposed to leave their bed until he did—by which time she wouldn't be able to. That was the way things were. Would be. From now on.

This morning, however, he'd have to go for a long ride.

Chapter 17

Success bred success. Late the next night, as he let himself into his hall, Devil reflected on that maxim. He'd successes on more than one front to celebrate; only one major item on his personal agenda remained unfulfilled—and he was making slow progress even there.

Picking up the waiting candlestick, he headed for the library, crossing directly to his desk. A folded letter sat prominently displayed. He broke the plain seal. In the flickering candlelight, he scanned the single sheet, and the enclosures, then smiled. Heathcote Montague, his man of business, had, as usual, delivered the goods.

Devil drew the two notes of hand he'd extracted from Viscount Bromley that evening from his waistcoat pocket and dropped them on the blotter; selecting a key from his watch chain, he opened the middle drawer of the desk, revealing a stack of twelve other notes of hand bearing Bromley's signature. They joined the others—and the six notes discreetly bought by Montague from other gentlemen who, having observed Bromley taking a tilt at him, had been only too glad to convert the viscount's promises to hard cash.

Flicking through the stack, Devil calculated the total, then compared it with Montague's assessment of Bromley's true worth.

It wasn't difficult to gauge where the viscount now stood—in the mire, well on the way to being helplessly adrift on the River Tick. Precisely where he wanted him.

With a satisfied smile, Devil placed both letter and notes back in the desk drawer, locked it, and stood. Picking up the candlestick, he left the library and headed upstairs. To celebrate one victory he'd already won.

The house lay silent about him as he strode swiftly to his room. By the time he reached his door, anticipation had dug in its spurs; he was thoroughly aroused. Opening the door, he stepped through, shutting it behind him, his eyes immediately searching the shadows of his bed.

An instant later, his fist connected with the oak panels; he swore—violently. She wasn't there.

Breathing deeply, he stood stock-still, his gaze on the undisturbed covers, struggling to free his mind of the fog of disappointment, frustration—and a nagging discomfort centerd in his chest. He needed to think. Again.

Crossing to the tallboy, he plunked the candlestick atop it; and scowled at the bed. A familiar tension took hold.

Devil swore. Closing his eyes, he uttered one, comprehensive, utterly applicable oath, then, features hardening, shrugged out of his coat. It took less than a minute to strip. Donning a robe, he glanced down at his bare feet. He hesitated, then cinched the belt of the long robe tight. Cooling his overheated blood might help. Leaving the candle wavering on his tallboy, he closed his door and strode, purposefully, down the dark corridors.

He was finished with thinking. Whatever Honoria's reasons for not being in his bed, waiting, as he'd spent the whole evening fantasizing she would be, he did not wish to know. He wasn't going to argue or even discuss it. But surely not even a well-bred, gently reared twenty-four-year-old barely ex-virgin could imagine that once was enough? That he could survive until their wedding night going on as before—not after he'd sampled her body, her passion, the challenge of her untutored wantonness?

As he marched past his ancestors, Devil cast them a narrowed-eyed look. He left the gallery, then swung left, into the corridor leading to Honoria's rooms.

And collided with a wraith in ivory satin.

She would have bounced off him but he caught her, trapping her against him. His body knew her instantly. Desire lanced painfully through him, her satin-clad curves stroking him to throbbing life as he juggled her. Her instinctive shriek never made it past a first gasp—he stopped it, sealing her lips with his.

Instantly, she relaxed, wriggling her arms free, then twining them about his neck. She pressed closer, kissing him back, flagrantly inciting. She offered her mouth—he took it rapaciously. Swaying seductively, she caressed his chest with her breasts; one arm tightening about her, Devil closed his hand about one firm mound, finding it already swollen, the peak a hard pebble against his palm.

With a gasp, she sank against him, a melting surrender so delicious it left him reeling. Her hands slid beneath his robe, searching out the muscles of his chest, fingers tangling in the crisp hair. Each touch was driven, invested with urgency, the same urgency coursing his veins.

Swallowing a guttural groan, Devil cupped her bottom and drew her hard against him. He lifted her, tilting her hips so his aching erection rode heavily against her. Suggestively, he rocked her, his tongue mimicking the rhythm; she closed her lips and held him, warm and wet, soft and slick.

The deliberate temptation, the flagrant promise in the intimate caress, set his demons raging; the gentle tug as her fingers found the tie of his robe sounded a belated alarm.

Stunned, staggered, his control in shreds, Devil couldn't summon enough strength for even an inward groan. She was going to kill him. The door to his mother's bedroom lay across the corridor.

If she'd been more experienced, he'd have been tempted to do it anyway—to set her bottom on the top of the side table by his mother's door and bury himself between her thighs. The illicit pleasure, knowing they dared not make a sound, would have wound them both tight.

But they were already tight enough—and even if she could handle the position, she would never be able to keep quiet. She'd screamed last night, more than once, an achingly sweet sound of feminine release. He wanted to hear it again—and again. Tonight. Now. But not here.

Breaking their kiss, Devil scooped her up in his arms.

"What—?"

"Sssh," he hissed. His robe had parted; if he'd waited a second longer, she'd have touched him—and God only knew what might have happened then. Striding rapidly down the corridor, he made for her rooms.

Juggling her, he threw open the door to her sitting room and strode through. He turned to shut the door; Honoria wriggled in his hold until she was stretched against him, her arms about his neck. The door locked, Devil turned back—directly into her kiss.

He set her on her feet; relinquishing all restraint, he let his hands have their way. They already knew her—knew her intimately—

and wanted to know her again. The caresses he pressed on her were blatant, expressly gauged to set her need soaring. His followed; in self-preservation he fended off her hands. Their caresses—his successful, hers less so—quickly degenerated into a panting, heated game, rapidly fueling the conflagration that already had them in its grip.

With a sound of keen frustration, Honoria drew back from their kiss. "I want—"

"Not here," Devil ground out. "The bedroom." He took her mouth again; the game resumed, neither willing to break free.

In desperation, with a sound close to a scream, Honoria wrenched away from his roving hands. Her skin was alight, on fire, her body no less so. If he didn't fill her soon, she'd swoon. Grabbing one of his hands, she hauled him to her bedchamber door. Flinging it open, she dropped his hand and entered.

Halting in the pool of moonlight streaming through the window, she faced him; tugging the bow of her translucent over-robe undone, she shrugged the sheer garment from her shoulders. As it pooled at her feet, she held out her hands—Devil had closed the door, then paused. She felt his gaze, hot as the sun, slide over her body, still shielded by soft satin.

Devil kept his hand on the cool metal of the doorknob and clung to the moment like a drowning man. He tried to remind himself about control, and that he'd taken her only once, that she might still be sore, that she would certainly still need time to adjust to his invasion. The facts registered with his conscious mind, the small remnant that still functioned. The rest was centered on her, on the throbbing ache in his loins—on his desperate need to claim her.

Her nightgown was a fascinating creation—solid satin with

slits to her hips. The long line of her legs had showed briefly, tantalizingly, then she'd halted, and the skirts had fallen primly straight—an illusion of virtuous womanhood.

Her fingers flickered in entreaty—slowly, he strolled forward, letting his robe fall to the ground behind him. Naked, he ignored her hands, letting her touch him as she would. With his own, he cupped her face, then, slowly, stretching each moment until they both quivered, he bent his head and set his lips to hers.

He kissed her deeply, ravenously—forcefully—he needed to stay in control. He locked his muscles as her hands slid about his waist. They halted, gripping him as she accepted his kiss, opening herself to it without restraint. Then she slid her hands over his back; she pressed herself briefly against him, then, to his surprise, pulled away. Puzzled, Devil let her go.

Her gaze shadowed, mysterious, she took his hand and led him to the canopied bed. Halting beside it, she faced him; her eyes on his, she raised her hands and opened the shoulder clasps that anchored her gown. It slithered down, revealing the full globes of her breasts, pale ivory in the moon's faint light. The gown gathered at her waist; with a wriggle, she freed it, letting it whisper to the floor.

With no hint of reticence, of coyness or shyness—with a directness that stole his breath and much more—she stepped close. She placed her hands on his ribs, then sent them gliding upward; she stretched sensuously against him, wrapping her arms about his neck, lifting her lips for his kiss, pressing her breasts to his chest, sinking her hips against his thighs. Offering herself to him.

Something inside him shattered.

He reached for her and she was there—he wasn't certain if he'd hauled her hard against him or if she'd pressed closer. Her lips were under his, open and eager; their tongues twined, invoking all the devils of passion that ever were. Nothing else mattered.

Completion, fulfillment, was their only aim—the only thought in their fevered brains. Devil knew his horses had bolted but could summon no will to haul on their reins. She commanded his senses, his strength, every particle of his awareness; her needs, heightening to near frenzy, were the perfect counterpart of his own.

The desire to join flowed strongly through them, a powerful, fiery force. It beat in their veins, found expression in their gasping breaths; it invested each touch, each bold caress, with pleasure so intense it was close to pain.

Pulling back on a gasp, Honoria lifted one knee to the bed; Devil lifted her and placed her upon it, letting her draw him down. He let her feel his weight, reveling in the supple softness of the arms that slid around him, of her body undulating beneath him. She parted her thighs; he drew away only enough to reach down and stroke her, feeling the slickness of her need, the heat of her arousal.

An incoherent plea left her lips; she tilted her hips in unmistakable invitation. Her hands wandered down; they reached his ribs before Devil, settling fully upon her, his hips cradled between her thighs, caught them, one in each of his.

Her eyes, glinting from beneath weighted lids, met his. Deliberately, Devil anchored first one hand, then the other, on either side of her head. He was beyond thought, far beyond any concept of control—the force that drove him, consumed him, compelled him to possess her. Completely. Utterly.

The slick heat between her thighs bathed his throbbing staff; he nudged her thighs wider—she complied, but even in that, she managed to shake him, settling her hips deeper, perfectly positioned for his penetration, letting her thighs relax, leaving herself open. Vulnerable. Inviting him to take her.

The emotion that rolled through him was so powerful, so deep, Devil had to close his eyes briefly, holding back the storm. Opening them, he drew a deep breath, his chest pressing against her breasts, and bent his head to hers.

Their lips met, then melded; their fires ignited. With one powerful thrust, he joined with her—and the conflagration began.

He moved on her, within her; she moved beneath him, about him. Her body caressed him in so many ways, he lost the distinction between him and her. He stroked deeply within her and felt her rise, felt the fiery flight start.

Honoria surrendered to it, to the elemental heat that burned between them. It consumed them, a pure fire that burned away all pretense, leaving only truth and emotion forged in its searing flames. She felt him within her and accepted him eagerly, taking him in, both possessed and possessing. The sunburst rose and drew rapidly nearer; their bodies strove, racing to their fate.

Then it was upon them. It caught them in its heat, in its unquenchable delight, in sensation so exquisite she screamed. She clutched him tightly and he was with her. Locked together, they soared, gasped, then fractured—into a selfless void of aching peace beyond the reach of human senses.

Devil returned to the mortal plane first. Slowly, every muscle heavy with sated lust, he lifted away, then settled the pillows about them. His gaze roamed Honoria's face, serene, softly glowing. Gently, he smoothed her hair, drawing his fingers through the silken mass, letting it slip free to lie across the crisp linen. For long moments, silent and still, he studied her face. Then his gaze drifted down, skimming her body, fair skin glowing in the silvery light.

Seconds later, he reached for the covers, drawing them up to her chin. He settled on his back beside her, one arm behind his head, a frown tangling his black brows.

He was in that pose when Honoria stirred; from under heavy lids, she studied his face, dark features etched by the moonlight. He seemed pensive. Pensive herself, she let her gaze roam the broad expanse of his chest, dark hairs shading its width, each muscle band sharply defined. The covers reached to his waist; beneath them, she could feel the hair-dusted hardness of his leg beside hers.

She smiled, a cat savoring cream. Her skin was warmly flushed, her limbs deliciously weighted. She felt at peace, fulfilled—possessed. Deeply, thoroughly, possessed. Just the thought sent a *frisson* of pleasure through her.

The day was behind her. The unsettling uncertainty which had seized her the minute she'd regained her room after scurrying like a wanton maid through the corridors in the half light of dawn, had disappeared, eradicated by the night's fire. Her lips curved; she could still feel the inner glow. On the thought, she glanced up—Devil was watching her.

His hesitation was palpable, then he shifted, raising a hand to lift a lock of hair from her forehead. "Why weren't you in my bed?"

Honoria held his gaze, even though his eyes were too shadowed for her to see. "I didn't know whether you wanted me there."

Fleetingly, his frown deepened, then eased. But his lips did not curve as, with one finger, he lightly brushed her cheek. "I want you—and I want you there."

The deep words all but shimmered in the moonlight; Honoria

smiled. "Tomorrow." She heard him sigh and saw his quick grimace.

"Unfortunately not." He lay back, his eyes still on hers. "While I'd much rather have you in my bed, until we marry, I'll have to suffer the restrictions of yours." He lifted one foot, demonstrating that even high on the pillows as he was, his feet reached the footboard.

Honoria frowned. "Why can't we sleep in your bed?"

"Propriety."

She opened her eyes wide. "*This* is propriety?" Her sweeping gesture encompassed his naked presence, which took up quite half of her bed.

"You can't be seen wandering the corridors in your peignoir every morning—the servants wouldn't approve. If they see *me* wandering about in my robe, they'll accept the sight with unimpaired aplomb—this is, after all, my house."

Honoria humphed. Wriggling about, she settled on her side, facing away from him. "I suppose you know all the correct procedures."

She felt him shift; a second later, warm limbs surrounded her. The light stubble of his jaw grazed her bare shoulder; his lips touched her ear.

"Believe it." He settled behind her. "And speaking of correct procedures, I should send a notice to *The Gazette*, stating our wedding day."

Honoria studied the shadows. "When should it be?"

He kissed her nape. "That's for you to say—but I'd hoped for December first."

Four weeks away. Honoria frowned. "I'll need a gown."

"You can command any modiste—they'll scramble for the honor."

"Celestine will do." Honoria saw no reason not to avail herself of Celestine's flair just because he'd commanded the modiste's attention.

"All the other arrangements you can leave to *Maman* and my aunts."

"I know," Honoria replied with feeling. "I spent a wretchedly awkward morning—your mother decided to visit the old house-keeper who ran the Place when your parents married. The entire conversation concerned the hows and wheres of arranging a wedding at Somersham."

Devil chuckled. "How did she know?"

"I don't know," Honoria lied. It was, she was sure, her odd, utterly inexplicable blushes that had given her away. "I'll need to write to Michael."

"I'll be writing to him tomorrow—give me your letter and I'll enclose it with mine." Devil studied the back of her head. "Incidentally, I spoke to old Magnus this morning."

Honoria swung about. "Grandfather?" Incredulous, she stared. "Why?"

Devil raised his brows. "He is the head of your family."

"You don't need his permission to marry me."

"No." His lips quirked. "However, the Anstruther-Wetherbys and Cynsters go back a long way. We've been scoring points off each other since the Ark beached."

Honoria studied his face. "How did he take the news?"

Devil grinned. "Philosophically, in the end. He knew you were living within my household, so it wasn't a total shock."

Honoria narrowed her eyes, then humphed and turned her back on him.

Devil's grin dissolved into a smile. Leaning forward, he planted a kiss behind her ear. "Go to sleep—you'll need your strength."

His words held a definite promise. Smiling, Honoria settled her cheek into her pillow, snuggled her back against his chest—and did as she was bid.

The next day, their letters to Michael were duly dispatched. The day after, a notice announcing the marriage of Honoria Prudence Anstruther-Wetherby, eldest daughter of Geoffrey Anstruther-Wetherby and his wife Heather, of Nottings Grange, Hampshire, to Sylvester Sebastian Cynster, duke of St. Ives, appeared in *The Gazette*. The marriage would take place on December 1 at Somersham Place.

Despite the *haut ton*'s preoccupation with departing London, the news spread like wildfire. Honoria gave thanks that the only social events remaining were small, select afternoon teas and "at-homes"—farewells to friends before society adjourned to the shires for the shooting and subsequently to their estates for Christmas. The dustcovers had been placed over the chandeliers—the *ton* was in retreat from London and would not return until February.

As she and Devil had foreseen, his mother and the other Cynster ladies threw themselves into organizing the wedding with undisguised relish. The Dowager warned Honoria that it was family tradition that the bride, while making all the final decisions, was not allowed to do anything—her sole role, according to all precepts, was to appear to advantage and keep her husband in line. Honoria quickly decided there was much to be said for tradition.

Devil watched from a distance, reassured by her readiness to take on the position of his wife. She'd already impressed his aunts; with their encouragement, she took up the matriarchal reins—his mother was ecstatic.

By the end of five whirlwind days, they were ready to leave London; Devil's final chore was to reel in Viscount Bromley.

When the enormity of his losses, the perilous nature of his finances, was fully explained, Bromley, a hardened case, philosophically shrugged and agreed to Devil's terms. He was in a postion to ascertain the truth of "Lucifer's discreditable rumor," to identify the Cynster involved and learn all the facts. All this he agreed to do—by the first of February.

Satisfied, on every count, Devil laid aside his black armband and, with his wife-to-be on his arm, retired to Somersham Place.

Chapter 18

The ballroom at Somersham Place was filled to overflowing. Afternoon sunlight poured through the long windows, striking glints from the curls and coifs of damsels and dowagers, rakes and roué's, gentlemen and haughty matrons. Gowns of every hue vied with bright jewels and equally bright eyes. The full flower of the *ton* was present—to see, to witness, to appreciate.

"She's the last marriageable Anstruther-Wetherby female *and* as rich as bedamned—isn't it just like Devil to have such a pearl fall into his lap."

"*Such* a handsome couple—Celestine designed her gown expressly."

Surrounded by such comments, by felicitations and congratulations, Honoria circulated through the throng, smiling, graciously inclining her head, exchanging the required word with all those who'd come to see her wed.

She was now the duchess of St. Ives. The past months of consideration, the last weeks of frenetic activity, had culminated in a simple service in the chapel in the grounds. The church had been packed, the overflow surrounding it like a jeweled sea. Mr. Merryweather had pronounced them man and wife, then Devil had claimed his kiss—a kiss she'd remember all her life. The sun had broken through as the crowd surged forth, forming a long aisle. Bathed in sunshine, they'd run a gauntlet of well-wishers all the way to the ballroom.

The wedding banquet had commenced at noon; it was now close to three o'clock. The musicians were resting—only six waltzes had been scheduled, but she'd already danced more. The first had been with Devil, an *affecting* experience. She'd been starved of breath by its end, only to be claimed by Vane, then Richard, followed by Harry, Gabriel, and Lucifer in quick succession. Her head had been spinning when the music finally ceased.

Scanning the crowd, Honoria spied Devil talking to Michael and her grandfather, seated near the huge fireplace. She headed toward them.

Amelia bobbed up in her path. "You're to bring Devil to cut the cake. They're setting up the trestles in the middle of the room—Aunt Helena said Devil would toe the line more easily if you ask."

Honoria laughed. "Tell her we're on our way."

Thrilled to be involved, Amelia whisked herself off.

Devil saw her long before she reached him; Honoria felt his gaze, warm, possessively lingering, as she dealt with the continual claims on her attention. Reaching his side, she met his eyes briefly—and felt her tension tighten, felt anticipation streak through her, the spark before the flame. They'd shared a bed for four weeks, yet the thrill was still there, the sudden breathlessness, the empty ache of longing, the need to give and take. She wondered if the feeling would ever fade.

Serenely, she inclined her head, acknowledging her grandfather. At Devil's behest, they'd met briefly before leaving London; focused on her future, she'd found it unexpectedly easy to forgive the past.

"Well, Your Grace!" Leaning back, Magnus looked up at her. "Here's your brother going to stand at the next election. What d'you think about that, heh?"

Honoria looked at Michael; he answered her unvoiced question. "St. Ives suggested it." He looked at Devil.

Who shrugged. "Carlisle was ready to put your name forward, which is good enough for me. With the combined backing of the Anstruther-Wetherbys and the Cynsters, you should be assured of a sound constituency."

Magnus snorted. "He'll get a safe seat, or I'll know the reason why."

Honoria grinned; stretching up, she planted a kiss on Michael's cheek. "Congratulations," she whispered.

Michael returned her affectionate kiss. "And to you." He squeezed her hand, then released it. "You made the right decision."

Honoria raised a brow, but she was smiling. Turning, she met Magnus's eye. "I am come to steal my husband away, sir. It's time to cut the cake."

"That so? Well—lead him away." Magnus waved encouragingly. "I wouldn't want to miss witnessing this phenomenon—a Cynster in tow to an Anstruther-Wetherby."

Honoria raised her brows. "I'm no longer an Anstruther-Wetherby."

"Precisely." Devil met Magnus's gaze, a conqueror's confidence in his eyes as he raised Honoria's hand to his lips. He turned to Honoria. "Come, my dear." He gestured to the room's center. "Your merest wish is my command."

Honoria slanted him a skeptical glance. "Indeed?"

"Indubitably." With polished efficiency, Devil steered her through the throng. "In fact," he mused, his voice deepening to a purr, "I'm anticipating fulfilling a goodly number of your wishes before the night is through."

Smiling serenely, Honoria exchanged nods with the duchess of Leicester. "You're making me blush."

"Brides are supposed to blush—didn't they tell you?" Devil's words feathered her ear. "Besides, you look delightful when you blush. Did you know your blush extends all the way—"

"*There* you are, my dears!"

To Honoria's relief, the Dowager appeared beside them. "If you'll just stand behind the cake. There's a knife there waiting." She shooed them around the table; family and guests crowded around. Their wedding cake stood in pride of place, seven tiers of heavy fruitcake covered with marzipan and decorated with intricate lace. On the top stood a stag, pirouetting on the Cynster shield.

"Good God!" Devil blinked at the creation.

"It's Mrs. Hull's work," Honoria whispered. "Remember to mention it later."

"Make way! Make way!"

The unexpected commotion had all turning. Honoria saw a long thin package waved aloft. Those at the edge of the crowd laughed; comments flew. A corridor opened, allowing the messenger through. It was Lucifer, his mission to deliver the package to Vane, standing before the table opposite Devil. With exaggerated ceremony, Vane accepted the package—a sword in its scabbard—reversing it and presenting it to Devil. "Your weapon, Your Grace."

The ballroom erupted with laughter.

His smile beyond devilish, Devil reached for the hilt. The blade—his cavalry saber—came singing from its sheath. To cheers and all manner of wild suggestions, he brandished it aloft—a piratical bucanneer in the heart of the elegant *ton*.

Then his eyes met Honoria's. One swift step and he stood behind her, his arms reaching around her. "Wrap your hands about the hilt."

Bemused, Honoria did so, gripping the thick-ridged rod of the hilt with both hands. Devil wrapped his hands about hers— Honoria suddenly felt faint.

A deep, soft chuckle sounded in her right ear. "Just like last night."

Last night—when he'd spent the final night of his bachelor-hood with his cousins. Sighting Webster carrying a cask of brandy to the library, Honoria had resigned herself to spending her last night as a spinster alone. She'd retired to her bed and tried to fall asleep, only to discover that she'd become too used to having a large, warm, very hard body in the bed beside her. That same large, warm, very hard body had slipped quietly into her room in the small hours of the morning—and slid beneath the covers. She'd pretended to be asleep, then decided cutting off her nose to spite her face was no fun. She'd made her wishes known.

Only to be informed in a deep, sleepy chuckle, that he was too inebriated to mount her. Fiend that he was, he'd suggested she mount him—and had proceeded to teach her how. One lesson she would never forget.

Only when, utterly exhausted, sated to her toes, she'd collapsed on top of him, only to have him take control, pushing her on, possessing her so completely she had all but lost her mind, had she realized that, in keeping with the rest of their bodies, Cynster males also had hard heads. Not thick, not dense—just hard.

The memories poured through her, leaving her weak. Turning her head slightly, she met Devil's eyes—and was immensely glad she hadn't seen his smugly triumphant smile last night; she was seeing enough of it now. It took immense effort to stiffen her spine and close her hands, beneath his, about the saber's hilt, without recalling what it reminded her of. Drawing a deep breath, she poured every ounce of warning she could into her eyes, then looked at the cake. With his help, she raised the saber high.

The blade came singing down; guiding the swing, Devil drew her back, ensuring the saber cut a neat slice in each of the seven layers. Cheers and clapping erupted on all sides; ribald comments flew.

Her knees weak, Honoria fervently prayed everyone present thought those comments were the cause of her flaming cheeks. She prayed even harder that none bar the reprobate she'd married had noticed just where the rounded knob at the end of the sabre's hilt had finally come to rest. Hemmed in by the crowd behind them, they hadn't been able to move far enough back; the knobbed end of the hilt had slipped into the hollow between her thighs.

And for once, she couldn't blame him—the stillness that gripped him, the quick indrawn breath that hissed past her ear, exonerated him; he was as shaken as she. Their eyes met—were hers as nakedly wanting as his? Carefully, he drew the sword from her slackened grasp and handed it to Vane—then swiftly bent his head and brushed her lips with his. "Later."

The whispered word was a promise; Honoria shivered and felt an answering ripple pass through him. Again their eyes met—they both blinked, both drew breath—and turned aside, putting distance between their overcharged bodies.

In a daze, Honoria did the rounds of her Anstruther-Wetherby relations—the uncles and aunts she'd never known, the cousins who now regarded her with something akin to awe. It was a relief

to return to the Cynster circle, to the warm smiles, openly affectionate, to the reassuring nods and the unflagging support. She
stopped beside Louise; Arthur stood beside her.

Arthur took Honoria's hand. "You make a fine duchess, my
dear." Despite the lines grief had etched in his face, as he raised
her hand to his lips, Honoria glimpsed the debonair, devil-may-
care gentleman he must once have been. "Sylvester's a lucky man."

"I'm sure your nephew appreciates Honoria as he ought,"
Louise put in from between them.

Arthur smiled—a typical, slow Cynster smile. "Never heard
him described as a slow-top." He looked past Honoria. "Ah—
here's Charles."

Honoria turned, regally acknowledging Charles as he joined
them.

"And there's Lady Perry!" Louise put her hand on Arthur's
arm. "Honoria—please excuse us. We must talk to her ladyship
before she leaves."

With a smile for Honoria and a cool "Charles" to his son,
Arthur yielded to his wife's directions and steered her into the
crowd.

Bowing correctly, Charles watched them go, then turned to
Honoria. "I'm glad to have a moment to speak with you, Miss—"
His features hardened. "Your Grace."

Honoria didn't trust his smile. Their subsequent meetings had
not allayed her first instinctive dislike. He was the only Cynster
who affected her so—all the rest she instinctively liked. "I had
hoped to have the pleasure of a dance with you, sir, but I believe
all the dances are done."

He raised a brow, haughty arrogance one of the few Cynster
traits he possessed. "I'm afraid you forget, Your Grace—I'm still

in mourning." He smoothed his black armband. "The others, of course, have forgotten Tolly, but his loss still greatly affects me."

Biting her tongue, Honoria inclined her head. Of all the Cynsters present, only Charles and his father still wore black armbands.

"But I believe congratulations are *de rigueur.*"

Charles's odd phrasing had her regarding him in surprise. He nodded superciliously. "I'm sure you recall the substance of our earlier conversation—in light of the reservations I expressed to you then, I most sincerely hope you do not live to regret your new state."

Honoria stiffened.

Scanning the crowd, Charles didn't notice. "But however that may be, I do wish you well—if knowing Sylvester all his life makes me hesitant as to his constancy, I ask you to believe that that circumstance in no way lessens the sincerity of my hopes for your happiness."

"Yet, if I understand you correctly, you don't believe such happiness likely." Honoria watched as her words sank in—slowly, Charles brought his gaze back to her face. His eyes were pale, cold, oddly expressionless.

"Your actions have been most unwise. You should not have married Sylvester."

Quite what she would have replied to such an outrageous assertion Honoria never discovered—Amelia and Amanda, both still in alt, came rushing up in a froth of muslin skirts.

"Aunt Helena says you should move to the door—some of the guests are starting to leave."

Honoria nodded. From the corner of her eye, she saw Charles draw back.

"By your leave, Your Grace." With a half-bow to her and a curt nod for his half sisters, he turned on his heel and walked off.

Amanda pulled a face at his back, then linked her arm in Honoria's. "He's such a stuffy old shirt—he never enjoys anything."

"Sententious," Amelia pronounced, taking Honoria's other arm. "Now—where should you stand, do you think?"

The short December day drew swiftly to a close; when the clock on the stairs chimed five, it was full dark outside. Standing on the porch by Devil's side, waving the last of the carriages away, Honoria inwardly sighed. Meeting Devil's eyes, she smiled and turned back to the hall. He fell in beside her, capturing her hand, long fingers twining. Most of the family would remain until the next day; they'd retreated to the drawing room, leaving them to do the honors alone. Immediately before the door, Devil halted.

Honoria perforce halted, too, and looked up.

A slow smile greeted her. Raising her hand, Devil brushed a kiss across her knuckles. "Well, my dear duchess?" With his other hand, he tipped her chin up—and up; automatically she rose on her toes.

He bent his head and kissed her, gently at first, then more deeply. When he lifted his head, they were both heated once more.

Honoria blinked at him. "There's dinner yet."

His smile deepened. "They're not expecting us to show." He drew her across the threshold. "This is where we slip away."

Honoria's lips formed a silent "Oh"; the hall, empty but for Webster, busy closing the door, suggested that her husband, as usual, had the procedure right. When he raised a brow, she acquiesced with a nod; calmly serene, she climbed the stairs by his side. They'd retired together often enough in the past weeks for her to feel no qualms.

A state of affairs that lasted all the way to the top of the stairs. That was when she turned right, toward the corridor that led to her rooms.

Devil's hold on her hand brought her up short. She turned in surprise—only to see him lift one brow, his gaze very green. He shook his head. "Not anymore."

Realization hit. Honoria nodded. Head high, outwardly assured, she allowed him to lead her through the gallery, into the corridor leading to the ducal apartments. Inwardly, her nerves had come alive, fluttering in ever-decreasing spirals until they tensed into knots.

It was ridiculous, she told herself, and struggled to ignore the sensation.

She'd been to the duchess's apartments only once, to approve the new color scheme—all rich creams, soft topaz, and old gold, complementing the warm patina of polished oak. Opening her door, Devil ushered her in; Honoria blinked at the blaze that greeted her.

Lighted candelabra graced the dressing table, the mantel-shelf, a chest of drawers, an escritoire against one wall, and a tantalus set before one window. In their glare, the room appeared much as she'd last seen it, with the huge, canopied bed in pride of place between the long windows. The only new items were the urn of flowers, all yellow and white, that sat upon one chest, her brushes, gleaming silver on the polished dressing table, and her nightgown of ivory silk with its matching peignoir, laid out upon the bed.

Cassie must have put it there; Honoria certainly hadn't thought of it. She wondered if the candelabra were Cassie's idea, too—then noticed Devil seemed unsurprised. Strolling into the room, drawing her with him, he stopped before the fireplace, and drew her smoothly into his arms.

Any doubt of his intent fled before his kiss, full of barely restrained hunger and an ardor to set her alight. She sank against him, his instantaneous response driving her to take the pleasure he offered and return it fullfold. Her head was swimming, her limbs turned to water, when he raised his head. "Come. Our children can be born in your bed—we'll beget them in mine."

He swung her into his arms; Honoria twined her arms about his neck. With impatient stride, he carried her to a paneled door, left ajar, shouldering it open, revealing the short corridor that led to his room. "What was that all about?" she asked. "The candelabra?"

Devil glanced down at her; the corridor was dim, but she saw his teeth gleam. "Diversionary tactics."

She would have asked for clarification, but all thoughts of candles went winging from her head as he carried her into his room.

His room in London was large—this room was immense. The bed that stood against the near wall was the biggest she'd ever seen. Long windows marched along both sides and filled the wall opposite the bed; this room was at the end of the wing—with the curtains open, it was flooded with moonlight, turning the pale greens of the furnishings to muted silver.

Devil carried her around the bed, setting her on her feet where the moon cast a shimmering swath across the floor. Her wedding gown, layer upon layer of wide Mechlin lace, sparkled and shivered. He straightened, his gaze drawn to where the lace rose and fell; he cupped one soft mound and felt it firm. His fingers searched, finding the tightening peak and caressing it to pebbled hardness.

Honoria's breath caught; her lids fell as she swayed toward him. Devil supported her against his chest, his hand still at her breast, gently kneading. She shifted restlessly, turning so he could reach her back. "The laces are hidden beneath the lace."

Devil grinned and set to work, one hand caressing first one breast then the other, lips trailing kisses along the side of her throat. When the last knotted lace fell free and the gown, with his help, slithered to the floor, Honoria was soft and supple in his arms, arching back against him. He loved her like this, soft and womanly, abandoned but knowingly so—later, she'd be even more abandoned, but by then she would be beyond knowing anything other than the fever singing in her veins. Reaching around her, he filled both hands with her breasts, covered by a single layer of filmy silk—a low murmur of appreciation escaped her. When he rubbed the ruched peaks between thumb and forefinger, she shifted her hips suggestively against him.

"Not yet," he murmured. "Tonight should be an experience you'll never forget."

"Oh?" The single syllable was breathless. She turned and, twining her arms about his neck, pressed herself against him. "What are you intending to do?"

He smiled, slowly. "Extend your horizons."

She tried to look haughty, but only succeeded in looking fascinated. Devil stepped back, shrugging out of his coat and waistcoat. He let them fall and reached for her. She came into his arms like the siren she was—the siren he'd spent the past weeks releasing from the shackles of convention. She was still wildly innocent in so many ways, yet whatever he taught her she mastered with a wholehearted enthusiasm that sometimes left him weak. From where he now stood, his view colored by experience, the years ahead looked rosy indeed.

He was looking forward to every one of them. Right now, he was looking forward to tonight.

Her lips were open under his, her tongue twining, inciting, enticing. She stretched against him, on her toes, her body shielded only by her fine chemise. Letting desire have its way, he molded her to him, allowing his hands to know her curves again. When he slipped his palms under the back of her chemise, her skin was dewed.

Two heated minutes later, the chemise floated to the ground to puddle, ignored, in the moonlight.

Devil deepened their kiss—Honoria met him, urging and urgent. Her hands slipped from his nape and started to roam, splaying across his chest, then searching through the folds of his shirt to knead the muscles of his back, then firming about his waist, his hips, dropping lower.

Abruptly, Devil shifted, capturing her hands, forcing them to her back, locking them there in one of his. Their kiss unbroken, he drew her hard against him, letting her feel his strength, letting her know the seductive quality of her own vulnerability. He bent her back slightly, over the arm at her waist, her hips pressed hard to his. She moaned, the sound trapped in their kiss, and wriggled—not to win free but to get closer.

The restless shifting of her hips against him was more than he could stand. Breaking their kiss, he scooped her up and deposited her on the silk sheets. She stretched, her eyes on him, her hands questing.

Quickly he drew back, out of her reach. "If you love me, keep your hands to yourself." He'd fantasized about tonight for the past week; if he let her enthusiasm get the better of him—as it had on more than one occasion—he would have no chance of converting fantasy to reality.

Stretching luxuriously, draping her arms above her head, Honoria fixed him with a sultry gaze. "I only want to touch you." She watched as he stripped off his cravat. "You liked it last night."

"Tonight is going to be different."

His eyes left her only momentarily as he pulled off his shirt. Honoria smiled, shifting seductively under the heat of his gaze, relishing the sense of power his fascination with her naked form gave her. He'd made it very plain that he liked seeing her naked, totally nude, without any hint of modesty. Being that naked had been difficult at first, but familiarity and his abiding obsession had built her confidence so that now, being wantonly, wickedly naked with him seemed natural—how it should be—at least between them. "How?" she inquired, as he sat on the bed to remove his boots.

He flicked her a glance, his gaze sliding over her breasts, then down over her stomach and thighs. "Tonight it's going to be my pleasure to lavish pleasure upon you."

Honoria eyed him consideringly. He could make her scream— scream and moan and sob with pleasure. She was the novice—he the master. "Just what are you planning?"

He grinned and stood, unbuttoning his trousers. "You'll see— or rather," he amended, his voice deepening, "you'll feel."

The anticipation simmering in her veins abruptly heightened; Honoria's nerves flickered. That familiar tension had hold of her again, a sweet vise locking tight. A second later, as naked as she, he came onto the bed in a prowling crawl. Elementally male, fully aroused, on hands and knees he straddled her, then lowered his body to hers.

Honoria's breath fled. Eyes wide, she studied his, glittering in the weak light. Then his lids fell and he lowered his head; his lips found hers.

His searching kiss reached deep—deep to where her wanton self dwelled. He called her forth and she came, eagerly seeking his pleasure. She opened to him, enticing him in, her body soft- ening beneath his; she murmured his name and shifted beneath him, but he made no move to claim her. His hands locked about hers, one on either side of her head; as the kiss went on, her skin burned for his touch. Driven, she arched beneath him but his weight held her trapped; his legs outside hers, he held her immobile, granting her no relief from the heat building between them.

Then his lips left hers, trailing hot kisses down the column of her throat. Panting, Honoria pressed her head back into the pillows, eager for much more. He shifted and his lips traced her collarbone, then returned by way of her shoulder and upper breast. He repeated the maneuver, this time following the curve of her arm to her elbow, then on to her wrist, eventually ending with her fingertips.

Tickled by his lips, by the abrasion of his chest and chin against her smooth skin, Honoria giggled; she saw his brow quirk, but he said nothing, merely lifting her hand and draping her arm over his shoulder. He repeated the entire exercise on her other arm, until it, too, went to join its fellow. Locking her fingers at his nape, she settled back expectantly, and waited to see what came next.

His lips on her breasts was a familar sensation, sweet and full of promise. When his mouth fastened over one nipple and he suckled, she gasped; the caress continued, hot and wet, pulsing wildfire down her veins. She moaned, hips restlessly lifting, seeking. But he'd shifted lower; she could make no contact with that part of his anatomy most susceptible to persuasion. Premonition bloomed—his "tonight" would be a long-drawn affair.

He'd told her more than once that she rushed ahead too fast, that, if she let him spin out their time, the sensations would be better—more heightened, more intense. As she could barely cope with what she felt as it was, she wasn't at all sure "slower" was such a good idea. He was used to it—she was not. She wasn't even sure the exercise affected him in the same, mind-dazzling, soul-shattering, heart-twisting way in which it affected her.

His lips left her breasts; panting she waited, then felt him nuzzling beneath their fullness. His lips swept across her sensitive midriff and down to the hollow of her waist.

She was so caught by the novel sensations, by the heated tingling of her skin, that he'd flipped her onto her stomach before she had a chance to protest. He shifted, rising over her then lowering his body along the length of hers. His lips found her nape—he proceeded to cover her back with kisses, soft and warm across her shoulders, changing to soft nips as he worked his way down. Her fires had died to smouldering embers, but when he reached the full swell of her bottom, anticipation exploded into flame again. She squirmed, her breath coming in soft gasps. One heavy arm across her waist kept her still; when he pushed her knees wide apart and held them so, Honoria dragged in a shuddering breath—and waited. He was lying beside her, his weight no longer upon her. Cool air caressed her heated skin; she longed for him to cover her. Expectation welled; she willed him to shift and come between her thighs.

Instead, she felt the soft brush of his hair and the light graze of his stubble as he laid a line of warm kisses down the back of one thigh. He paid homage to the sensitive spot at the back of her knee, first one, then the other, then worked his way back up her other thigh. Honoria slowly exhaled, and waited to be allowed to roll over.

The next instant, her breath hissed in—and in. Her hands clenched on the pillow. In stunned disbelief, she felt tiny tender kisses dot their inexorable way up the inside of one thigh. Her skin shivered and flickered; as the kisses steadily neared the place where she burned, she let out a small shriek, stifled in the pillow.

She felt, rather than heard his deep chuckle. He swung over her and repeated the exercise on the inside of her other thigh. Honoria gritted her teeth, determined not to repeat her shriek; her whole body quivered with mounting need. When he reached the limit of his trail, pressing one last lingering kiss to skin that had never before felt a man's lips, she sighed—then shrieked, as his tongue swept tender, pulsing flesh—just once, but it was more than enough.

He seemed to think so, too; he drew back, rolling her onto her back, his weight pinning her again as his lips returned to hers, his kiss searing, conflagrationary—exactly as she wished it. Wrapping her arms about his neck, Honoria gave him back fire for flame, passion for desire, in a frenzy of escalating need. This time, her thighs were spread and he lay between; she could feel his throbbing staff nudging her thigh.

Abruptly, he drew back, onto his knees. Dazed, she saw him seize a fat pillow. Lifting her, he wedged it under her hips, then, leaning over her, he found her lips again. When he lifted his head she was panting in earnest, every nerve in her body alive, every vein afire. One hand was on her breast; swiftly, he lowered his head and suckled until she moaned.

"Please—now." Honoria reached for him but he shifted back.

"Soon."

He lowered his body to hers again, but too low—his head was at her breasts. He laved each burning peak until she could take no more, then trailed kisses to her navel. He circled the dimple with his tongue, then probed; the slow, repetitive thrusting brought tears of frustration to her eyes. She twisted and arched, her hips lifted high by the pillow.

"Soon." He whispered the word across the sensitive skin of her stomach, and followed it with a kiss. And another and another, slowly descending; when the first kiss fell amongst her soft curls, Honoria's eyes flew wide.

"Devil?"

The sensations streaking through her were unlike any she'd yet experienced, sharper, stronger, fiercer. More kisses followed the first and she gasped, hands reaching, fingers locking in his hair.

"*Oh God!*" The exclamation was wrung from her as his lips touched her softness. The sudden bolt of sensation was enough to melt her mind. "No." She shook her head.

"Soon," came the answer.

His lips left her swollen flesh to trail kisses along the inside of her thighs, lifting them as he slid still lower, draping a knee over each shoulder.

Well-nigh mindless, Honoria felt his breath caress her throbbing flesh. Speech was beyond her; she was going to die. From excitement—from pleasure so intense it was frightening. Gripping the sheets convulsively, she hauled in a huge breath, and shook her head violently.

Devil took no notice. Deliberately, he set his lips to her soft flesh, hot and swollen, intimately caressing each soft fold; a strangled sound, neither shriek nor scream, was his reward. He found her throbbing nubbin, already swollen and tight; he laved it gently, swirling his tongue, first this way then that, about the sensitive spot. He wasn't surprised by the subsequent silence; he could hear her ragged breathing, could feel the tension that gripped her. As usual, she was rushing—he set himself to slow her down, bringing her to that plane where she could appreciate his expertise, savor all he could give her, rather than fly headlong to her fate.

He repeated his caresses, again and again, until she grew familiar with each new sensation. Her breathing slowed, deepened; her body softened beneath his hands. She moaned softly and twisted in his hold, but she no longer fought him; she floated, senses alive to each explicit caress, receptive to the pleasures he wished her to know.

Only then, deploying every ounce of his considerable expertise, did he open the door and introduce her to all that might be. With lips and tongue, he pressed on her caresses that sent her soaring, anchoring her with an intimacy that could not be denied. Again and again, she rose to the heavens; again and again, he drew her back. Only when she could take no more, when her breathing grew frantic and every muscle in her body quivered, begging for release, did he let her fly free, filling her with his tongue, feeling her hands clench tight in his hair—then relax as ecstasy washed through her. He savored her, taking pleasure in the warm piquancy that was her, letting her essence sink to his bones. When the last of her rippling shudders had died, he slowly rose over her.

Pressing her thighs wide, he settled between—with one slow, powerful thrust he filled her, feeling her softness, slick and hot, stretch to take him, feeling her body adjust to his invasion, to being his.

She was fully relaxed, fully open; he moved within her, powerfully plundering, unsurprised when, scant moments later, she stirred and, eyes glinting beneath weighted lids, joined him in the dance. He watched her until he was sure she was with him, then, closing his eyes, letting his head fall back, he lost himself in her.

The explosion that took them from the mortal plane was stronger than any he'd felt before—just as he had known it would be.

Hours later, he awoke. Honoria lay soft and warm by his side, her hair a tangled mass on his pillow. Devil allowed himself a smile—a conqueror's smile—then carefully edged from the bed.

In her room, the candles were still burning. Warmed by recent memory, he padded, naked, to the tantalus before the window. Watered wine had been left waiting, along with suitable sustenance. He poured a glass of wine and swallowed half, then lifted the lid of the serving dish, grimaced and replaced it. He was hungry, but not for food.

On the thought, he heard a sound behind him—turning, he watched Honoria emerge, blinking, from his room. Wrapped in one of his robes, her hand shading her eyes, she squinted at him. "What are you doing?"

He held up the glass.

Lowering her hand, she came forward, holding the robe closed with one hand. "I'll have some, too."

In the garden below all was silent and still. From the distant wilderness, six pairs of startled eyes fastened on the lit window of the duchess's bedchamber, screened by lacy gauze. Six men saw Devil turn and raise his glass in salute; all six lost their breaths when Honoria joined him. The idea of what was happening in that brilliantly lit chamber exercised all six minds.

They watched, breath bated, as Honoria, cloaked in a flowing robe, her hair an aureole about her head, took the glass from Devil and sipped. She handed the glass back; Devil drained it. Setting the glass down, he lowered his head as Honoria went into his arms.

Eyes on stalks, six watched their cousin and his wife share a lengthy, amazingly thorough kiss; five shifted uncomfortably when it ended, then were struck to stillness, paralyzed anew, when Honoria raised her hands and let her robe fall. Her shadow merged again with Devil's, her arms about his neck, his head bent to hers as they resumed their kiss.

Silence filled the wilderness—not even an owl hooted. Then Devil's head rose. His arm about Honoria, their shadows still one, they moved away from the window.

"*God!*" Harry's stunned exclamation said it all.

Richard's eyes were alight. "You didn't seriously imagine Devil married purely to ensure the succession?"

"By the looks of it," Gabriel dryly observed, "the succession's in no danger. If they've got that far in five hours, then St. Valentine's Day's odds-on for our wager."

Vane's deep chuckle came out of the dark. "I hesitate to mention it, but I don't believe Devil started from scratch five hours ago."

Four heads turned his way.

"Ah-hah!" Lucifer turned to his brother. "In that case, I'll sport my blunt on St. Valentine's Day definitely. If he's got a head start, then he'll have more than three months to accomplish the deed—*more* than enough."

"True." Gabriel fell into step beside Lucifer as the party turned toward the house. Their impromptu stroll had been unexpectedly revealing. "Given Devil's reputation, it's fair to assume anyone could guess as much, so we don't need to be overly concerned about taking bets against St. Valentine's Day as the limit for conception."

"I think," Richard said, following in Gabriel's wake, "that we should be rather careful about letting any of the ladies learn about our book—they're unlikely to appreciate our interest."

"Too true," Harry replied, joining the straggling line back through the bushes. "The female half of the species has a distinctly skewed view of what's important in life."

Vane watched them go, then raised his eyes to the blazing windows in the east wing. After a moment, he shifted his gaze to the unlit windows of the large bedroom at the end of the wing.

Silent and still in the dark, he considered the sight, his grin deepening to a smile. Hands in his pockets, he turned—and froze. His eyes, adjusted to the dark, picked out the square figure of a man moving slowly through the wilderness, heading toward the house.

Then the tension left his shoulders. Hands still in his pockets, he strolled forward. "What ho, Charles? Getting a breath of fresh air?"

The heavy figure came to a sudden halt, swinging to face him. Then Charles inclined his head. "As you say."

It was on the tip of Vane's tongue to ask whether Charles had caught the ducal exhibition; Charles's propensity to lecture kept the words from his lips. Falling into step as Charles gained the path back to the house, he asked instead: "You planning to stay for a few days?"

"No." Charles walked a few steps before adding: "I'll be returning to town tomorrow. Do you have any idea when Sylvester plans to return?"

Vane shook his head. "I haven't heard it mentioned, but I'd be surprised to see them up before Christmas. It's to be held here as usual."

"Really?" There was genuine surprise in Charles's voice. "So Sylvester intends to take on the role of 'head of the family' at all levels?"

Vane sent him a cool glance. "When has he not?"

Charles nodded vaguely. "True—very true."

Chapter 19

When, years later, Honoria looked back on the first months of her marriage, she wondered what benevolent fate had ordained they would marry on December 1. The season was perfect, fine-tuned to her needs—December and January, cold and snowy, kept society at bay; the week of Christmas, when the whole family descended, was a happy interlude. Those quiet winter months gave her time to find her feet, to assume the mantle of the duchess of St. Ives, to learn what she needed to go on.

Taking up the reins of the ducal household was of itself easy enough. The staff was excellent, well trained and well disposed; she faced few difficulties there. However, the decisions it fell to her to make were wide-ranging, from cows to flower beds to preserves to linens. Not just for the Place, but for the three other residences her husband maintained. The organizational logistics were absorbing. Within the family, she was expected to play the matriarch, a demanding yet satisfying role.

All this and more fell to her lot in that first December and January, yet throughout that time, the aspect of her life that commanded her deepest attention remained her interaction with Devil.

Quite what she'd expected, she couldn't have said—she had come to her marriage with no firm view of what she wanted from it beyond the very fact of laying claim to the role, of being the mother of his children. Which left, as she discovered during those long quiet weeks, a great deal to be decided. By them both.

Time and again, as their wills crossed in daily life, their eyes would meet and she would see in his an expression of arrest, of calculation, consideration—and know the same emotions were visible in her eyes.

There were adjustments in other spheres, too. Like finding time to be alone, to be easy in each other's company, to discuss the myriad matters affecting their now-mutual life, all within the framework of who they were and what they were and what they could both accept. Some adjustments came easily, without conscious effort; others required give-and-take on both sides.

And if their nights remained a constant, an arena where the lines had already been drawn, where they'd already made their decisions, even there, while their physical need of each other continued, a steady, unquenchable flame, with each night that passed, their involvement deepened, became more profound, more heavily invested with meaning.

By the time January waned and the thaws set in, they were both conscious of, not only change, but the creation of something new, some palpable entity, some subtle web within which they both now lived. They never discussed it, nor in any way alluded to it. Yet she was conscious of it every minute of the day—and knew he felt it, too.

"I'm for a ride."

Seated at a table by one window, a pile of chandler's accounts before her, Honoria looked up to see Devil strolling across the back parlor.

His gaze swept her, then returned to her face. "The going will be heavy—very slow. Do you care to chance it?"

The ice in the lanes and the general bad weather had vetoed riding for the past few weeks. But today the sun was shining—and if he was the one suggesting it, riding had to be safe once more. "I'll need to change." Forsaking her accounts without a second thought, Honoria rose.

Devil grinned. "I'll bring the horses to the side door."

They were away ten minutes later. In perfect amity, they rode across his fields, taking a roundabout route to a nearby rise. They returned by way of the village, stopping to chat with Mr. Postle-thwaite, as ever in the vicarage garden. From there, their route home was via the track through the wood.

Gaining the straight at the top of the rise, they fell silent, slow-ing from a canter to a walk. They passed the spot where Tolly had fallen; reaching the track to the cottage, Devil drew rein.

He glanced at Honoria—halting beside him, she held his gaze. He searched her eyes, then, without a word, turned Sulieman down the narrow track.

In winter, both cottage and clearing appeared very different. The undergrowth was still dense, impenetrable, but the trees had lost their leaves. A dense carpet of mottled brown blanketed the earth, muffling hoofbeats. The cottage was neater, tidier, the stone before the door scrubbed; a wisp of smoke curled from the chimney.

"Keenan's in residence." Devil dismounted and tied his reins to a tree, then came to Honoria's side.

As he lifted her down, she recalled how distracted she'd felt when he'd first closed his hands about her waist. Now his touch was reassuring, a warmly familiar contact. "Will he be inside?"

"Unlikely. In winter, he spends his days in the village."

He secured her reins, and together they walked to the cottage. "Is it all right to go in?"

Devil nodded. "Keenan has no real home—he simply lives in the cottages I provide and keeps my woods in trim."

Opening the door, he led the way in; Honoria followed. She watched as he crossed the small room, his ranging stride slowing as he neared the raised pallet on which Tolly had died. He came to a halt at its foot, looking down on the simple grey blanket, his face a stony mask.

It had been a long time since she'd seen his face that way— these days, he rarely hid his feelings from her. She hesitated, then walked forward, stopping by his side. That was where she belonged—sometimes he needed reminding. With that aim in mind, she slid her fingers across his palm. His hand remained slack, then closed, strongly, firmly.

When he continued to stare at the uninformative bed, Honoria leaned against him. That did the trick—he glanced at her, hesitated, then lifted his arm and drew her against him. And looked frowningly back at the pallet. "It's been six months, and we've not got him yet."

Honoria rested her head against his shoulder. "I don't imagine the Bar Cynster are the sort to accept defeat."

"*Never.*"

"Well, then." She glanced up and saw his frown deepen.

He met her gaze, the tortured frown darkening his eyes. "That something I've forgotten—it was something about *how* Tolly died. Something I noticed—something I should remember." He looked back at the pallet. "I keep hoping it'll come back to me."

The intensity in his eyes, his words, precluded any light reassurance. A minute later, Honoria felt his chest swell, felt his arm tighten briefly about her, then he released her and gestured to the door. "Come—let's go home."

They rode slowly back through the gathering dusk. Devil did

not mention Tolly's killer again; they parted in the hall, he heading for the library, Honoria climbing the stairs, considering a bath before dinner.

Attuned as she now was to his moods, she knew immediately when he returned to the subject. They were in the library, he in a well-stuffed armchair, she on the *chaise*, her embroidery on her lap. The fire burned brightly, warming the room; the curtains were drawn against the night. Webster had supplied Devil with a glass of brandy, then retreated; the Dowager had gone up.

From beneath her lashes, Honoria saw Devil take a long sip of brandy, then he looked at her. "I should return to London."

She looked up, studied his face, then calmly asked: "What information do you have regarding Tolly's death that necessitates our going back now?"

His gaze locked on hers. She held it steadily, calmly, without challenge, even when the green eyes narrowed and his lips compressed. Then he grimaced and leaned back against the chair, his gaze shifting to the ceiling. Setting aside her needlework, Honoria waited.

Devil thought long and hard, then thought again, yet she *was* his duchess—and too intelligent and too stubborn to swallow any glib tale. He lowered his gaze to her face. "Viscount Bromley is currently working for me."

Honoria frowned. "Do I know him?"

"He's not the sort of gentleman you need to know."

"Ah—that sort of gentleman."

"Precisely. The Viscount is currently endeavoring to discover the truth of 'Lucifer's discreditable rumor.' He's due to report next week."

"I see." Frowning, Honoria looked at the fire, then, absentmindedly, gathered her silks. "We have no engagements here—

I'll speak to Mrs. Hull and Webster immediately." She rose, then glanced back. "I assume we'll be leaving tomorrow?"

Devil held her wide gaze for a pregnant moment, then, sighed and inclined his head. "Tomorrow. After lunch."

With a nod, Honoria turned away; Devil watched her hips sway as she walked to the door. When it closed behind her, he drained his glass—and wondered, not for the first time, just what had come over him.

"How far beyond his limit did Bromley go?"

Vane asked the question as he eased into the chair before Devil's desk. Viscount Bromley had left a bare minute before, looking decidedly green.

Locking the viscount's notes of hand back in his desk drawer, Devil named a sum; eyes widening, Vane whistled. "You really did him up in style."

Devil shrugged. "I like to be thorough."

The door opened; glancing up, Devil deduced from the distracted expression in Honoria's eyes that she'd overheard his last remark. His smile when he met her gaze was unambiguously rakish. "Good morning, my dear."

Honoria blinked, then inclined her head regally.

He watched while she exchanged greetings with Vane; she was dressed to go out in a golden merino pelisse, a velvet bonnet with a ruched rim dangling by its ribbons from her hand. The same hand, gloved in ivory kid, carried a muff of golden velvet lined with swansdown; the inner face of her pelisse's upstanding collar was trimmed with the same expensive stuff. Her hair was swept up in a sleek knot—no longer the wild tangle it had been that morning when he'd left her in their bed. The memory raised a warm glow, which he knowingly allowed to infuse his smile.

Tucking the key to the desk drawer into his waistcoat pocket, he strolled, smugly satisfied, to her side. She turned as he approached—and raised her brows. "Did the viscount have the information you expected?"

Devil halted, his eyes steady on hers. He didn't need to look to be aware of Vane's surprise. "As it happens, no. Bromley needs more time."

"And you gave it to him?"

After a fractional hesitation, Devil nodded.

Honoria raised her brows. "If his lordship's so tardy, isn't there someone else you could employ in his place?"

"It's not that simple." Forestalling the question he could see in her eyes, Devil went on: "Bromley has certain attributes that make him ideal for the job."

Honoria looked even more surprised. "I only caught a brief glimpse, but he didn't strike me as the sort to inspire any great confidence." She paused, frowning slightly, looking up at Devil's uninformative face. "Now we're here, couldn't you dispense with Bromley and investigate the matter yourself? There's quite a crowd already in residence; if you tell me what it is you need to know, I might be able to learn something myself."

Vane choked—and tried to disguise it as a cough.

Honoria stared at him; capturing Vane's gaze, Devil frowned.

Witnessing that silent exchange, Honoria narrowed her eyes. "What, precisely, is Bromley investigating?"

The question brought both men's gazes to her face; Honoria met their eyes, read their instinctive response and lifted her chin. Devil eyed the sight for a bare second, then flicked a loaded glance at Vane.

Suavely, Vane smiled at Honoria. "I'll leave you to your questions." She gave him her hand; he bowed over it, then, with a speaking look for Devil, he turned to the door.

As it closed behind him, Devil looked down, into Honoria's eyes. Her expression spoke of unshakable resolve. "You don't need to know the details of Bromley's task."

He would have shifted nearer, but her quiet dignity held him back. She searched his eyes—what she read there he couldn't tell; despite all, he was conscious of admiration of a sort he'd never thought to feel for a woman—he fervently hoped it didn't show.

Honoria straightened, her chin lifting fractionally. "I'm your wife—your duchess. If something threatens *our* family, I need to know of it."

Devil noted her emphasis; she did not look away but continued to face him with unwavering resolution.

The moment stretched, charged, thick with unspoken argument. She was challenging his authority and she knew it—but she would not back down. Her eyes said so very clearly.

Devil narrowed his eyes. "You are an exceedingly stubborn woman."

Haughtily, Honoria raised a brow. "You knew that before we wed."

He nodded curtly. "Unfortunately, that trait was an integral part of the package."

His clipped accents stung; Honoria tilted her chin. "You accepted me—for better or worse."

Devil's eyes flashed. "You did the same."

Again, their gazes locked; after a moment's fraught silence, Honoria, very slowly, lifted an imperious brow. Devil eyed the sight with undisguised irritation—then, with a low growl, gestured to the *chaise*. "The matter is hardly one fit for a lady's ears."

Hiding her triumph, Honoria obediently sat; Devil sat beside her. Briefly, concisely, he told her the essence of Lucifer's rumor—how a number of contacts had reported that a Cynster had been frequenting the "palaces."

"Palaces?" Honoria looked blank.

Devil's jaw set. "Brothels—highly exclusive ones."

Honoria looked him in the eye. "You don't believe it's one of the Bar Cynster."

A statement, not a question; grimly, Devil shook his head. "I *know* it isn't one of us. Not one of us would cross the threshold of such a place." He saw no reason to edify Honoria with details of what transpired at the "palaces"—the worst excesses of prostitution was not something his wife needed to know. "It's possible Tolly attended out of curiosity and, while there, saw or heard something that made him a threat to someone." He met Honoria's eyes. "Patrons of the 'palaces' are necessarily wealthy, most are powerful in the true sense of the word. The sort of men who have secrets to hide and the capability to silence those who learn them."

Honoria studied his face. "Why do you need Bromley?"

Devil's lips twisted. "Unfortunately, the opinions of the Bar Cynster on that particular topic are widely known. The proprietors are careful; none of us could get answers."

After a moment, Honoria asked: "Do you really think it was Tolly?"

Devil met her gaze, and shook his head. "Which leaves . . ." He frowned, then grimaced. "But I believe that even less than that it was Tolly."

They both frowned into space, then Honoria focused—and glanced at the clock. "Great heavens—I'll be late." Gathering her muff, she rose.

Devil rose, too. "Where are you going?"

"To call on Louise, then I'm due at Lady Colebourne's for lunch."

"Not a hint of any of this to Louise—or *Maman*."

The glance Honoria sent him was fondly condescending. "Of course not."

She turned to the door—Devil halted her with one finger beneath her chin, turning her back to face him, tilting her head up. He looked into her eyes, waited until he saw awareness blossom, then bent his head and touched his lips to hers.

As a kiss, it was a whisper, a tantalizing, feathering touch, too insubstantial to satisfy yet too real to ignore.

When he raised his head, Honoria blinked wildly, then she saw his smile and only just stopped her glare. She drew herself up and regally inclined her head. "I will bid you a good day, my lord."

Devil smiled, slowly. "Enjoy your day, my lady."

Throughout her afternoon, Honoria cursed her husband—and the lingering effects of his devilish kiss. Unable to explain the occasional shivers that racked her, she was forced to humor Louise's supposition and drink a glass of ratafia to drive away her chill. Seated on the *chaise* in Louise's drawing room, the twins on footstools at her feet, she grasped the opportunity to air the idea that had taken root in her mind. "I'm thinking of giving a ball." She felt it imperative to publicly stamp her claim as the new duchess of St. Ives—an impromptu ball seemed the perfect solution.

"A ball?" Amanda's eyes grew round. She swung to face her mother. "Will we be allowed to attend?"

Observing her daughters' glowing faces, Louise struggled to hide a smile. "That would depend on whether you were invited and what sort of ball it was to be."

Amanda and Amelia swung back to face Honoria; she pretended not to notice, and spoke to Louise. "I believe it should be an *impromptu* ball—just for family and friends."

Louise nodded. "Not many of the *ton* are yet in residence—it would hardly do for the duchess of St. Ives to hold her first formal ball when fully half of society is still on the hunting field."

"Indeed—tantamount to social indiscretion. A sure way of putting the *grandes dames'* noses out of joint. Too many would be offended if I held my first formal ball now—but an *impromptu* ball should raise no ire."

Louise sat back, gesturing magnanimously. "As business has necessitated your return to town, no one would question your right to a little informal entertainment. And, of course, Helena has yet to come up—you couldn't hold your first formal ball without her."

"Precisely." Honoria nodded; the Dowager had gone to visit friends and was not expected to join them until the start of the Season proper. "And if it's just for friends . . ."

"And family," Louise added.

"Then," Honoria mused, "it could be held quite soon."

Amanda and Amelia looked from one distant expression to the other. *"But will we be invited?"* they wailed.

Honoria blinked and regarded them with apparent surprise. "Good heavens! You've put up your hair!"

Louise laughed; the twins pulled faces at Honoria, then leapt up from their footstools to flank her on the *chaise*.

"We promise to be models of decorum."

"The most proper young ladies you ever did see."

"And we've plenty of cousins to dance with, so you won't need to be forever finding us partners."

Honoria studied their bright eyes, and wondered how they would view their magnificant cousins once they saw them in their true colors, their true setting, prowling a *ton* ballroom. Her hesitation earned her two abjectly imploring looks; she laughed. "Of course you'll be invited." She glanced from one ecstatic face to the other. "But it will be up to your mama to decide if you should attend or not."

They all looked at Louise; she smiled fondly but firmly at her daughters. "I'll reserve my decision until I've spoken with your father *but*, given you're to be presented this Season, an *impromptu* family ball, particularly one at St. Ives House, would be an excellent start to your year."

Expectation took flight; the twins glowed with delight.

Leaving them in alt, already badgering Louise over their ball gowns, Honoria traveled on to Lady Colebourne's town house, to partake of luncheon amidst a host of young matrons. Any lingering reservations over the need for her ball were swiftly laid to rest. Considering gleams appeared in too many eyes at the news that her husband had returned to town, a married gentleman now, far safer, in terms of dalliance, than the unattached rake he used to be.

Smiling serenely, Honoria considered stamping her claim on him, too. Perhaps with a tattoo?—on his forehead, and another relevant part of his anatomy. The *ton*'s bored matrons could look elsewhere for entertainment. Devil was hers—she had to fight an urge to declare the point publicly.

By the time she climbed into her carriage to return to Grosvenor Square, rampant possessiveness had taken firm hold. The strength of the feeling shocked her, but she knew well enough from whence it sprang. Within the *ton*, there was more than one way to lose a husband.

Not since the night of the storm, when she'd woken to find him in her room, had she thought again of losing him. Despite her fears, despite the fact Sligo and Devil's head stableman had shared her suspicions, nothing further had occurred—it now seemed likely that Devil had been right, and the disintegration of his phaeton nothing more than freakish accident.

Staring at the streetscape, Honoria felt a totally unexpected determination well. She recognized it for what it was—it surprised her, but she did not fight it. Too many people had told her that it was her fate to be his bride.

Which meant he was hers—she intended keeping it that way.

Devil lunched with friends, then dropped in at White's. It was their third day back in the capital; despite the acquisition of a wife, the comfortable regime of former days was slowly settling into place. "The only difference," he explained to Vane as they strolled into the reading room, "is that I no longer need to exert myself over the matter of warming my bed."

Vane grinned. Nudging Devil's elbow, he nodded to two vacant armchairs.

They settled companionably behind newssheets. Devil gazed at his, unseeing. His mind was full of his wife and her stubbornness. Quite how he had come to marry the one woman in all the millions impervious to intimidation, he did not know. Fate, he recalled, had arranged the matter—his only option seemed to be to hope fate would also provide him with the means to manage her *without* damaging the subtle something growing between them.

That was unique, at least in his experience. He couldn't define it, could not even describe it—he only knew it was precious, too valuable to risk.

Honoria was also too valuable to risk, at any level, in any way.

He frowned at the newssheet—and wondered what she was doing.

Later that afternoon, having parted from Vane, Devil strolled home through the gathering dusk. He crossed Piccadilly and turned into Berkeley Street.

"Ho! Sylvester!"

Devil halted and turned, then waited until Charles joined him before strolling on. Charles fell into step; he had lodgings in Duke Street, just beyond Grosvenor Square.

"Back to your old haunts, I take it?"

Devil smiled. "As you say."

"I'm surprised—I thought Leicestershire would hold you rather longer. They've had excellent sport, so I've heard."

"I didn't go to the Lodge this season." Manor Lodge was the ducal hunting box. "I went out with the Somersham pack but the runs were hardly worth it."

Charles looked puzzled. "Is Aunt Helena well?"

"Perfectly." Devil shot him a sidelong glance; his lips twitched. "I've had other distractions to hand."

"Oh?"

"I married recently, remember?"

Charles's brows rose briefly. "I hadn't imagined marriage would cause any change in your habits."

Devil merely shrugged. They circumnavigated Berkeley Square, then turned down a alleyway that ran between two houses, connecting the square with Hays Mews.

"I take it Honoria remained at Somersham?"

Devil frowned. "No. She's here—with me."

"She is?" Charles blinked. After a moment, he murmured: "I must remember to pay my respects."

Devil inclined his head, unwilling to commit Honoria to any transports of delight. He knew perfectly well how his other cousins viewed Charles; for his part, he'd always tried for tolerance. They strode on, eventually halting at the corner of Grosvenor

Square. Duke Street lay ahead; Devil was but yards from his door.

Abruptly, Charles swung to face him. "I hesitate to allude to such a delicate matter, but I feel I must speak."

Coolly, Devil raised his brows—and took a firm grip on his tolerance.

"Bringing Honoria to London, so early in her tenure, to require her to countenance your wider liaisons within months of your marriage, is unnecessarily cruel. She may not be experienced in *ton*nish behavior but her understanding is, I believe, superior. She will doubtless realize you're bestowing your interest elsewhere. Women are sensitive to such matters—if you had left her at Somersham, she would not be exposed to such hurt."

His expression blank, Devil looked down at Charles; he'd lost all touch with tolerance—instead, he was battling to keep the lid on his formidable temper. If Charles had not been family, he'd be choking on his teeth. It took concerted effort to keep a snarl from his face. "You mistake the matter, Charles. It was Honoria's wish that she accompany me, a wish I saw no reason to deny." His rigidly even tone had Charles stiffening; his gaze would have frozen hell. "Furthermore, you appear to be laboring under a misapprehension—at present, I have no intention of seeking any 'wider liaison'—my wife holds my interest to the exclusion of all others."

It was the truth, the literal truth, stated more clearly than he'd allowed his own mind to know it.

Charles blinked—he looked stunned.

Devil's lips twisted in chilly self-deprecation. "Indeed—there's more to marriage than even I foresaw. You should try it—I can recommend it as a challenging experience."

With a curt nod, he strode for his door, leaving Charles, blank-faced, staring after him.

Chapter 20

The next morning, as soon as he was free of his most urgent business, Devil climbed the stairs to the morning room.

Honoria looked up as he entered; she smiled warmly. "I thought you'd be busy for hours."

"Hobden's on his way back to the Place." Devil strolled to the *chaise* and sat on the arm beside her. Resting one arm along the *chaise*'s back, he picked up one of the lists from Honoria's lap. "Our guests?"

She peeked. "That's the connections. These are the friends."

Devil took the lists and scanned them. They'd discussed her notion of an impromptu ball the evening before. Reasoning that the exercise would keep her occupied—distracted from Bromley and his doings—he'd readily concurred. "There are a few names you might add."

Honoria picked up a pencil and dutifully scribbled as he reeled off a short list of his own. When he said "Chillingworth" she looked up in surprise. "I thought the earl was no favorite of yours?"

"On the contrary—he's a prime favorite." Devil smiled, one of his Prince of Darkness smiles. "Who would I taunt if I didn't have Chillingworth by?"

Honoria looked her reply but left the earl on the list. Chilling-worth could look after himself.

"I had wondered," Devil said, studying her profile, "if you were free to come for a drive?"

Honoria looked up, her arm brushing his thigh. Her eyes touched his, then she grimaced. "I can't." She gestured to the writing materials on the table. "If the ball's to be next Friday, I need to send the invitations out today."

Devil had never written a ball invitation in his life. He was about to suggest he might learn, when Honoria continued: "Louise is bringing the twins by to help."

With a swift smile, Devil uncoiled his long legs. "In that case, I'll leave you to your endeavors."

His fingers trailed against her cheek as he stood, then he grinned and strolled to the door; Honoria watched it close behind him. She stared at the panels, her expression wistful, then she grimaced and went back to her lists.

The next morning, when the morning room door opened, Honoria looked up with an eager smile. Only to discover it was Vane who sought an audience.

"Devil said I'd find you here." Smiling charmingly, he strolled forward. "I've a request to make."

The gleam in his eye suggested just what that request might be; Honoria eyed it with matriarchal disapproval. "Who?" she asked.

"Lady Canterton. And Harry suggested Lady Pinney."

Honoria held his gaze for a pregnant moment, then reached for her pencil. "I'll send the invitations today."

"Thank you."

"With one proviso." She looked up in time to see wariness creep into his eyes.

"What proviso?"

There was a hint of steel in the question; Honoria ignored it. "You will each dance one dance with each of the twins."

"The *twins*?" Vane stared at her. "How old are they?"

"Seventeen. They'll be presented this year—Friday will be their first ball."

Vane shuddered.

Honoria raised a brow. "Well?"

He looked at her, grim resignation in his eyes. "Very well— one dance each. I'll tell Harry."

Honoria nodded. "Do."

Her next visitors followed in quick succession, all on the same errand. Gabriel succeeded Vane; Lucifer followed. The last through the morning-room door was Richard. "I know," Honoria said, reaching for her much-amended list. "Lady Grey."

"Lady Grey?" Richard blinked. "Why Lady Grey?"

Honoria blinked back. She'd seen him slip away from Horatia's ball with the dark-haired, alabaster-skinned beauty. "Isn't she . . . ?" She gestured with her pencil.

"Ah, no." Richard's grin was reminiscent of Devil at his worst. "That was last year. I was going to ask for Lady Walton."

Ask for—like a treat. And, like a treat, Lady Walton would doubtless fall, a ripe plum into his lap. Honoria decided it was useless disapproving; she added Lady Walton to her list.

"And I dutifully promise to stand up with both Amanda and Amelia."

"Good." Honoria looked up in time to witness Richard's insouciant bow.

"A very good idea, this ball of yours." He paused at the door, a Cynster smile on his lips. "We were all looking for a way to get the Season rolling. Nothing could be better than an *impromptu* ball."

Honoria shot him a warning look; chuckling, he left.

She went on with her planning, trying not to listen for footsteps beyond the door, trying not to wonder whether Devil would drop by to hear of his cousins' selections, to ask her what she was doing, to offer his views.

He didn't.

When she entered the breakfast parlor the next morning, she was pleased to find Devil still present, sipping coffee and scanning *The Gazette*. Her place was now at the table's other end, an expanse of polished mahogany between them. Taking her seat, she beamed a warm smile across the silver service.

Devil returned the gesture, the expression more evident in his eyes than on his lips. Folding *The Gazette*, he laid it aside. "How are your plans progressing?"

Although he'd dined at home the previous night, he'd been preoccupied with business; he had come to bed late, conversation very far from his mind. Between sipping tea and nibbling toast, Honoria filled him in.

He listened attentively, interpolating comments, ending with: "You're setting a new fashion, you know. I've already heard of two other hostesses who are planning early, *impromptu* entertainments."

Smiling radiantly, Honoria shrugged. "Where St. Ives leads, the others will follow."

He grinned appreciatively, then his eyes locked on hers. "I've had the horses brought up from the Place. It's fine outside—I wondered if you'd care to ride?"

Honoria's heart leapt—she sorely missed their private hours. "I—"

"Your pardon, Your Grace."

Turning, Honoria watched as Mrs. Hull bobbed a curtsy to Devil, then faced her. "The caterers have arrived, ma'am. I've put them in the parlor."

"Oh—yes." Happiness deflating like a pricked balloon, Honoria smiled weakly. "I'll join them shortly." The florists were also due that morning, as were the musicians.

Mrs. Hull withdrew; Honoria turned back to meet Devil's eyes. "I'd forgotten. The supper menu needs to be decided today. I won't have time to ride this morning."

With a suave smile, Devil waved dismissively. "It's of no account."

Honoria held back a frown—that smile did not reach his eyes. But she could think of nothing appropriate to say; with an apologetic smile, she stood. "By your leave."

Devil inclined his head, his superficial smile still in place. He watched Honoria leave, then set down his cup and stood. Slowly, a frown replaced his smile. He walked into the hall; behind him, Webster gave orders for the parlor to be cleared. An instant later, he appeared at his elbow.

"Shall I send for your horse, Your Grace?"

Devil focused, and found his gaze resting on the stairs up which Honoria had gone. "No." When he rode alone, he rode early, before others were about. His features hardening, he turned to the library. "I'll be busy for the rest of the morning."

The day of the duchess of St. Ives's impromptu ball dawned crisp and clear. In the park, wispy mist wreathed beneath the trees; shrill birdcalls echoed in the stillness.

Devil rode along the deserted tan track, the heavy thud of his horse's hooves drumming in his ears. He rode with single-minded abandon, fast yet in absolute control, his body and his mount's in fluid concert as they flew through the chill morning. At the end of the track, he hauled the snorting chestnut's head about—and rode back even faster.

Nearing the end of the tan, he eased back, pulling up before a stand of oak. The deep-chested horse, built for endurance, blew hard, and dropped his head. Devil loosened the reins, chest swelling as he drew the air deep.

There was no one in sight, nothing but trees and well-tended lawns. The tang of damp grass rose as the chestnut shifted, then settled to crop. Devil filled his chest again, and felt the cold reach his brain. And, as often happened in this solitude, his unease, the nagging disquiet that had gnawed at him for days, crystallized, clarified. The insight was not encouraging.

The idea that he was irritated because his wife was so busy organizing her ball that she had no time for him did not sit well— yet denying his jealousy, the waiting, the wanting to be with her, was pointless. Even now, he could feel the black emotion roiling inside. Yet he had no justifiable cause for complaint. Duchesses were supposed to give balls. Honoria was behaving precisely as a wife should—she'd made no awkward demands, no requests for attention he didn't wish to give. She hadn't even accepted the attention he'd been only too willing to bestow.

That fact rankled. Deeply.

Frowning, Devil shook his shoulders. He was being unreasonable—he'd no right to expect his wife to be different, to comport herself by some different code—one he couldn't, even now, define. Yet that was precisely what he did want, the desire at the heart of his dissatisfaction.

Unbidden, his mind conjured up that moment when, in his woodsman's cottage, she'd leaned against him. He'd looked down, seen the warmth and understanding in her eyes, and felt her weight, soft and womanly, against him. And realized just how much he now had that Tolly would never have, never have a chance to experience.

He drew a deep breath; the crisp cold sang through his veins. He wanted Honoria—had wanted her from the first—but his want was not quite what he'd thought it. The physical want, the possessive want, the protective want, the need for her loyalty, her commitment—all these he'd fulfilled. What remained?

Something, certainly—something strong enough, powerful enough, to unsettle him, to obsess him, to undermine effortlessly his normally unassailable control. Something beyond his experience.

Brows quirking, he examined that conclusion and could not fault it. Lips firming, he took up his reins. He wasn't going to get any real peace until he fulfilled this want, too.

Both he and the chestnut had cooled. Leaning forward, he patted the horse's sleek neck and dug in his heels. The chestnut obediently stepped out, shifting fluidly into a loping canter.

The bark of the tree before which they'd stood splintered. The sound reached Devil; glancing back, he saw the fresh lesion in the trunk, level with his chest. In the same instant, a telltale "cough" reached his ears.

He didn't stop to investigate; he didn't rein in until he reached the park gate where others were now gathering for their morning ride.

Devil halted to let the chestnut settle. Guns were not permitted in the park. The keepers were exempt, but what would they shoot at—squirrels?

The chestnut had calmed; deadly calm himself, Devil headed back to Grosvenor Square.

The duchess of St. Ives's impromptu ball was an extravagant success. Held, not in the large ballroom, but in the relative intimacy of the music room, the evening overflowed with laughter, dancing, and an easy gaiety not often encountered within the rigid confines of the *ton*.

Many present, of course, were related; the rest were long-standing acquaintances. The tone was set from the first, when the duke and duchess led the company in a vigorous, breathless waltz. All hundred guests took the hint, setting themselves to enjoy the relaxed atmosphere, the champagne that flowed freely, the excellent supper and the similarly excellent company. Some five hours after the first had arrived, the last guests, weary but smiling, took their leave. Webster shut the front door, then set the bolts.

In the center of the hall, Devil looked down at Honoria, leaning on his arm. Lights still danced in her eyes. He smiled. "A signal success, my dear."

Honoria smiled back, resting her head against his arm. "It went very well, I think."

"Indeed." His hand over hers where it lay on his sleeve, Devil turned her toward the library. It had become their habit to end their evenings there, sipping brandy, exchanging comments. They halted on the threshold; footmen and maids were clearing glasses and straightening furniture. Devil glanced at Honoria. "Perhaps, tonight, we should take our drinks upstairs."

Honoria nodded. Devil accepted a lighted candelabrum from Webster; together they started up the stairs.

"Amelia and Amanda were exhausted."

"For quite the first time in their lives."

Honoria smiled fondly. "They danced every dance bar the waltzes. And they would have danced those if they could have." Glancing up, she noted the slight frown marring her husband's handsome countenance; looking forward, she inwardly grinned. The twins' presence had triggered an intriguing reaction in their male cousins—repressive looks had been *de rigueur*. She could foresee certain interesting scenes as the Season unfolded.

The thought reminded her of another interesting scene, one in which she'd participated. "Incidentally, I give you fair warning, I will not again invite Chillingworth if you behave as you did tonight."

"*Me?*" The look of innocence Devil sent her would have done credit to a cherub. "*I* wasn't the one who started it."

Honoria frowned. "I meant both of you—*he* was no better."

"I could hardly let him get away with casting a slur on my ability to satisfy you."

"He *didn't!* It was you who twisted his words that way."

"That was what he meant."

"Be that as it may, you didn't have to inform him that I—" Honoria broke off, cheeks flaming—again. She caught the gleam in Devil's green eyes. Pulling her hand from under his, she pushed him away; he didn't even stagger. "You're *incorrigible*." Lifting her skirts, she climbed the last stairs. "I don't know why you insisted on inviting him when all the conversation you exchanged was a litany of thinly veiled insults."

"*That's* why." Retaking her arm, Devil drew it through his as they crossed the gallery. "Chillingworth's the perfect whetstone to sharpen my wit upon—his hide's as thick as a rhinoceros's."

"Humph!" Honoria kept her chin high.

"I did let him waltz with you."

"Only because I made it impossible for you to do otherwise." She'd used the waltz to separate the two dueling reprobates—unsuccessfully as it transpired.

"Honoria, if I do not wish you to waltz with a particular gentleman, you won't."

She looked up, a protest on her lips. The undercurrent beneath his words registered, she met his eye—and decided it was safer simply to humph again.

When she looked forward, Devil grinned. He'd enjoyed the evening without reservation; even the emergence of the twins as budding Aphrodites couldn't tarnish his mellow mood. As they turned toward the ducal apartments, he slid his arm about Honoria and drew her against him.

Honoria let him, enjoying his nearness. She remained puzzled by his relationship with Chillingworth. While waltzing with Vane, she'd asked his opinion; he'd smiled. "If they weren't so busy being rivals, they'd be friends." Their rivalry, now she'd viewed it at close quarters, was not entirely facetious, yet neither was it serious. From any distance, however, they appeared deadly rivals.

"Is Charles always so subdued?" She'd noticed him watching as she waltzed with Chillingworth; his expression had been oddly blank.

"Charles? Now there's one who won't approve your innovation—unfettered gaiety was never his strong suit."

"Your other cousins reveled in 'unfettered gaiety.' " Honoria cast him a pointed glance. "*Totally* unfettered." Each one of the Bar Cynster, excepting only Devil, had disappeared from the festivities at some point, reappearing later with smug, cat-who-had-found-the-cream smiles.

Devil grinned. "Gabriel tendered his felicitations along with the firm hope that you'll make your impromptu ball a yearly event."

Honoria opened her eyes wide. "Are there really that many accommodating ladies within the *ton*?"

"You'd be surprised," Devil held his door wide.

Honoria threw him a speaking glance, then, nose high, swept over the threshold. But she was smiling as she glided deeper into the room, lit by a fire burning cheerily in the grate. The candelabra held high, dispelling the shadows, Devil crossed to the tallboy, setting the candlestick beside a silver tray holding a crystal decanter and two glasses.

Pouring brandy into one glass, he handed it to Honoria. Warming the glass between her hands, she waltzed to the armchair by the hearth and sank onto its well-stuffed arm. Raising the glass, she breathed in the fumes.

And froze. She blinked. Across the rim of her glass, she saw Devil grasp the second glass, half-full of amber liquid. He raised it.

"*No!*"

Her breathless shout made him turn. But the glass still rose— any second, he'd swallow his usual first gulp.

Honoria dropped her glass; it fell, amber liquid splashing across the jewel-hued rug. Vocal cords paralyzed, she flung herself at Devil, striking the glass from his grasp. It shattered against the tallboy.

"What—?" Devil lifted her, swinging her clear of the shards raining down. White-faced, Honoria clung to him, her gaze fixed on the liquid dripping down the tallboy.

"What's wrong?" Devil stared at her; when she didn't answer, he looked around, then, grasping her arms, set her from him and looked into her face. "What?"

She drew a shaky breath, then looked into his face. She gulped. "The brandy." Her voice was weak, quavery; she hauled in another breath. "Bitter almonds."

Devil froze—literally. The cold started at his feet and spread upward, claiming muscle after muscle until he was chilled through. His hands fell from Honoria as she pressed close, sliding her arms around him, clinging so tight he could barely breathe. Breathing, indeed, was an effort. For one instant, he stopped altogether—the instant when he realized he'd handed her a glass of poison. His gut clenched tight. He closed his eyes, resting his cheek against her curls, closing his arms about her. Her perfume reached him; he tightened his hold, feeling her body, warm and alive, against his.

Suddenly, Honoria looked up, nearly hitting his chin with her head. "You were nearly *killed!*" It was an accusation. Her expression mutinous, she clutched his waistcoat, and tried to shake him. "I told you before—I *warned* you! It's *you* they're trying to kill."

A conclusion he could hardly argue. "They didn't succeed. Thanks to you." Devil tried to draw her back into his arms. Honoria resisted.

"You were one gulp away from death—I *saw* you!"

Her eyes were fever-bright, her cheeks flushed. Devil bit back a curse—not at her, but at his would-be murderer. "I'm not dead."

"But you nearly *were!*" Her eyes flashed blue fire. "*How dare they?*"

Devil recognized shock when he heard it. "We're both alive."

His calming words fell on deaf ears; Honoria swung away and started to pace. "I can't believe it!" She threw out one hand. "This is utterly *wrong!*"

Devil followed as she paced toward the bed.

"I won't allow it—I *forbid* it! You're *mine*—they can't have you." She swung around; finding him close, she grabbed his lapels. "Do you hear?" Her eyes were silver saucers, sheened with tears. "I am *not* going to lose you, too."

"I'm here—you won't ever lose me." Devil slid his arms about her; she was so tense she was quivering. "Trust me."

She searched his eyes; tears spangled her lashes.

"Hold me," he commanded.

She hesitated, then obeyed, slowly unclenching her fists, sliding her arms about him. She rested her head against his shoulder but remained tense, taut—determined.

Framing her jaw, Devil lifted her face, looked down on pale cheeks, at eyes awash with tears, then he bent his head and kissed her set lips. "You'll never lose me," he whispered. "I'll *never* leave you."

A shudder rippled through her. Damp lashes lowered, Honoria lifted her face, offering her lips. Devil took them, then took her mouth. The caress lengthened, deepened, slowly, inexorably spiraling into passion. He needed her—she needed him—an affirmation of life to chase away death's specter.

Honoria drew back only long enough to wrap her arms about his neck. She clung to him, to the vibrant life enshrined in their kiss. His arms locked about her, his chest hard against her breasts, his heartbeat a heavy, repetitive thud reverberating through her. Her defensive tension shifted, transmuted; she pressed herself to him. She answered his kiss and desire rose, not in passionate frenzy, but as a swelling presence impossible to deny. Like rivers unleashed, it welled from them both, merging to a torrent, carrying all thought, all conscious will before it, impelling, compelling, not with need but with the need to give.

Neither questioned its rightness, neither attempted to fight it—a force more than strong enough to deny the deaths they'd faced. Surrendering, to it, to each other, they stripped, barely aware of the clothes they left strewn across the floor. The touch of skin against warm skin, of hands searching, of lips and tongues caressing, played on their senses, feeding the swelling crescendo.

Naked, aroused, they took to their bed, limbs twining, then parting, only to close intimately again. Soft murmurs rose, Devil's deep rumble beneath Honoria's breathless gasps. Time stretched; with freshly opened eyes and heightened senses, they learned each other anew. Devil revisted every soft curve, every square inch of Honoria's ivory skin, every fluttering pulse point, each and every erogenous zone. No less ensorcelled, Honoria rediscovered his hard body, his strength, his perception, his unfailing expertise. His commitment to her fulfilment—matched only by hers to his.

Time suspended as they explored, lavishing pleasure on each other, their murmurs transmuting to soft cries and half-suppressed groans. Only when there was no more left to give did Devil lie back, lifting Honoria over him. Straddling him, she arched and took him in, sinking slowly down, savoring every second, until he was buried deep.

Time fractured. A crystal moment, it hung between them, quivering, invested with sensation. Gazes locked, they both held still, then Honoria let her lids fall. Heart thundering, hearing—feeling—his heartbeat deep within her, she savored the strength that had invaded her, silently acknowledging the power that held her in its coils. Beneath her, Devil closed his eyes, his mind awash with the softness that had accepted him, that now held him so powerfully he could never break free.

Then they moved, their bodies in perfect communion, their souls committed beyond will or thought. Too experienced to rush, they savored each step down the lengthy road, until the gates of paradise opened before them. Together, they entered in.

"Under no circumstances is Her Grace to be left unattended at any time." Devil reinforced that edict with a flat look, trained impartially on the three retainers ranged before him on the library rug.

All three—Webster, poker-straight, his expression more impassive than ever, Mrs. Hull, rigidly upright, lips pinched with concern, and Sligo, his face more mournful than ever—looked uncertain.

Grudgingly, Devil amended: "Other than in our apartments."

That was where Honoria presently was and, if experience was any guide, where she'd remain for a good few hours yet. She'd been deeply asleep when he'd left her—after fully sating his senses and hers; the exercise had left him feeling more vulnerable than he'd ever felt before. But she was safe in their rooms, given the burly footman stationed within sight of the door.

"When I'm absent from the house, Webster, you'll admit no one other than one of my aunts or Vane. If any call, Her Grace is indisposed. We will not be entertaining in the immediate future—not until this matter is resolved."

"Indeed, Your Grace."

"Both you and Mrs. Hull will ensure no one has any chance to tamper with any food or provisions. Incidentally," Devil's gaze fixed on Webster's face, "did you check the rest of that brandy?"

"Yes, Your Grace. The rest of the bottle was uncontaminated." Webster straightened. "I can assure Your Grace I did not fill that decanter with poisoned spirits."

Devil met his gaze directly. "So I had assumed. I take it we've hired no new staff lately?"

Webster's stiffness eased. "No, Your Grace. As is our habit, we brought up more of our people from Somersham to assist last night, hands already familiar with our ways. There were no strangers amongst the staff, m'lord." Fixing his gaze on a point above Devil's head, Webster continued: "Last night, every member of the staff had some prescribed activity they had to perform at virtually any given time." Webster let his gaze drop to meet Devil's eyes. "The long and the short of it is that none of our staff were missing from their duties long enough to have reached your apartments and returned undetected. We must assume, I believe, that some guest aware of the location of the ducal apartments introduced the poison, my lord."

"Quite." Devil had already thought through that point, that and a great deal more; he shifted his gaze to Sligo. "You, Sligo, will accompany Her Grace wherever she goes. If she should decide to walk in public, you will be by her side—not behind her." He met Sligo's gaze levelly. "You're to guard her with your life."

Sligo nodded; he owed Devil his life several times over and saw nothing odd in the request. "I'll make sure no one gets to her. But . . ." He frowned. "If I'm to be with Her Grace, who's to be with you?"

"I've faced death before—this is no different."

"If I could suggest, Your Grace," Webster intervened. "At least a footman—"

"No." The single word cut off all protest. Devil eyed his servitors straitly. "I'm more than capable of protecting myself." His tone dared them to contradict him; naturally, none of them did. He nodded a dismissal. "You may go."

He stood as they filed to the door; Webster and Sligo left, but Mrs. Hull hung back. When, tight-lipped, she looked at him, Devil, resigned, lifted a brow.

"You're not really invincible, you know."

Devil's lips twisted wryly. "I know, Hully, I know. But for God's sake, don't tell Her Grace."

Mollified by his use of his childhood name for her, Mrs. Hull sniffed. "As if I would. You just busy yourself finding whoever was so lost to all proper feeling as to put poison in that decanter—*we'll* look after Her Grace."

Devil watched her leave, and wondered if any of the three had any idea how much he was entrusting to their care. He'd told them true—he'd faced death many times. Honoria's death he couldn't face at all.

"I'm putting my trust in you to ensure that no harm comes to His Grace." Pacing before the morning-room windows, Honoria sent a raking glance over the three servitors lined up on the rug—Webster, Mrs. Hull, and Sligo. "I assume he's already spoken to you regarding the incident last night?"

All three nodded; Webster acted as spokesman. "His Grace gave us orders to ensure no repetition of the incident, ma'am."

"I'm sure he did." Devil had left the house before she'd awoken, an occurrence delayed by him. He'd kept her awake into the small hours—she'd never known him so demanding. When he'd stirred her awake at dawn, she'd applied herself wholeheartedly to appeasing his considerable appetite, assuming, with what little wit she'd been able to command, that it was some long-overdue realization of his mortality that made him so hungry for life.

She'd expected to discuss the shocking incident of the poison with him over breakfast—instead, she'd missed breakfast altogether.

"It is not my intention to counteract any of His Grace's orders—whatever he has decreed must be done. *However*"—

pausing, she glanced at the three faces before her—"am I right in assuming he gave no orders for his own protection?"

Webster grimaced. "We did make the suggestion, ma'am—unfortunately, His Grace vetoed the idea."

"Flat," Sligo corroborated, his tone making it clear what he thought of that decision.

Mrs. Hull's lips thinned to a prim line. "He always was exceedingly stubborn."

"Indeed." From the way all three were watching her, Honoria knew she had only to say the word. The context, however, was somewhat delicate—she could not, in all conscience, contradict her husband's edicts. She looked at Webster. "What was the suggestion His Grace vetoed?"

"I suggested a footman as a guard, ma'am."

Honoria raised her brows. "We have other suitable men in our employ, do we not—men who are not footmen?"

Webster blinked only once. "Indeed, ma'am. From underbutlers to scullery boys."

"And there's the grooms and stablelads, too," Sligo added.

Honoria nodded. "Very well." She met each pair of eyes. "To preserve my peace of mind, you will ensure you are always in a position to tell me where His Grace is at any time while he is absent from this house. Nothing, however, must be done against His Grace's expressed wishes. I trust that's clear?"

Webster bowed. "Indeed, ma'am. I'm sure His Grace would expect us to do all possible to keep you from fretting."

"Precisely. Now, do you have any idea where he is at present?"

Webster and Mrs. Hull shook their heads. Sligo looked at the ceiling. "I believe he said"—he rocked slightly on his toes—"that the Cap'n's with Mister Vane." Lowering his gaze, he met Honoria's eyes. "At his lodgings in Jermyn Street, ma'am." When

Honoria, along with both his peers, looked their question, Sligo opened his eyes wide. "A lad from the stables had to go that way with a message, ma'am."

"I see." For the first time since smelling bitter almonds, Honoria felt a touch of relief. She had allies. "Do you think this stable-lad might still be about his business when His Grace leaves his cousin?"

Sligo nodded. "Very likely, ma'am."

Honoria nodded back, decisively, dismissively. "You have your orders, from both myself and His Grace. I'm sure you will carry them out diligently."

Sligo nodded; Mrs. Hull curtsied. Webster bowed low. "You may rely on us, Your Grace."

Chapter 21

Vane stared at Devil, unfeigned horror in his face. "Just how many attempts on your life have there been?"

Devil raised his brows. "If Honoria's supposition is correct, three. There's still nothing to suggest my phaeton was tampered with, but, given these other two episodes, I'm inclined to think she may be right." They were in Vane's parlor; seated at the table, Devil raised a tankard of ale and took a long sip.

Standing before the windows, Vane was still staring. "The phaeton, the poison—what was the third?"

"Someone took a shot at me in the park yesterday morning."

"You were out early?"

Devil nodded. Vane's gaze blanked; he turned to stare, unseeing, out of the window. Devil waited. After the dramatic events of the night, he felt deadly calm. In between making love to his wife, he'd spent the night thinking. Near death was a wonderful focuser—nearly losing Honoria had eradicated all pretense, exposed all the logical reasons he'd used to justify their marriage as the facade they actually were. What he felt for his wife had nothing to do with logic.

Abruptly, he shifted, and glanced at Vane—then inwardly, mockingly, shook his head. At himself. Whenever his thoughts even touched on that point—that emotion he could not, would not, define—he pulled back, edged away. That unnameable emotion left him feeling so vulnerable he found it near impossible to countenance, to even admit its existence. It opened up a gaping hole in his defenses; his instinctive response was to rebuild his walls with all speed.

But he would have to face it soon. Insecurity lay, a leaden weight in his gut; the uncertainty was driving him insane. Honoria cared for him—last night had proved that. She might even care in the way women sometimes did, at some different level from any sexual interest. On some other plane. He desperately needed to know.

Finding out without asking, without revealing his intense interest in the answer, was a challenge he intended to devote his entire attention to—just as soon as he'd dealt with his would-be murderer.

Who'd very nearly murdered his wife.

He looked up as Vane turned, fixing him with a worried look. "This is more than serious." Vane started to pace. "Why only in London?" He shot a glance at Devil. "There weren't any other suspicious happenings at the Place?"

Devil shook his head. "London because it's safer—more people about. Cambridgeshire is open country, and my fields are rather full of my workers."

"That didn't help us locate Tolly's killer."

Devil looked down, swirling the ale in his tankard.

"To sabotage your phaeton, they had to get into your stables undetected, know which carriage, and how best to make it look like an accident, which presupposes some knowledge of your driving habits. Whoever shot at you in the park must have known you make a habit of riding that early. And whoever put the poison in the decanter"—his expression grim, Vane met Devil's eye—

"whoever did that had to know where the ducal appartments lie as well as your peculiar method of drinking."

Devil nodded. "If they hadn't known that, they'd have been far more circumspect in their dosage—there was enough in one mouthful to fell an ox, which was why Honoria detected it so easily."

"So," Vane said, "whoever it is knew all the above, but—" He broke off and looked at Devil.

Who grimaced. "But didn't know that Honoria shares my brandy as well as my bed."

Vane grimaced back. "Even I didn't know that, so it doesn't help us thin the ranks." He paused, then asked: "So was Tolly killed because he was coming to warn you?"

Slowly, Devil nodded. "That scenario makes sense of what he said at the cottage as well as, if not better, than any other."

Both fell silent, then Vane asked: "What will you do?"

"Do?" Devil raised his brows. "Precisely what I was planning before, only with both eyes fully open."

"*And* with me to cover your back."

Devil grinned. "If you insist."

It was a familiar sally between them; some of Vane's tension eased. He sat in the chair opposite Devil's. "So, has Bromley finally turned up trumps?"

"Not yet—but he thinks he's laid his hand on a winning card. He came by yesterday with the offer of a meeting—the madam in question wanted certain guarantees. I told him what she could have—he's gone off to negotiate time and date."

"Place?"

"The palace itself."

Vane frowned. "You'll go?"

Devil shrugged. "I can see why she'd want it that way."

"It could be a trap."

"Unlikely—she's got more to lose by siding against me rather than with me. And Bromley's too enamored of his comforts to encourage any double-dealing."

Vane didn't look convinced. "I don't like any of this."

Draining his tankard, Devil shook his head. "No—but I'd rather not miss any clue for want of looking." He glanced at Vane. "I still haven't remembered that something I've forgotten about Tolly's murder."

"You're still positive it's something vital?"

"Oh, yes." His expression grim, Devil rose. "It was something so vital I noticed it particularly, but Tolly dying wiped it from my mind."

Vane grimaced. "It'll come back."

Devil met his eyes. "But will it come back in time?"

Firm footsteps approached the morning room; Honoria left the window and sat on the *chaise*. She'd spent the day methodically analyzing the attempts on Devil's life. And had reached the only logical conclusion. While her immediate impulse was to lay her findings before Devil, further consideration had suggested he might not, in this case, accept her conclusion readily. After considerable cogitation, she'd sent a message to the one person she knew he trusted without question.

Her "Come in" coincided with a peremptory knock. The door opened; Vane strolled in. His gaze found her; closing the door, he strolled forward, his gait reminiscent of Devil's prowl. "How are you?"

Honoria grimaced. "Distracted."

He nodded and sat in the chair facing her. "How can I help?" One brown brow rose. "Your note said the matter was urgent."

Lips compressed, Honoria studied his face. "I've been thinking over all that's happened. There has to be a reason someone's trying to kill Devil."

His gaze on her face, Vane nodded. "Go on."

"There's only one compelling reason I know of connecting Devil and a person who would know enough to tamper with his phaeton and put poison in his brandy. The inheritance—which, after all, is more than considerable. That might also explain why the attacks only started after it became obvious we would wed."

Light dawned in Vane's face. "Of course. I've been concentrating on Tolly—I didn't think of that angle."

"You agree?" Honoria leaned forward. "You agree it must be Richard?"

Vane stared in blank astonishment. "Richard?"

Honoria frowned. "Devil's heir."

"Ah." Swiftly, Vane searched her face. "Honoria, your logic's impeccable—unfortunately, Devil's neglected to give you all the details necessary to arrive at the correct outcome." He hesitated, then shook his head. "I'm sorry, but it's not my place to explain—you'll have to ask Devil."

Honoria eyed him straitly. "Ask him *what*?"

Vane's eyes turned hard. "Ask him who his heir is."

"It's not Richard?"

Lips compressed, Vane rose. "I must go—but promise me you'll tell Devil your conclusions."

Honoria's eyes flashed. "I can give you an absolute assurrance on that point."

"Good." Vane met her gaze. "If it makes it any easier, I'd wager he's already followed the same train of thought."

"You think he knows?" Honoria held out her hand.

"He knows, but, as he does with such matters, he won't say

until he's sure—until he has proof." Vane released Honoria's hand. "By your leave, I've an idea to pursue—the sooner we get your husband the proof he requires, the sooner we'll be free of this murderer."

Unwilling to do anything to delay that outcome, Honoria nodded and let him go. Long after the door had closed behind him, she sat staring at the panels, unable to make head or tail of what was going on.

Cynsters—a law unto themselves. With a disgusted humph, she stood and headed upstairs to change.

His Grace of St. Ives dined at home that evening. Honoria waited until they retired, then stripped off her gown, donned her night-gown, scurried like an eager chambermaid into the ducal chamber, dropped her peignoir, kicked off her slippers, and scrambled beneath the covers.

From the other side of the room, engaged in untying his cravat, Devil watched her performance with interest—an interest she ignored. Propped against the pillows, she fixed her gaze on his face. "I've been thinking."

Devil's hands stilled, then he drew the white linen from about his throat. Unbuttoning his waistcoat, he approached the bed. "What about?"

"About who would want you dead."

He shrugged out of his waistcoat, then sat on the bed to pull off his boots. "Did you reach any conclusion?"

"Yes—but Vane told me my conclusion wasn't right."

Devil looked up. "Vane?"

Honoria explained. "Naturally, I thought your heir was Richard."

"Ah." Devil dropped his second boot. He stood, stripped off

his shirt and trousers, then slid beneath the covers. Honoria tumbled against him; he settled her beside him. "I suppose I should have told you about that."

Honoria squinted through the shadows; she was almost sure he was grinning. "I suspect you should have. What is it I don't know?"

Devil lay back against the pillows. "You know Richard's nickname?"

"Scandal?"

Devil nodded. "Like mine being a shortened form of 'That Devil Cynster,' Richard's is also a truncation. His full sobriquet is 'The Scandal That Never Was.' "

"*He's* a scandal?"

"Richard's my brother, but he's not my mother's son."

Honoria blinked. "Ah." Then she frowned. "But you look so alike."

"We look like my father—you've seen his portrait. Only our coloring, and in my case my eyes, come from our respective mothers—Richard's was also dark-haired."

This was scandal on a major scale—Richard was younger than Devil. Yet Honoria had detected not the slightest whiff of disapprobation in any of the *ton*'s dealings with Richard Cynster. "I don't understand." She looked up in time to see Devil's teeth gleam.

"The truth of Richard's birth has been an open secret for three decades—it's very old news. *Maman*, of course, is the key."

Honoria crossed her arms on his chest and fixed her gaze on his face. "Tell me."

Devil settled his arms about her. "When I was three, my father was asked to undertake a diplomatic mission to the Highlands. There'd been an outbreak of dissaffection and the Court boffins

wanted to rattle sabers without sending troops. Sending a Cynster was considered the next best thing. *Maman* decided not to
accompany him. She was told at my birth that she wouldn't be
able to have more children, so she was hideously overprotective
of me, much to my disgust. So m'father went north alone. The
laird he was sent to . . ." He paused, searching for words.

"Intimidate?" Honoria suggested.

Devil nodded. "This laird, a redhead, had recently married—
an arranged marriage with a lowlands beauty."

"She would be a beauty," Honoria muttered.

Devil glanced at her. "We Cynsters have standards, you know."

Honoria humphed and poked his chest. "What happened next."

"Strangely enough, we're not entirely sure. We do know my
father's mission was a success; he was home within four weeks.
Richard appeared twelve months later."

"*Twelve* months?"

"His mother died a few months after his birth. Whether she
confessed or whether her husband simply assumed from his coloring that Richard was none of his, we don't know. But there was
no doubt, even then, that Richard was my father's—he looked
exactly like me at the same age, and there were enough about
who remembered. Whatever, Richard's fate was sealed when
Webster picked him up from before the front door—a carriage
had driven up, the wrapped bundle deposited, and the horses
whipped up immediately. No message—just Richard. Webster
carried him in and Richard immediately started squalling.

"The sound was *horrendous*—I remember because I hadn't
heard it before. *Maman* was brushing my hair in the nursery—we
heard it all the way up there. She dropped the brush and rushed
downstairs. She beat me down. I reached the last landing to see
her descend on Webster and my father, who were trying to hush

Richard. *Maman* plucked him out of their arms—she cooed and Richard stopped crying. She just smiled—brilliantly—you know how she can."

Her chin on his chest, Honoria nodded.

"I realized immediately that Richard was a godsend—*Maman* was so caught up with him she forgot about the knots in my hair. From that moment, Richard had my full support. My father came up—I think he was about to attempt an explanation— in retrospect I'm sorry I didn't hear it, even if I wouldn't have understood it then. But *Maman* immediately told him how immensely clever he was to have provided her with the one, truly most important thing she wanted—another son. Naturally, he kept quiet. From there on, *Maman* rolled over any objections— she'd been my father's duchess for five years and was an eminent social power. She publicly decreed Richard was her son—none were game, then or now, to contradict her." Honoria heard the smile in his voice.

"There's no doubt that having Richard to rear really did make *Maman* happy. The matter caused no one any harm; my father acknowledged him and made provision for him in his will." Devil drew a deep breath. "And that's the story of The Scandal That Never Was."

Honoria lay still; Devil's hand stroked her hair. "So now you know Richard's not my heir." His hand slid to her nape. "He's not the one trying to kill me."

Honoria listened to the steady thud of his heart. She was glad it wasn't Richard—she liked him, and knew Devil was fond of him. Without lifting her head, she murmured: "Your mother's a fascinating woman."

Devil rolled, rolling her under him; on his elbows, he brushed her hair from her face. "She certainly fascinated my father." Honoria felt his eyes on her face, then his head dipped. His lips brushed hers. "Just as my duchess fascinates me."

They were the last logical words said that night.

She needed to have a long, serious talk with her husband. Clad in a translucent ivory peignoir trimmed with feathers, Honoria paced the ducal bedchamber and waited for him to appear.

They'd met at breakfast and again at dinner, but she could hardly interrogate him in front of the servants. He was presently at White's, meeting with Viscount Bromley. That much she knew, that much he'd told her. What he hadn't told her was what he thought, who he suspected.

As Richard was illegitimate, he couldn't inherit, not with so many legitimate males in the family. After learning how Scandal had come by his name, she hadn't needed to ask who Devil's heir was. In the weeks before their marriage, she'd questioned Horatia about Devil's father—in passing, Horatia had mentioned that George, her husband, Vane's father, was a bare year younger than Devil's father. Which meant that, with Richard ineligible, George was Devil's heir, with Vane next in line.

Not in her wildest dreams could she imagine George as the villain of the piece. Devil treated him as a surrogate father, an affection George openly returned. And Vane's devotion to Devil was beyond question. So the killer wasn't Devil's heir, but as soon as she'd drawn Vane's attention to the point, he'd seen a blinding light.

With a frustrated growl, Honoria kicked her feathered hem aside. "So what is it about the heir that makes all obvious?"

Devil knew; Vane was sure he'd followed the same reasoning

and come up with an answer. Presumably, as it wasn't the heir, some process of elimination illuminated the true killer. Who was . . .

Honoria glared at the clock. And tried not to think of the other reason she was pacing, eager to set eyes on her husband again. Someone was trying to kill him. This house was a safe haven; he was safe here. But outside . . . ?

She wanted him here, safe in her arms.

Honoria shivered; she wrapped her arms about her and, frowning, looked at the clock again. Lips setting, she made for the door. Opening it, she listened; as the clock on the mantel had correctly foretold, the clock on the stairs whirred, then chimed. Twelve deep booms resonated through the house. Midnight—and Devil was still not back.

She was closing the door when the front knocker sounded—a curt, peremptory summons. Honoria paused, her frown deepening. Who would come calling at midnight? Devil had a latchkey, so . . .

The blood drained from her face. Her heart stuttered, then started to race. She was halfway down the corridor before she realized she'd moved. Then she picked up her skirts and flew.

She raced through the gallery to the top of the stairs. Breathless, she clutched the wide banister and looked down. Webster swung the door wide, revealing a shadowy figure. The figure stepped forward; the light from the hall lamps burnished Vane's chestnut locks.

He handed his cane to Webster. "Where's Devil?"

Accepting the cane, Webster shut the door. "His Grace has not yet returned, sir."

"He hasn't?"

Even from the top of the stairs, Honoria heard Vane's surprise.

"I believe he went to White's, sir."

"Yes, I know." Vane sounded vague. "I left before him—I had to call at a friend's, but he intended leaving on my heels. I would have thought he'd be here by now."

Her heart thumping, Honoria watched the men stare at each other—the black specter she'd held at bay all day suddenly swirled closer. She leaned over the banister. "Vane?"

He looked up, then blinked. Surprise leached from his face, leaving it curiously blank. Webster glanced up, too, but immediately lowered his gaze.

Vane cleared his throat, and tried not to focus. "Yes, Honoria?"

"Go and look for him. *Please*?" The last word was heavy with latent fear.

Vane tried an unfocused frown. "He probably fell in with some friends and was delayed."

Honoria shook her head violently; inside, a familiar panic was rising. "No—something's happened. I *know* it." Her fingers tightened on the banister; her knuckles showed white. "*Please—go now!*"

Vane was reaching for his cane before her last words had died—the emotion investing her "please" was compelling. Infected by her concern, her fear overriding the logical excuses his mind freely concocted, he turned to the door.

Webster, reacting with similar speed, opened it. Swiftly, Vane descended the steps. His stride lengthening, he mentally retraced Devil's habitual route home from his favorite club. Ten yards from the steps, Vane remembered the alleyway between Berkeley Square and Hays Mews. Cursing, he broke into a run.

Back inside St. Ives House, Honoria clutched the banister and fought down her panic.

Closing the door, Webster briefly glanced her way. "By your leave, ma'am, I'll notify Sligo."

Honoria nodded. "Please do." She remembered she'd odered Devil watched—with relief, she grasped that branch and hung on. Sligo, protective, watchful Sligo, would have made sure his "Cap'n" was well guarded.

Beneath her, the baize door was flung open, crashing against the wall. Sligo rushed into the hall, flung open the front door and raced down the steps. As he disappeared, Honoria felt the slim branch she'd clutched ripped from her grasp—and found herself facing the black pit of her fears again.

"Hah!" Devil didn't waste breath putting much force into the shout—the alleyway was long and narrow; there were no windows in the tall brick walls. Swinging the thin blade of his sword-stick in a wide arc, he grabbed the moment as his three attackers flinched back to reach down and tug the body slumped on the alley's cobbles within his guard.

Leaving room for his feet, he straightened immediately, sword flicking back and forth, steel tip scenting blood. In his other hand, he held the empty scabbard, the rigid rod a foil against another weapon. With a feral grin, he gestured with the scabbard. "Well, gentlemen? Who'll be first?"

His challenging glance swept the faces of the men sent to kill him. They'd waited until he was in the alley, striding along, thinking of other things. Two had followed him in, the third had closed from the other end. All three were brawny, hulking brutes—sailors from their ill-fitting garments. All three carried swords—not slim blades like the one keeping them at bay but long, straight, single-sided weapons.

His gaze steady, his expression taunting, Devil mentally

searched for escape. And found none. Chance—in the form of two large barrels left in the usually empty alley, and a man who'd chased the sailors into the dimly lit passage—had kept him alive this far. With a yell, the man had thrown himself at the pair, alerting him to their presence. The man's intervention had been more heroic than wise; after momentarily grappling with him, one sailor had raised his arm and, with his sword grip, struck him down.

But by then he'd had his back against the wall, unsheathed sword and scabbard in his hands, the barrels immediately to his left restricting the front he had to defend. "Come along," he taunted, waving them forward. "No need to feel reticent about dying."

Their eyes shifted one to the other, each waiting to see who'd be first. It was his only hope—to keep them hanging back in indecision. From the corners of his eyes, he kept watch on the ends of the alley, lit by the flares in the street and square beyond. If anyone passed, their shadows would be thrown in—he'd have to hold his attackers back until that happened, and he could call for help. Unfortunately, it was past midnight in an area of fashionable residences with the Season yet to start. There were few people abroad.

Feet shifted on the cobbles; the largest of the sailors, the one directly in front, tried a slashing thrust. Devil blocked, catching the blade on his scabbard, sword hissing forward to slice the man's forearm. With a curse, the man jumped back, scowling, piggy eyes considering.

Devil prayed he wouldn't consider too hard—one on one, he could win, or hold them off forever. They were all heavier, but he was taller and had a longer, more flexible reach. If they rushed him all at once, they'd have him. Indeed, he couldn't understand why they hadn't already overwhelmed him; despite his black coat, his snowy cravat and white cuffs marked him clearly. Then he saw all three exchange another wary glance; inspiration dawned. He smiled, devilishly. "Hell's not such a bad place—take my word for it. Fiendishly hot, of course, and the pain never ends, but I can guarantee you'll all be found a place."

The three exchanged another glance, then the leader tried a less-than-successful sneer. "You may look like Satan, but you ain't him. You're just a man—your blood'll run free enough. 'Tisn't us slated to die tonight." He glanced at the others. "C'arn—let's get this done."

So saying, he raised his sword.

His warning, of course, was not wise. Devil met them, front and right; the man on his left, impeded by the barrels, predictably hung back. Sparks flew as one sword met the sweetly tempered steel of the swordstick and slid away; blocking the leader's stroke with his scabbard, Devil followed up with a swift thrust that pierced flesh.

He disengaged, simultaneously blocking the leader's second blow; the sword, wielded with force, sheered along the polished wood and struck his hand, clenched around it. The cut was not serious, he'd been pulling back at the time, but the scabbard quickly turned sticky beneath his fingers. Suppressing all reaction to the wound, Devil sent his thin blade reaching for the leader. The man jumped back as the fine point pricked his chest.

Devil cursed; the man to his left pressed closer, anxious to be in on the kill. The three assassins regrouped, all raising their weapons.

"Hi! *Hold hard!*"

A tall figure blocked out the light from Hays Mews. Running

footsteps echoed from the walls; a second figure followed the first.

Devil grabbed the moment, striking cleanly at the leader.

The man yelped, then staggered back, clutching his right arm. His sword dropped from nerveless fingers. The clatter shocked his comrades—they looked around, then dropped their weapons. All three turned and fled.

Devil started in pursuit—and tripped over the slumped form of his would-be savior, still lying at his feet.

Vane, his own scabbard and unsheathed sword in his hands, skidded to a halt beside him. "Who the hell were they?"

Side by side, the cousins watched the three burly shadows disappear into the glare of Berkeley Square. Devil shrugged. "We didn't exchange introductions."

Vane looked down. "You got one." Bending down, he turned the man onto his back.

"No." Devil peered at his comatose good Samaritan. "He tried to help and got a clout over the ear for his pains. Strange to tell, I think he's one of my undergrooms."

Puffing, Sligo clattered up. His gaze swept Devil, then he slumped against the wall. "You all right?"

Devil raised his brows, then sheathed his swordstick, clicking the blade into place. Transferring the innocent-looking cane to his right hand, he examined his left. "Other than a cut, which doesn't seem serious."

"Thank Gawd for that." Propped against the wall, Sligo closed his eyes. "The missus would never forgive me."

Devil frowned—first at Sligo, then at Vane.

Vane was studying the three discarded swords. "Funny business." Bending, he scooped them up. "Not your usual backstreet weapon."

Devil took one of the swords and hefted it. "Odd indeed. They look like old cavalry issue." After a moment, he added: "Presumably they knew I carry a swordstick and would use it."

"They also knew they'd need three to get the job done."

"If it hadn't been for him," Devil indicated the man on the ground, "they'd have succeeded." He turned to Sligo. "Any idea what he's doing here?"

The tone of the question was mild; Sligo clung to the shadows and shook his head. "Most likely out for the evening and on his way home. Saw you and the others—you're easy enough to recognize."

Devil humphed. "You'd better get him home and make sure he's cared for. I'll see him tomorrow—such timely devotion shouldn't go unrewarded."

Making a mental note to explain to the second undergroom that he'd had the night off, Sligo hefted the man over his shoulder. Wiry and used to such loads, he started off up the alley, plodding steadily.

Devil and Vane strolled in his wake. As they left the alley, Devil glanced at Vane. "Speaking of opportune events, what brought you two here?"

Vane met his look. "Your wife."

Devil's brows rose. "I should have guessed."

"She was frantic when I left." Vane glanced at him. "She worries about you."

Devil grimaced; Vane shrugged. "She may jump to conclusions, but too often they've proved right. I decided not to argue. The alley was an obvious place for an ambush."

Devil nodded. "Very obvious."

Vane looked ahead; Sligo was making his way about Grosvenor Square. Vane slowed. "Did Honoria speak to you about your heir?"

Devil sent him a sidelong glance. "Yes."

Eyes narrowing, Vane sent the glance right back. "How long have you known?"

Devil sighed. "I still don't *know*—I suspect. I can't say exactly when I realized—I just suddenly saw the possibility."

"So?"

Devil's features set. "So I want to find out what I can from this madam—tie up that loose end, if loose end it proves. Bromley confirmed the where and when of the meeting. After that—" He grimaced. "We've precious little evidence—we may need to draw him into the open."

"A trap?"

Devil nodded.

Vane's expression hardened. "With you as bait?"

They'd reached the steps of St. Ives House. Devil looked up at his door. "With me—and Honoria Prudence—as bait."

The suggestion stunned Vane; when he refocused, Devil was climbing the steps. Webster opened the door as Sligo, lugging his burden, reached it. Setting the door wide, Webster called for assistance, then helped Sligo.

Pacing in the gallery, wringing her hands with frustrated impotence, Honoria heard the commotion. In a froth of silk and feathers, she rushed to the balustrade. The sight that met her eyes was not designed to reassure.

Webster and Sligo were carrying a body.

Honoria paled. For one instant, her heart stopped; her chest squeezed so tight, she couldn't breathe. Then she realized the body wasn't Devil's—relief hit her in a dizzying wave. The next instant, her husband strolled over his threshold, ineffably elegant as always. Vane followed.

Vane was carrying three swords and his walking cane.

Devil was carrying his silver-topped cane. The cane was streaked with blood; the back of his left hand was bright red.

Honoria forgot everything and everyone else. In a whisper of silk, feathers scattering in her wake, she flew down the stairs.

Sligo and two footmen had the unconscious groom in charge; Webster was closing the door. It was Vane who saw her first; he jogged Devil's elbow.

Devil looked up—and only just managed not to gape. His wife's peignoir was not transparent but left little to the imagination; the soft, sheer silk clung to gently rounded contours and long sleek limbs. Abruptly, his face set; biting back a curse, he strode for the stairs. He only had time to toss his cane to Webster before Honoria flung herself against him.

"Where are you hurt? What happened?" Frantic, she ran her hands across his chest, searching for wounds. Then she tried to draw back and examine him.

"I'm fine." With his right arm, Devil locked her to him. Lifting her, he continued up the stairs, his body shielding her from the hall below.

"But you're *bleeding*!" Honoria wriggled, trying to pursue her investigation of his hurts.

"It's just a scratch—you can tend it in our room." Devil gave the last three words definite emphasis. Reaching the top of the stairs, he glanced down at Vane. "I'll see you tomorrow."

Vane met his gaze. "Tomorrow."

"Is the wound on your hand or your arm?" Honoria half tipped in Devil's hold, trying to see.

Devil swallowed a curse. "On my hand. Stay still." Tightening his hold, he headed for their chamber. "If you're going to work yourself into a frenzy waiting up for me, you'll need to invest in more suitable nightwear."

The terse comment didn't even impinge on Honoria's consciousness.

Resigned, Devil set her down in their room and surrendered to the inevitable. Obediently stripping off his shirt, he sat on the end of the bed and let her bathe his cut. He answered all her questions—truthfully; she'd hear the details from her maid tomorrow anyway.

Mrs. Hull appeared with a pot of salve and bandages. She joined Honoria in clucking over him. Together, they bandaged the cut, using twice as much bandage as he deemed necessary. However, he kept his tongue between his teeth and submitted meekly; Mrs. Hull cast him a suspicious glance as she left. Honoria rattled on, her voice brittle and breathless, her gaze skittish.

"*Swords!* What sort of ruffians attack gentlemen with swords?" She gestured wildly. "It shouldn't be allowed."

Devil stood, caught her hand and towed her across the room. He stopped before the tallboy, poured two glasses of brandy, then, taking both in one hand, towed Honoria, her litany of exclamations gradually petering out, to the armchair before the fire. Dropping into the chair, he drew her down onto his lap, then handed her one glass.

Taking it, she fell silent. Then she shivered.

"Drink it." Devil guided the glass to her lips.

Cradling the glass in both hands, Honoria took a sip, then another. Then she shuddered, closed her eyes and leaned against him.

His arm about her, Devil held her close. "I'm still here." He pressed his lips to her temple. "I told you I won't leave you."

Dragging in a breath, Honoria snuggled closer, settling her head in the hollow of his shoulder.

Devil waited until she'd drained her glass, then carried her to their bed, divesting her of her *peignoir* before putting her between the sheets. Moments later, he joined her, drawing her into his arms. And set about demonstrating in the most convincing way he knew that he was still hale and whole, still very much alive.

Honoria slept late the next morning, yet when she awoke she felt far from refreshed. After tea and toast on a tray in her chamber, she headed for the morning room. Her head felt woolly, her wits still skittish. Settling on the *chaise*, she picked up her embroidery. Fifteen minutes later, she'd yet to set a stitch.

Sighing, she put the canvas aside. She felt as fragile as the delicate tracery she should have been creating. Her nerves were stretched taut; she was convinced a storm was brewing, roiling on her horizon, poised to sweep in and strike—and take Devil from her.

He meant so much to her. He was the center of her life—she couldn't imagine living without him, arrogant tyrant though he was. They were *growing* together so well, yet someone was not content to let them be.

The thought made her frown. She might think of the murderer as a black cloud, billowing ever higher, yet he was only a man.

She'd woken early to find Devil sitting beside her on the bed, stroking her hair. "Rest," he'd said. "There's no reason you need be up and about." He'd searched her face, then kissed her. "Take care. I won't approve if I find you peaked and wan." With a twisted smile, he'd stood.

"Will you be about?" she'd asked.

"I'll be back for dinner."

Which was all very well, but dinner was hours away.

Honoria stared at the door. Something was about to happen—she could feel it in her bones. A chill stole down her spine; she shivered, but didn't let go of her disturbing thoughts. Yet she could identify no action, nothing she could do to avert the impending doom. She was impotent. Helpless.

A tap on the door interrupted her dismal reverie. Sligo entered, balancing a tray. "Mrs. Hull thought as you might like her special tea. Makes it up herself, she does." He set the tray on the sidetable and deftly poured a cup.

Honoria's instant reaction was a definite veto—her stomach felt as fragile as her mental state. The soothing aroma that rose with the steam changed her mind.

"Chamomile, it is." Sligo handed her the cup.

Honoria took it and sipped, then remembered the groom.

"How is Carter?"

"Better. Got a lump the size of an egg, but the Cap'n thanked him special this morning—Carter says as how he hardly feels it now."

"Good. Please convey my thanks to him as well." Honoria sipped. "Did Carter have any idea where the men who attacked His Grace hailed from?"

Sligo fiddled with the doily on the tray. "Not as such. He did say they looked like sailors."

Honoria fixed her gaze on his face. "Sligo—did Carter overhear anything?"

Sligo shifted. "He heard the two he followed agree to meet up later at the Anchor's Arms."

"The Anchor's Arms?"

"A tavern by the docks."

A demon prodded Honoria to act; she ignored it. "Has His Grace been informed of Carter's recollections?"

"No, ma'am. Carter only fully came to his wits an hour ago."

Honoria chose the course of wisdom. "Inform His Grace immediately of Carter's information."

Sligo bit his lip and shifted his weight.

Honoria studied his unprepossessing features in dawning disbelief. "Sligo—where is he?"

Sligo straightened. "The Cap'n must've fallen to our plan. When the lads set out to follow 'im this morning, he lost 'em. Neat as you please."

"Neat!" Honoria sat bolt upright. "There's nothing neat about it."

Here they were, with a potentially valuable avenue to explore, and her husband had taken himself off. Away from their watchful eyes. She handed Sligo her teacup, inwardly congratulating herself on not having thrown it. She wasn't so lost to all sense as to wax hysterical over someone trying to kill Devil in the middle of London during the day. She did, however, want his would-be-murderer caught without delay. Narrow-eyed, she considered Sligo. "Where does His Grace normally lunch?"

"One of his clubs, ma'am—White's, Waitier's, or Boodles."

"Send footmen to wait at all three. They are to inform His Grace immediately he arrives that I wish to speak with him as soon as may be."

"Very good, ma'am."

Chapter 22

By two, Honoria had started to pace. At four, she summoned Sligo.

"Have you located His Grace?"

"No, ma'am. I've men at White's, Waitier's, and Boodles—we'll know the instant he shows."

"Would Carter recognize the ruffians he followed?"

"Aye—he'll know them again, so he says."

"How long do ships normally remain at the docks?"

"Two, three days at most."

Honoria drew a deep breath. "Have the carriage brought around—the unmarked one."

Sligo blinked. "Ma'am?"

"I presume Carter's well enough to assist us?"

"Assist us?" Sligo's expression blanked.

Honoria frowned. "To identify the men who attacked His Grace should they be at the Anchor's Arms."

"The *Anchor's Arms*?" Horror replaced Sligo's blankness. "You can't go there, ma'am."

"Why not?"

"You . . . you simply can't. It's a dockside tavern—not the sort of place you'd feel comfortable."

"At present, my comfort is not of great importance."

Sligo grew desperate. "The Cap'n wouldn't approve."

Honoria transfixed him with a look as baleful as any of his master's. "Sligo, your 'Cap'n' isn't here. He's slipped his leash and taken himself off God knows where. We are presently in receipt of information which, if acted on promptly, might identify his would-be killer. If we wait until your Cap'n deigns to return, our opportunity might have sailed with the evening tide. In His Grace's absence, we—you and I—will accompany Carter to the Anchor's Arms. I trust I've made myself clear?"

Sligo opened his mouth—then shut it.

Honoria nodded. "The carriage. I'm going to change."

Ten minutes later, attired in a deep brown carriage dress, she crossed the gallery. Mrs. Hull was standing by the stairs. "Begging your pardon, ma'am, but I heard as you were planning to visit that inn by the docks. A terrible rough area, it is. You don't think, perhaps, that it would be better to wait . . . ?"

"Mrs. Hull, you can't expect me to allow my husband's would-be murderer to continue to stalk him for want of a little courage. The Anchor's Arms may be all you fear, but I'm sure I'll survive."

Mrs. Hull grimaced. "I'd do the same meself, ma'am—but the master's not going to like it."

Honoria started down the stairs. Webster was waiting on the landing; he fell into step beside her. "I would like to suggest, ma'am, that you permit me to go in your stead. If we discover the blackguards who attacked His Grace, Sligo and I will persuade them to return here and speak with His Grace."

"There!" Mrs. Hull, following on Honoria's heels, leaned forward. "That's another way to scour the pot."

Honoria stopped on the last stair. Sligo stood waiting by the newel post. "Webster, neither you nor Sligo can offer sufficient inducement to secure such men's cooperation. Should we discover them at the Anchor's Arms, it is my intention to offer them a sizeable reward if they will swear to the name of the man who hired them. They will not fear me because I'm a female—they'll consider my proposition. When they ask for the reward, it's my intention to repair to Child's Bank. Mr. Child will assist me in any negotiations."

She paused, her gaze touching each concerned face. "While His Grace is unlikely to approve of my involvement, I do not approve of someone trying to kill him. I would rather face His Grace's displeasure than risk His Grace's death." She stepped down from the stair. "I'm taking you into my confidence because I appreciate your concern. I am, however, determined on my course."

After an infinitesimal hesitation, Webster followed her. "Indeed, ma'am. But please—take care."

With a haughty nod, Honoria swept out of the door and down the steps. Sligo had to scurry to open the carriage door because, at that moment, there was not a single footman, or groom, left within St. Ives House.

The hitch in Honoria's plan became apparent the instant they reached the Anchor's Arms, in a mean, narrow street close by the docks. Sulfurous fog, dense and thick, wreathed the inn's low eaves. A rumble of male voices rolled out through the open door, punctuated by occasional female shrieks.

Sligo and Carter had traveled up top; descending nimbly to the cobbles, Sligo glanced around, then eased open the carriage door.

Her face lit by one of the carriage lamps, Honoria raised a brow.

"There's a problem."

"Problem?" Honoria glanced through the door at the inn

beyond. The carriage's leather window flaps were down. "What problem?"

"This area's not safe." Sligo scanned the shadows. "We should have brought more men."

"Why? I'll remain here while you and Carter go in. If the men are there, bring them out to me here."

"Who's going to watch over you while we're in the inn?"

Honoria blinked. "John Coachman's up top." Even as she said it, Sligo's unease reached her.

He shook his head. "He'll have his hands full with his team. If any wanted to grab you, all they need do is spook the horses. And I don't want to send Carter in alone. If those men are there, he might not come back."

Honoria understood, yet she had to find out if the men were there. "I'll come in with you. It's not particularly well-lit—if I cling to the shadows, no one will pay any attention to me." On the words, she left her seat.

Sligo gaped—Honoria scowled and he let down the steps. Defeated he handed her down, then beckoned Carter closer. "If we walk in front, shoulder to shoulder, you'll be less noticeable, ma'am."

Honoria nodded curtly. She followed close on Sligo's heels as he and Carter crossed the tavern's threshold.

They entered a smoke-filled, low-ceilinged room—a deathly silence fell. Every conversation was suspended, instantly cut off. Sligo and Carter halted; Honoria sensed their defensiveness. Men lounged, slumped over a long counter; others sat on crude benches about rough tables. All heads had snapped their way; eyes used to sifting shadows focused without difficulty on her. The expression on some faces was surprised; most quickly turned calculating. Some turned malevolent. Danger, palpable, cloying, hung on the smoky air. Honoria tasted it, felt it crawl across her skin.

The barman, a harrassed-looking individual, reacted first. "You've come to the wrong place." He shooed them back. "We don't have what you want."

"Now, now." A beefy arm stopped him in his tracks. A body to match the arm heaved its way off a bench. "Don't be so hasty, Willie. Who's to say wha' the fancy want?"

The leer that went with this, directed at Honoria, convinced her the barman was right.

"Tha's right. Lady walks in—must know what she's alookin' for." Another grinning navvy, wide as a tug, lumbered to his feet. "Any number of us 'ere might have wha' she's after."

Honoria looked him in the eye. "You're quite right." The only way out was through sheer, brazen bluff. Pushing Carter aside, she stepped forward. "You might well be able to assist me. However"—she let her gaze roam the tables—"I must warn you that my husband and his cousins—the Bar *Sinister*, as they're called—are presently on their way here. All six of them." She considered the navvy. "They're all taller than you."

She turned to the barman: "I daresay you can imagine how their group got its name. And now they've learned that three of your patrons attacked one of them last night. They're coming for revenge, but when they get here, they're not going to waste time on identification."

Barman and patrons struggled through her words; Honoria inwardly sighed. "I think they're going to wreck this tavern—and everyone in it as well."

The navvies bristled; rebellious rumblings flew. "If it's a roughhouse they're after, we'll give it 'em," one brawny salt declared.

"I'll complain to the magistrate," the barman bleated.

Honoria eyed the navvies measuringly. "Six of them—all rather large. And . . ." She looked at the barman. "Did I mention my husband's a duke?" The man's face blanked; she smiled. "His nickname's Devil. Lucifer and Demon will be with him." She peered out through the open door. "I didn't see the Watch out there."

The navvies exchanged glances. Tales of the forays mounted by the less civilized of society's males were commonplace; the poorer classes bore the brunt of such destructive routs. The crowd in the Anchor's Arms were too old to risk getting their skulls cracked unnecessarily.

The man who'd spoken first eyed her challengingly. "And just what might *you* be a-doing 'ere, then? A duchess an'all?"

Honoria looked down her nose at him. "My dear man, surely you've heard that duchesses are required to do charitable deeds? Saving the Anchor's Arms is my deed for today." She paused. "Provided, of course, that you tell me what I need to know."

The navvy glanced at his cronies—many nodded. Still suspicious, he turned back to her. "How d'we know if'n we help you, you'll be able to stop this 'ere Devil from laying waste anyway?"

"You don't." Honoria held his gaze. "You can only hope."

"What'd you want to know?" came from the back of the room.

Honoria lifted her head. "Three sailors met here recently. I need to talk to them. Carter—describe the two you saw."

Carter did; more than a few remembered them.

"In here yesterday evenin'—off the *Rising Star*."

"*Rising Star* upped anchor this mornin' for Rotterdam."

"You're sure?" Confirmation came from several points in the room.

Then silence fell. Dense, cold, it chilled the air. Even before she turned, Honoria knew Devil had arrived.

She swung to face him—and only just stopped her blink. She swallowed instead. It was him, but not the man she habitually saw. This man filled the space before the door with a menacing presence; barely restrained aggression poured from him in waves. His elegant attire did nothing to conceal his powerful frame, nor the fact that he was fully prepared to annihilate anything or anyone unwise enough to give him the slightest excuse. He fitted the image she'd created to perfection.

His eyes, cold and flat, left her, scanning the room, holding not challenge but a promise, an intent every man could feel. Vane stood at his shoulder; just the two of them made the tavern seem uncomfortably overcrowded.

As Devil's gaze fastened on the wide-eyed barman, Honoria conjured a smile and swept into the breach. "There you are, my lord. I fear the men you seek are not here—they sailed this morning."

Devil didn't blink. His gaze fastened on her face—flames replaced the chill in his eyes but they remained oddly flat. One brow rose fractionally. "Indeed?"

The single word, uttered in his deep voice, gave no hint of his thoughts. For one definable instant, the entire tavern held its breath. Then he nodded at the barman. "In that case, you must excuse us."

On the words, Devil turned, catching Honoria's arm, propelling her over the threshold, lifting her through the carriage door Sligo raced to open and into the safety beyond.

Vane swung out of the inn behind them; he loomed at Devil's shoulder as he paused, one boot on the carriage steps. "I'll take the hackney." Vane nodded to where the small carriage waited.

His expression beyond grim, Devil nodded—he followed Honoria into the carriage. Sligo slammed the door; John Coachman flicked the reins.

It took three tense, silent minutes before the coach maneuvered its way free of the narrow street. And a further, equally silent half-hour before it drew up in Grosvenor Square. Devil alighted. He waited until Sligo let down the steps, then held out his hand. Honoria placed hers in it; he helped her down and led her up the steps.

Webster opened the door, his relief so intense it showed in his face. Then he saw his master's face—immediately his expression leached to impassivity. Gliding into the hall, her fingers on an arm more like rock than human flesh, Honoria held her head high.

Devil halted in the hall. "If you'll excuse me, my dear, I must speak with Sligo." His tone was glacial, bleak, and not quite steady, the icy surface rippling with barely suppressed rage. "I'll join you shortly. Upstairs."

For the first time that evening, Honoria saw his face clearly, lit by the chandelier high above. It was paler than usual, each harsh plane starkly edged, the whole no more animated than a death mask in which his eyes burned oddly dark. She met that black gaze directly. "Sligo was acting on my orders."

Devil raised a brow, his expression cold. "Indeed?"

Honoria studied his eyes, then inclined her head. And turned for the stairs. In the mood he was in, saying anything further might be counterproductive.

Rigid, Devil watched her ascend. When she passed from sight, he switched his gaze to Sligo. "In the library."

Sligo scurried in; Devil followed more slowly. Crossing the threshold, he paused; a footman closed the door. Sligo stood at attention to one side of the desk. Devil let silence stretch before slowly closing the distance.

Normally, he would have sat at his desk; tonight, the rage consuming him would not let him rest. He halted before the long windows giving onto the dark courtyard.

Words filled his head, jostled for prominence on his tongue, a ranting rave of fury clamoring to spill free. Jaw clenched, he fought to hold it back. Never before could he recall such rage—so fraught he was chilled to the marrow, so powerful he could barely contain it.

He glanced at Sligo. "I was informed by a footman who chanced upon me in St. James that Her Grace was on her way to the Anchor's Arms. Before I could summon a hackney, three others of my household appeared, bearing like tidings. It appears that fully half my staff were scouring the streets for me, instead of *obeying my orders and looking after my wife! How the devil did she even hear about the Anchor's Arms?*"

Sligo flinched. "She asked—I told her."

"What in all the saints' names did you mean by taking *her there?"*

The door opened at the height of that roar. Devil glared balefully at Webster. "I do not wish to be disturbed."

"Indeed, Your Grace." Webster stepped around the door, held it open for Mrs. Hull, then closed it. "Mrs. Hull and I wished to make sure you were not laboring under any misapprehension."

"It is exceedingly difficult to misapprehend discovering my wife in a dockside tavern."

The words had an edge like cut glass; Webster paled but persevered. "I believe you wish to learn how that came about, my lord. Sligo did not act on his own. We were all, myself, Mrs. Hull, and Sligo, aware of Her Grace's intent. We all attempted to dissuade her, but, having heard her reasons, we couldn't legitimately stand in her way."

His fists clenched so tight they hurt, his jaw all but locked, Devil spoke through his teeth. "What reasons?"

Webster outlined Honoria's plan; Mrs. Hull elucidated her reasons. "Perfectly understandable, to my mind." She sniffed defensively. "She was worried—as were we. It seemed a perfectly sensible thing to do."

Devil swallowed the tirade that leapt to his tongue. His temper seething, roiling behind the flimsy façade of civilized behavior, he eyed them narrowly. "*Out!* All of you."

They went, carefully shutting the door. Swinging around, Devil stared into the night. Sligo didn't approve of *ton*nish women, Webster was as starchily devoted as they came, and Mrs. Hull was an arch-conservative—yet all had been suborned by his wife. And her reasons.

Ever since marrying Honoria Prudence *Anstruther*-Wetherby, he'd been knee-deep in reasons—her reasons. He had reasons, too—good, sound, solid reasons. But it wasn't his staff he need to share them with. Having reached that conclusion, Devil swung on his heel and stalked out of the library.

Striding toward the ducal apartments, he reflected that Honoria had succeeded in shielding her three co-conspirators from his anger, without even being present. Of course, if he'd been able to lose some of the red-hot fury swirling inside him by venting it on them, she wouldn't be about to face it all herself. As it was . . .

Reaching the end of the corridor, he threw open the door, then slammed it shut behind him.

Honoria didn't even jump. She stood before the fireplace, head erect, unshakable resolve in every line. The skirts of her brown velvet carriage dress were gilded by the fire behind her; the soft chestnut curls atop her head glowed. Her hands were loosely clasped before her; her face was pale but composed, her eyes wide, the soft blue-grey showing no hint of trepidation. Her neatly rounded, Anstruther-Wetherby chin was set.

Deliberately, Devil stalked toward her, watching her chin rise as she kept her eyes on his. He stopped directly before her. "You gave me your word you would not actively pursue Tolly's killer."

Calmly, Honoria raised a brow. "*Tolly's* killer—I gave no undertaking to sit idly by while someone tried to kill *you*."

Shadows flitted through Devil's darkened eyes. He inclined his head. "Very well—you may give me such an undertaking now."

Honoria straightened. Devil still towered over her. "I can't do that."

His eyes mere slits, more black than green, he shifted closer. "Can't—or won't?"

Honoria held her ground. "Can't." Her eyes on his, her jaw slowly firmed. "*And* won't. You can't seriously expect it of me."

For three heartbeats, Devil held her gaze. "I'm deathly serious." He braced one hand on the mantelpiece, his body settling closer, his face nearer hers. "Women—wives—are supposed to sit quietly at home and embroider, *not* actively hunt villains. They're *supposed* to be at home when their husbands get in, *not out courting danger on the docks!*" Briefly closing his eyes, he fought down the impulse to roar. Then he trapped Honoria's gaze and continued: "I want your promise that you will not again indulge in any escapade such as today's, that you will remain safely at home and that you will not further concern yourself with tracking *anyone's* killer." His eyes locked on hers, he raised one black brow. "Well?"

Honoria held his gaze steadily. "Well what?"

Devil only just managed to hold back a roar. "*Well give me your promise!*"

"When hell freezes!" Honoria's eyes flashed. "I will *not* sit tamely by while someone tries to take you from me. I'm your *duchess*—not some disinterested spectator. I will *not* sit quietly embroidering, waiting for news when that news could tell of your death. As your wife, I have a duty to help you—if in this case that means walking a dangerous path, so be it." Her chin, defiantly high, rose another notch. "I'm an Anstruther-Wetherby—I'm every bit as capable of facing danger and death as you are. If you wanted a tame, complaisant wife, you shouldn't have married *me*."

Momentarily stunned, more by her vehemence than her words, Devil stared at her. Then, his frown deepening, he shook his head. "No."

Honoria frowned back. "No what?"

"No to all the above, but most especially no, you do not have a duty to assist me in hunting a murderer. As my wife, you have no duties other than those I deem proper. In my eyes, there's nothing—no duty, no reason whatever—that could justify you placing yourself in danger."

Their faces were six inches apart; if Honoria had not sensed the throttled fury investing his large frame, radiating from it, she could not have missed the jagged edge to his words. Her eyes narrowed. "That I do not accept." She was not about to bow before his rage.

Devil's lips curved slightly; his voice, when he spoke, was mesmerically low. "*That* you *will* accept."

It was an effort not to shiver, to submissively shift her gaze from his, so penetrating, so compelling, it resembled a physical force. By sheer will, sheer stubbornness, Honoria met that intimidating gaze levelly. "You're wrong on all counts. I've lost others before, to forces I could not influence—I couldn't help them, I couldn't save them." Her jaw set; momentarily, her teeth clenched. "I *will not* sit by and let you be taken from me."

Her voice quavered; flashes of silver lit Devil's eyes. "Damn it!—do you think I'm going to *let* myself be taken?"

"Not intentionally, but it was *me* who detected the poison."

Devil waved that aside. "That was here." He studied her face, her eyes. "Within this house, you may watch over me to your heart's content, but you will *stay away from all danger*. You spoke of duty—it's *my* duty to protect you, *not* yours to protect me."

Honoria went to shake her head; Devil caught her chin on the edge of his hand and trapped her gaze with his. "Promise me you'll do as I ask."

Honoria drew as deep a breath as her tight chest would allow, then shook her head. "No—leave duty aside—we spoke also of reasons, a reason to justify my doing all and anything to safeguard your life." She spoke quickly, breathlessly; she *had* to make him understand. "My reason is one that will stand against any objection."

Devil's face hardened. His hand fell; he drew back. Her eyes locked on his, Honoria clung to the contact, refusing to let him withdraw totally behind his mask. She drew a swift breath, and let it out on the words: "I love you—more than I've ever loved anyone. I love you so profoundly it goes beyond all reason. And I could *never* let you go—let you be taken from me—that would be the same as letting life itself go, because you are life to me."

Devil stilled. For one, heart-stopping moment, he looked into Honoria's eyes; what he saw there locked his chest. He wrenched his gaze free and swung away. He paced toward the door, then stopped. Hands in fists by his sides, chest swelling, he dropped his head back, and stared at the ceiling. Then exhaling, he looked down. He spoke without turning. "Your reason's not good enough."

Honoria lifted her chin. "It is to me."

"*Damn it woman!*" Furious, Devil turned on her. "How by all that's holy do you imagine *I'm* supposed to function, knowing that, at any instant, *you* may be courting heaven knows what danger—all in the name of keeping *me* safe?" His voice rose to a bellow that literally shook the chandelier. Gesticulating violently, he paced viciously, like some trapped jungle cat. "Do you have any *idea* what I felt when I learned where you'd gone today?" Brilliant with accusation, his eyes raked her. "Can you even *conceive* what I felt when I walked in that tavern door?" He halted directly before her.

Honoria caught her breath as his eyes locked on hers.

"Do you know what might have happened in such a place?" His voice had lowered, his tones chillingly prophetic.

Honoria didn't move.

"They could have knifed Sligo and Carter—killed them without a qualm. Then they'd have raped you—one after another. If you'd survived, they'd have slit your throat."

Devil spoke with deadpan conviction; it was the truth—a truth he'd had to face. The muscles across his shoulders rippled; he tensed, holding back his reactive rage, clinging grimly to the reality of the woman standing slim, straight, and unharmed before him. A second later he caught himself reaching for her— abruptly, he swung away, pacing again, then he stopped.

His back to Honoria, he dragged in a deep breath. "How the hell do you think I would have felt *then*?—if anything had happened to you?" He paused, then flatly stated: "I cannot countenance you putting yourself in danger over me. *You* can't ask that of *me*."

Silence fell; Devil looked back at Honoria. "Will you give me your word you will not knowingly go into danger?"

Honoria held his gaze, then, slowly, shook her head. "I can't."

He looked forward immediately, his fury clearly delineated in the rigid lines of his back, clearly expressed in a single, violent expletive.

"I simply *can't*." Honoria spread her hands. "I'm not trying to be wilful, but you must see I can't—" Her words were drowned out by a half-strangled roar; the next instant, Devil flung open the door. Honoria stiffened. "Where are you going?"

"Downstairs."

"Don't you *dare* leave." If he did, would he come back? "I haven't finished—"

His hand on the doorknob, Devil turned, his green gaze impaling her. "If I *don't* leave, you won't sit comfortably for a sennight."

Before she could react, he slammed the door shut. Honoria listened to his footsteps, uncharacteristically heavy, retreat. She stood before the fire, her gaze fixed unseeing on the panels of the door, for a very long time.

Reaching the library, Devil flung himself into an armchair. An instant later, he sprang up and fell to pacing. He never paced— the action was too indicative of lost control for his liking. If he kept on as he was, he'd wear a track in the rug.

Uttering a long-drawn groan, he halted; eyes closed, he dropped his head back and concentrated on breathing, on letting his impotent rage settle. Into the morass of emotions that swirled inside him, all called forth by the woman he'd taken to wife.

Both jaw and fists clenched; then again he forced himself to relax. One by one, tensed muscles uncoiled; eventually, he stood easy. Eyes still closed, he looked inward, sifting through his reactions to what lay beneath.

When he saw what it was, he wasn't impressed.

Honoria was dealing with this unexpected development far better than he. Then again, she'd been through it before, albeit unhappily. He'd never experienced the like before.

He hadn't, in fact, known real fear, even on the battlefield. He was a Cynster; fate took care of Cynsters. Unfortunately, he wasn't sanguine enough to assume fate's benevolence extended to Cynster wives. Which left him battling a fear he'd no idea how to combat.

Exhaling slowly, he opened his eyes. Spreading his fingers, he studied them. They were almost steady. His muscles, tensed for so long, now felt chilled. He glanced at the decanter, then grimaced. Switching his gaze to the flames cheerily dancing in the hearth, he paused, then, deliberately, opened the door of his memory. And let Honoria's words warm him.

He stared at the flames for so long that when he heaved a long sigh and turned to the door, they still danced before his eyes.

Honoria shivered beneath the unfamiliar covers of her bed. After much mental debate, she'd returned to her apartments, undressed, and climbed between the sheets. She hadn't had any dinner—not that it mattered; she'd lost her appetite. Whether she'd find it again was moot, but if she could relive her scene with Devil, she would not change one word she'd said.

Her declaration had been necessary—she hadn't expected him to like it. She had no idea how he viewed her confession—he'd turned from her the instant he'd seen her words confirmed in her eyes.

Frowning, she stared into the dark, trying, for the umpteenth time, to make consistent sense of his reaction. On the surface, he'd appeared his usual tyrannical, domineering self, insisting without quarter that she fall in with his dictates, resorting to intimidation when she stood firm. Yet not all he'd said fitted that image—the mere thought of her being in danger had agitated him to a remarkable degree. It was almost as if . . .

The nebulous thought went round and round in her head, and followed her into sleep.

She woke to find a very large, dense shadow looming over her.

"Damn fool woman—what the devil are you doing here?"

His tone made it clear the question was rhetorical; Honoria valiantly stifled a giggle. He sounded so put upon—poor aggrieved male—not one of the most powerful men in the land. Her eyes adjusted to the dark, she saw him, hands on hips, shake his head. Then he leaned over her.

He loosened her covers, then pressed down on the soft mattress and slid his hands under her. He lifted her easily; Honoria played dead.

"*And* a bloody nightgown."

The disgust in his voice made her jaw ache.

"What the hell does she think she's about?"

He shouldered through the door into the short corridor; seconds later, very gently, she was deposited in his bed. Honoria decided a murmur and a wriggle were required for authenticity.

She heard him humph, then listened to the familiar sounds of him undressing, her mind supplying what she could not see.

The relief she felt when he slid into bed beside her, curling around her, warm, hard, reassuringly solid, made her chest ache. Carefully, he slid one arm over her waist; his hand gently pushed between her breasts, long fingers draping possessively over the lower.

She felt him heave a long, deep sigh; the last of his tension left him.

Minutes later, before she could decide whether or not to "wake up," his breathing deepened. Smiling, still wondering, Honoria closed her eyes.

Chapter 23

The next morning, Honoria woke late, alone, Devil long gone, up and about his business. His unflagging energy struck her as unfair—the events of the night had left her drained. Her gaze, unfocused, fell on the swath of ivory silk adorning the richly hued carpet. Her nightgown.

They'd engaged in a midnight tussle—half-asleep, she'd been reluctant to relinquish the gown's warmth. He, however, had insisted, then compensated admirably. Even now, she felt pleasurably aglow, inside and out. Smiling, she sank deeper into the bed, luxuriating in the lingering sense of warm fulfilment.

Who'd made the first move she neither knew nor cared; they'd turned to each other and let their bodies seal their unvoiced commitment that, regardless of any differences, they remained man and wife, their alliance rock-solid, as enduring as the Place.

The door from her apartments cracked open; Cassie peeked, then bustled in. "G'morning, ma'am." She swiped up the nightgown. "It's nearly eleven."

"Eleven?" Honoria blinked her eyes wide.

"Webster asked if you wanted any breakfast kept. Having missed dinner and all."

Honoria sat up. "We ate later." An hour after her nightgown had hit the floor, Devil's mind had turned to food. She'd been sound asleep again; he'd made a trip to the kitchens, then ruth-lessly harried her awake, insisting she eat morsels of chicken, ham, and cheese, all washed down with white wine.

"There's kedgeree, boiled eggs, and sausages."

Honoria wrinkled her nose. "I'll take a bath."

The bath suited her mood: lazy, disinclined to move. She stared through the steam, reviewing the previous evening—and heard in her mind, in the depths of the night, her husband's deep voice as, sated, replete, he'd slumped beside her. *"You can't fear losing me half as much as I fear losing you."* It had been a grudging admission; he'd thought her already asleep.

Why would he fear losing her even more than she feared losing him?

The minutes ticked by, the water grew cold, and still she could find only one answer. As she rose from the bath, her spirits soared—she spent the next half hour sternly lecturing herself on the unwisdom of leaping to conclusions, especially conclusions like that.

She retired to the morning room but couldn't settle, idly drift-ing between window and fireplace, consumed by a longing to see her husband again. To look into his face; to study his clear eyes. Mrs. Hull brought up a pot of herbal tea. Grateful, she accepted a cup, but it grew cold while she stared at the wall.

Louise and the twins provided a welcome diversion; they came to lunch, the girls eager to describe their latest gowns. Honoria toyed with a portion of steamed fish and listened with half an ear. She'd canceled all her other engagements, although the news that the new duchess of St. Ives was indisposed was certain to lead to speculation.

In this instance, speculation would be accurate. She'd hesi-tated to let the thought form in her mind, but it now seemed

beyond question. Her dullness every morning, her fragile appetite, all testified to the fact.

She was carrying Devil's child.

The very thought made her giddy with happiness, with eager
anticipation tinged only by understandable apprehension. Real
fear had no chance of intruding, not with Devil and his family so
constantly about her.

As if to emphasize that last, with the twins on the front steps,
Louise glanced at her affectionately. "You're looking well, but if
you have any questions, there's me or Horatia or Celia—we've all
been there before you."

"Oh—yes." Honoria blushed—she hadn't told Devil; she
could hardly tell his aunts first. "That is—" She gestured
vaguely. "If . . ."

Smiling, Louise patted her arm. "Not if, my dear. *When.*"
With a nod and a wave, she left, the twins falling in behind her.

Climbing the stairs, Honoria debated just how to tell Devil
the news. Every time she imagined doing so, the specter of his
would-be murderer intruded. They were closing in; before he'd
left that morning, Devil had told her that he and Vane were
searching for proof, precisely what he hadn't said. He'd promised to reveal all tonight. The last thing they needed now was a
distraction—announcing the impending birth of his heir would
create a major stir, focusing society's rabid interest on them.

Entering the morning room, Honoria inwardly shook her head.
She would inform Devil of his impending fatherhood *after* they'd
caught his would-be killer. Until then, his safety consumed
her—not even his child meant more to her than he. Besides, she
wanted the telling to be a happy event, a memorable moment
between them, not overshadowed by a killer.

As she sank onto the *chaise*, Webster knocked and entered. "A message, ma'am." He proffered a silver salver.

Lifting the folded sheet, Honoria saw black lettering, conservative, precise, not her husband's extravagant scrawl. "Thank you, Webster." Breaking the plain seal, she returned the knife to the tray and nodded a dismissal. Webster left as she unfolded the note.

> *To Her Grace, the duchess of St. Ives:*
>
> *Should you wish to learn more of he who intends your husband ill, come at once to No. 17 Green Street. Come alone—tell no one of your errand, else all will be lost. Most especially destroy this note that none may chance upon it and follow you, scaring away the little bird that would whisper in your ear.*
>
> *A Well-wisher.*

For a long moment, Honoria stared at the note, then she reread it. Then, drawing a steadying breath, she sank back against the *chaise*.

Devil wouldn't want her to go. But if she didn't?

There was clearly a potential threat to herself, but that she dismissed out of hand; far more relevant was how Devil would react. Not, of course, that such a consideration would sway her— her fear was more compelling than his.

Glancing at the note's thick black script, she grimaced. Devil's words of the night replayed in her mind; if she understood them correctly, then his fear was a mirror image of hers. There was only one emotion which gave rise to such fear. That emotion, if he felt it, demanded her consideration, her care. The same emotion impelled her to go to Green Street. How to do both?

Five minutes later, she stood and crossed to the escritoire. Fifteen minutes later, she shook sand across her letter, folded it, and sealed it with the seal Devil had given her—the Cynster stag rampant imposed on the Anstruther-Wetherby chevrons. Blowing on the wax, she rose, crossed the room, and tugged the bell-pull three times.

Sligo answered her summons. "Yes, ma'am?"

Honoria glanced at the clock on the mantelpiece. Nearly three o'clock. "Where is His Grace at present?"

"At White's with Master Vane." Sligo almost smiled. "He didn't try to lose the men I set to follow him today."

"Good." Honoria held out her letter. "I want this delivered into His Grace's hands with all possible speed."

"Right away, ma'am." Accepting the letter, Sligo turned for the door.

"And have Webster call up a hackney for me."

"A hackney, ma'am?" Sligo turned back, his expression watchful. "John Coachman can have the carriage around in a trice."

"No." Honoria let authority tinge her tone. "A hackney. I'm only going a short distance—there's no need to get the carriage out." With a regal nod, she dismissed Sligo. "Tell Webster I wish to leave in ten minutes."

Sligo departed. Honoria picked up the letter from her "well-wisher." She glanced at it again, then, folding it neatly, headed upstairs.

Ten minutes later, arrayed in her golden pelisse and clutching an ivory-beaded reticule, she settled in one corner of the hackney. The footman bowed and started to close the door. It was wrenched from his grasp—Sligo bundled himself into the carriage, then shrank back in the other corner. Honoria stared at him. "Where's my letter?"

Sligo watched her like a chicken shut in with a vixen. "On its way—I sent Daley with it. He'll see it into His Grace's hands, just like you wanted."

"Indeed? And what are you doing here?"

"Ah . . ." Sligo blinked. "I thought as how it wasn't right you going about alone—you might get lost, not being used to Lunnon an' all."

Lips compressed, Honoria straightened her skirts. "I'm only going a few streets away to visit an acquaintance."

Sligo swallowed. "Be that as it may, ma'am, I'll go with you— if you don't mind."

Looking up, Honoria was about to inform him that she did mind, when suspicion dawned. "Did His Grace order you to stay with me?"

Glumly, Sligo nodded.

Honoria sighed. "Very well—but you'll have to remain in the carriage."

The hatch above opened; the jarvey peered down. "We goin' somewhere? Or did you just want to use me carriage for a chat?"

Honoria silenced him with a glare. "Green Street. Drive along it slowly—I'll tell you where to stop."

"Right you are." The jarvey dropped the hatch; an instant later, they were off.

Green Street was where her grandfather lived, at Number 13. Number 17 was closer to the park. The jarvey walked his horse along; Honoria studied the facades. Number 17 was an elegant residence, a gentleman's abode. She waited until they'd passed two more houses before saying: "Have the jarvey pull up. Wait for me here."

Sligo relayed her orders. The hackney drew up; Sligo leapt down and helped her out. Beside the hackney, screened from Number 17 on the other side of the road, Honoria fixed Sligo with a commanding look. "Wait for me here—*inside* the carriage."

Sligo blinked. "Shouldn't I walk you to the door?"

"Sligo, this is Green Street, not Billingsgate. You will stay in the carriage."

Mournfully, Sligo nodded; Honoria waited until he resumed his seat, then turned on her heel, walked back a short distance, and swiftly crossed the road. Briskly determined, she climbed the steps of Number 17. Reaching for the knocker, she froze, her hand in midair. The brass knocker was a sylph—a naked sylph. Honoria frowned, then closed her gloved hand about the indiscreet figure and beat an imperious tattoo.

She waited, clutching her reticule, trying not to think of the expletives her husband would utter when he read her letter—she hoped the committee of White's would understand. Then footsteps approached on the other side of the door. Not the measured tread of a well-trained butler but a slow, familiar, prowling gait. Even before the door opened, Honoria knew she would not be facing a butler.

When she saw who held the door wide, her jaw dropped.

The earl of Chillingworth's jaw dropped, too.

For one instant, they stood stock-still, staring at each other. Honoria mentally reeled, possibilities and conjectures whirling wildly.

Then Chillingworth scowled. "For God's sake, don't just stand there! Someone might see you."

Honoria blinked dazedly and remained rooted to his front step. Smothering a growl, Chillingworth grabbed her arm and hauled her inside. He shut the door, then faced her.

Although he was not as tall as Devil, Chillingworth was not a small man. In the narrow hall, Honoria was acutely conscious of that fact. Straightening, without a clue as to what was going on, she fixed him with an imperious look. "Where's your butler?"

Chillingworth returned her look with one she found unreadable. "My butler is out. As are the rest of my staff." Honoria's eyes widened; grimly, Chillingworth shook his head. "I can't believe you're serious." He searched her face, her eyes.

Honoria tilted her chin defiantly. "Of *course* I'm serious."

Chillingworth's expression showed a medley of disbelief and disillusionment, then hardened into a mask very like his greatest rival's. Fluidly, he shrugged. "If you insist."

Without further ado, he bent his head to Honoria's.

Uttering a strangled shriek, she jerked back and hit him.

Just before two o'clock, Devil had absentmindedly climbed the steps of White's. On the threshold, he'd literally run into Vane.

"*There* you are!" Vane had dropped back. "Where in all hell have you been? I've been looking all over."

Devil had grinned. "Surprising you didn't find me then, for that's where I've been. All over."

Frowning, Vane opened his lips—Devil waved the question aside. "Have you eaten?"

Still frowning, Vane nodded. Devil handed his cane to the doorkeeper; Vane did the same. "I'll talk while you eat."

The dining room was companionably crowded with gentlemen lingering over their brandies. Served with remarkable promptness, Devil started on the sole—and lifted an inquiring brow.

Vane grimaced at the bodies about them. "I'll tell you later."

Devil nodded and applied himself to his meal, pleased to have an excuse not to talk. Explaining why he'd spent the whole morning roaming the town, exercising the two grooms Sligo had set to tail him, was beyond him. He suspected it would always be beyond him—his affliction wasn't improving with time. And he could hardly tell Vane he was avoiding his wife because she'd said she loved him.

Said it, declared it, in unequivocal terms, with absolute conviction. Pausing, Devil quaffed half his glass of wine.

It was heady stuff, to know your wife felt that way. About you. That she would face danger without a blink, and refuse to back down, even when faced with sufficient intimidation to break a troop sergeant—all because she loved you.

There was only one snag, one fly in the ointment.

Taking another sip of wine, he returned to his sole. And the dilemma with which he'd spent all morning wrestling. If he told Honoria how he felt about her loving him, if he even acknowledged her declaration, he would simultaneously acknowledge the validity of her "justification" for going into danger. Which was something he could never do.

In times of trouble, as far as he and, he was quite sure, all his ancestors were concerned, Cynster wives were supposed to retreat to the donjon, there to remain in safety while their husbands manned the walls. Honoria's vision was apparently different—she wanted to be on the walls with him.

He understood her point—he simply couldn't accept it.

Explaining that was not going to be easy, not even after he'd made the confession he'd convinced himself he was honor-bound to make.

Feeling vulnerable was bad enough—admitting to vulnerability, out loud, in words, was infinitely worse. And, once said, the words couldn't be taken back. He would, in essence, be handing her a *carte blanche* of a kind he'd never used before. Given how she reacted to his being in danger, he wasn't at all sure that was wise.

Whether she suspected his state he did not know—he did know he couldn't count on her remaining in blissful ignorance for long. Not his Honoria Prudence. Which meant that the only way he could keep her out of danger was to remove the danger—by laying Tolly's killer by the heels.

Pushing aside his plate, he looked at Vane. "What have you learned?"

Vane grimaced. "Let's go into the smoking room."

They found a deserted nook and settled in; Vane began without preamble. "Basically, I was right. My source has checked every—"

"Excuse me, Your Grace."

They both looked up; one of the club's footmen stood at Devil's elbow, proffering a salver bearing a folded note. "This arrived a moment ago, Your Grace. The man was most insistent it be delivered to you immediately."

"Thank you." Taking the letter, Devil broke the seal, absentmindedly nodding a dismissal. Unfolding the letter, he scanned it—Vane saw his face harden. Devil's eyes flicked back up to the start of the letter; his face unreadable, he read it through again.

"Well?" Vane asked, when Devil looked up.

Devil's brows rose. "Something's come up." He didn't meet Vane's eyes. "An unexpected development." Refolding the letter, he rose. "You'll have to excuse me—I'll send for you as soon as I'm free."

With that, he turned and, putting the letter in one pocket, walked out.

Stunned, Vane stared after him. Then his face hardened. "Honoria Prudence—what the devil have you got up to now?"

"No! Wait! You can't just walk out the door."

"Why not?" Honoria swung around.

Holding a cold compress to the bridge of his nose, Chilling-worth followed her up the hall. "Because there's no sense in taking unnecessary chances. Your husband's not going to ap-preciate this as it is—there's no sense in making things worse." Setting the compress down on the hall table, he looked her over. "Your bonnet's not straight."

Lips compressed, Honoria swung to face the mirror. Adjusting her bonnet, she studied Chillingworth's reflection. He was still very pale; she wasn't sure it was wise to leave him—his servants had not yet returned. On the other hand, she could understand his insistence that she leave without delay. "There!" She turned. "Does that meet with your approval?"

Chillingworth narrowed his eyes. "You'll pass." He met her gaze. "And don't forget—show that note to Devil as soon as you see him. *Don't* wait for him to ask."

Honoria lifted her chin.

Chillingworth eyed it with open disapproval. "Thank the heavens you're his and not mine. Wait here while I check if any-one's about. Like your grandfather or his butler."

Honoria watched as he opened the door; standing on the front step, he looked up and down the street.

"All clear." Chillingworth held the door open. "Other than your hackney, there's no one in sight."

Head high, Honoria swept out, then stopped and looked back. She frowned. "Don't forget to lie down with your feet higher than your head. And for goodness sake put that compress back, or your eye will be worse than it need be."

For the second time that day, Chillingworth's jaw dropped. Momentarily. Then he glowered. "Good God, woman—get *going!*"

Honoria blinked. "Yes, well—take care of yourself." With that, she turned and briskly descended the steps. Gaining the pavement, she saw her hackney waiting. She glanced the other way—a black carriage rolled slowly around the corner into Green Street. Behind her, Chillingworth's latch clicked. It was after four; dusk was drawing in. As Chillingworth had said, there was no one about. With an inward sigh, Honoria started along the pavement.

She didn't see the dark figure, cloaked in black, who emerged from the area stairs beside Chillingworth's steps. She had no inkling, felt no presentiment of danger, when the figure drew close, looming behind her. Harness jingled, hooves clacked as the black carriage drew abreast of her, blocking out the hackney. Honoria glanced at the carriage—a black pall dropped over her, cutting off the light, wrapping her in impenetrable folds. She gasped, and grasped the material, only to feel it wind tighter. She opened her mouth to scream; a hard hand clapped over her lips.

Honoria froze. An arm like steel wound about her waist and lifted her.

She didn't struggle but patiently waited for Devil to set her down. He eventually did—on the carriage seat. The carriage jerked and picked up speed. "Wait!" Still enveloped in what she assumed was Devil's cloak, Honoria struggled to break free. "What about Sligo?"

Silence.

Then, "Sligo?" Devil sounded as if he couldn't believe his ears.

"You ordered him to watch over me, remember?" Honoria wrestled with the cloak. The next instant, it was lifted from her—she let out an explosive breath, and discovered her husband watching her with an expression she couldn't read at all. "He's in the hackney, waiting for me."

Devil stared at her, then, frowning dazedly, shook his head. "Wait here."

He tapped on the hatch and ordered John Coachman to pull over, then leapt down. Honoria heard him stride back along the pavement. She couldn't see anything; the flaps were all down.

Two minutes later, the carriage dipped as Sligo scrambled up behind.

"Around the park until I say otherwise." Devil yanked open the door, climbed in, closed the door, then resumed his seat beside her.

The carriage lurched into motion; Devil met Honoria's wide, totally open gaze. He drew a careful breath, trying to disguise the tension that still held him. "Perhaps you'd better tell me what's going on."

He'd obviously made a horrendous mistake—he didn't want her to guess what he'd thought, how he'd felt, when he'd seen Chillingworth, stripped to his shirt, look out of his door, then seen her come waltzing out, turning back for a few last words before strolling away.

From the depths of the area, he hadn't been able to hear her words; his imagination, however, had supplied words enough, with actions to match. Her betrayal had chilled him; the thought that her declaration of love had been worthless—mere words without meaning—had struck him to the heart. Black rage had consumed him, far beyond mere temper; he could barely remember following her. He could remember the instant when he'd held her trapped before him—and thought how easy it would be to put an end to the torment before it began. The recollection left him chilled, even as relief poured through him. Guilt over his lack of trust made him inwardly ache.

Honoria was watching him, a frown forming in her eyes. Devil cleared his throat. "Sligo said you got a note?"

He threw out the question to get her talking—instead, she frowned more definitely. "I told you about the note in my letter."

Devil slowly blinked. "What letter?"

Rummaging in her reticule, Honoria dragged a sheet from the clutter. "I got this—"

Devil took it and scanned it, then glanced accusingly at her.

She tilted her chin. "It said I had to come immediately, so I wrote you a letter explaining and asked Sligo to deliver it; he knew you were at White's. I didn't know you'd ordered him to stay by me—he sent Daley to deliver my letter so he could obey your orders."

Devil frowned, then looked down at the note. "I didn't get your letter—I must have left before Daley arrived." The admission was past his lips before he'd considered.

"But—" Honoria's brow was a mass of furrows. "If you didn't get my letter, why are you here?"

Devil stilled. A minute passed; slowly, he lifted his head and met Honoria's puzzled gaze. She searched his face—abruptly, he looked down. "I came because I got this." He forced himself to draw the folded note from his pocket. He didn't want to give it to her, but her straightforwardness, her honesty—her love—left him no choice. His heart a leaden weight in his chest, he handed it over.

Honoria unfolded the note, then read it. When she got to the end, she paused and drew an unsteady breath. A vise locked painfully about her chest; her heart beat heavily. Without lifting her head, she read the note again.

As she worked out what must have happened, her hands, holding the note, shook—she fought to steady them. Then, very slowly, she raised her head—and looked straight at Devil, into those eyes that usually saw too much but could also be blinded by fury. Time stretched; she stared into his eyes, her own full of pleading and disbelief. "It's not true—I would *never* do that. You *know* I wouldn't." In a painfully soft whisper, she added: "I *love* you."

Devil closed his eyes. "I *know.*" His jaw clenched; savage rage swirled within him, directed at his would-be killer who had struck through the one, truly vulnerable chink in his armor—and hurt her. He dragged in a huge breath; opening his eyes, he locked them on hers. "I didn't think—I reacted. When I got that note, I *couldn't* think. Then I saw you come out of Chillingworth's—" He broke off; his jaw clenched tighter, but he forced himself to hold Honoria's gaze. Very low, he said: *"I care for you—too much."*

His words reached Honoria; what she saw in his eyes wiped away her pain. The vise about her chest eased; she drew a deep breath. "That's only fair." Shifting along the seat, she slid her arms about him and laid her head against his chest. "I love you so much it hurts, too."

If he couldn't say the words, she'd say them for him; the truth was there, shining in his eyes. His arms closed about her, then locked painfully tight; after a moment, he rested his cheek on her curls. He was so tense, his muscles flickered. Gradually, as the carriage rolled on, she felt his tension ease, felt the muscles in his arms unlock.

His warmth enveloped her; his heart beat steadily beneath her cheek. He drew in a deep breath, then slowly exhaled; long fingers found her chin and tipped her face up.

Their eyes met, and held, then he lowered his head. Honoria's lashes fell as Devil touched his lips to hers in a gentle, inexpressibly sweet kiss.

He drew back, one brow rising. "I don't suppose you'd like to tell me just what *did* happen?"

No command or demand, just a mild request; Honoria couldn't help but grin. "Actually, Chillingworth was very insistent that I tell you all, which must be a first."

"Very likely. Start at the beginning—when you knocked on his door. Was he expecting you?"

"Not exactly." Honoria wriggled upright. "He'd received a note, too—I saw it. Written in the same hand as ours." She placed the note she still held next to the one on the seat beside Devil. "See? You can't tell if it's a man or a woman."

"Hmm—so he knew you were coming to see him?"

"No." Honoria spoke distinctly, mindful of Chillingworth's instructions—and her husband's propensities. "His note was from a mysterious unnamed lady, making an assignation for this afternoon. It was quite . . ." she gestured airily, "titillating."

Devil narrowed his eyes. "By which you mean Chillingworth was raring to go—what did he say when you arrived on his front stoop?"

Honoria shot Devil a mischievous look. "Actually, I think he was even more surprised than I was. He was almost disapproving."

Devil raised his brows skeptically. "And?"

"What followed was actually my fault—he told me I couldn't possibly be in earnest. Naturally, I assured him I was."

"*And?*"

Honoria held Devil's gaze. "He tried to kiss me—and I hit him."

Devil blinked—then blinked again. "You *hit* him?"

Honoria nodded. "Michael taught me how before he allowed me to go governessing." She frowned. "I suppose I should have used my knee, but I didn't think of it at the time."

Devil only just managed not to choke. "I think," he said, his voice not entirely steady, "that Chillingworth is probably quite grateful you hit him." Honoria was uncommonly tall, and Chillingworth was shorter than he was. Devil's lips twitched. "I must remember to inform him of his close escape."

Honoria frowned. "Yes, well—unfortunately that's not all. When I hit him, his nose started to bleed."

It was too much; Devil succumbed to gales of laughter. "Oh, God," he said, when he could speak again. "*Poor* Chillingworth."

"He seemed to think so, too. His waistcoat was ruined."

One hand pressed to his aching ribs, Devil fisted Honoria's left hand. "You must have used your left."

Honoria nodded. "How did you know?"

Devil's grin was pure devilish delight. "I caught him with a left at Eton—the same thing happened. He bled like a stuck pig."

"Precisely." Honoria sighed. "I'm afraid he's feeling rather put-upon."

"I can imagine."

Devil's tone had hardened; Honoria looked up inquiringly.

He met her eyes. "He and I will have to sort this out."

Honoria straightened. "What do you mean?"

Devil's lips softened as he drew her back into his arms. "Just that we'll need to make sure we've got our stories straight in case someone noticed or starts a rumor." He hugged Honoria close. "Don't worry—I'm hardly likely to call a man out because my wife bloodied his nose."

Honoria frowned. "Yes—but is *he* likely to call *you* out because I bloodied his nose?"

Devil's chest quaked. "I really don't think that's likely." Grinning, he tilted Honoria's face up. "You're a remarkably resourceful woman, you know."

She blinked her eyes wide. "Naturally—I was raised an Anstruther-Wetherby."

Smiling, Devil lowered his head. "You were raised to be a Cynster."

He kissed her—and kept kissing her. The carriage rolled slowly through the gathering gloom, through the quiet shadows beneath the trees.

Breathless moments later, Honoria discovered that he could be remarkably resourceful, too. *"Great heavens!"* She had barely enough breath to whisper the words. "We *can't*—" Her hands closed tightly about Devil's wrists; her head fell back as she struggled for breath. "Where are we?"

"In the park." Intent on what he was doing, Devil didn't raise his head. "If you look outside, you'll see a number of carriages slowly rolling around the circuit."

"I can't *believe*—" A burst of pleasure stripped the thought from Honoria's mind; she struggled to hold back a moan. The thought that replaced the first had her blinking her eyes wide. "What about John and Sligo?" On a gasp, she met Devil's eyes. "Won't they realize?"

The grin on her husband's lips could only be described as devilish. "The trick's in the timing—trust me, they won't feel a thing."

They didn't—but she, and he, certainly did.

It seemed like hours—an infinite number of panting, gasping, *desperately* silent minutes later—when, slumped against Devil's chest, Honoria wriggled, then wriggled again. Frowning, she sat up and examined the buttons on his coat.

"Horrible things—they're sticking into me." She turned the mother-of-pearl buttons about. "They're not as big as the ones Tolly had, but they're quite bad enough."

Devil's eyes, closed in blissful peace, snapped open. "What?"

"These buttons—they're too large."

"No—what else did you say?"

Honoria frowned even more. "That they're like the one on Tolly's coat?"

Devil stared into the distance, then he closed his eyes—and closed his arms about Honoria, drawing her close. "That's it." He spoke the words into her hair. "That's what I've been trying to remember about Tolly's death."

Honoria held him. "The button deflecting the ball? Does it help?"

His chin resting in her hair, Devil nodded. "It helps. It's the final nail in our would-be-murderer's coffin."

Honoria tried to look at Devil's face, but he held her too tightly. "You're sure who it is?"

Devil sighed. "Beyond doubt."

Three minutes later, their clothes precisely correct once more, the duke and duchess of St. Ives headed back to Grosvenor Square.

Chapter 24

Vane was waiting in the library when Honoria and Devil entered. He searched their faces, then relaxed.

"The end is nigh." Devil handed Honoria to the *chaise*, then sat beside her.

Vane sat in an armchair. "What happened?"

Devil gave him a severely edited account, proffering only the note Honoria had received. "The one I got was in the same hand." Vane studied the note, then frowned. Devil suggested: "Look at the writing itself, not the style."

Vane's face cleared. "The nib! He always uses those wide nibs so his writing looks heavier. We've got him!"

"Yes, and no. Everything we've discovered is circumstantial. Given what I've remembered today—"

"*And* my news, which I've yet to tell you," Vane cut in.

"Put it together," Devil continued, "and the murderer's identity's obvious. Obvious, however, isn't proof."

Vane grimaced; Devil's expression was bleak. Honoria glanced from one to the other. "But *who is it?*" When they looked at her blankly, she nearly ground her teeth. "You haven't told me yet."

Devil blinked. "But it was you who told me. You were the first to put it into words."

"I thought it was Richard, remember? You *both* told me I was wrong."

"Well, you were," Vane said. "It isn't Richard."

"You suggested the murderer was my heir." Devil waited until Honoria looked his way. "Effectively, he is."

Honoria's eyes flew wide. She glanced at Vane, then looked back at Devil. "But . . . You mean *George* . . . ?"

"George?"

"*Father?*"

Devil and Vane stared at her. "Why George?" Devil asked. "He's not my heir."

"He's *not?*" It was Honoria's turn to stare. "But Horatia told me he's a bare year younger than your father was."

"He is," Vane corroborated.

"Great heavens!" Honoria's eyes couldn't get any wider. "How many Cynster skeletons are there? Is George another Cynster like Richard?"

"You've missed a vital point—George and Arthur are twins." Devil caught Honoria's gaze. "Arthur's the elder twin—and no, it's not him either."

"*Charles?*" Honoria's expression blanked, then hardened. "How . . ." For a full minute, words failed her, then her eyes flashed. "How *cowardly*." She met Devil's eyes. "He killed his younger brother."

"Half brother," Devil corrected. "As he used to be very quick to point out. He's also now tried to kill me."

"Several times," Vane put in.

"He's also tried to kill you." Devil reached for Honoria's hand. "And it now looks like he's killed his previous man, Holthorpe."

Devil and Honoria looked at Vane. "What did you discover?" Devil asked.

"Circumstantial evidence still, but I've had all the shipping lists checked—no Holthorpe embarked for America, or anywhere else. Holthorpe never left England."

Devil frowned. "Let's start at the beginning. Tolly left Mount Street the evening before he died. As far as we can tell, he headed home on foot. His lodgings were in Wigmore Street, so he'd walk past here. According to Sligo, he called in and learned I'd gone up to the Place. He continued on in good spirits—"

"And stopped in to see Charles," Vane said. "Around the corner in Duke Street."

"Given Holthorpe's disappearance, that seems a reasonable assumption." Devil's frown grew. "Presumably Tolly learned something, possibly overheard something—something that told him Charles was planning to kill me. Let's take that as read—what would Tolly do?"

"Tax Charles with it," Vane replied. "Tolly wouldn't have paused to think of any danger—he was too open and honest and naive to imagine others might be less so."

"We'll presume Charles didn't recant, so Tolly left."

"Probably saying enough on his way out to seal Holthorpe's fate." Vane looked grim. "The next morning, as soon as he could, Tolly left for the Place."

"But Charles took the faster route—we know he did. We didn't find anyone who could place Charles near the lane when Tolly was shot, but we did exhaustively prove no one else was in the area. No other gentleman arrived from London that day." Devil glanced at Vane.

"Right. So Charles shot Tolly—"

"That's what I'd forgotten. The button on Tolly's coat."

Vane looked puzzled. "What about it?"

Devil sighed. "The shot that killed Tolly was nothing short of perfect—the only reason he didn't die immediately with a hole through his heart was because one of his coat buttons"—Devil glanced down at the buttons on his coat—"like these, only larger, deflected the shot." He met Vane's eyes, then glanced at Honoria. "Charles's one real talent is that he's an exceptional marksman."

"Particularly with a long-barreled pistol." Vane nodded. "All right—so we have Tolly dead. Charles 'arrives' at the Place then plays the grieving brother the next day."

"Very convincingly." Devil's face hardened.

"He must have got one hell of a shock when he realized Tolly had lived long enough to talk to you."

Devil nodded. "But he kept mum and saw it through, Tolly's funeral and all."

"But then came the biggest shock of all." Vane looked from Devil to Honoria. "Charles learned you were going to marry Honoria."

Honoria frowned. "Actually, no. Not then. I put him off." When Devil looked his question, she grimaced. "He came to see me in the summerhouse after the wake. He offered to marry me in your stead, assuming I was concerned over protecting my name."

"He *what?*" Devil stared at her.

Honoria shrugged. "I told him I'd no intention of marrying you or anyone."

"He believed you," Vane said. "He was taken aback later, at Mama's ball, when Gabriel and I suggested you'd changed your mind."

"Hardly surprising." Devil glanced at Honoria. "He'd stopped us in the park not long before and you as good as assured him you were off to Africa in a few weeks."

Honoria shrugged again.

"And that," Vane said, "was when the attacks on you started."

"Your phaeton accident." Honoria paled.

Devil squeezed her hand. "An impulsive first attempt. I was very busy after that, then came our wedding."

Honoria shivered. "I just remembered—Charles warned me on our wedding day that I shouldn't have married you."

Devil drew her against him. "While we remained at the Place, he didn't attempt anything."

"Too dangerous," Vane said. "Too likely he'd be spotted there."

"But as soon as we returned to town, he started plotting in earnest." Devil looked at Honoria. "First, he tried to convince me to send you back to the Place." His lips twisted. "I'm afraid I told him precisely where you stood in my affections. So, from then on, you, too, were in his sights—he wouldn't risk a posthumous heir."

Turning to Vane, Devil missed Honoria's startled expression. "The episode with the brandy came next, then the three sailors with swords who knew my route home. Both attempts were well within Charles's capabilities."

Vane held Devil's gaze. "That brandy should have done for you, you know."

Feeling Honoria shiver, Devil shot him a warning glance. "But it didn't, so he persevered. The sailors, I suspect, was an opportunity he couldn't pass up—he's walked home with me from White's often enough."

Vane frowned. "What about this business with the palaces? Where does that fit?"

Devil grimaced. "It might not—but I'll wager it'll turn out to be Charles. Whatever, I'll find out tonight."

"Tonight?" Vane blinked. "What with everything else, I'd forgotten. What's our plan?"

Devil glanced at Honoria; absorbed with her own thoughts, she eventually felt his gaze. Looking up, she blushed. "I was just recalling," she said, her eyes locking on Devil's, "something Lady Herring mentioned."

Devil's expression blanked. "Lady Herring?"

Honoria nodded. "She said Charles approached her— something about replacing her last paramour. She refused him— from the sound of it, quite contemptuously."

"Hmm." Devil looked thoughtful.

"That wouldn't have helped Charles at all." Vane shook his head. "He always resented your successes—apparently on that level, too."

The look Devil shot him was sharply reproving; Vane simply raised his brows. "It might explain why he started frequenting the palaces—the timing's right. A Cynster couldn't patronize such places for long without us hearing of it, and we heard of it soon after Tolly's funeral."

Devil nodded. "But I still want to know definitely."

"When's the meeting?"

"Midnight."

Vane looked at the clock. "I'll drive—Sligo can travel behind. Lucifer'll keep watch from the street—Scandal'll be at the corner." Devil stared; Vane raised his brows. "You didn't seriously imagine we'd let you waltz in there without pickets?"

Honoria kept her lips firmly shut on the response she knew Devil would not, in this instance, appreciate—"Thank God for the Bar Cynster" was not what he was thinking.

Devil scowled. "What *else* have you organized?"

"Nothing." Vane's expression was mild. "But there's no earthly use imagining we'll let Charles take another easy crack at you. If you die, he'll be the head of the family—there's not one of us can stomach the thought."

Devil glanced at Honoria; when she said nothing, he looked back at Vane. "All right. But I don't want the cavalry charging in before the bugle sounds—we need to let Charles run with his master plan and let him take enough rope to hang himself."

"His master plan." Vane glanced at the note in his lap. "Is that what this is?"

Devil nodded. "It fits. I'd worried that all the other attempts were too simple, too spontaneous—simply not like Charles. You know how he thinks. Any plan of his is convoluted and complicated. He's also very conservative, socially rigid. This latest effort has his character stamped all over it. Involved, heavy with intrigue, and solidly based in society's view of me, Honoria, and Chillingworth."

"Chillingworth?" Vane frowned. "Why him?"

"Because he *appears* to be the perfect goad."

"For what?"

Devil smiled—chillingly. "My temper."

Vane blinked, remembering the note Devil had received, the note he hadn't been allowed to see. His expression leached. "Oh."

"Indeed. This time, Charles has outdone himself—it's really a very good plan. It might have worked." Devil glanced at Honoria. "If things had been otherwise."

Studying his eyes, she raised a brow. "I'm not well acquainted with Charles's mental processes—could you explain his master plan to me?"

Devil's lips twisted; raising her hand, he brushed a kiss across her knuckles. "Charles needs to kill me—and now you as well—

to take the title. He's tried to avoid direct action; the phaeton, the brandy, the sailors—there's no way of connecting them with him. But such chancy methods haven't succeeded. So, consider—he needs both me and you dead *with a reason*. After Tolly's death, accidental shooting of even one of us would cause a furore."

"No one would swallow that twice," Vane put in. "And he knows the rest of us wouldn't let your death under suspicious circumstances rest."

"Which is why he's focused on the one type of death for both of us that society will swallow without a qualm, and, even more importantly, the family will not only accept, but work with him to hide."

Vane's jaw firmed. "I don't like what I'm thinking, but if that's how he's set it up, he's read us very well."

Devil nodded. "He's clever. Not wise, but clever."

"I still don't understand," Honoria said. "What exactly is this death Charles has planned for us?"

Devil looked at her, his expression bleak. "Charles has known me all my life. He knows of my temper, of the scope of my rage; he has a reasonable idea of what might touch it off. With his three carefully structured notes, he arranged for me to find you coming out of Chillingworth's house."

"I'd worked that much out."

"From there on, he's relying on me—and my rage—to set the scene. He's counting on me to enact the role of jealously furious husband to the hilt, so he can kill us both and blame it on my sufficiently well-known temper."

Honoria held his gaze. "He's going to make it appear that you killed me in a jealous rage, and then killed yourself?"

Devil nodded.

Honoria's eyes narrowed, then flashed. Her chin firmed.

"Charles," she declared, "is clearly not a Cynster." She looked at Devil. "How do we plan to catch him?"

"The only way we can—by letting him show his hand."

"So what's our next move?" Vane handed the note back to Devil.

"Our next move is to make our own plans, which must include all the right actions to make Charles believe *his* plan is succeeding. In any good play, the villain only reveals himself in the last scene; Charles won't appear unless we, the intended victims, play out the earlier scenes correctly." Devil glanced at Vane, leaning forward, intent, then looked at Honoria, calmly expectant by his side. He smiled, coldly. "We've already completed the opening scene in our melodrama. For the next . . ."

At six o'clock the next morning, wreathed in mist, two tall figures, pistol in hand, faced each other on Paddington Green. Their seconds stood aside; a scrap of white drifted down. Two shots rang out. One of the principals crumpled to the ground; the other, clothed in black, waited while the doctor swooped down on his patient, then handed his pistol to his second and stiffly turned away.

He and his second climbed into a black, unmarked carriage and departed the scene.

The third scene in the tragedy was played out later that morning.

Gentlefolk taking their morning stroll in Grosvenor Square— nurses and their charges, governesses and young misses, old and young alike—all witnessed the unexpected sight of the St. Ives traveling carriage rolling into the square. It drew up before St. Ives House; an army of footmen descended to strap on a mountain of luggage.

Diverted, many watched, wondering, then the door opened; His Grace of St. Ives, his face like stone, appeared, leading a heavily veiled woman. Given her height, there were few who did not recognize his duchess; her stiff manner and the way she held her head led most to speculate that there'd been some falling-out, some possibly scandalous rift in what had, until then, appeared a remarkably felicitous relationship.

Before a host of round eyes, the duke handed the duchess into the carriage and followed her in. A footman shut the door; the coachman whipped up his horses.

The word was winging, on whispers uttered with wide eyes, on hushed confidences traded behind elegantly gloved hands, long before the carriage had quit the fashionable precincts. The St. Iveses had left London unexpectedly, just before the beginning of the Season. What was the *ton* to think?

Predictably, the *ton* thought—and said—precisely what had been intended.

Four powerful blacks drew the St. Ives carriage rapidly into Cambridgeshire. Leaning against Devil's shoulder, Honoria watched the countryside flash by. "I've been thinking."

Devil opened his eyes only enough to look down at her. "Oh?"

"We'll have to give a formal ball as soon as we return to town. To dispel the mistaken impression we've been at such pains to instill."

Devil's lips twitched. "You'll have to invite Chillingworth, of course."

Honoria flicked him a warning glance. "I suppose that's unavoidable."

"Quite." Devil studied the weak sunlight playing across her

features. "Incidentally, I should warn you that, despite its being midnight, it's possible someone might have seen me at the palace last night." The unknown Cynster had proved to be Charles; the madam's story had been utterly convincing.

Honoria lifted a haughty shoulder. "If any should think to mention your presence there to me, I can assure you they'll meet with a very cool reception."

Observing the imperious tilt of her chin, Devil decided it was unlikely even the most thick-skinned gabblemonger would dare—his wife was fast becoming as matriarchally intimidating as his mother.

"Do you think anyone was watching at Paddington Green this morning?" Honoria asked.

"Gabriel spotted a fellow resembling Charles's new man, Smiggs."

"So we assume Charles knows you and Chillingworth met?"

"It's a reasonable bet." Devil settled her more comfortably against him. "Try to rest." When she looked at him blankly, he added: "Tomorrow might be exhausting."

Honoria frowned vaguely. "I'm not sleepy." She looked away and so missed Devil's exasperated grimace.

After a moment, he ventured: "I just thought—"

"When do you think Charles'll appear?"

Devil inwardly sighed. "Either tonight, in which case he'll come up to the house and announce his presence, or sometime tomorrow, in which case he might not." *When* was she going to tell him? "I'll send a couple of grooms to Cambridge, to warn us the instant he arrives there."

"You think he'll use his usual route?"

"There's no reason for him to do otherwise." Studying her

profile, noting her firm, not to say resolute, chin, Devil stated: "Incidentally, whatever transpires, you'll need to keep one point uppermost in your mind."

Tilting her head, Honoria blinked up at him. "What?"

"You're to obey my orders without question. And if I'm not about, then I'll have your promise that you'll do what Vane tells you, without giving him a headache in the process."

Honoria searched his eyes, then looked forward. "Very well. I'll abide by your edicts. And Vane's in your absence."

Devil drew her back against him and touched his lips to her hair. "Thank you." Beneath his confident facade, he was deeply uneasy. The need to allow Charles to act and thus incriminate himself, to have to follow his lead and so enter the fray with no plan at all, was risky enough; having Honoria involved made it a hundred times worse. Tightening his hold on her, he settled his cheek on her hair. "We'll need to work together—rely on each other, and Vane—if we're going to spike Charles's guns."

Clasping her hands over his at her waist, Honoria humphed. "Given guns are Charles's favorite weapon, we may literally have to do so."

Devil closed his eyes and prayed it wouldn't come to that.

To his relief, Honoria nodded off, lulled by the swaying of the carriage and the mild sunshine bathing the countryside. She woke as the carriage halted before the front steps of the Place.

"*Ho-hum.*" Stifling a yawn, Honoria allowed Devil to lift her down.

Webster was there to greet them. "No trouble, Your Grace?"

"None." Devil glanced around. "Where's Vane?" Vane had left for Cambridgeshire the instant they'd quit Paddington

Green; Webster and Mrs. Hull had left Grosvenor Square at first light.

"Trouble with the windmill at Trotter's Field." Webster directed the footmen to the luggage. "Master Vane was here when Kirby reported it—he went to take a look."

Devil met Honoria's eye. "I should go and check. It's only a few fields away—I won't be long."

Honoria waved him away. "Go and shake the fidgets from that black demon of yours. He's probably scented your return—he'll be pawing up the pasture with impatience."

Devil chuckled. Capturing her hand, he pressed a kiss to her wrist. "I'll be back within the hour."

Honoria watched him stride away, then, with a contented sigh, trod up the steps to her home. And it was home—she felt it immediately she entered. Throwing off her bonnet, she smiled at Mrs. Hull, passing with a bowl of open bulbs for the drawing room. Drawing a deep breath, she felt calm strength infuse her—the strength of generations of Cynster women.

She took tea in the back parlor, then, restless, wandered the downstairs rooms, reacquainting herself with the views. Returning to the hall, she paused. It was too early to change for dinner.

Two minutes later, she was climbing the summerhouse steps. Settling on the wickerwork settee, she studied the house, the imposing facade that had so impressed her at first sight. Recalling how Devil had hauled her along that day, she grinned. The thought of her husband increased her restlessness; he'd been gone for nearly an hour.

Rising, she left the summerhouse and headed for the stables. There was no one about when she entered the yard, but the stables were never unmanned. The stablelads would be out exercising her husband's prize cattle; the older men were probably assisting with the broken mill. Melton, however, would be hiding somewhere; he would come if she called, but otherwise tended to remain out of sight.

Honoria entered the main stable block—neither Devil nor Sulieman was there. Unperturbed, she spent the next five minutes communing with her mare. Then she heard hoofbeats. Lifting her head, she listened—a horse clattered into the yard. Smiling, she fed the mare one last dried apple, then, dusting her hands on her skirts, walked quickly back down the stable and swung through the archway into the yard.

And ran into a man.

She fell back, eyes widening, a shriek stuck in her throat.

"Your pardon, my dear. I didn't mean to startle you." With a brief, self-deprecatory smile, Charles stepped back.

"Ah . . ." One hand pressed to her palpitating heart, Honoria couldn't think what to say. Where was Devil? Or Vane? They who were supposed to tell her the plan? "I . . . er . . ."

Charles frowned. "I've truly overset you. I apologize. But I fear I bring grave news."

The blood drained from Honoria's face. "What news?"

"I'm afraid . . ." Lips pinched, Charles's gaze swept her face. "There's been an accident," he finally said. "Sylvester's hurt—he's asking for you."

Eyes wide, Honoria searched his face. Was it true—or was this the first step in his final scene? If Devil was hurt, she didn't care—she would go to him regardless. But was Charles lying? She steadied her breathing, and tried to rein in her racing heart. "Where? Where is he?"

"At the cottage in the wood."

She blinked. "The one where Tolly died?"

"Alas, yes." Charles looked grave. "An unhappy place."

Indeed—but the broken windmill was in the opposite direction. "Oh dear." Striving for blankness, Honoria wrung her hands, something she'd never done in her life. In Devil's and Vane's absence, she'd have to script the scene herself. Delaying tactics came first. "I feel quite faint."

Charles frowned. "There's no time for that." When she tottered sideways and slumped against the stable wall, his frown deepened. "I wouldn't have thought you the sort to have the vapors."

Unfortunately, Honoria had no idea what succumbing to the vapors entailed. "What—what happened? To Devil?"

"He's been shot." Charles scowled with what was obviously supposed to be cousinly feeling. "Clearly some blackguard with a grudge against the family is using the wood as his cover."

The blackguard was facing her; Honoria struggled to hide her reaction. "How badly is he hurt?"

"Severely." Charles reached for her. "You must come quickly—God knows how long he'll last."

He grasped her elbow; Honoria fought the impulse to twist free. Then she felt the strength in his grip and was not sure she could. Half-lifting her, Charles propelled her into the stables. "We have to hurry. Which horse is yours?"

Honoria shook her head. "I can't ride."

Charles glanced at her sharply. "What do you mean?"

Pregnant women did not ride. Honoria blinked blankly. "I'm nervous of horses." As far as she could recall, Charles had never seen her ride. "And Devil's horses are impossible." She managed to wriggle her elbow free. "We'll have to take the gig."

"Gig!" Charles's scowl was quite real. "There's no time for that!"

"But—but—then I won't be able to go!" Honoria stood in the middle of the stable and stared at him helplessly. Pathetically. Charles glared at her; she wrung her hands.

He ground his teeth. "Oh—*very well!*" He flung out of the stable and headed for the barn.

Honoria stopped in the yard. As soon as Charles disappeared into the barn, she searched, scanning the connecting yards, peering into the dimness of the opposite stable block. Where was Melton? Then she heard the rumble of wheels. "Damn!"

She scurried back across the yard. Her role was clear—she should go along with Charles's plan and let him incriminate himself. Panic feathered her nerves and tickled her spine; mentally, she stiffened it. They had to catch Charles—he was like a sword hanging over their heads, Devil's, hers, and the child she carried. But how would Devil rescue her if he didn't know where she was? Weakly, she slumped against the stable wall.

And saw Melton in the shadows of the stable directly opposite.

Honoria swallowed a whoop of joy; she hurriedly blanked her features as Charles maneuvered a light gig from the barn.

He threw her a black scowl. "Come hold the shafts while I fetch a horse."

Softening her chin, hiding any hint of resolution, Honoria limply complied. Charles entered the stable; Honoria glanced at the one opposite. Melton's cap was just visible through the open stable door; he was hugging the shadows to one side of the entrance.

Then Charles was back, leading a strong grey. "Hold the shafts steady."

Honoria dropped them once, then surreptitiously jostled the

horse so he shouldered them loose again. Face set grimly, Charles worked frantically, buckling the harness, clearly conscious of time passing. Honoria fervently hoped she'd judged that commodity correctly, and that Devil would not decide to go for a longer ride.

Charles tugged on the final buckle, then stood back, scanning the rig. For one instant, his expression was unguarded—the smile that twisted his lips, oozing anticipation, Honoria could have done without. In that instant, she saw the killer behind the mask.

Melton might be old but his hearing was acute, which was how he so successfully avoided Devil. Honoria fixed Charles with her most helpless look. "Is Keenan with Devil?" She kept her expression vague, distracted. "You did say he's at Keenan's cottage, didn't you?"

"Yes, but Keenan's not there." Charles sorted the reins.

"You mean he's alone?" Honoria let her eyes grow round. "Dying in Keenan's cottage all alone?"

"*Yes!*" Charles grabbed her arm and all but forced her into the gig. "He's dying there while you're having hysterics here." He shoved the reins into her hands. "We have to hurry."

Honoria waited until he was mounted on his chestnut, turning toward the stable entrance before asking: "Are you going to ride back direct?"

Charles frowned back at her. "Direct?"

"Well . . ." She gestured weakly at the gig. "This can't go through the arch in the wall—I'll have to leave by the main gate and then find the bridle path back to the cottage."

Charles audibly ground his teeth. "I had better," he said, enunciating slowly, "stay with you. Or else you might get lost."

Dumbly, Honoria nodded. Meekly, she clicked the reins and set the gig rolling. She'd done all she could—delayed by all means she dared. The rest was up to Devil.

Chapter 25

Devil knew something was desperately wrong the instant he spied Melton, standing beneath the stable yard arch, wildly waving his cap. Cursing, he set his heels to Sulieman's sides; Vane's exclamation died behind him, then hooves thundered as Vane followed in his wake.

"What?" he asked, hauling Sulieman to a sliding halt.

"Master Charles." Melton clutched his cap to his chest. "Your lady went with him—he told her you were shot and a-dying in Keenan's cottage."

Devil swore. "How long since they left?"

"Five minutes, no more. But your lady's a bright one—she insisted on taking the gig."

"The gig?" Devil sat back. "Charles went with her?"

"Aye—he wanted to make sure she didn't lose her way."

Slamming a mental door on the chill fear that howled inside him, Devil flicked a glance at Vane. "Coming?"

"Nothing on earth could stop me."

They made straight for the cottage; there was no one there. Tethering their horses down the bridle path leading south, opposite the one Charles and Honoria would use, they scouted the area. Within the wood facing the cottage, they discovered a ditch, deep enough to hide them. It ringed the clearing on either side of the track from the lane. They were considering how best to use it when hoofbeats approached. Scrambling into the ditch, they watched.

Charles rode up. He dismounted by the stable, checked that Honoria was still following, then led his horse inside.

Halting the gig before the cottage, Honoria made no attempt to leave it. The instant Charles was out of sight, she looked wildly about. Both action and expression spoke of real fear.

In the ditch twenty-five yards away, Devil swore softly. "This time, I *am* going to beat you!" He didn't dare wave; he would bet his entire fortune Charles had come armed. Both he and Vane had loaded weapons in their hands, but he wanted no shooting with Honoria in the line of fire.

Dusting his hands, Charles came out of the stable. He frowned when he saw Honoria still in the gig, the reins lax in her hands. "I would have thought you'd be eager to see your husband." He waved to the cottage.

Honoria met his cold gaze. "I *am* keen to see him." She knew in her bones Devil was not in the cottage—for one fleeting instant, she'd thought he was in the wood, close, but she'd seen nothing. But he had to be coming—and she'd gone far enough with Charles. Charles slowed, his frown deepening. Drawing a deep breath, Honoria straightened her shoulders. "But he's not in the cottage."

Charles stilled; for one instant, there was no expression of any sort on his face. Then his brows rose, condescendingly superior. "You're overset." Stepping to the gig's side, he reached for her arm.

"No!" Honoria jerked back. The planes of Charles's face shifted. What she saw in his eyes had her swallowing her panic; this was no time to lose her head. "We *know*. Did you think we wouldn't realize? We know you've been trying to kill Devil—we know you killed Tolly."

Charles paused; as she watched, the veneer of civilization peeled, layer by layer from his face, revealing an expression of blank calculation, dead to any human emotion. "Knowing," Charles said, his voice unnaturally level, "isn't going to save you."

Honoria believed him—her only hope was to keep him talking until Devil arrived. "We know about your man Holthorpe—and about the sailors you set on Devil, about the poison in the brandy." What else did they know? Her recital wouldn't hold Charles for long. Fired by fear, she tilted her head and frowned. "We know everything you've done, but we don't know why you did it. You killed Tolly so he wouldn't warn Devil that you planned to kill him. But *why* are you so intent on taking the title?"

Desperate, she called up everything she'd ever felt about Charles, every intuitive hint she'd gleaned. "It isn't for money—you're rich enough as it is. You want the title, but you hold the family in contempt. Why, then, do you want to be their head?" She paused, hoping he would read true interest in her face. "What deep reason drives you?"

Charles regarded her without expression; Honoria felt her heart slow. Then he lifted one brow in typically arrogant Cynster style. "You're very perceptive, my dear." He smiled, a slight curve of his lips. "And, as you'll die shortly, I don't suppose there's any harm telling you." He looked directly into her eyes. "My name may be Cynster, but I've never been one of them—I've always felt closer to my mother's family. They're all dead now."

Bracing one hand on the gig, Charles looked into the wood, his eyes glowing. "I'm the last of the Butterworths—an infinitely superior breed, not that any Cynsters would admit that." His lips curved mockingly. "Soon, they won't have a choice. Once I take over the reins, I plan to change the family entirely—not just in the behavior associated with our name, but I'll change the name, too." He looked at Honoria. "There's nothing to stop me."

Honoria stared in openmouthed amazement. Smiling, Charles nodded. "Oh, yes—it can be done. But that was how it was meant to be—the Butterworths were destined to become the main line; my mother was to be the duchess. That's why she married Arthur."

"But—" Honoria blinked. "What about . . ."

"Sylvester's father?" Charles's expression turned petulant. "Mama didn't expect him to marry. When she married Arthur, it seemed all clear—eventually Arthur would inherit, then his son. Me." His frown grew black. "Then that slut Helena wriggled her hips and Uncle Sebastian fell for it, and Sylvester was born. But even then, my mother knew all would eventually be well—after Devil, Helena couldn't have any more brats, which left father, then me, next in line." Charles trapped Honoria's gaze. "Do you want to know why I left it so long? Why I waited until now to make away with Sylvester?"

Honoria nodded.

Charles sighed. "I was explaining that point to Mama, to her portrait, when Tolly came in that night. I didn't hear him—that cretin Holthorpe let him show himself in. Fitting enough that because of his laziness, Holthorpe had to die." His voice had turned vicious; Charles blinked, then refocused on Honoria. "As I told Mama, I needed a reason—I couldn't simply kill Sylvester and hope no one noticed. When he was young, Vane was always with him—the accidents I engineered never worked. I waited, but they never grew apart. Worse—Richard joined them, then the rest." Charles's lips curled. "The Bar Cynster." His voice strengthened, his features hardened. "They've been a thorn in my side for years. I want Sylvester dead in a way that will wean them, *and* the rest of the family, from their adulation. I want the title—I want the *power*." His eyes glowed. "Over them all."

Abruptly, his face changed, his features leaching of all expression. "I promised Mama I'd take the title, even if she wasn't here to see it. The Butterworths were always meant to triumph—I explained to her why I'd held off for so long and why I thought, perhaps, with Devil becoming so restless, the time might, at last, have come."

Again, he was with his past; Honoria sat perfectly still, content to have his attention elsewhere. The next instant, he turned on her viciously. "But then *you* came—and my time ran out *completely*!"

Honoria shrank back; the horse shifted, coat flickering. Charles's eyes blazed; for an instant, she thought he might strike her.

Instead, with a visible effort, he drew back, struggling to control his features. When he was again composed, he continued, his tone conversational: "Initially, I thought you too intelligent to fall for Devil's tricks." His gaze flicked her contemptuously. "I was wrong. I warned you marrying Sylvester was a mistake. You'll lose your life because of it, but you were too stupid to listen. I'm not going to risk being moved further from my goal. Arthur's old—he'll be no trouble. But if you and any son you bear survive Devil, I'll have all the rest of them to contend with—they'll never let Devil's son out of their sight!"

Clutching the back of the gig tightly, Honoria kept her eyes locked on Charles's, and prayed that either Devil or Vane had arrived in time to hear at least some of his ranting. He'd taken the rope she'd handed him and run, unreeling enough to hang himself twice over.

Charles drew a deep breath and looked away, into the woods.

He straightened; letting go of the gig, he tugged his coat into place.

Honoria grabbed the moment to look around—she still had the feeling someone was watching. But not even a twig shifted in the wood.

She'd achieved her primary objective. Her disappearance and death would give proof enough of Charles's guilt; Melton could testify Charles had lured her away. Devil would be safe—free of Charles and his endless machinations. But she'd much rather be alive to share the celebrations, and to enjoy their child. She definitely didn't want to die.

Charles grabbed her—Honoria shrieked. Dropping the reins, she struggled, but he was far too strong. He hauled her from the gig.

They wrestled, waltzing in the leaves carpeting the clearing. Snorting, the grey backed; Charles bumped the gig. The horse bolted, the gig rattling behind it. Honoria saw it go, caught by a sense of *déjà vu*. Another grey horse bolting with another gig, this time leaving her stranded with the murderer, not his victim. *She* was to be the next victim.

Locking one arm about her throat, Charles hauled her upright. *"Charles!"*

Devil's roar filled the clearing; Honoria nearly fainted. She looked wildly about; holding her before him, Charles swung her this way, then that, but couldn't locate Devil's position. Charles cursed; the next instant, Honoria felt the hard muzzle of a pistol pressing beneath her left breast.

"Come out, Sylvester—or do you want to see your wife shot before your eyes?"

Pushing her head back, Honoria glimpsed Charles's face, full of gloating, his eyes glittering wildly. Frantic, she tried struggling; Charles squeezed her throat. Raising his elbow, he forced her chin up; she had to stretch on her toes, losing all purchase on the ground.

"Devil?" Honoria spoke to the sky. "Don't you *dare* come out—do you hear? I'll never forgive you if you do—so don't." Panic gripped her, sinking its talons deep; black shadows danced across her eyes. "I don't want you to save me. You'll have other children, there's no need to save me."

Her voice broke; tears choked her. A dull roaring filled her ears. She didn't want to be saved if the price was his life.

In the ditch, Devil checked his pistol. Vane, brows nearly reaching his hairline, stared at him. "*Other* children?"

Devil swore through his teeth. "Fine time she picks to announce her condition."

"You *knew*?"

"One of the prime requirements of being a duke—you have to be able to count." His face grimly set, Devil stuck his pistol into the back of his waistband and resettled his coat. "Make for the other end of the ditch, beyond the track."

Honoria was babbling hysterically; he couldn't afford to listen. He pulled Tolly's hip flask from his pocket; he'd carried it since Louise had given it back to him, a reminder of his unavenged cousin. Working feverishly, he wriggled the flask into the inside left breast pocket of his coat; swearing softly, he carefully ripped the lining—finally, the flask slid in. Resettling his coat, he checked the position of the flask.

Vane stared. "I don't believe this."

"Believe it," Devil advised. He looked up; Honoria was still in full spate. Charles, his pistol at her breast, scanned the wood.

"I don't suppose there's any point trying to talk you out of it?" On his back, Vane checked his pistol. When Devil made no reply, he sighed. "I didn't think so."

"Sylvester?"

"Here, Charles."

The answer allowed Charles to face in their general direction. "Stand up. And don't bring any pistol with you."

"You do realize," Vane hissed, wriggling onto his stomach, "that this wild idea of yours has the potential to severely dint the family's vaunted invincibility?"

"How so?" Devil unbuttoned his coat, making sure the buttons hung well clear of his left side.

"When Charles kills you, I'll kill Charles, then your mother will kill me for allowing Charles to kill you. This madness of yours looks set to account for three of us in one fell swoop."

Devil snorted. "You're starting to sound like Honoria."

"A woman of sound sense."

Getting ready to stand, Devil shot a last glance at Vane. "Cover my back?"

Vane met his gaze. "Don't I always?" Then he swung about; crouched low, he started for the far end of the ditch.

Devil watched him go, drew in a long breath, then stood.

Charles saw him—he tightened his hold on Honoria.

"Let her go, Charles." Devil kept his voice even; the last thing he wanted was to panic Charles—the one he was counting on to shoot straight. "It's me you want, not her." He started forward, stepping over the scrubby undergrowth, sidestepping new canes and saplings. He didn't look at Honoria.

"Go back!" she screamed. "Go *away!*" Her voice broke on a sob. "Please . . . no." She was crying in earnest. "No . . . No!" Shaking her head, she gulped back sobs, her eyes pleading, her voice trailing away.

Devil walked steadily forward. He neared the edge of the clearing and Charles smiled—a smugly victorious smile. Abruptly, he flung Honoria away.

She screamed as she fell; Devil heard the scuffling of leaves as she frantically tried to free her feet from her skirts. Calmly, he stepped into the clearing. Charles raised his arm, took careful aim—and shot him through the heart.

The impact was greater than he'd expected; it rocked him back on his heels. He staggered back, hung motionless for a split second—the second in which he realized he was still alive, that Charles had clung to habit and aimed for his heart, not his head, that Tolly's hip-flask had been up to the task—then he let himself fall, slipping his right hand under the back of his coat as he went down. He landed on his left hip and shoulder; beneath him, his right hand held his pistol, already free of his waistband. Artistically, he groaned and rolled onto his back, his boots closest to Charles. All that remained was for Honoria—for once in her life—to behave as he expected.

She did; her scream all but drowned out the shot—the next instant, she flung herself full length upon him. Tears streaming down her cheeks, she framed his face; when he didn't respond, she sobbed and frantically searched—for the wound he didn't have.

Beyond thought, beyond all rational function, Honoria pushed aside Devil's coat—and found nothing but unmarked white shirt covering warm hard flesh. Gasping, her throat raw from her scream, her head pounding, she couldn't take it in. Devil was dead—she'd just seen him shot. She pulled his coat back—a wet stain was starting to spread. Her fingers touched metal.

She stilled. Then her eyes flicked up to Devil's; she saw green gleam beneath his long lashes. Beneath her hand, his chest lifted fractionally.

"*Such* a touching scene."

Honoria turned her head. Charles strolled closer, stopping ten paces away. He'd dropped the pistol he'd used to shoot Devil; in his hand was a smaller one. "A pity to put an end to it." Still smiling, Charles raised the pistol, pointing it at her breast.

"*Charles!*"

Vane's shout had Charles spinning around. Devil half rolled, coming up on his left elbow, freeing his right arm, simultaneously flinging Honoria to the ground, shielding her with his body.

Charles's head snapped back; his lips curled in a feral snarl. He raised his pistol. And paused for an infinitesimal second to correct his aim.

Neither Devil nor Vane hesitated. Two shots rang out; Charles jerked once. The look on his face was one of stunned surprise. He staggered back; his arm slowly fell. The pistol slid from his fingers; his eyes closed—slowly, he crumpled to the ground.

Devil swung around—a stinging blow landed on his ear.

"*How dare you?*" Honoria's eyes spat fire. "How *dare* you walk out to be killed like that!" Grabbing his shirt, she tried to shake him. "If you ever do that again, I'll—"

"*Me?* What about you? Happily going off with a murderer. I should tan your hide—lock you in your room—"

"It was *you* he shot—*I* nearly died!" Honoria hit his chest hard. "How the hell do you think I could live without you, you impossible man!"

Devil glared. "A damned sight better than I could without *you!*"

His voice had risen to a roar. Their gazes locked, sizzling with possessive fury. Honoria searched his eyes; he searched hers. Simultaneously, they blinked.

Honoria dragged in a breath, then flung her arms about him. Devil tried to cling to righteous fury, then sighed and wrapped his arms about her. She was hugging him so tightly he could barely breathe. He lifted her into his lap. "I'm still here." He stroked her hair. "I told you I'll never leave you." After a moment, he asked: "Are you all right? Both of you?"

Honoria looked up, blue-grey eyes swimming; she searched his face, then hiccupped. "We're all right."

"You didn't get hurt when you fell?"

She shook her head. "I don't think so. Nothing *feels* amiss."

Devil frowned. "I'll take you home." To Mrs. Hull, who knew about such things. "But first . . ." He glanced at Charles, sprawled on the leaves.

Honoria looked, then, sniffing, flicked her skirts straight and struggled up. Devil helped her up, then stood. Drawing a deep breath, he stepped forward—Honoria pressed close. Devil hesitated, then put his arm around her and felt hers slide about his waist. Together, they walked to where Vane stood, looking down on Charles.

Two bullets ripping into it from different angles had made a mess of Charles's chest. It was instantly apparent he couldn't survive. But he hadn't yet died. When Devil halted at his right hip and looked down, Charles's lids flickered.

"How?" he whispered, his voice hoarse.

Devil pulled Tolly's flask from his pocket. It would never hold liquid again; the ball had pierced one side and lodged in the other. He held it out.

Charles stared. Recognition dawned; his features twisted. "So," he gasped, each word a fight. "My little half brother won through in the end. He was so set on saving you—" A cough cut him off.

Devil quietly said: "Tolly was a far better man than you."

Charles tried to sneer.

"If I was you," Vane said, "I'd use what time you have left to make your peace with God. Heaven knows, you'll never make it with the Cynsters." So saying, he walked away.

His expression supercilious, Charles opened his mouth to comment—his features contorted, his eyes opened wide. He stiffened. Then his lids fell; his head lolled to one side.

Honoria tightened her hold on Devil, but did not take her eyes from Charles's face. "Is he dead?"

Devil nodded. "It's finished."

Hoofbeats approached, coming from the south. Vane came out of the cottage and looked at Devil. Devil shrugged. They moved to intercept the newcomers. Honoria moved with Devil; she wasn't yet ready to let him go.

Horsemen appeared on the bridle path, riding briskly. The next instant, the clearing was overflowing with Cynsters.

"What are you doing here?" Devil asked.

"We came to help," Richard replied, in the tone of one offended to be asked. Looking at the body sprawled on the ground, he humphed. "Looks like you've managed without us. He was so damned sure he had you dancing to his tune, he left London before you did."

"What next?" Gabriel, his horse tied to a tree, came to join them.

"You can't seriously consider passing this off as an accident." Lucifer followed on his heels. "Aside from anything else, I, for one, will refuse point-blank to attend Charles's funeral."

"Quite." Harry ranged himself beside Vane. "And if you can stomach burying Charles next to Tolly, I can't."

"So what do we do with the body, brother mine?" Richard raised his brows at Devil.

They all looked at Devil.

Honoria glanced up, but he had his mask on. He glanced down at her, then looked at the cottage. "We can't risk burying him—someone might stumble across the grave." His gaze lingered on the cottage, then swept the wood around them. "There hasn't been much rain. The wood's fairly dry."

Vane studied the cottage. "It's yours after all—no one would know except Keenan."

"I'll take care of Keenan—there's a widow in the village who's quite keen to have him as a boarder."

"Right." Richard shrugged out of his coat. "We'll have to bring the roof down and push the walls in to make sure it burns well enough."

"We'd better get started." Gabriel glanced at the sky. "We'll need to make sure the fire's out before we leave."

Honoria watched as they stripped off coats, waistcoats, and shirts, Devil and Vane included. Richard and Gabriel unearthed axes from the stable; Harry and Lucifer led the horses away, taking Charles's hired chestnut with them.

"Turn him loose in the fields closest to the Cambridge Road," Devil called after them.

Harry nodded. "I'll do it this evening."

Moments later, the sound of axes biting into seasoned timber filled the clearing. Devil and Vane each took one of Charles's hands; they dragged his body into the cottage. Honoria followed. From the threshold, she watched as they manhandled Charles onto the bare pallet on which Tolly had died.

"Most appropriate." Vane dusted his hands.

Honoria stepped back—a woodchip went flying past her face.

"What the—!" Richard, axe in hand, glared at her, then raised his head. "Devil!"

He didn't need to explain what the problem was. Devil materialized and frowned at Honoria. "What the devil are you doing here? Sit down." He pointed to the log across the clearing—the same log he'd made her sit on six months before. "Over there—safe out of the way."

Six months had seen a lot of changes. Honoria stood her ground. She looked past his bare chest and saw Vane, with one blow, smash a rickety stool to pieces. "What are you doing with the furniture?"

Devil sighed. "We're going to bring this place down about Charles's body—we need lots of fuel so the fire burns hot enough to act as his pyre."

"But—" Honoria stepped back and looked at the cottage, at the wide half logs of the walls, the thick beams beneath the eaves. "You've got plenty of wood—you don't need to use Keenan's furniture."

"Honoria, the furniture's mine."

"How do you know he isn't attached to it by now?" Stubbornly, she held his gaze.

Devil pressed his lips together.

Honoria's chin firmed. "It'll take two minutes to carry it out. We can use the blankets to cover it, then Keenan can take it away later."

Devil threw up his hands and turned back into the cottage. "All right, all right—but we'll have to hurry."

Vane simply stared when Devil explained. He shook his head, but didn't argue. He and Devil shifted the heavier pieces; Honoria gathered the smaller items into baskets and pails. Harry and Lucifer returned—and couldn't believe their eyes. Honoria promptly conscripted Lucifer; Harry escaped on the pretext of fetching Devil's and Vane's horses and taking them upwind of the cottage.

While Richard and Gabriel weakened the joints, the pile of

Keenan's possessions grew. Finally, Harry, whom Honoria had collared and sent to clear out the stable, came back with an old oilcloth and dusty lamp. He put the lamp on the pile, then flicked the oilcloth over the whole.

"There! Done." He looked at Honoria, not in challenge, not in irritation, but in hope. "*Now* you can sit down. Out of the way."

Before she could reply, Lucifer pulled the big carved chair out from under the oilcloth, picked up the tasseled cushion, and plumped it. Coughing furiously, he dropped it back down and made her a weak but extravagant bow. "Your chair, madam. *Please* be seated."

What could she say?

Her slight hesitation was too much for Gabriel, strolling up to hand his axe to his brother. "For God's sake, Honoria, sit down—*before* you drive us all demented."

Honoria favored him with a haughty stare, then, sweeping regally about, she sat. She could almost hear their sighs.

They ignored her thereafter, as long as she stayed in the chair. When she stood and strolled a few paces, just to stretch her legs, she was immediately assailed by frowning glances—until she sat down again.

Swiftly, efficiently, they pulled the cottage down. Honoria watched from her regal perch—the acreage of tanned male chests, all gleaming with honest sweat, muscles bunching and rippling as they strove with beams and rafters, was eye-opening, to say the least. She was intrigued to discover that her susceptibility to the sight was severely restricted.

Only her husband's bare chest affected her—that particular sight still held the power to transfix her, to make her mouth go suddenly dry. One thing that hadn't changed in six months.

Between them, little else was the same. The child growing

within her would take the changes one stage further—the start of their branch of the family. The first of the next generation.

Devil came over once they'd got the fire started. Honoria looked up, smiling through her tears. "Just the smoke," she said, in reply to his look.

With a sudden "swhoosh," the flames broke through the collapsed roof. Honoria stood; Devil put the carved chair back under the oilcloth, then took her hand. "Time to go home."

Honoria let him lead her away. Richard and Lucifer remained to ensure the fire burned out. Harry rode off, Charles's hired horse in charge. The rest of them made their way back through the wood, riding through the lengthening shadows. In front of Devil, Honoria leaned back against his chest, and closed her eyes.

They were safe—and they were heading home.

Hours later, chin-deep in the ducal bath, soothed by scented steam, Honoria heard sudden mouselike rustlings. Cracking open her eyes, she saw Cassie scurry out, closing the door behind her.

She would have frowned, but it was too much effort. Minutes later, the mystery was solved. Devil climbed into the bath. It was more than big enough for both of them—he'd had it specially designed.

"*Aarrghhh.*" Sinking into the water, Devil closed his eyes and leaned back against the bath's edge.

Honoria studied him—and saw the tiredness, the deep world-weariness, the last days had etched in his face. "It had to be," she murmured.

He sighed. "I know. But he was family. I'd rather the script had been otherwise."

"You did what had to be done. If Charles's deeds ever became known, Arthur's life, and Louise's, would be ruined, let alone

Simon, the twins and the rest—the whispers would follow them all their lives. Society's never fair." She spoke quietly, letting the truth carry its own weight, its inherent reassurance. "This way, I presume Charles will simply disappear?"

"Inexplicably." After a moment, Devil added: "Vane will wait a few days, then sort out Smiggs—the family as a whole will be mystified. Charles's disappearance will become an unsolved mystery. His soul can find what peace it can, buried in the woods where Tolly died."

Honoria frowned. "We'll have to tell Arthur and Louise the truth."

"Hmm." Devil's eyes gleamed from beneath his lashes. "Later." Lifting his arm, he reached for the soap, then held it out to Honoria.

Opening her eyes, she blinked, then took it. Softly smiling, she came up onto her knees between his bent legs. This ranked as one of her favorite pastimes—soaping his chest, washing his magnificent body. Quickly raising a lather in the crisp mat of hair on his chest, she splayed her hands, caressing each heavy muscle band, lovingly sculpting each shoulder, each arm.

I love you, I love you. The refrain sang in her head; she let her hands say the words, give voice to the music, infusing every touch, every caress, with her love. His hands rose in answer, roaming her curves, unhurriedly possessing every one, orchestrating an accompaniment to her song.

She'd only let him use the soap on her once; the room had ended up completely flooded. To her abiding delight, his control was stronger than hers.

One large palm splayed over her gently rounded belly. Looking up, Honoria caught the gleam of green eyes beneath his lashes; she frowned. "You knew."

One brow lifted in his usual arrogant way; his lips slowly curved. "I was waiting for you to tell me."

She raised her brows haughtily. "Tomorrow's St. Valentine's Day—I'll tell you then."

He grinned—his pirate's grin. "We'll have to devise a suitable ceremony."

Honoria caught his eye—and struggled not to grin back. She humphed and clambered over one rock-hard thigh. "Turn around."

She soaped his back, then lathered his hair and made him duck to rinse it. She'd returned to sit before him, between his thighs, her back to him, soaping one long leg, when Devil leaned forward, his arms closing around her. He nuzzled her ear. "Are you sure you're all right?"

"I'm perfectly well, and so's your son. Stop worrying."

"*Me* stop worrying?" He snorted. "That's a fine thing coming from you."

Dropping his leg, Honoria smiled and leaned back, luxuriating in the feel of the warm, hard, wet wall of his chest against her shoulders and back. "Oh, I've given up worrying about you."

Devil gave vent to an excessively skeptical sound.

"Well—just consider." Honoria gestured with the soap. "In recent times alone, you've been thrown from a disintegrating phaeton, poisoned, attacked with swords, and now shot through the heart. And you're still here." Dramatically, she spread her arms wide. "In the face of such trenchant invincibility, it's obviously wasted effort to worry about you. Fate, as I've been told often enough, quite clearly takes care of the Cynsters."

Behind her, Devil grinned. She would stop worrying about him on the same day he stopped worrying about her. Closing his hands about her waist, he lifted her, drawing her hips back against him. "I told you you were fated to be a Cynster wife—an *invincible* husband was obviously required." He underscored his emphasis by nudging the softness between her thighs, his erection sinking a tantalizing inch into that familiar haven.

Dropping the soap over the edge of the tub, Honoria arched— and drew him deeper. "I warn you, the staff are going to start wondering if we have to paint the downstairs ceiling again."

"Is that a challenge?"

She grinned. "Yes."

He chuckled, the sound so deep she felt it in her bones.

"Not a single splash," she warned him.

"Your desire is my command."

It was; he rose to her challenge—in every way—rocking her in the cradle of his hips until she thought she'd go mad. His hands roamed, fondling her swollen breasts, teasing her aching nipples. The slight ripples caused by their movement lapped at the sensitive peaks, a subtle, thoroughly excruciating sensation. Sweet fever blossomed, heating her skin, making the cooling water seem colder, impressing her with her own nakedness, sensitizing her skin to the crisp abrasion of his hair-dusted body rubbing so intimately against her.

Steadily, the fever built; Honoria shifted her knees to the outside of his. She tried to rise higher—he held her down, his hands firming about her hips. "No splashing—remember?"

She could only gasp as he pulled her lower, his hot hardness pressing deeper. Three restricted yet forceful thrusts later her fever exploded. She gasped his name as her senses soared; eyes shut, she savored the flight, hung briefly in the selfless void at the peak, then drifted gently back to earth.

He hadn't joined her; his arms came around her, holding her safe as her senses returned. Blissfully content, Honoria smiled and inwardly embraced him as possessively as he embraced her. He hadn't said he loved her, but after all that had happened, she didn't need to hear the words. He'd said enough, and, like any Cynster, his actions spoke loudest.

She was his; he was hers—she needed nothing more. What had grown between them, what was growing within her, was theirs—their life from now on. As her mental feet touched earth, she concentrated and caressed him, expertly, intimately—encouragingly.

And felt his muscles lock. Abruptly, he lifted her from him; the next instant, he stood and scooped her into his arms. As he stepped from the bath and headed for their bedroom, Honoria's eyes flew wide. "We're still wet!"

"We'll dry fast enough," replied her thoroughly aroused spouse.

They did, rolling, twisting, tangling amidst their silken sheets in a glorious affirmation of life, and the love they shared. Later, as he lay flat on his back, Honoria slumped fast asleep on his chest, Devil's lips quirked.

True Cynsters—all the male ones—died in their beds.

Stifling a chuckle, he peered down at his wife. He couldn't see her face. Gently, he shifted her to the side, settling her against him; she snuggled closer, her hand sliding across his chest. He touched his lips to her temple, and closed his arms about her.

"To have and to hold" was the family motto—it was also in the wedding vows. One of his ancestors had paid a horrific sum to put it there. Having married Honoria Prudence, Devil could understand why.

The having was very nice; the holding—the loving, the never letting go—was even better.

Epilogue

Somersham Place, Cambridgeshire
September 1819

The Bar Cynster was in session.

They were all there, lounging about the library, languorously at ease like so many well-fed predators. Devil had pushed the chair back from his desk and propped one boot on his knee to make a makeshift cradle for his heir. Sebastian Sylvester Jeremy Bartholomew Cynster. The star attraction of the present gathering of the clan had been baptized several hours before; he was now getting his head wet in a different temple.

Vane was in the armchair by the desk; Gabriel and Harry occupied the *chaise*. Lucifer lay sprawled in one armchair by the hearth, Richard a mirror image in its mate. Each held a brandy balloon well filled with His Grace of St. Ives's best; a somnolent air of deep male satisfaction permeated the room.

The staccato click of feminine heels in the hall was the first intimation of impending fate. Then the door flew open; Honoria swept in. One look at her face, one glance at her flashing eyes, was enough to inform them that *someone* was in deep trouble.

Secure in the knowledge that, whatever was exciting her ire, *he* had to be innocent, Devil gave her a vague smile. Honoria returned it with a brief, ominously serious nod; when the others made to rise, she waved them back to their seats. Skirts swishing, she marched across the room, then whirled before Devil's desk. Crossing her arms, she faced them, her gaze impartially distributing her ire. *Only* Devil was safe.

"It has come to my notice," Honoria intoned, her words clipped and precise, "that a set of wagers—I believe the term is a book?—was run on the question of, not the date of Sebastian's birth, which would have been bad enough, but on the date of his conception." Her gaze settled on Gabriel; she raised her brows. "Is that correct?"

Gabriel eyed her warily; a tinge of color crept into his lean cheeks. He flicked a glance at Devil, who merely raised his brows back. Frowning, Gabriel looked at Honoria. "Your information is accurate."

"Indeed?" Honoria's eyes flashed pure steel. "And exactly how much did you—all of you—win?"

Gabriel blinked. To his left, Sebastian gurgled—there was no point looking to Devil for help; His Grace of St. Ives was besotted with his son as well as his wife. At the edge of his vision, Gabriel saw colors gathering in a phalanx by the door—Honoria's supporters, their mothers. Nearer to hand, he sensed Harry's tension. Vane shifted, uncrossing his legs; Richard and Lucifer both slowly sat up. Gabriel had no difficulty interpreting their silent message.

Which was all very well—they weren't the ones facing Her Grace of St. Ives's fire.

"Seven thousand, six hundred and forty-three pounds."

Honoria's brows flew. Then she smiled. "Mr. Postlethwaite *will* be pleased."

"Postlethwaite?" Richard's tone reflected their escalating unease. "What's he got to do with it?"

Honoria opened her eyes wide. "The village church needs a new roof. Mr. Postlethwaite's been at his wit's end—good lead is becoming so costly. And, of course, as we endow the chapel here, he didn't like to approach us."

Gabriel glanced at Vane; Vane looked to Richard, who was looking at Harry. Lucifer bent a look of disbelief on his brother. Jaws aching, Devil kept his head down, his gaze locked on his son's cherubic countenance.

It was Vane who stepped into the breach. "So?" The single syllable was steeped in unchallengeable superiority; with any other woman, it might have worked.

Honoria merely turned her head, looked Vane in the eye, then turned back to Gabriel. "You will donate the entire proceeds from your enterprise, with any interest accrued, to Mr. Postlethwaite, to use as he sees fit. As you were in charge of this infamous book, I will hold you responsible for collecting the funds and conveying them to the vicar." Her tone was that of a magistrate pronouncing sentence—it left no room for argument. "Furthermore, as a final penance, you will all attend the dedication." She paused; her gaze swept the gathering. "I trust I've made myself clear?"

Her eyes challenged them to gainsay her; each considered it— none did.

Briskly, Honoria nodded.

Sebastian cried, an eloquent warning of impending hunger. Honoria immediately lost interest in wagers, lead roofs, and in-delicate speculation. Turning, she held out her arms commandingly; Devil handed his son over, an unholy smile lighting his eyes, lifting the corners of his lips.

With Sebastian at her shoulder, Honoria headed for the door, utterly ignoring the five large males she passed. She swept straight out of the room, the ladies closing ranks behind her.

Six males watched her go—one with glowing pride, the other five with uneasy trepidation.

They paid up without a whimper. Mr. Postlethwaite was delighted.

One month later, they attended the dedication; each uttered a prayer that fate wouldn't, just yet, turn her attention their way.

Unfortunately for them, fate wasn't listening.

The World of Stephanie Laurens

Enter the unforgettable world of
#1 *New York Times* bestselling author

STEPHANIE LAURENS

with a sneak peek at the Cynster novels!

Read on for a look at the complete series!

Devil's Bride

When Devil Cynster, the Duke of St. Ives and leader of the Cynster males, is caught in a compromising position with governess Honoria Wetherby, some scandalous behavior follows . . .

A Rake's Vow

Vane Cynster vowed he'd never marry, until he encountered irresistible Patience Debbington, a young woman who tempts him as no other. Soon he has seduction—and more—on his mind!

Scandal's Bride

Catriona Hennessy, honorable Scottish Lady of the Vale, receives the prediction that Richard "Scandal" Cynster will father her children. So she forms a daring plan to avoid this fate . . . but she can't resist him!

A Rogue's Proposal

Demon Cynster has seen love bring his fellow Cynsters to their knees. He decides not to share that fate—until he spies Felicity Pargeter riding one of his horses!

A Secret Love

Gabriel Cynster cannot resist a lady in distress, and when Lady Alathea Morwellan appears before him—her face hidden by a veil, begging for his help—he cannot refuse her!

All About Love

Lucifer Cynster is still unclaimed—so he escapes to the country, believing he can keep himself unattached. Instead he meets his destiny in Phyllida Tallent . . .

All About Passion

Fate has deemed Gyles, the Earl of Chillingworth, be welcomed into the Cynster clan, an honorary member of that tribe. He is determined to control his own destiny; then he discovers a daring wedding-day deception!

The Promise in a Kiss

Sebastian Cynster, head of the Cynster family, literally falls at the feet of Helena de Stansion. He believes that this gently bred miss could be no match for his wicked ways . . . and he would be wrong!

On a Wild Night

Where, oh where, are the exciting London men? Amanda Cynster wonders. So she takes matters into her own hands, goes where no woman dares, and is unexpectedly rescued by the Earl of Dexter.

On a Wicked Dawn

Amelia Cynster risks scandal with Lucien Ashford by appearing at his doorstep, unchaperoned, at dawn. Yet even she is shocked when he accepts her marriage proposal—before falling in a dead faint at her feet!

The Perfect Lover

Sometimes the perfect lover and the perfect wife are one and the same. Simon Frederick Cynster is determined to find a woman who could be both! He is astonished that his youthful nemesis Portia Ashford is the lady he seeks . . .

The Ideal Bride

Those "honorary Cynsters," such as Michael Anstruther-Wetherby, cannot help but follow their ways. Michael's future in Parliament seems assured, however he requires a biddable wife. But Caroline Sutcliffe is far from what he thinks he needs!

The Truth About Love

Cynster protégé Gerrard Debbinton is one of the most eligible gentlemen of the *ton*. Besieged by offers to paint one of his amazing creations, he is tantalized by the idea of re-creating the famous, but never seen, gardens of Hellbore Hall, but can do so only if he also paints Jacqueline Tregonning, the daughter of the manor. But secrets haunt the hall, and Jacqueline is the key to discovering the truth about many of them . . .

What Price Love?

Just how much will you risk for love? Dillon Caxton, only son of General Caxton and cousin-by-marriage to Demon Cynster, finds himself asking this question. Priscilla Dalloway asks for his help in rescuing her twin brother from a swindle she fears he is involved in, and Dillon soon finds himself becoming involved in a risky affair of the heart . . .

The Taste of Innocence

Charles Morwellan, the eighth Earl of Meredith must marry, so he offers for his neighbor, Sarah Conningham. But as a lady of independent means with a life of her own, Sarah is unwilling to surrender her independence unless it be for unbounded love . . .

Temptation and Surrender

Jonas Tallent, who has taken the reins of his family's rural estate, never expected a delectable morsel like Miss Emily Beauregard to apply for a position at the village inn. But Emily has her reasons and doesn't plan to share them, even with someone as seductive as Jonas.

The Cynster Sisters Trilogy

Viscount Breckenridge to the Rescue

Determined to hunt down her very own hero, one who will sweep her off her feet and into wedded bliss, and despairing of finding him in London's staid ballrooms, Heather Cynster steps out of her safe world and boldly attends a racy soiree.

In Pursuit of Eliza Cynster

Brazenly kidnapped from her sister Heather's engagement ball, Eliza Cynster is spirited north to Edinburgh. Desperate and determined to escape, she seizes upon the first possible champion who happens along—gentleman scholar Jeremy Carling.

The Capture of the Earl of Glencrae

Angelica Cynster is certain she'll recognize her fated husband at first sight and when her eyes meet those of a mysterious nobleman across a candlelit ballroom, she knows beyond doubt that he's the one. But her heart is soon pounding for an entirely different reason—when her hero abducts her!

The Cynster Sisters Duo

And Then She Fell

Famously known in London society as "The Match-breaker," Henrietta Cynster's uncanny skill lies in preventing ill-fated nuptials—*not* in falling victim to Cupid's spell. But then she disrupts one match too many and feels honor-bound to assist dashing James Glossup in finding a suitable bride . . .

The Taming of Ryder Cavanaugh

As the last unwed Cynster of her generation, Mary is determined to remain in charge of her life. At the very bottom of her list of potential husbands is Ryder Cavanaugh, the daring and devastating Marquess of Raventhorne, an overwhelming and utterly unmanageable lion of the ton. But destiny has a different plan . . .

And don't miss the new series by

#1 *New York Times* bestselling author

THE CASEBOOK OF BARNABY ADAIR

Where the Heart Leads

The Masterful Mr. Montague

Loving Rose: The Redemption of Malcolm Sinclair

Available now in print and e-book

from Avon Books!